DEDICATION

*This book is dedicated to my mother, Betty Smith, who told me
I could achieve anything and to my husband, Grant Young, who
makes me believe it. It is also for my children, Stephanie and Gregor.*

May God thy gold refine, and all success be nobleness, and every gain divine.

America the Beautiful

CHAPTER 1

The last sound Lucie heard was her own scream.

She lost her footing and pitched forward onto the hard ground. As if somebody had flicked the switch on the city, the light went out. With the blackness came silence.

When Lucie opened her eyes, the world was monochrome. White shadows drifted through a strange, cloying darkness she could smell and taste. A weak beam of light swung towards her, a halo through the dust. Didn't dying people speak of a tunnel of light? Lucie wasn't ready to be drawn in to whatever lay beyond. She closed her eyes to concentrate on staying alive, leaving her brain to scan for memories.

Images flickered and faltered on her eyelids like some old movie. Gaping mouths screaming silently, pedestrians spilling off sidewalks into the path of cabs, disgorged drivers pointing at the sky.

Where no sky should be.

Just a thunderhead of smoke billowing upwards, filling the blue space. Blotting out the sun over Manhattan.

Lucie lay on the street, trying to make sense of it all, head throbbing, breath rasping. There was something wrong with that picture. Only smoke where the South Tower should be. Then she remembered the collapse, right before her eyes. The tsunami of smoke had raced towards her, funnelling between blocks, stealing the air. The sound wave, loud enough to feel, crashed down a canyon of tall buildings.

Men and women were running in a hurricane of paper, a storm of detritus. Lucie stood, frail as a sapling, till a man bundled into her, his mouth shaping an apology as he stumbled away. A teenage boy, bandana clutched to his mouth, grabbed her arm as

1

he passed, trying to drag her with him. Her legs refused to move. He ran on, saving himself. An elderly couple jogged sedately into her line of vision, and disappeared into the windstorm.

But her feet were set in concrete.

A running snowman swooped like a hawk to snatch a young child up into his embrace and ran on, without breaking stride. A dark-haired woman, chic and slim, stopped by Lucie's side. She removed her shoes and cast them away, their red soles gazing at the sky as they fell onto the dusty concrete to lie with the others. She caught Lucie's eye, tearful, then ran on.

Lucie looked down at her own shabby courts. She was loath to leave the only pair of heels she possessed, but knew the other woman was right; she'd run much faster without them. So Lucie broke into a run, clutching her shoes to her chest until someone crashed into her, knocking her to her knees. People piled up behind her, logs in a river.

A strong hand took her elbow, pulling her to her feet. Galvanised, she ran on. At last she was keeping up with the crowd, racing the unraceable.

She sensed the cloud catching up. Felt its force push her in the back, propel her forward. Getting closer. Then she smelt it, saw it, tasted it. Was engulfed by it. Swallowed up. Cut off from everything and everyone around her. And still running. Her legs, once so reluctant to move, now refused to stop. Running and running till blinded and lost, she tripped and hurtled into darkness.

How long had that been?

She opened her eyes. The beam of light had gone and the murk was clearing. Around her, shadowy outlines moved, grey ghosts in the silence. Blinking hard, she tried to clear her vision. Her throat hurt when she tried to swallow and she tasted bitter ash on her tongue. She tried to spit but her mouth was dry-coated and no saliva would come.

Then the silence became sound with a brutality that hurt her ears, a cacophony of sirens, alarms, and screaming. And more screaming. A baby cried and random names were shouted over and over. One persistent voice was finally answered with a weak, 'I'm here, Bob. Over here.' And tears.

The whole city was crying.

Lucie wiped away a stray tear, temporarily blinding herself with the ash and grit she rubbed into her eyes. Her hands, arms and legs were all coated in a thick layer of fine, grey powder, as if her whole body had been dredged in talcum.

Lucie looked around, desperate for an explanation. Vague, indistinct shapes stirred and moved, every one the same pale, greyish white. All colour had been erased in an instant.

She tried to sit, disentangling her legs from the obstacle that had sent her sprawling. Through the ash rain Lucie made out a woman's legs, slim, tight-skirted and splayed at odd angles. No shoes.

With a muttered apology, Lucie pushed herself away. When the woman did not move, Lucie knelt by her side and tried to roll her over but although she was pencil thin, she felt heavy. Dead weight.

'Hey, you okay?' whispered Lucie hoarsely, as she manoeuvred the woman onto her side. Despite how badly it hurt to talk, Lucie persevered. 'Hello. Can you hear me? Can you open your eyes?' The woman's eyes remained closed as if in sleep and, for the second time that day, Lucie thought she might be touching a corpse. Horrified, she let go and the woman flopped, face down, into the ash snow.

Feel for a pulse. That's what she *should* have done this morning, instead of running away. With tentative fingers, Lucie touched the woman's neck. Nothing. She moved her fingers leaving petal patterns in the fine dust on the warm skin. There was no movement beneath her fingertips, no reassuring beat of life, nothing to feel.

Lucie needed to find help.

The grey ghosts had moved away and for a moment the world seemed strangely empty.

Then, the sound of another voice, indistinct, but close by. A huge white outline of a person appeared, barely visible.

'Help me,' Lucie said, her voice rough. The shape did not react. She coughed and tried again, 'Please?'

'Somebody there?' The diffused, muggy beam of a flashlight shone in her face, the same light she'd seen earlier. 'Ma'am, you can't stay here.'

'This woman needs help.' Lucie's words came out in a pathetic whisper.

'You have to leave. Go north and keep moving.'

Lucie was hauled to her feet and given a push. She tried to resist, then saw the man's face, shocked beyond belief. His eyes were empty. 'We can't just leave her.'

'I have to clear the street.' He pushed her again, none too gently, then pleaded, 'Please. Please get going …'

'Just let me get my purse.'

He stood while she dropped to her knees and crawled around in the ash, scrabbling till her hand snagged a leather strap, then she got to her feet and started to run.

Lucie ran till her rasping lungs told her she could run no more and she slowed reluctantly to a walk, joining the ranks of a grey army that marched forward while glancing back every few seconds as if afraid of being followed.

She couldn't remember dropping her shoes, but they'd gone. Her bare feet stung from slapping against asphalt and every bone in her legs ached.

'What the hell just happened?'

Lucie found herself face to face with a human snowman. Every part of the man's body was dusted in fine, grey powder. Only the deep voice gave a clue to his gender.

'What the hell *was* that?' he asked her. Lucie stared at him. Inside grey lips his mouth was an obscenity of bright red. Lucie looked at his eyes, two hollows in day-old snow. A tear carved a clean channel down his cheek, only to disappear like a raindrop in the desert. 'What's going on?'

Lucie shook her head but the man paid no attention; he was dazed, staring somewhere over her shoulder, deep into the dust cloud, his senses trying to make sense of something that made no sense.

Lucie walked past him, she needed to keep moving. There was nothing she could say, and her mouth was so dry she doubted she could form a word. The dust ate at her throat, her nose, her lips. She badly needed to sneeze, she reached for her handbag to get a tissue. When the bag wouldn't open, she dusted it off with her hand and realised why. It wasn't hers. The shape was much the same, a brown leather bag on a single shoulder strap, but this bag felt softer and more expensive, even with its coating of dust and ash. Hers was a cheap, drugstore imitation, a very rare gift from Curtis.

She'd picked up the other woman's bag. 'Oh no,' groaned Lucie. She couldn't afford to lose her bag. Not today. Her entire life was in that bag. She needed to get that bag.

Fighting off her panic, Lucie turned and raced back the way she'd come. She felt like a minnow swimming against the tide. Struggling to make headway through the masses heading north, she charged and shoved.

'Hey! Watch out,' scolded a small man as she barrelled into him and bounced off like a pinball.

'Sorry,' she mouthed and ran on into the dust cloud. It was thicker here, catching in her raw throat. Every instinct told her to turn back to clearer air. Spectral figures appeared out of the ash fog for a few seconds then vanished again. She was the only one heading south.

Lucie took a few more steps then stopped, covered her mouth with her hand and looked around. She could see nothing. The bright blue sky had disappeared and with it the tall buildings that defined the skyline. Lucie had no point of reference other than the flow of people heading north. She might never find the woman. Even if she were still lying in the street, Lucie had no idea where. She was lost and Lucie's bag was lost with her.

Wandering around like this, breathing ash into her lungs, was solving nothing. She started to cry, everything was gone.

When the next surge of people passed, Lucie joined them.

Running north.

CHAPTER 2

Dylan had just scored the winning touchdown in the Superbowl when his phone woke him. He buried his head under the pillow but the tinny ringtone was too insistent. He cursed the phone's inventor and checked caller ID.

Why was Mom phoning on his day off? She knew he never surfaced before lunchtime.

'Dylan. You awake?'

'I am now. What's up?'

'Switch on the TV, right this minute.'

'I'm trying to get some sleep here, Mom. Can I call you back?'

No answer.

'You okay?'

'Dylan, you'll never believe this. One of the Twin Towers just collapsed.'

'No way!'

'It's gone. A plane flew right into it. People were trapped. Inside of it. Some were jumping. It was awful. Lanie next door called to tell me to switch on the TV and I saw a man jump. With my very own eyes.' Her voice spiralled into a wail.

'Hey, Mom, it's okay,' Dylan had no idea what she was talking about. Maybe she'd made an early start on the cocktails.

'Switch on your TV, son. I need you to see this.'

'I don't have a TV. Maddy took it. Remember?'

'Go find a television. Oh my God. Sweet Jesus, no!'

The line went dead.

* * *

Dylan was torn between comforting his mother and making sure Lucie was okay. In the end he decided his mom would have Lanie next door to keep her company and besides, Curtis and Lucie's place was quicker to get to. He tried their phone but couldn't get through. Curtis never paid the damn bill on time.

The screen door was hanging from one hinge. Same as the last time he'd been here. Dylan pushed it aside and banged on the front door. Flakes of paint peeled off like dead skin and dropped at his feet.

He tried the handle. It was never locked. Nothing worth stealing, Curtis said.

'Anyone home?'

The living room seemed dark after the bright sunshine. The smell reminded him of the locker room at the end of a hard circuit session. Dylan tried to breathe through his mouth.

Somewhere a bluebottle buzzed. When it stopped, the house fell silent.

A rip in the blind admitted a shaft of light that slanted across the kitchen floor. Curtis lay face down, the fly droning round his head. Passed out and sleeping it off. Pretty normal behaviour for Good Ole Curtis these days, unfortunately.

Dylan bent and patted his shoulder. 'Hey, buddy! Wake up. It's morning.'

Curtis didn't react.

Dylan batted the bluebottle away. It rose, circled and came back in to land.

'Come on, pal. Wake up. We need to switch on the TV. Where's the remote?' He peered through the gloom towards the La-Z-Boy where Curtis spent his days. And sometimes his nights.

The TV burst into life, showing some crappy disaster movie. Dylan skipped to the next channel, then the next. Every screen showed a tower belching black smoke into a perfect sky. A plane appeared from nowhere and flew straight into the second tower. It burst into flames as Dylan watched in fascination.

'Jee-suss, I don't believe this.'

Dylan knew better than to wake Curtis, but Mom was right. He had to see this.

'Curtis!' he shouted, 'You have to see this. There's guys jumping from, like, a hundred storeys.'

Dylan knelt on the floor, unable to drag his eyes off the TV, where a shell-shocked anchorman was doing his best to describe the chaos.

'Man, people are dying. In Manhattan. It's like a horror movie.' He shook his friend by the arm. The bluebottle flew off. And Dylan saw blood, dark as treacle, clotted in Curtis's hair and congealed on the floor.

'Shit.'

'Lucie!' Dylan got to his feet and stumbled to the bedroom door. The bed was empty. Its poor, threadbare covers lay jumbled on the floor.

He heard a groan and dashed back to the living room. Curtis hadn't moved an inch.

'Curtis, you okay? I got you, buddy,' he said, dropping to his knees. He took Curtis's hand and squeezed. 'Curtis, it's Dylan. Can you hear me?'

Curtis opened his eyes and blinked a few times. 'Hell you doing here?'

'You passed out. Banged your head. Looks pretty bad.' He laughed nervously and sat back on his heels. 'Shit, I thought you were, like, dead. You really scared me, man. I need to call nine one one.'

'No, leave it. I'll be okay. Give me a hand here.'

'You sure? Your head's bleeding. I think we should call an ambulance.'

'I said I'll be okay. Lucie'll clean me up. Lucie? Lucie, you get in here.'

'She's not here, Curtis. I already looked.'

'Well, where is she?'

'How should I know? She's your wife.' A familiar anxiety gnawed at Dylan's guts. 'Tell me you didn't hurt her.'

'Aw, maybe I roughed her up a little last night. But man, she was asking for it.'

'You're an asshole, Curtis. Lucie's the best thing that ever happened to you.'

'Yeah, yeah, yeah. You planning to help me up or what?'

On TV the NBC reporter was shouting hysterically into camera.

'What is this crap?' asked Curtis.

'A plane hit the Twin Towers. Looks like the second one just collapsed.'

'No shit! Let me see.' Curtis pushed up on his arms, as if he were doing a press-up, then crashed back to the floor.

'Dylan, I can't move my legs.'

CHAPTER 3

Lucie ran, stumbling and lurching blindly through the dust. Hoping she was heading north. Following the snowpeople up ahead till they melted into white and disappeared.

Her throat was on fire, her feet stinging.

She heard voices. Women crying. Men shouting. She followed the sound, her arms held out in front. A sinister game of Blind Man's Buff.

As the dust began to clear, it felt easier to breathe and she could see sky again. Bright, beautiful, blue sky.

The Manhattan street looked more like Vail in mid-winter. White powder lay inches deep on car roofs and their parking meters wore peaked caps. The blacktop of the road was white, confusing as a negative photo.

Lucie's bare feet kicked up mini-clouds around her ankles as she padded through the dust. She leaned against the first wall she came to and her legs gave way. She sank to the ground and wept.

'Excuse me? Could you tell me what street this is?'

Lucie looked up at the woman and tried to speak, but her mouth felt like she'd swallowed a bag of flour. She coughed and tried again. On the third attempt she managed to whisper, 'Sorry, no idea.'

'Pardon me?'

It really hurt to talk but Lucie persevered. 'Heading south. On Greenwich. Before.' She gestured at the alpine scene, the unrecognisable cityscape.

'Speak up, dear. I can't hear you.'

Lucie swallowed hard, soothing her throat a little. 'Don't know.'

The woman shook her head impatiently, cascading a flurry of dust onto Lucie's face.

She covered her mouth with her hand and asked through her fingers, 'Ma'am?' It came out like a croak. She lifted a handful of white powder. 'What happened?'

'The World Trade Center collapsed. Some kind of plane crash. Young man I spoke to, can you believe it, he sees a plane fly right smack into one of those towers. We're standing talking, the two of us, just looking up at the sky and he's telling me all about it. The tower's been lit on fire, by the plane, I guess, and flames are burning out the walls and chunks of metal are falling to the ground and pieces of paper, all floating around and then suddenly the whole tower just kind of crumbles and disappears. Right there, while we're watching. Can you credit that? People are screaming and yelling. Some of them shouting cuss words. Some of them saying "Oh my God," over and over, like it's a prayer. Then all of a sudden this dust is coming at us. A huge cloud of it, coming along the street. And people are going crazy. It was bedlam. I just ran and ran. Till I could run no more.'

When Lucie was sure the woman had stopped talking, she asked, 'You okay?'

'I'm fine, thank you. Bless your heart for asking.'

Lucie leaned her head against the wall and closed her eyes, considering her options. She was in the middle of the city, shoeless, covered in white dust and minus her bag. No bag meant no money. No money meant no way of getting home.

She pictured Curtis, flat out on the kitchen floor. She'd hit him pretty hard.

She should have checked on him. Instead of sneaking out in a panic in case he'd wake up and stop her getting to her interview.

He'd be fine. Of course he would. How many times had she seen him out of his face on drink and drugs?

Except this time was different.

One thing was certain. She didn't want to be there when he woke up. If he recalled her hitting him with the skillet, he'd be mad as a bull with its balls in barbed wire, as he liked to put it.

It might be wise to lie low for a day or two, give him time to calm down a bit.

Maybe she could find some sort of refuge for the night. She had enough bruises to prove she was a victim of domestic violence. The black eye alone would be enough to cinch it.

Lucie looked up at the woman.

'Ma'am? Would you know where I could find a Women's Refuge?'

'Oh my dear lord, no. I'm from out of town. I wouldn't know anything about that kind of a place.' The woman sounded offended.

Lucie took a deep breath which triggered a coughing fit. Spluttering and gasping for air, she rasped, 'I'd never normally ask, but do you think you could give me ten dollars, please? I'd be happy to pay it back. It's just that, I need to find somewhere to stay and I've lost my purse, my ID, everything.'

The woman looked down at the leather bag in Lucie's lap and tucked her own tightly under her arm. 'I'm afraid I can't help one little bit. Sorry.' She backed away, as if Lucie had become a danger to her. Lucie watched her grey figure disappear into the grimy air.

Lucie couldn't sit here begging for money. She brushed the dust off the bag in her lap.

What harm would it do to take a few dollars? It wasn't like she'd stolen the bag. And if the woman who owned it was dead … She let that thought slide away, not wanting to go there.

More and more white-dusted people were gathering, crowds milling around, though many continued to run past, pushing their way through. Lucie checked to see if anyone was watching her then flicked the catch and opened the bag.

She felt for a pocketbook or a wallet. Her fingers touched soft leather and she pulled her hand away as if she'd been scalded.

She couldn't do it. She was no thief.

She tried to reason with herself. Don't think of it as stealing. How about *borrowing*? She could take a note of the woman's address and return the money later. Get it off Curtis, one way or another, when she got home and mail it. Nothing wrong with that.

She thrust her hand into the bag. Her fingers touched hard plastic. She pulled out an inhaler, like people take for asthma. Pictured the woman lying on the street, gasping for breath, suffocating, knowing she was going to die in the dust. If only Lucie had found her earlier, she could have helped, maybe saved her life.

Lucie couldn't take this woman's money. It would be like robbing a grave. She dropped the inhaler and searched the bag till she found a small, leather Filofax. The woman's name, C J Gillespie, and her address, right here in Manhattan, were on the first page.

She could take the bag to the woman's family, explain what happened and express her condolences. Maybe she could even tell them where to find their loved one's body. Then, if they seemed kind, she'd ask to borrow the cab fare to a women's shelter.

The dust was clearing from the air, and a bright blue sky was gradually reappearing above the tall buildings.

Lucie spotted a couple of cops running towards the World Trade Center, walkie-talkies in hand.

She scrambled to her feet and stepped into their path. 'Officer, I'm lost.' Her voice had all but disappeared again. 'Can you help me, please?'

'Lady, we don't have time for this right now,' said one and pushed by her. The other, a younger guy, stopped and asked how he could help.

'Fitzgerald Square? It's urgent.' She held up the bag for him to see. Trying to save words. 'Need to return this.'

The cop cut her off but gave her the directions she needed then sprinted to catch up with his partner.

Lucie walked as fast as she could through the dust. Every breath clogged her nose and coated her tongue. Her throat was closing again.

Progress was slow as people suddenly stopped, gasping for air, or stood around in dazed groups, but the further she got from WTC the clearer the air and the sidewalks became. Trees were dressed in white as if winter had come overnight and Christmas had moved to September. Nothing made sense anymore.

All the apartment buildings looked the same to Lucie. Black marble, stainless steel and glass. She caught sight of her reflection and stood, staring. A pale, grey ghost of a woman stared back.

'Miss Gillespie? That you?'

A tall, elderly man in a doorman's uniform clasped his hands as if in prayer and looked skywards. 'Thank God you're safe, Miss Gillespie. I thought for sure you must be gone.' He shook his head as if in wonderment.

When he took her hand and clasped it in both of his, Lucie felt tears threaten. This unexpected kindness from a complete stranger was too much for her. With his hand on her elbow, he guided her into a stylish lobby. The conditioned air tasted like the top of a mountain and Lucie took a greedy breath, deep into her lungs. It made her cough and choke.

'Pretty hard to breathe out there, huh?'

Lucie nodded. Tried to control the spluttering.

'Don't you worry, Miss Gillespie. You're safe now. Come on.'

Lucie let herself be led to the elevator. She looked at her benefactor as the doors opened and he stepped back and waited for her to go in first. She was unused to such courtesy and hesitated for a moment, noticing how his sleeve was covered in white dust from her clothes. She tried to wipe the man's arm, whispering a silent 'Sorry.' Her throat had closed up again. Her voice was gone.

'Oh, that's nothing. Old Tommy will soon get spruced up once he sees you safely into your apartment.'

A robotic voice announced 'Fortieth floor' and the elevator came to a smooth stop. Lucie hadn't felt it move, but when the doors slid silently open she could see a different hallway. A mass of fresh blooms stood tall in a glass vase. She could smell stocks and lilies.

'Here we are. Home sweet home.'

Lucie fumbled for the bag and held it out to him but the doorman said, 'No need, Miss Gillespie. I have my pass right here.'

He unlocked a pale wooden door which swung open without a sound.

'Now, is there anything Tommy can do for you, Miss Gillespie?'

Lucie stood dumbfounded, her brain struggling to keep up. She shook her head. He'd got it wrong. She wasn't Miss Gillespie.

'Is there anyone I could call for you? I don't like to leave you all alone after what's happened today.'

Lucie felt a gentle pressure on her lower back. Tommy ushered her through the door into the apartment. She looked at him and shook her head again, keen to explain that he'd made a mistake. She opened her mouth to speak but her throat was dry as Death Valley.

'Lost your voice? Well, I can't say I'm surprised with all that dust. Lordy, what is this world coming to? I never thought I'd live to see such a day.'

He reached for the door handle and drew it towards him. With one foot on the threshold he hesitated, seemed to change his mind and opened the door again.

'You take care, Miss Gillespie. I'll see you tomorrow. And if you need anything meantime, you know where I am.' He smiled and touched one finger to his cap then closed the door.

Lucie stood and stared like she'd never seen a door before.

CHAPTER 4

It was early evening before Diane would let him out of her sight. She'd been tearful all day, crying and clinging to him since she got back from the hairdressers, her hair uncut and uncoloured. The news had interrupted the classical music station that Ronaldo's clients favoured. Apparently Diane hadn't heard it right away, with her head under a shower. She said she'd realised something awful must have happened when the stylist abandoned her halfway through her shampoo.

Diane had asked for her hair, still soapy and wet, to be wrapped in a towel while she called him. She'd tried his offices, all of them, but there were no calls getting through. Networks were crashing right, left and centre. No matter how many times she dialled, the response was the same frustrating 'We are unable to connect your call.'

So she'd rushed back here and found him glued to the TV.

He hadn't expected such a hysterical reaction. At least, not once she knew he'd never made it into the office. She didn't question the migraine that had forced him to turn back before he'd driven a mile. He'd been feigning headaches for months now, a plausible excuse for changes to his routine.

It was her reaction to the deaths that surprised him. He'd expected her to be frightened and emotional until she knew he was safe, but how could anyone shed so many tears for complete strangers? Sure, Diane supported all the bleeding-heart charities, like other women in their social circle, but he hadn't realised how genuinely troubled she was by the plight of those less fortunate.

Every so often, just when he thought she was calming down, some new footage on screen would set her off again. If he heard one more anguished wail of 'Oh, those poor, poor people' he would go mad. Normally he never tired of hearing her honeysuckle voice and her Southern Belle accent, but he'd had enough tearful outbursts for one day.

Early reports were tentative, but as news came in of each new flight disaster, every finger in the media pointed towards a terrorist attack.

'Terrorists,' Diane had wailed. 'In this country? How did that happen? I thought we were safe. Didn't you believe we were safe?'

He'd folded her into his arms, wrapped the cashmere blanket tightly round her shoulders and petted her like a fretting child. 'Yes, I did, my darling. We all did, but those bastards will stop at nothing to bring down Western civilisation. Forgive my language, but those damn terrorists make me so angry.'

Finally, she'd fallen asleep on the sofa where they'd spent the day and he was free to make the necessary phone calls. He wouldn't rest until he knew all loose ends had been tied up, nice and tidy, just the way he liked them.

'Well?' he demanded, the moment the connection was made.

'Man! What a day! Have you seen the news?'

'Of course I've seen the news.'

'Can you believe these fuckin' terrorists, man? Right here on American soil?'

He let the guy rant a bit more then interrupted. 'Did you get the job done?'

'Chill out! I got the job done. But man, you *owe* me. Big time.'

He'd expected as much. 'Why would that be?'

'Because, when we made our deal, nobody knew today was gonna be like the day Kennedy got shot, only worse. Don't you watch TV, man?'

'From what I saw on TV, I would have thought your job was a piece of cake. How hard can it be when every person on the sidewalk is staring at the sky? Not a single witness. I should be paying you less than we agreed, not more.'

'Fuck that. Did you even see that dust cloud? I could've killed the wrong woman.'

'Did you?'

The guy didn't answer. Probably treating it as a stupid question.

'Did you get the proof I asked for?'

'Yeah, I got proof. So when do I get my money?'

'You'll get it.'

'When? I got bills to pay.'

He tried not to imagine what kind of bills this lowlife would have to pay. 'I said you'll get it. Maybe even a bonus. Once I see the proof.'

'I already told you. I got the proof. Okay?' The guy was starting to raise his voice. Not good.

'Okay. I hear you. Same bench in Central Park. Tomorrow. Same time as before.' He paused. All he could hear at the other end of the line was street noise. 'You listening?'

'Tomorrow. Same park. Same bench. Same time. I got it. I ain't stupid, man.'

'That's why we're doing business. You start getting stupid, you stop getting paid.'

'Hey, how do I know you'll show up? It's crazy in Manhattan. What if Central Park's shut tomorrow?'

'Trust me, Central Park will be open. All you have to worry about is getting there on time and following instructions. You got that?'

'Okay, okay. Just tell me what to do. I need that money.'

'Wait until no one else is around. Make sure you do. Then, walk by the bench, drop the key and keep walking. Go around the Bethesda Fountain and come back. The next time you walk by the bench, there'll be a styrofoam sandwich box sitting on it. Your money will be inside, under the sandwich. And we'll be done.'

'Can you make it a pastrami on rye?' The dude laughed a deep rumble, then said, 'Boss, you mentioned a bonus?'

'You'll get your bonus.'

'Yeah?'

'Yeah, extra pickle on the pastrami.'

He terminated the call, put his cell phone beside the others in his briefcase and locked it.

Diane was awake when he got back into the snug. The TV was still on, but showing new footage.

'Honey,' she cried, 'where were you?'

'Right next door. Had some calls to make.'

'Number Seven's just collapsed.'

He looked at the antebellum clock on the mantelpiece. Twenty after five. American Airlines Flight 11 had taken off just before eight in the morning. He did a quick calculation. Ten hours of terror, just as predicted.

Supper was light, Diane claiming she had 'no appetite whatsoever'. He felt it appropriate to feign lack of hunger too. He could always grab a snack from the fridge later, when the cook and maid had left for the night.

Diane rose from the table, pausing to kiss his forehead as she passed on the way to their bedroom. 'I'm quite exhausted. It's just too sad. All those poor, poor people!'

Sighing, he stood and took her in his arms. 'Try to have a good night's sleep, my darling. Perhaps tomorrow things won't look so bleak and we can start to think about how we can help.'

She rewarded his patience with a teary smile. 'You're such a good man. Thank God you're safe.'

He hugged her tightly. Then, his arm around her shoulder, directed her towards the door. 'Goodnight, my love. Sleep well.'

She stopped on the threshold. 'I am so grateful my daddy didn't live to see this day. Everything he worked for turned to dust.'

He smiled a tight smile and held it until she turned away. Everything her daddy worked for? Her daddy may have toiled for his first million, but he wouldn't have made his subsequent millions without the help of a son-in-law working his butt off from dawn till dusk. Langdon Associates had earned its place in the World Trade Center thanks to him and him alone.

He was still smarting from his wife's comment when the phone rang.

'Thank you, sweet Jesus! You're alive.'

He laughed. 'I sure am.'

'God, I can't tell you how good it is to hear your voice, little brother. I saw those towers crumble and just prayed you weren't in any of your offices.'

'No, I was miles away. Stunned, like the rest of the world. Watching it at home, on TV.'

'How come?'

'Another of those damned migraines. Hit me just before I joined the freeway. Turned around and came straight back home.'

'Well, thanks be to God.'

He heard his brother release a huge sigh and asked, 'Bad day?'

'Don't even go there. Sorry I couldn't call earlier.'

'I get it. Don't worry about it.'

'Diane okay?'

'Pretty shaken up. A bit tearful. Relieved I'm safe.'

'That makes two of us. Say, I have to go. It's crazy here.'

'Any idea how many casualties?'

'Classified. Talk soon.'

What a day. Most of his workforce missing and his main business headquarters reduced to rubble and dust. Still, his brother was safe, his wife was safe, and with Charlotte out of the way, he was safe.

He reckoned the occasion demanded a dram of something special. It might be time to draw the cork on the Macallan 1926. Bottled fifteen years ago after sixty in the cask. Only forty bottles produced and he owned one of them. He'd been waiting for a moment like this to taste the whisky inside.

He poured a generous measure into a Waterford crystal glass whose sides were as thin as a bubble. From a matching jug he dribbled a meagre amount of water, no more than a few drops. The water did its job, releasing the celestial vapour he'd heard called the angels' share. It smelled of majestic mountains and rushing rivers. For fifty grand, it should. Glass in hand, he walked towards the television and settled in his favourite armchair. A lazy plume of smoke rose from the ashes of the towers.

'Slàinte,' he said, and raised the Scotch in a toast to absent friends.

CHAPTER 5

Silence. Complete silence. After the bedlam of the street, the lack of sound felt strange.

'Hello?' Lucie sounded like a frog with strep throat. 'Hello?' Louder this time. 'Anyone at home?'

She took a few steps, then, remembering the mess she'd made of the doorman's uniform, looked guiltily at the floor. A track of white footprints followed her across black tiles.

'Hello,' she called again, her voice stronger.

She slipped the Gillespie woman's bag from her shoulder and set it on the floor. Perhaps she ought to just leave it and go. There was obviously no one here to listen to her explanation. She could tell Tommy the story on her way out. Let him explain to the family when they came home.

Her hand was on the door when she realised how strange that story was going to sound. As well as taking another woman's bag she was now guilty of entering her apartment. Tommy might feel inclined to call the police. Who could blame him?

She'd only made her situation worse by coming here.

And she still had no money to get home.

Lucie burst into tears, telling herself it was the shock to blame. She hated self-pity. She wiped her eyes with one fingertip and looked around for something to wipe her face. She pushed gently at a door and reached for the light switch. She grabbed a handful of toilet tissue from the roll and blew her nose. The tissue came away dirty, filled with foul, grey debris. How long had she been breathing this stuff?

She threw the soiled paper in the toilet and reached for more tissue, catching sight of herself in the mirror. Her hair was coated and colourless, her make-up and bruises lost under fine powder. Even her eyebrows and lashes were white. Her jacket and skirt might be ancient and well-worn but, obliterated by dust, they looked no different from the Ted Bakers or Ralph Laurens that thronged Manhattan's business district. She could be any one of ten thousand women.

Lucie turned on the faucet and splashed water on her face. It tasted sweet and refreshing. She drank as if she'd returned parched from a desert, the water healing her dust-dried throat.

Long after her thirst was quenched, she continued to wet her face and watch dirty, grey water sluice down the drain. She leaned her elbows on the basin and wished she could wash away the last twenty-four hours.

When Lucie raised her eyes to her reflection, the mark of Curtis's hand was as clear as a brand on her wet cheek. The swelling round her eye was less obvious than it had been this morning but the familiar black-and-blue stain had started to appear. Lucie touched the bruise and winced. She shook her head. She would never allow him to do this to her again.

When she came out of the bathroom the sun was streaming through an immense plate-glass window that dominated the living room. Lucie stood in the sunlight and savoured its warmth until the billowing clouds of smoke in the distance reminded her why she was here.

She looked around, checking for signs of life. The apartment was as perfect and glossy as an ad in a magazine. Lucie made for the television set and switched it on. The screen burst into life, filling the space with sights and sounds of chaos. Sirens screamed in the background and air horns blasted from fire trucks. A news anchorman stopped his report mid-sentence while a huge armoured vehicle blared and bullied its way through the traffic behind him. Manhattan looked like a war zone.

'Sorry about that,' the news reporter said. 'Yes, as I was saying, where once the iconic Twin Towers dominated our New York skyline, nothing remains but smoking wreckage.'

Lucie turned up the sound and watched the towers crumble over and over again. Her legs went weak and she half sat, half collapsed onto an enormous sofa. If she'd made it to that interview, if Curtis hadn't tried to stop her, if they'd not fought this morning, if she hadn't missed her train. The ifs were too many and too horrific to think about.

Curtis had been outraged that she'd go after a job without telling him. And mortified at the thought of his wife working as a cleaner. So he'd beaten her up. And inadvertently saved her life.

She switched channels. NBC was showing footage of the dust cloud. Hard to believe she'd been down there, running in a crowd like the one on screen. No one outran something that powerful. Crazy to think anyone could.

Lucie couldn't bear to watch. She switched off the television, sat back and closed her eyes, trying to block out the images of mayhem and terror she'd witnessed.

Curtis. She still remembered the day she'd first set eyes on him.

'Morning, ladies,' he'd said, when the college Principal finished introducing Coach Curtis Jardine as 'one of the finest sprinters of his generation and the youngest track coach in US collegiate athletics'. He'd been leaning against the wall of the gymnasium, one foot crossed over the other, arms folded and head bowed, as if too modest to look at them while his boss recited his resumé. Lucie knew she wasn't the only one impressed by the guy's credentials. Around her she could hear other athletes murmuring their appreciation. She was wondering why he'd 'tried out for the ninety-six Olympics', but 'tragically didn't make it to the starting blocks' when he pushed off the wall and stepped forward. The limp was not pronounced, but it was enough evidence of a serious injury to make Lucie feel an immediate sympathy for him. She couldn't imagine not being able to run and compete. It was the very reason for her existence and why she'd won a coveted scholarship to the States.

Her Scottish blood made her immediately distrustful of someone so good-looking and sure of himself. His hair was dark, thick and cut close to his scalp, like a pelt. Lucie wanted to stroke it. See if it would feel soft like a spaniel. He was at least six foot 'in his stocking soles' as her Glasgow granny would have put it, and 'built like a brick shithouse' – Scottish shorthand for the classic sprinter's build.

Their relationship had been strictly coach and athlete to begin with, and boy, could he coach. He pushed his runners hard with track sessions and gym work that left them aching all over. The other girls smiled and simpered to his face and moaned behind his back, but Lucie responded to his style of teaching. Her coach back in Scotland was a sergeant major type who terrified his runners into training and performing well, but here each session was filled with words of encouragement and Coach Jardine always found something to praise in every one of his athletes. Like a flower that had been starved of sunlight, Lucie blossomed under Coach Jardine's guidance. She trained so hard and ran so competitively that she soon became his and the college's best hope of a medal at the NCAA games. When she smashed her personal best and the college record for fifteen hundred metres, gold did not seem like an impossible dream.

She smiled at the memory of that day. The best day of her life. Without stopping to think, Lucie had dipped for the tape and run straight through the finish line into her coach's arms. It was only when she overheard the other girls bitching about her in the locker room that she wondered if the hug was inappropriate.

The following day she'd been going into her local coffee shop as he was coming out, coffee in hand. Classic boy bumps into girl scenario, or in their case, girl bumps into boy. Except he wasn't a boy. He dropped his paper cup, splashing her legs with coffee. No matter how hard she tried to reassure him she was okay, he took complete control and insisted on escorting her to the ER.

He'd been charming and solicitous. Made her laugh while they waited in the triage area with crazy, made-up stories about the other patients' lives. Whispering them to her, his lips thrillingly close to her ear.

The very next day he called her.

'Lucie?'

'Hi, who is this?'

'It's Curtis.'

'Sorry?'

'Curtis? Curtis Jardine.'

'Oh. Coach Jardine. Hi. How are you?'

'I'm good, yeah. More to the point, how are you?'

When she assured him her legs were none the worse for their coffee shower, he asked if she'd like to meet. 'We could have coffee. See if I can actually drink it this time? There are some new training programs I'd like to run by you.'

And so, they'd met up that evening, and, over coffee, she'd told him about her boyfriend Josh, a medical student at Cornell and how she'd met him when they were both working the summer at Camp America. She'd been there for the money and he for 'the experience of working with kids so I can be a great paediatrician one day.'

Coach Jardine had pulled a face at this and she'd giggled, suddenly aware of how pompous she'd made Josh sound.

To change the subject she'd said, 'Which school did you go to?'

He'd laughed. 'Harvard.'

'Really?' Lucie had been impressed and surprised in equal measure. He seemed a little rough round the edges for Harvard.

'Yeah. Law,' he replied, without missing a beat.

Lucie dreamed for a moment of introducing a Harvard law graduate to her father. 'Wow,' she said, 'That's impressive.'

'Sorry, Lucie, I was kidding. The closest I ever got to Harvard was gatecrashing a party. Hey, I'm so dumb it takes me two hours to watch *60 Minutes*.'

After weeks with the staid and preppy Josh, Lucie liked Curtis's infectious chuckle. Clearly he didn't take himself, or life, too seriously.

He'd been so easy to talk to that, over a second coffee, she'd told him all about the major fallout with her dad over her scholarship.

'Are you serious?' Curtis said. 'It's every athletic kid's dream in the States, to win a scholarship to a good school. Your old man should be super proud. We don't give these places away. Especially to foreigners. No offence.' He held his hands up.

Lucie laughed. 'None taken. My mum was pleased for me. She understands me and my need to run, knows what a big deal it was to win a place at NYU.'

'And on a full scholarship.'

'I *had* to get that. My dad refused to pay for me.'

'Why, Lucie?'

'Oh, it's a long story. And boring. I don't really want to talk about it. Let's just say he had his own agenda. He was mad at me for "wasting my brains".'

'Well, I never knew my dad, but I imagine any father would be proud fit to bust of a kid like you.'

'Hey!' She poked him in the ribs. 'Not so much of the kid, if you don't mind.'

He rubbed his side. 'God, you Scottish women are fierce. I think you've bruised me.' Curtis had pulled up his T-shirt and checked his skin for damage, oblivious to the admiring glances his six-pack was attracting.

Hard to imagine him as the same guy who lay sprawled in a La-Z-Boy last night, rubbing his belly and scratching a hairy and unattractive paunch.

'Lucie,' he'd bawled. 'You planning on cooking any time soon?'

'I'd love to, but there's nothing to cook.'

'Why don't you quit being a smart-ass and go get me something to eat?'

She'd tried to keep her voice reasonable, non-accusatory. Knew how easy it was to antagonise him these days. How little it took for his temper to flare like phosphorous. And she wanted him in a good mood so she could tell him about her job interview. She'd been putting it off, scared of his reaction. And even more scared he'd find out about her backup plan.

'There's no food, Curtis. Sorry.'

'Damn right you're sorry. What the hell have you done with all the food money?'

Most of the 'food' money he'd spent on cans of beer, but Lucie thought it unwise to remind him of that. 'It's gone, Curtis.'

'You kidding me? Already?'

She'd seen that as the ideal opportunity to mention the cleaning job she was planning to get in Manhattan the next morning. He hadn't been impressed.

Her stomach gurgled a protest. Almost twenty-four hours had passed since her last meal. She had to eat something or she'd faint. 'Miss Gillespie,' she announced to thin air, 'I'm really sorry, but I need to take some of your food.'

The refrigerator was like a Who's Who of New York food suppliers. Garden of Eden fruit and dairy carrying the Beecher's logo. Dean and Deluca, Citarella, Grace's Market. Luxury food she'd heard of but never tasted.

Lucie's mouth filled with saliva as she stood in the waft of cold air and touched one packet after another. In the end she took only a Greek yogurt and a plump, purple fig, surprised to find her appetite had disappeared. She carried her stolen food and a coffee cup of water to a high stool and sat at the breakfast bar. She ate the yogurt in tiny mouthfuls, thinking about all that food in the fridge. Easily enough to feed a family and yet this didn't look like a home with children in it. There wasn't a toy or a drawing to be seen, far less a grubby fingermark on the plate glass.

The fig was ripe and luscious, but it proved too much for her ravaged throat. After a single bite she put it and the yogurt carton in the trash and washed up her spoon and cup.

When Lucie returned to the living area, the room was bathed in a golden glow. The sun had dipped low in a blood orange sky and smoke from the disaster drifted lazily in gilded clouds. Far too pretty for a tragedy. Nature's joke. Drawn to the window, she leaned her forehead against the glass and felt it cool on her brow. Way below she could see tiny people still streaming out of Manhattan, a river of humanity lost without their public transportation system. How they would ever get home, these New Yorkers who'd set out this morning for a normal day at the office. Nothing would ever be normal again. Scotland had never seemed farther away and she suddenly longed for her home and her mother.

She needed to phone them. Let them know she was okay. They'd definitely be worried about her, wouldn't they, if they'd flown all this way to see her? Why would her dad agree to come, unless he cared?

She remembered his face the last time they'd spoken, as red and frustrated as a toddler's. She'd thought he was going to have a heart attack when she refused to call off her plans. The night before she was due to leave. What did he expect, that she'd just give up on her dream, because he didn't want her to go?

Lucie found a phone on the kitchen wall and dialled 192.

Engaged. She hung up, waited, then dialled again. Still engaged. When she got the same result a third time she remembered. Everyone in the country would be trying to contact someone in New York City.

CHAPTER 6

All afternoon she'd been waiting. No one had come home. No one had phoned. The doorman had called her *Miss* Gillespie, not Mrs, but that didn't mean a woman was single. What else was it he'd said? Something about not wanting to leave her alone. And hadn't he asked if there was anyone he could call?

If no one else lived here, there was little point in waiting any longer. Trying not to shed too much dust as she went, Lucie explored the apartment, room by room. The clothes in the closet belonged to one very slim woman, and even the razor and shaving foam in the shower were a women's brand. A single expensive-looking electric toothbrush stood on its charger in the bathroom. This was a one-woman home.

Lucie had wasted precious hours of daylight. Beyond the window, darkness was falling fast and although she used to come into New York City regularly, it was a long time since she'd walked the streets alone, especially at night. What if she left the apartment and found she couldn't get out of the city? What if she couldn't find somewhere to stay? She'd be forced to spend the night on the street, like some down and out.

She wondered if Curtis was watching TV, worried about her. Maybe he was weeping on Dylan's shoulder, believing her dead. Maybe, if someone else was paying, he was drowning his sorrow. Or maybe he was sprawling in that La-Z-Boy, waiting for her to show up. Ready to punish her for beating him in a fight.

She was so tired, the journey back out to the suburbs seemed as impossible as a coast-to-coast run. By morning the trains would be running and Curtis would have had time to calm down.

The phones would be fixed and she could call her parents and set up that meeting with her mum. Maybe, now, her dad would let bygones be bygones and come too.

It made sense to stay here. Try to get some sleep. In the morning, she'd get up and clear out. She could leave a note explaining how she'd found and returned Miss Gillespie's bag. She'd take enough money to get home and no one would be any the wiser. Lucie made sure the door was locked then turned and leaned on it, frowning at the mess she'd made of the hall floor. She was gradually shedding her mantle of dust, and it was settling all over this beautiful apartment. She could clean up the apartment before she left in the morning, but right now, showering this dust off her skin was the main priority.

As if stripping herself of painful memories, she peeled off her clothes in a corner of the bathroom and rolled them into a tight bundle. A cloud of dust rose to the ceiling and sparkled in the beam of recessed spotlights. Lucie made a mask of her hand and held her breath till she was under the shower.

Miss Gillespie's good taste extended to her toiletries. Jo Malone body wash. Forty dollars a bottle. Once, in Bergdorf-Goodman, Lucie had sampled all the fragrances, longing to own one, until a snotty assistant had enquired whether she intended to make a purchase. She squeezed the tiniest amount onto her hand and washed the dust from her body. The citrus-scented steam was as cleansing as fresh air and she breathed deeply for the first time in hours.

Afraid to linger in the shower, Lucie wrapped an immense bath sheet around her body and tucked the end in tightly. With her hair turbaned in a towel, she wiped down Miss Gillespie's bathroom and left it unsullied, apart from the poor bundle of dusty old clothes dumped on the floor. There was no point in putting them back on, but she couldn't wander around draped in luxury towels like a client in some high-end spa.

A door off the bedroom opened into a space as big as the one she slept in with Curtis. Hanging rails ran along two sides and the rest of the wall space was given over to shelves of sweaters, piles of shoeboxes and drawers full of gorgeous underwear.

A quick look at a few labels confirmed a lot about Miss Gillespie. She had very expensive taste and the income to indulge it. She wore a small size, the same as Lucie, and probably most of the women in Manhattan. One rail held nothing but black suits, dresses and coats – the unofficial uniform of city businesswomen. Lucie felt no sense of envy until she saw Miss Gillespie's collection of casual and sportswear. It had been a long time since Lucie had owned anything so cool. She chose a pair of soft sweatpants and a slouchy top from Pineapple. Both fitted perfectly. That was one advantage of her life with Curtis; living on nervous energy and very little food meant she never gained weight.

When she was dressed she tied her hair in a tight knot on the top of her head. Her granny would be appalled. 'Never go to sleep with wet hair, hen,' she always said. 'Ye'll catch yer death of cold.'

The bed was piled with plump pillows and covered in a quilt as pale and soft as whipped cream. The sheets felt smooth and silky to the touch. The temptation to crawl between them and curl up in a ball was hard to resist, but Lucie couldn't. Stealing the woman's food and using her Jo Malone was one thing. Borrowing her clothes was even okay. But sleeping in her bed was too intimate, too intrusive, too wrong.

Lucie double-checked the door was locked and paid a visit to the bathroom, where she found some Tylenol. She forced two over her aching throat, wincing as she swallowed. Then she took a pillow and a soft comforter from the bed and lay down on the sofa, alert to the slightest sound.

Every time she closed her eyes a cloud of dust raced towards her, shrouding her in white and clogging her throat. She didn't expect to get much sleep.

CHAPTER 7

Lucie's sleep, when it came, was disturbed by dreams of suffocating dust. Each time she woke, the huge window showed the same sky in a different colour. When daylight came, she could see the ghost of smoke rising and drifting, a reminder of the horrors of the day before. She'd relived them countless times in the night. The dust chasing her down, choking her. The running, screaming crowds. Her fall and loss of consciousness. The policeman's flashlight reaching out towards her through the blackout. Waking her. Saving her. Several times she'd startled, sure she'd heard a key turn in a lock, or a door open, someone tiptoeing into the apartment. At one point, just before dawn, it seemed, she heard the elevator working and lay there, paralysed with fear. When she slept again, Curtis was chasing her through the dust cloud. Curtis locking his hands round her neck as vast towers crashed around them. People, running to save themselves, paying no attention to a strangled wife.

Lucie wondered where *he'd* slept last night. If he'd woken eventually and crawled to bed with the dregs of his hangover. Despite the nightmare she'd lived through to get here, it felt good to be free of him. Lucie imagined the luxury of sleeping alone every night, even on a couch. No snoring, farting man to wake her at any hour demanding she satisfy his need for sex. In the early days he'd been loving and gentle, patient with her and eager to please. It wasn't hard to identify when he'd started to change.

Now if she tried to refuse him during the night, Curtis claimed it was his right as a husband to have sex where and when he wanted. She had no rights. He made that clear in as many ways as he could think of. The only time he'd left her alone was when she was carrying the baby. He refused to touch her at all during the pregnancy, even when she craved hugs of reassurance. She never allowed herself to wonder where or how he'd got his satisfaction during those months. Afterwards, he had made up for lost time, telling her how much he'd missed her body.

That was one of the reasons she'd never left, apart from the obvious fact that she'd nowhere else to go. Curtis *could* be the most loving man, making her feel cherished and needed. Sometimes, it felt as good as their first months together and she dared to hope they could fall in love again.

He always said sorry for hurting her. Sometimes he looked at the marks he'd made on her poor body as if he couldn't believe *he* was responsible. He'd cuddle up to her, seeking forgiveness, often weeping till she hugged him and told him it was okay. She'd managed, almost, to forgive him the blows that cost the baby's life, but she'd never forgive the words he'd used. Funny how his verbal abuse had hurt more than punching and kicking. Granny had taught her a chant when she was wee and some girl at school had been giving her a hard time. 'Sticks and stones may break my bones, but names will never hurt me.' Not true, Granny. Words can wound as surely as fists and feet, you just don't see the damage.

Lucie rose from the sofa and walked to the window. The sky was a clear blue and the river gleamed like polished silver in the morning sun. It was difficult to imagine the mayhem of the day before and the awfulness of what was happening down below in Manhattan. This apartment was a haven where all sounds from the street were silenced and horrors were confined to the TV screen.

She picked up the remote. There was no need to select a channel to find coverage of the story. Flicking through several, she saw the same images again and again. The towers intact against a sky of perfect blue. A plane hurtling into a wall of windows. Flames raging from a vast gash in one tower and a plume of black smoke rising from the other. Desperate people clawing at windows higher than the flight path.

Only one scene made any sense to her – the one she'd lived through. People racing along the street trying to run away from the cloud of smoke and dust. She watched it catch up with runners as if they were standing still, obliterating them and everything around them. She switched channels looking for the same footage, longing to understand what had happened to her and to the city. No matter how often she looked, it seemed surreal. And yet Lucie knew exactly how real it had been.

Live coverage was showing the rescue operation in full swing. Thousands of people were missing, feared dead. She could have been one of them.

She turned up the volume, just a little, afraid of being heard next door. Snippets from the different channels began to fit together and tell the story. An attack on the World Trade Center by terrorists, thought to be Muslim. Osama something or other thought to be behind it. She couldn't make out the name. Knew she'd never heard it before. Planes had been hijacked, it seemed, and flown straight into the Twin Towers.

As Lucie watched them implode and collapse, a gush of acid flooded her stomach. Her cleaning job was with an employment agency based on the fifty-second floor of the South Tower. Had she been on time for her nine o'clock interview, she'd have been inside that tower when the plane hit. She'd be dead.

The newscasters talked on, but their voices faded in her head, lost in the morass of her thoughts. When she heard the familiar strains of 'God Bless America' she focused on the screen. In a show of solidarity and defiance, a crowd of Congressmen stood singing on the steps of the Capitol. The last time she'd heard the song had been way back in January. Curtis, drunk before the Superbowl even kicked off, had stood to attention, hand on heart. She remembered laughing at him singing with the Backstreet Boys as they pelted out the national anthem.

She also remembered the beating he gave her when the Giants lost. She could feel his hands closing round her neck. Squeezing.

Lucie's throat ached on the inside and her neck on the outside. Last night's medication had worn off. She touched her scalp, tender where she'd banged it on the sidewalk.

She fetched more Tylenol and a bottle of orange juice from the fridge. Wincing as she swallowed, she drank down the tablets. The juice was sweet and zesty, and she gulped, greedy till her thirst was quenched.

Like Goldilocks stealing the bears' porridge, she foraged and nibbled, exalting in the delicious food. She banished the thought that she was thieving and concentrated on the need to appease her hunger.

She had slept in this woman's home, eaten her food, used her bathroom and she didn't even know her first name. Was she Carol Gillespie? Christina Gillespie? Carrie-jo Gillespie?

Lucie retrieved the bag from the hall floor. She wiped away the dust with her sleeve and opened it. The Filofax was still there, of course, and a bunch of keys. A pack of tissues and a small make-up bag. A soft leather pocket book, fat with twenty-dollar bills. A separate little wallet, that looked and felt handmade, contained store and credit cards, all registered to Charlotte Gillespie. Lucie breathed out a long, sad sigh. 'Charlotte,' she whispered, 'Charlotte Gillespie.'

When Lucie found Charlotte's driving licence, she shivered. She'd often seen Granny do the same thing and say, 'Somebody just walked on my grave.' Lucie had never understood what it meant. Now she did. The woman staring back from the tiny photo was so familiar and yet Lucie knew she'd never met this Charlotte Gillespie. It was like looking at a photo of herself and yet not herself. More like a cousin who shared the family colouring and bone structure. Her hair was darker than Lucie's, at least in the photo, and the style was shorter, expensively cut and expertly styled.

The address shown was for this apartment. Miss Gillespie's date of birth was given as May third, 1972. That would make her three years and a bit older than Lucie. Twenty-nine.

As she tucked Charlotte's licence back into her wallet, Lucie spotted a photo, so small she almost missed it. One single image, torn from a strip, its edges softened and creased. Lucie remembered the photo booth she and her pals used to visit in the local station. It had been a challenge to see how many girls could squash into one photo before the camera flashed and the crabby wee stationmaster came along and chased them.

This photo, passport sized, had plenty of room for two smiling faces, cheek to cheek. Charlotte and a boy. A special boy, judging by the sparkle in their eyes. In a caption competition, every entry would have been a variation of 'Young and in love'. Lucie wasn't sure she and Curtis had ever radiated joy like this.

She turned the photo over. 'Me and Matthew 7/3/90'. She fished the licence back out and checked Charlotte's date of birth. She'd have been seventeen in the photo. About the same age Lucie was when she fell for Curtis. It seemed a long lifetime ago. Lucie took a last look at the young, vibrant Charlotte and couldn't help a sad smile. Then she realised how devastated this Matthew would be. And that she might have to be the one to tell him Charlotte was dead.

Lucie put the photo back where she found it and packed the stranger's belongings into her bag. She was fastening the clasp when the doorbell rang.

Lucie stiffened.

It rang again.

When it rang for a third time she still hadn't moved. Or breathed.

CHAPTER 8

Central park would normally be bustling with people at this time of the day. Workers grabbing some fresh air and open space to eat their lunch. Keep-fit nuts skipping lunch so they could fit in multiple laps of the pond before swapping their shorts and singlet for a business suit. Childminders blocking the paths with traffic jams of strollers and gangs of wayward toddlers; but today the park was eerily quiet. Emergency vehicles could be heard every now and again, heading for the ruins at Ground Zero, as the media had taken to calling WTC. He thought it ironic, knowing the origins of the phrase 'Ground Zero'. First used for the Manhattan Project and the bombing of Japan. A strategy employed to put an end to war, whereas the events of 9/11 were more likely to kick-start a war. The war against terrorism. One that would prove very lucrative for him. Not that he was about to feel guilty. Hell, didn't all wars make money for some guy? Whoever happened to be in the right place at the right time, with grand ambitions and enough invested to see them to fruition.

He pushed back his cuff and checked his Rolex. His contact was twenty minutes late. Getting here had been a bit of a nightmare, admittedly, even for him, but he wasn't prepared to wait all day. Just when he'd decided it was time to make a call, the man appeared at the bench they'd identified as the pick-up point.

From a safe distance he watched the character walk on, the swagger in his stride a clear message – don't mess with me.

Others might be intimidated by this guy, but not him.

He sat down on the bench, stooping low to sweep up the ribbon that lay in a soft loop at the edge of the path, as if carelessly dropped. He stuffed the ribbon into his pocket, his fingers moving along the silken band till they curled around the key. The last thing that could connect him to Charlotte. And proof she was dead.

Hard to believe, sitting in the park, that Charlotte and countless others were gone. Some of them he knew; the rest were nameless, faceless strangers. There was little here to suggest the pandemonium a few miles away. Trees and bushes bore a light dusting of powder, the only clue. It glistened like a mild frost, out of place on this sunny autumn day. Rain forecast for tomorrow would wash them as clean as his conscience.

Pity about Charlotte. They'd had some good times and he would miss their 'business meetings'. A different luxury hotel each time, but always the finest suite. A bottle of Dom Pérignon on ice, her favourite. Long-stemmed flutes waiting by the bubble-filled bathtub.

Charlotte came straight from work and usually kept him waiting, his anticipation growing like the bulge in his pants.

'My God, woman, you look sexy in a suit,' he would say, barely allowing her through the door before he started stripping her. First the sharp black jacket. Then the starched white shirt. He liked to pull it up out of her waistband before undoing one button at a time to reveal her breasts cupped in white lace. Once he'd ripped a button off her shirt in his haste to get his mouth on her nipple and she had become angry, which only excited him all the more.

'That's a three-hundred-dollar shirt you just ruined, you schmuck.'

'Oh, come on, Charlotte honey,' he'd tried to cajole her, 'it's just a little button. Surely a smart girl like you can sew on a button?'

She'd pushed his hands away. 'I do not sew on buttons. Nor do I tolerate anyone ripping my clothes.'

'But you're so sexy, I can't keep my hands off you. Serves you right for keeping me waiting. Feel this.' He'd taken her hand and placed it on his crotch. She massaged him for an agonising few moments then leaned into him, giving him permission to peel off her blouse, carefully this time. He kissed her neck, just the way she liked it.

When she was naked, he carried her to the bed. As they lay in the tub afterwards, sipping champagne, she'd whispered, 'I'd die for you, my darling. You know that, don't you?'

Yes, pity about Charlotte. Pity she got so damned greedy. Why couldn't she be happy with things as they were? She was the only one he'd ever committed to. Before Charlotte, all the others had been one-night stands, meaning nothing. Not even worthy of the name adultery. Just a wicked temptation, as harmless as a glass of champagne or a handmade chocolate. And equally meaningless. But Charlotte had been different, the only one he'd ever been prepared to cheat on Diane with.

He wound the silky ribbon round his fingers, recalling the moment he'd put it round Charlotte's neck. 'This is the key to our future,' he'd whispered.

'Our future *together*,' she'd insisted.

'Guard it well.'

'I'll keep it close to my heart.'

He'd kissed her mouth to stop her talking and tucked the key inside her bra. Her breast felt as smooth as the ribbon itself and his fingers had followed it, delving down into the lacy cup. She'd stopped him, removing his hand as she spoke. 'Uh-uh,' she'd teased. 'I want to wait till we're together forever. I want to feel like a bride on her first night.'

'I'm sorry, I just can't get enough of you. I'm not sure I can wait.' Poor Charlotte. She would never know the reason he'd been so keen to have her was because he knew it would be the last time. Ever.

Ultimately it was Charlotte who brought about her own downfall, so he wasn't about to feel guilty. She'd still be alive if she hadn't become so demanding and clingy. So 'in love'. He didn't do love. It was far too complicated.

When, a few weeks ago, she accused him of waiting too long to end his marriage, she'd threatened to tell Diane everything.

Desperate to hold things together until the middle of September, he'd had no option but to let her in on the deal, promising it would guarantee the financial independence that would allow him to walk away from Diane. He'd been taking a risk, aware that sharing his knowledge with Charlotte made her dangerous, but he hadn't anticipated her late change of heart. Now she was gone. She would complicate his life no more.

Like any businessman on his lunch break, he removed a sandwich container from a bag and placed it on the seat beside him. When his contact reappeared at the far end of the path, he stood and walked away in the other direction. He didn't look back.

CHAPTER 9

When she felt brave enough to move, Lucie tiptoed to the door and pressed her ear to the wood. She kept her eyes fixed on the handle, watching for the slightest movement. Had she locked the door properly?

'Okay, I guess I'll just leave them here.' A man's voice. Matthew? Lucie knew she should open the door, break the bad news, hand over the bag and get out of there. Instead she listened to the guy's footsteps receding, then waited for the elevator to come and take him away. Whoever he was.

When she was one hundred per cent sure he'd gone, she quietly opened the door and peeped out. A bouquet of roses lay on the mat. She reached out one arm and grabbed them. Clasping the flowers to her chest, she closed the door and leaned back against it, breathing as if she'd just dashed through sniper alley.

A tiny envelope was tucked in amongst twelve long-stemmed roses, all different shades of pink. Inside was a printed card that bore the message, *'Last Rose of Summer'* – *the September Selection, from your friends at The Bloom Room. Your next delivery, due September 26, will be 'Autumn Glory' a fiery collection of golds, reds and umbers, reminiscent of New England in the fall. Enjoy!* A handwritten note at the bottom apologised for the bouquet being much smaller than usual due to a shortage of roses following the sad events at WTC.

Lucie thought of people trying to buy roses for lost loved ones and felt guilty about keeping this whole bunch for herself. Except they weren't for her. They were for Charlotte, one of the lost. And not from Matthew.

Lucie was starting to build up a picture of Miss Gillespie. A stylish, single woman, who bought her own flowers. The only sign she'd ever loved and been loved, a dog-eared photo from a previous millennium. A woman who bought designer labels and cashmere sweaters. A woman who chose to live alone in a million-dollar apartment in Lower Manhattan, and could afford to do so. Renting a place like this would cost thousands of dollars a month. Charlotte was either from a very wealthy family or held down a job that carried a six-figure salary.

Lucie might have become a successful businesswoman like Charlotte, had she taken a different direction, made other choices. Listened to her father. If only he'd let her do it her way. She'd have been happy to follow him into the transport business her granddad had started with one ancient lorry. She'd have been proud to take over one day, and build the business. Lucie had always preferred lorries to dollies. She first got behind the steering wheel of a truck when she was twelve years old, having charmed Old Sandy into letting her have a go. By fourteen, although her dad didn't know it, she could reverse a twelve-wheeler on the forestry roads where they picked up the logs. At sixteen she was ready to cast off the calf-length kilt and unflattering blazer of her all-girls school and start earning the men's respect as she learned the haulage business.

Her father would have none of it. Weighed down by a chip on his shoulder about his own lack of education, he was determined she'd continue with hers. He wanted her to study accountancy. She could be trusted to do the books, but running the business? No chance. That was man's work.

Lucie had rebelled, of course, but looking back, would it have been such a terrible mistake to do things his way? The advent of open-cast mining in Scotland meant thousands of tons of coal being hauled by road and McBride Hauliers had been astute enough to be ready for the bonanza. By now Dad would own a huge fleet of trucks, worth millions of pounds. Lucie could have had a challenging, satisfying job and a small fortune due to come her way.

Maybe it wasn't too late to make up with her dad. How hard could it be? He was right here in New York City. How Mum had managed to convince him to come after all these years was a mystery. Maybe he was ready to forgive her? Granny always said they were too alike, Lucie and her dad. 'Thrawn as a wulk, you pair.' Like a whelk refusing to be winkled out of its shell, neither one was ever prepared to give an inch. But Lucie was more than ready to capitulate now. She would beg her father's forgiveness, if it got her away from Curtis.

Maybe, if she arranged to meet Mum at their hotel, Dad would agree to join them. If things went well, Lucie could be on a plane home to Scotland by the end of the week.

This time the operator answered on the first ring.

The hotel also answered on the first ring. A good omen.

'I'd like to speak to one of your guests, please. Her name's Margaret McBride?'

'Let me just put you on hold.'

Lucie crossed her fingers, hoping her father wouldn't come to the phone. She wasn't quite ready for that.

'I'm sorry. We have no one here of that name.'

'Would you look again, please? Under McBride. John Bradford McBride.'

'Our system shows a reservation in the name of McBride. Arriving September tenth.'

Lucie had arranged to meet her mother on the eleventh, so that would be right. 'Yeah, that's them. Can you put me through to their room, please? Ask for Mrs McBride, if you don't mind.'

'I'm sorry. Mrs McBride hasn't checked in.'

CHAPTER 10

'Is this the Crowne Plaza? In Times Square?'

'Yes, it is.'

'Well, I think there must be some kind of a mistake. Would you mind checking again, please?'

Lucie heard the receptionist sigh. 'I already have, ma'am. I'm afraid your friend hasn't arrived.'

'Not my friend. My parents. And they must have arrived. Mum said they were flying into New York on the tenth. I was supposed to meet her for coffee yesterday after my interview but I got caught in the ash cloud when the towers collapsed and I couldn't make it.' Lucie realised she was babbling. 'Sorry,' she said, feeling ridiculous, and very close to tears.

'Would you like to leave a number? Who should I say called?'

'I don't have a number. Can you please tell them Lucie rang? And I'll call back.'

'Certainly. I'll make sure that message is passed on.'

When she put the phone down, Lucie felt as flat as a week-old balloon. She hadn't realised how much she'd been pinning on this chance of a reconciliation. She should have swallowed her pride sooner. Written home years ago.

She'd been pinning a lot on that job interview too. It had given her a legitimate reason for going into Manhattan on her own, one that Curtis couldn't object to. Or so she'd thought. His temper had flared before she even got to the bit about seeing her mother afterwards.

She'd hoped to meet Mum with a job offer in her pocket so she wouldn't appear to be a complete loser, but with the South Tower gone, Lucie had no job prospects. And the tiny amount of money she had scrimped together was lying in the street somewhere, along with her driver's licence whose address was way out of date. She and Curtis had moved around so much, from one squalid rental to another, that Lucie had stopped trying to keep personal paperwork up to date. Besides, with no car to drive, she only ever used her ID to buy his beer.

She had no job, no money and no ID. The complete loser package.

It made sense to stay here for now. Grab a couple of days' breathing space.

Space to breathe. Exactly what she needed after escaping a dust cloud. And exactly what she needed after escaping from Curtis.

One of his regular complaints was that she'd let herself go. 'What happened to that bright-eyed, shiny-haired, hot, sexy babe I married?' he would whine. 'When did you turn into such a tramp?' Last week he'd grabbed her ponytail and tugged it viciously. Lucie did her best not to wince but she couldn't keep her eyes from watering.

'Oh, don't start in with that blubbering,' he said. 'What man wants to listen to that?'

Lucie had attempted a smile.

'That's better.' He patted her rear and his face clouded again. 'When did your ass get so skinny? I used to love your booty in tight jeans. Didn't your momma teach you to look good for your man?'

'It takes money to look good, Curtis, but you're right, I could use a haircut. Maybe you could lend me a few dollars to have my hair trimmed, buy some new jeans, so I can look good for you?'

Mistake. Big mistake.

Lucie dismissed Curtis from her mind. He'd been controlling her thoughts, her life, for far too long.

From now on, Lucie was in charge. First she trimmed her hair, evening up the scraggy broken ends with scissors she found in a drawer in the kitchen. Not ideal, but she managed to get it fairly even, then blew it dry and smooth with Charlotte's hairdryer. The result was pretty good for a novice hairdresser and, in spite of her battered face, Lucie thought she looked okay. No, not just okay, she looked a whole lot better than she had for a long time.

She opened a drawer under the bathroom mirror. It slid out silently to display a collection of make-up that would grace the cosmetics counters in Fraser's, Glasgow's most glamorous department store. Lucie remembered Mum and Granny taking her on the underground train to Buchanan Street. She could still recall the smell of damp earth and oil hanging in the air and the way that air would funnel down the track when a train approached. She used to hang on tightly to Mum's hand, terrified of being sucked off the edge of the platform and into the endless tunnel. Every Christmas they took her to see Santa and Granny bought her a party dress. Then they'd have lunch in the restaurant on the top floor. When it was time to go home, Lucie had to be dragged away from the central hall, with its soaring Christmas tree and balconies festooned in garlands of gold and white.

Lucie chose some foundation and applied it to her face. It failed to cover her bruises, but it did add some colour to her pale cheeks. She admired the effects in the mirror. Out of the corner of her eye she spotted the jumble of dusty clothes she'd dumped on the floor. Time to do something about those.

She stuffed her suit and shirt in the kitchen trash can and pushed them right to the bottom, out of sight. Then she turned on the faucet and watched the last of the dust flow off her hands and down the drain.

Over the sound of the water, she heard a buzzing, insistent as a hungry wasp. Lucie turned off the faucet and listened, not recognising the sound and trying to work out where it was coming from. Some kind of intercom, connecting the apartment with the lobby.

Someone seemed very keen to come up and see Charlotte.

The intercom continued to buzz while she stood and looked at it, not knowing what to do.

Abruptly, mid-racket, it stopped. In the silence that followed, Lucie's bravado vanished. This could all end very badly and she'd been treating it like a game, a kid playing dress-up in clothes and make-up that didn't belong to her.

She should get her own clothes back on, pronto, and get the hell out of here. Take nothing of Charlotte's, not even the train fare. No one need ever know she'd lived another woman's life for a day. What on earth made her think she could get away with this hare-brained idea?

She'd have to go back to Curtis, of course. But this time she'd be stronger. This near-death experience would help her stick to her resolution never to let a man control her again. Maybe he'd be glad to see her back. He must be worried about her by now. It would be better this time, different. She'd make certain of it.

Lucie picked her clothes out of the trash, shook off the worst of the dust and started to put them on. She'd have to say sorry for hurting Curtis, and he wouldn't be happy with the idea of his woman hitting back, knocking him over. The best she could hope for was that he might not remember the fight. He was out cold when she left, after all.

It started at her fingertips, the realisation of what she'd done. It was a numbing, black fear that crept up her hands and arms till it reached her chest and clawed at her heart.

CHAPTER 11

*T*hat's why he was lying so still.

She hadn't thought to stop and check. Hadn't been too concerned. She'd often seen him pass out with drink or drugs, then lie motionless till he sobered up.

When she'd told him there was no food in the house, he'd grudgingly handed over some loose change and sent her to the 7-Eleven for cheap burgers. She'd cooked them in the huge cast-iron skillet that was a pain in the ass to wash up. She needed two hands to lift it but Curtis insisted she always use it because he liked the way its ribbed surface made griddle marks on his burgers. She couldn't really remember what wound him up. She'd started to tell him about the cleaning job but she never got to finish. Something set him off. Some little thing she'd said or done, or not said or not done. Hard to tell at the time and impossible to remember now. Whatever it was, maybe the cocktail of drink and drugs he'd taken earlier, who knew, something made him seem extra threatening.

Desperate to avoid riling him further, Lucie had served up his burgers, just the way he liked them. Then she made herself scarce while he had his meal in front of the TV.

She couldn't believe her luck when she woke alone. She managed to shower and dress without disturbing him, and would have made it out the door if she hadn't decided to grab an instant coffee. She'd planned to drink it lukewarm rather than risk the scream of the boiling kettle. She'd have got away with it, too, had she not left her bag in the bedroom. The kettle started to whistle, gently at first, but building to a crescendo. Lucie grabbed her bag and sprinted. Abruptly, the whistling stopped.

He was waiting for her, traitorous kettle in hand. Fearing he might throw it at her, she ducked back into the bedroom, but a violent slam of metal on metal told her he'd dumped it back on the stove.

Lucie had checked her watch. She couldn't afford to hide too long or she'd miss her interview. She waited a minute, counting off the seconds in her head, then, thinking the danger had passed, she ventured out, a nervous smile on her face. 'Morning, honey,' she chirruped, hating the toadying in her voice.

Curtis looked her up and down, as if appraising her. He grinned and she relaxed a little.

'Well, don't you look fine?' he said, admiringly.

She brushed down her dark skirt and picked at a speck of white that caught her eye. Quick as a snake, he pounced, grabbing her by the throat. His fingers tightened till she could hardly breathe. Without a word, he pushed her back against the kitchen cabinets. Leaned his weight on her till she was terrified her spine would snap. If she didn't choke first. Somehow she knew that this time he was going to kill her.

His breath was stale and rancid on her face, but she knew better than to react. He growled at her, his voice low and filled with menace. 'Hell you think you're going, all dressed up like a city girl?'

With her windpipe crushed, she couldn't breathe, far less answer.

'You really think I'm gonna let you waltz off into Manhattan every morning?' Her silence seemed to madden him further. 'You're goin' nowhere! Hear me?' He squeezed tighter. When she couldn't loosen his fingers, she tore at his face but he didn't seem to feel a thing. She was about as effective as a fly, irritating but harmless. With no time to make a fist, Lucie lashed out with her flat hand and struck him on the ear.

He let her go. She breathed, gasping in great lungfuls of precious air that made her cough and retch. Curtis staggered back, like a cartoon drunk, then dropped to his knees. She'd seen him fall over before and knew the pattern. He'd clamber back onto his feet and beat her twice as hard, as if she'd deliberately humiliated him. Usually she would brace herself, scared to do anything but take whatever revenge he chose to dole out. God alone knew what it would be this time. The first time she'd had the temerity to fight back.

She didn't wait to find out. Her arm stretched along the counter looking for a weapon, a knife, anything she could use to protect herself. Her fingers found metal and closed around the handle of the skillet. She pulled it to her and, with a strength she didn't know she possessed, Lucie raised that skillet with both hands, as high as she could, and brought it down like an axe on his back. She could have gone for his head. But she didn't want to kill him, just stop the beating. Curtis dropped to the floor, his head smacking the stone tiles with a thud that made her stomach heave. She backed away, clutching her neck.

Without taking her eyes off him, she gathered her bag, stepped over his body and left.

It was all clear to her now. He must be dead. Why else would he just lie there and let her leave?

Lucie looked at the old skirt she'd been pulling on and let it drop to the floor, sending up little puffs of dust.

She couldn't go back. They'd be waiting to arrest her. She wasn't prepared to face a murder charge for Curtis. He'd robbed her of one life. She wasn't about to let him take all she had left of this one. She could claim self-defence, but with no witnesses, there wasn't a jury in the land who would believe her. What would any self-respecting citizen think of a woman who clubbed her husband with a cast-iron pan and went calmly about her business?

Why hadn't she called nine one one? That's the question any prosecutor would ask. Maybe she wanted him to die? After all, she'd made no attempt to check for vital signs, no effort to summon assistance. She didn't even scream. She had silently and cold-bloodedly left the scene of the crime.

The TV burbled quietly in the background. Lucie savaged her fingernails while she considered her options. She didn't have many to choose from.

She could go back and face a murder rap.

She shook her head. Not going to happen.

She could take off and start again elsewhere.

Impossible. She had no ID, no money, no skills. And anyway, where would she go?

The intercom buzzed again. Lucie kicked her feet free of the dusty skirt that tethered her to her old life and lifted the receiver.

'Hello? Ms Gillespie?'

CHAPTER 12

'**M**s Gillespie?'
　　　　Lucie couldn't answer.
　　　　'Is this Ms Gillespie?'
Lucie didn't know what to say.

'Ma'am, I'm sorry to bother you. I called earlier. I hope I didn't disturb you.' The caller, his voice that of a young man, sounded nervous. 'It's just that I'd like to introduce myself to as many residents as possible and I wondered if I could come up and say hello.'

Lucie felt a sweat break out and knew a red rash would be racing up her neck. Who was this guy?

He seemed to read her mind.

'Oh, I'm so sorry, ma'am. I'm Tommy's replacement.'

She scanned her brain for a match that would make sense of these words and, fortunately, came up with the answer before the pause became too long. Tommy, the doorman who'd let her in yesterday.

'Oh yes,' she murmured.

'So, would that be okay?'

'I guess,' she said, because no seemed the wrong thing to say.

'Thank you, ma'am. I'll be right there.'

Lucie hung up the phone and stood there, stunned. She had just said she was Charlotte Gillespie. Not in so many words, maybe, but the implication was clear.

Sweat trickled between her breasts. She swiped it away and felt bare skin. She needed to get dressed. And fast. Before this guy turned up at the door.

She grabbed the first things she could find – the clothes she'd worn the night before. As she pulled the other woman's sweatshirt over her head, Lucie imagined she was pulling on a new skin, turning into someone else.

The doorbell rang.

A tall, fair-haired young man stood in the hallway, looking somewhat uncomfortable in the liveried uniform of a doorman. He was holding his hand out, waiting for Lucie to take it.

'Hello, Ms Gillespie. I'm Rob. For the foreseeable future, I'll be your replacement doorman. Or concierge, if you prefer.' His smile was self-deprecating and Lucie couldn't help smiling back as she shook his hand.

'What happened to Tommy?'

'I heard he lost someone real close, his son, maybe? Worked in one of the towers. Don't know any details, but I sure feel sorry for him.'

Lucie nodded, knew she ought to say something. 'That's so sad,' was all she could manage.

Rob's young face was sombre. 'Well, ma'am. I'd like to assure you of my best service at all times. Anything I can do for you, please don't ever hesitate to call me.'

'Thank you, Rob,' she said and started to close the door.

'Ma'am?' He touched the side of his face then pointed at hers. 'Your face, ma'am. Are you okay?'

'Thanks, I'm okay.' She nodded. 'Got caught in the dust cloud yesterday and fell over. But I'm fine, really. Lucky to be alive.'

'Ain't that the truth! Well, Ms Gillespie, you know where I am, if you should need anything.'

The door clicked shut. Lucie's shoulders slumped. This was no good.

She had to get hold of her folks and get out of here. The sooner, the better.

CHAPTER 13

'I'm sorry,' said a receptionist who sounded anything but. 'We haven't heard from Mrs McBride. In fact, we've re-allocated the room.'

'You can't do that. What if they turn up?'

'I'm afraid it's company policy when clients don't check in within forty-eight hours.'

'Have you any idea where else they might be?' Lucie asked. What a stupid question.

'You should speak to our central reservations team. They may be able help you.'

One more call was all it took for Lucie to learn that her parents hadn't checked in at any hotel in the chain. But then, why would they go elsewhere when their reservation was for Times Square. Every visitor to New York wanted to see Times Square.

Maybe something had happened back home. Some emergency that meant they couldn't come after all. More likely Dad changed his mind at the last minute. She should have expected as much. The only thing bothering him would be that he didn't cancel the reservation in time to get his money back.

This not knowing would drive her daft. She could try the airport, ask if someone would check the passenger lists for her. It was a long shot, but worth a phone call.

The guy who answered the airport helpline almost choked when Lucie made her request. 'Lady, are you for real?'

'Sorry?'

'After what happened yesterday?'

'Sorry, I didn't think.'

'No, ma'am, you sure didn't. You have a nice day now.' He hung up.

There was one more call she could make. Her parents' home number, the only phone number in the world she could remember off by heart. As she'd expected, it was 'unavailable'. Years ago she had asked what that meant. It meant Dad had changed their number and gone ex-directory.

CHAPTER 14

Dylan woke with a jolt. A nurse was shaking his arm, repeating his name.

'What's happened? Is he dead?'

'We've brought your friend out of the induced coma. Would you like to see him for a few minutes?'

'Please,' Dylan muttered, still half-sleep. 'Is he okay?' He rubbed at his three-day growth. His eyes felt as if he'd only just closed them but the clock on the waiting room wall said different.

He stood, unsteady on his feet, and the nurse touched his elbow. 'Do you need a moment?'

He shook his head. 'Just got up too fast. I'm good. What about Curtis? What shape's he in?'

'You'll probably find him a bit woozy to begin with.' The nurse turned away before he could ask any more, but woozy was fine. He could handle woozy.

She showed him into a room full of people in hospital garb. I hope Curtis has insurance to pay for this level of attention, he thought.

The lighting in the room was low and subdued and machines bleeped and flashed in the background. The medical staff were speaking to each other in hushed tones and as they moved aside Dylan caught his first sight of Curtis. Dylan thought he'd been brought to see the wrong patient. The man on the bed had more wires attached than a marionette. Bags of liquid hung above the bed and underneath another contained murky fluid that Dylan preferred not to look at. Curtis's pale cheeks were clean-shaven and someone had flattened his hair into something resembling a style. His chest was bare and dotted with electrodes and seemed far too skinny and frail. Lying there with his eyes closed, Curtis looked like an old man, closer to sixty than thirty.

No one spoke and Dylan didn't know what was expected of him. He was there in lieu of next of kin, Curtis being alone in the world now that Lucie seemed to have disappeared. He stepped up to the bedside and looked at one of the doctors for permission.

'Go ahead and talk to him. He'll hear you.'

Dylan leaned close to his friend. 'Curtis,' he whispered, self-conscious. 'Hey, buddy. It's Dylan.'

No response. Was Curtis brain damaged? Dylan looked to the nurse, wordless.

'Mr Jardine,' she said in a bossy, no-nonsense voice. 'It's time to wake up now. You have a visitor and the doctors would like to speak to you.'

Without opening his eyes, Curtis said in a rasp so hoarse it was hard to make out, 'Lucie?'

'Sorry, buddy,' said Dylan. 'Hate to disappoint you, but it's only me.' When there was no reaction, he said, 'It's Dylan, Curtis.'

Curtis squinted as if the light was too much for him. 'Dylan?'

'Yeah, that's right. Dylan. You know me. We've been best buddies since kindergarten. Remember Miss Rosie?'

No response.

'Our first-grade teacher? She just loved you. You remember?'

'Miss Rosie.'

'Man, she must be about a hundred years old by now.' Dylan laughed at his own joke and was delighted when Curtis laughed too, but the laugh was short-lived. It turned into a hacking cough and Curtis raised a pale hand to his throat.

A tall, middle-aged man in a white coat stepped forward and said, 'I'm Doctor Fernandez, Neurology. Your throat may be a bit tender for a few days, Mr Jardine. We had to intubate you, I'm afraid, just to help you breathe for a while.'

'What happened?' Curtis looked at Dylan, appealing for an answer. 'Dylan?'

'I don't know, buddy. I came round to your house and found you out cold. Thought you were sleeping off the night before. Then when you wouldn't wake up, I got a bit freaked. Finally, you came to and said a few words. But you passed out again, and that's when I called nine one one.'

'When?' Curtis asked.

'You've been here three days, Mr Jardine,' said the doctor.

'Three?'

'You were seriously injured.'

'Feel fine now. When can I go?'

'Not for a while, I'm afraid. You've suffered severe trauma to your spine.'

'My spine?' Curtis narrowed his eyes, trying to understand. 'But I'm okay, yeah?'

'Unfortunately we were unable to repair the damage.'

'What does that mean?'

'You appear to have sustained severe trauma to the thoracic spine which has caused damage between T11 and T12.'

'Speak plain English!'

'I'm sorry to have to tell you …' The doctor paused.

'Tell me what?'

'It's unlikely you'll walk again.'

CHAPTER 15

'**D**octor Fernandez, sir,' said Dylan quietly. 'Are you sure about that?'

'I'm afraid so,' the doctor answered, nodding slowly. He sounded genuinely upset.

Curtis howled like an injured dog. The sound chilled Dylan to his core. Then, just as suddenly, Curtis went quiet. He turned his head away as if to shut them out.

The nurse laid her hand on Curtis's arm but he flung it off and tried to move across the bed.

'My legs won't move. Somebody help me!'

Curtis had never asked for help in his life. He'd borrowed money, scammed beers, but always demanded whatever it was he wanted, as if he were taking his dues. The beseeching look in his eyes was new and just about the most heartbreaking sight Dylan had ever seen.

Curtis turned on the doctor. 'You saying you're just giving up on me? There has to be something you can do. For chrissake, man, guys with no legs run marathons these days. I've seen them.'

'I'm terribly sorry, Mr Jardine. The spinal column is less protected and very vulnerable at the point where the trauma occurred. That has very serious implications. And, although it grieves me to have to say this, there's nothing we can do to reverse the damage. I'm so very, very sorry.'

Dylan could listen to no more. Afraid Curtis would see his tears, he turned his back and stepped away from the bedside. As he left the room he glanced at the shrunken figure in the bed. Curtis did not appear to notice him leaving.

* * *

It took two cups of coffee and a chat with the kind nurse before Dylan could face going back in. When she offered to go with him for moral support, he accepted.

Curtis was staring at the ceiling.

'Hi, pal.' Dylan said. 'You feeling any better?'

Curtis turned his head to look at him. Dylan tried to read his expression.

'Help me out here, Dylan. I'm trying to remember what happened. There's a block in my head, and it's driving me crazy. I remember an argument with Lucie and then it all goes blank on me. The next thing I remember is waking up on the floor and you're there, watching some goddamn disaster movie on our TV.'

Dylan and the nurse exchanged a look but neither spoke.

'What?' said Curtis.

'There was no movie, Curtis. That was real. Some terrorist group ordered an attack on the World Trade Center that morning. The Twin Towers collapsed.'

'Come on, man. You don't expect me to believe that.'

Dylan said nothing.

'You're not kidding, are you?'

Dylan shook his head, his face solemn.

'Is anyone hurt?'

Before Dylan could answer, Curtis said, 'Sorry, dumb question.'

'They reckon thousands of people could be dead.'

Curtis tried to sit up in bed, and when he couldn't he cursed loudly and looked to the nurse for help. She shook her head sadly, her eyes full of compassion. 'I'll go get some help.'

'Listen to me, Dylan. I could be wrong about this, but I'm pretty sure Lucie said she was going to World Trade Center. Something about getting a job. Is that right?'

'I don't know, Curtis. I don't know anything about Lucie looking for a job.'

'Is she okay?'

Dylan rubbed at his chin, and looked away.

'Dylan, look at me. Is Lucie okay? Why isn't she here?'

'I'm not sure.' Dylan nibbled on his lip.

'Hell you talkin' about, you're not sure?'

Dylan found it hard to look his friend in the face. 'I'm not sure where she is. I'm sorry, man. I haven't seen her.'

'You been round the house?'

'Yeah, a couple times, but she wasn't there.'

Curtis started to cry. Not a manly cry with silent sobs and heaving shoulders. Dylan thought it was the saddest sound. He looked at the nurse. Do something, he wanted to say.

She gave Curtis a quick check over and quietly left the room. Dylan didn't know what to do. He sat on the side of the bed and patted Curtis on the shoulder. To his horror, his tough-guy friend pulled at him and hugged him close, like a child seeking comfort.

When the weeping died down, Dylan extricated himself and got to his feet.

'I'm gonna go now, buddy, and leave you to get some rest. I could use a freshen up and a shave. Okay, pal? I'll see you tomorrow, okay?'

Curtis didn't respond.

CHAPTER 16

The television reports were full of distraught relatives desperately seeking the tiniest shred of evidence that their loved ones were alive. People had gathered with home-made placards, each showing the face of a lost relative, friend or lover. Lucie scanned the crowd and turned up the volume. Those interviewed told of phone calls from the towers made by loved ones who knew their death was inevitable and imminent. Some calls had been cut off mid-word while horrified relatives watched the drama unfold on screen like some far-fetched disaster movie. This was a comment made by many. For a few seconds they'd been watching a gruesome reality without knowing it was real.

Perhaps, among the throng, someone was holding a placard with Charlotte's face on it?

Maybe someone was out there looking for Lucie Jardine?

Curtis? Not impossible. The more she thought about it, the more she managed to convince herself he was alive. She hadn't hit him that hard. Maybe he was down there on the streets of Manhattan, looking for her. Worried she'd come to harm.

He'd been so proud of her in the early days. She was his protégée, his hope for glory. He saw her potential and was determined to take her right to the top of collegiate athletics, and beyond. The night he'd told her he loved her, he'd also told her she could win Olympic gold. Something he had never been able to achieve. Later they'd made love for the first time. Lucie knew it was crazy to get mixed up with her coach but it was too late. She'd have done anything to please him. She trained harder than anyone else on the squad, she never cheated on the prescribed diet even when she longed for some Häagen-Dazs. Her dedication paid off and her times got better and better. Curtis made Lucie feel like the queen of the world.

Then it all went sour.

She shouldn't think about Curtis. He'd been the toxic air she'd breathed for too long, and now she was free. Or at least she could be, if she were brave enough.

A wee voice kept whispering in her head. She ignored it at first but the whispering continued, persistent as tinnitus and equally maddening.

This could be her way out. Her escape route from the prison of her life with Curtis. She'd fought back, and defiantly come to Manhattan yesterday morning. Hadn't that been her first step towards freedom? Now Fate had given her a great big push in the right direction. Like jumping from the poorest to the richest street on a Monopoly board without passing Go.

Lucie began to see the merit in what the voice in her head was saying. Perhaps she *could* stick around here for a while. Lie low, just till the dust settled. She smiled grimly at the metaphor that had come so easily to mind. No dust-associated clichés would ever be the same for New York citizens. Especially those who'd lived and breathed it.

As she dumped her old clothes in the trash for the second time, Lucie felt she had turned a corner, but if she were going to become Charlotte Gillespie, even for a few weeks, she'd need to find out all she could about her.

Another look in Charlotte's bag revealed nothing new, but she was struck by the fact that such an affluent businesswoman didn't carry a cell phone.

This apartment must have information to share. All she had to do was look in the right places. She'd make a start soon. Right after she raided that fridge again.

With a plate stacked high with deli and salads, Lucie looked at the bottle of Riesling chilling on the refrigerator door.

'Why the hell not?' she announced, opening tall cupboards till she found Charlotte's glassware. It was beautiful, the same quality as the rest of her belongings, but each glass stood beside only one that matched. Two red wine, two white wine, two flutes, all with dangerously slender stems. Two tumblers and two high-ball, lined up with precision. Charlotte wasn't one for entertaining large numbers. Or perhaps when she entertained, the caterers brought everything. Lucie reached for a wine glass and poured the pale wine, enjoying the joyous way it gurgled out of the bottle. She lifted her glass and raised it in a toast. 'Cheers, Charlotte. Here's to you. And me. One and the same.'

Lucie ate, trying to enjoy the first good food and wine she'd tasted for years.

Since Curtis failed to find work she'd been making ends meet on a tight budget. For the last few months it had got even tighter as she'd tried to save a little each week and stash it below the mattress. The only way she could do that was by cutting down the amount she ate.

'I'm just not hungry,' she explained, the one time he'd remarked on the small amount on her plate. He never asked again. A dime here and a quarter there soon added up until she had enough for her fare into Manhattan and the first step on her escape route.

Who would blame her if she indulged herself for a few days in the good things Charlotte enjoyed. Lucie felt like a child, playing house with someone else's belongings. What harm could there be in that, as long as she didn't damage or steal anything?

The only problem that Lucie could foresee in the immediate future was food. The supplies in the fridge wouldn't last for ever. At some point she would need to venture out or go hungry.

The thought of leaving Charlotte's place made her insides cramp like a monthly pain. After the madness on the street, being cocooned in this luxury apartment was balm to her soul.

When she walked away from Curtis she swore she'd never let anyone or anything scare her again, but she'd been living with fear for so long, she'd forgotten how to be brave.

The intercom buzzed. Lucie startled like a nervous kitten. A bizarre giggle emerged with her out breath as she tried to decide if she should answer. Stuffing the fear down into a corner of her mind, she picked up.

'Ms Gillespie, I have a guy here says he always delivers your grocery order. I just have to check with you before I let him bring it on up? Excuse me one second, ma'am.' His voice became less audible, as if he'd turned away to speak to someone.

'He says he's from Shop around the Block. That mean anything to you, ma'am?'

Lucie recognised the logo from the packaging in the refrigerator. The groceries had come to the right place.

Lucie's stomach flipped. The delivery guy would know Charlotte. She couldn't let him in. But turning away a regular delivery would look very suspicious. And she needed to get food from somewhere.

Lucie did the quickest thinking of her life.

'Okay, send him up, but warn him he may get a shock when he sees me.'

She ran to the bathroom, stuck a shower cap on her head and grabbed a pot of face mask. Liberally smearing the expensive goo all over her face, she listened for the doorbell. It rang just as the last bit of bare skin disappeared under a dollop of green slime.

Her heart thundering, she undid the locks and opened the door.

'Hi, Miss Gillespie. How are you today?' Without giving her a second glance, the young delivery man, laden with boxes, sailed through the doorway and headed for the kitchen.

'Good,' she said, in as neutral a voice as she could manage. She was conscious of her hand shaking on the door handle and clasped it tightly in her fingers.

He placed the boxes of food on the counter and apologised for having no asparagus this week. Pointing to the gloop stuck to her face she made a gesture of apology.

He laughed, but made no move to leave. Lucie hoped Charlotte wasn't the chatty type. Why didn't he go now he'd made the delivery? She was still standing by the open door, hoping he'd take the hint. Perhaps Charlotte was one of those sad bored-housewife types who invited delivery boys to join her for a coffee? Or worse.

When he finally said, 'Well, I'd better get going,' but still didn't leave, she remembered the protocol. Of course, he was waiting for a tip. It had been so long since she'd been in a position to tip anyone that Lucie had forgotten how it was done.

She held up her hand as if to say, 'Hang on,' and ran to the bedroom closet where she grabbed Charlotte's bag from a shelf behind the door and rifled through it for her wallet.

The delivery guy was staring at the TV.

'Horrendous,' he said. 'Sure makes you feel lucky to be alive.'

She nodded vigorously and handed him a ten-dollar bill. His surprise showed her tip was more generous than Charlotte's usual, but hey, given they had all just diced with death a little generosity did not seem inappropriate.

'Wow, thanks, Miss Gillespie,' he said, stuffing the money into the front pocket of his jeans. 'You have a nice day now. I'll see you next week. That's if I recognise you!'

Lucie's body language must have shown some reaction to his remark, for he added, as if by way of explanation, 'I mean, if the facemask hasn't made you look ten years younger by then.'

Lucie couldn't laugh through the rigor mortis of the drying mask.

The young man responded to her silence by becoming terribly embarrassed. He muttered and mumbled apology after apology.

Before he could say any more, Lucie gave him a gentle pat on the back followed by a little push towards the door.

The relief when he'd gone left her feeling weak and she flopped on the sofa and stared out of the window. The plume of smoke was thinner now and drifting in a different direction. There was a change in the wind. Lucie felt a change in herself, too. She'd just had an encounter with someone who saw Charlotte regularly, once a week, it seemed, and she'd got away with the deception. Even if she had cheated a bit with the face mask, she'd survived the ordeal. And it had taught her something.

The guy had bustled in with the groceries and, if she'd been ready with his tip, he'd have bustled straight out again. Nobody wastes time examining people they encounter every day. She tried to remember what the checkout girl at her local grocery store looked like. Apart from a few sketchy details – tall, heavy, darkish hair – Lucie could not give a description that would find the girl in a police enquiry. She was sure most folk were in the same position. Keen to get on with their lives and concerned with their own problems. Neighbours were another example. All those years she was with Curtis she could hardly tell you who lived next door. The likelihood of the inhabitants of a Manhattan apartment block being friendly with their neighbours was slimmer than their floor to ceiling windows.

She could get away with this. Go on living here for as long as she wanted. Pretty much everything she needed could be ordered in and delivered to the door. She had enough of Charlotte's cash to tip delivery boys for weeks.

She'd never get bored. Charlotte had an amazing collection of DVDs packed with episodes of TV shows and movies. There was wine in the fridge and candy and popcorn in the kitchen cupboards. What more could a girl ask?

When Lucie went to the bathroom to remove the mask, it had dried into more cracks than a Mexican riverbed and her skin felt tight and very clean. She patted it dry with a towel and smeared on some of Charlotte's expensive face cream.

Feeling more pampered than she had in years, Lucie settled down for the afternoon with series one of *Sex and the City* and a bowl of freshly popped corn.

Then the phone rang again.

'Ms Gillespie, your cleaners are here.'

CHAPTER 17

Dylan felt a lot better for his shave and shower, the first he'd had since the morning he'd found Curtis out cold. The morning the towers came down. His mum always claimed to remember exactly where she was and what she was doing the day Kennedy got shot. Dylan had thought it was just something older folks said, but now he knew what she meant. He would never forget the morning of 9/11. It was as if something in his brain had been recording in high definition. He'd heard some of the nurses saying the same sort of thing while he'd been waiting for Curtis to wake up.

For Lucie's sake, if not his own, he was glad to see Curtis recover consciousness. Curtis could be a real mean S.O.B. at times, and Dylan would have been done with him, years ago, if it hadn't been for Lucie. He would never understand, not if he lived to be a thousand years old, how any man could be mean to her.

The first time he'd met her he thought she was the prettiest girl he'd ever seen. Something about the way she laughed and the sparkle in her eyes. She was like one of those trees you see in the springtime, all covered in bursting buds. You know there will be a mass of flowers all over that tree the next time you walk by. That was Lucie, so full of vitality you wanted to be near her, so you could pick up some of her energy.

Living with Curtis had diminished Lucie. First the sparkle went, when the baby died. Then her energy seemed to seep away, a little bit at a time, leaving a poor defeated woman who looked nothing like the vibrant girl she'd been.

They were so happy, to begin with. Lucie had been warm, friendly and kind, not a bit jealous of Curtis's friendship with

Dylan. Instead of losing his best buddy, he gained a good friend. For a while he spent most of his free time going to track meets with them, cheering Lucie on and celebrating her wins over pizza and a pitcher of Bud.

Knowing Curtis could not afford to get romantically involved with another student, Dylan had hoped for a while that he might have a chance with Lucie, but she only ever had eyes for Curtis. How could it be any different? Although they were both tall and athletic, Dylan was a skinny distance runner, not muscled and bulky like the sprinters. With his pale, freckled skin and mousy hair he was no match for the dark, swarthy Curtis and his charismatic personality. Dylan knew he could never compete, so he settled for Lucie's friendship, his heart singing when she laughed at his quiet humour. He was glad to have her in his life and was sure she liked having him around.

When he found out they were sleeping together, Dylan had felt a double let-down and accused Curtis of using their threesome as a smokescreen to hide his inappropriate relationship with Lucie. He'd even threatened to report Curtis to the college and to NCAA.

'Don't, Dylan. Please, man, I'm begging you.'

'Because you'll lose your job? Well, you should have thought of that before you started messing with Lucie.'

'I didn't mean to. I swear on my mother's life.'

'Your mother's already dead, Curtis.'

'You know what I mean.' Curtis was pacing up and down, trying to think of a way out of this. Dylan knew the behaviour. He'd seen it a hundred times since kindergarten. Curtis in trouble. Curtis blaming someone else. Curtis charming the teacher. Curtis getting away with it. 'Lucie's just so damn gorgeous and when she smashed the record that time in Minneapolis, we had a bit too much to drink that night and, well, she came on to me, man.'

'Shut your mouth, Curtis!' Dylan could feel his hands forming fists. If Curtis started in with the details, Dylan would beat his face to a pulp.

'What the hell was I supposed to do?' He threw his arms wide, palms up.

'You were supposed to keep it in your fucking pants. She's your student, for chrissake! You're in a position of trust. She's just a kid.'

Curtis laughed. 'She's no kid, believe me.'

'You're a piece of shit. You disgust me.' In that moment, Dylan meant every word. 'Did you learn nothing the last time? The Principal warned you. You'll lose your job if this gets out.'

Curtis had hung his head. 'You're right. Sorry. And I'd deserve it. I'm an asshole.'

'You got that one right.'

'But Dylan, this isn't about me. Think about Lucie. If this gets out, she'll lose her scholarship.'

'No, she won't. Lucie's the injured party here. You took advantage of her.'

Curtis looked like he was going to contradict him, then thought the better of it. 'She might not lose her place here, but if they fire me, she'll lose her coach. Think about it. She could be NCAA Champion if she keeps going at this rate. After all the work she's done, would you take that away from her?'

Dylan thought about it, just long enough for Curtis to see his chance and go for it.

'I believe she's Olympic material. Maybe even gold.'

Dylan knew how much Curtis wanted this for Lucie. And for himself. It would be a life-changing victory for Curtis, albeit vicarious.

'You really think she's that good?'

'I know she is. Please don't rob her of the chance to prove it, just to punish me.'

'Promise me you won't lay another finger on her.'

'I promise. Sorry, man.' He'd held out his hand and Dylan, fooled again, shook it and gave him a hug.

Last night, as Curtis had lain unconscious in hospital, Dylan had lain awake. Worrying about Lucie. Worrying about Curtis.

Worrying about Lucie again. In the lonely, early hours between night and day, his mind drove him close to madness.

Curtis deserved some payback for all the times he'd hurt Lucie. But what if Curtis had died?

Dylan could never have testified that Lucie Jardine had struck her husband with a blunt instrument thereby causing his death. When they and the doctors asked him if he had any idea how Curtis might have sustained his injury, Dylan simply shook his head. He'd rather die and go to his grave with her secret locked in his heart than betray Lucie.

It was a blessing that Curtis's memory seemed to have erased completely the scene where Lucie had struck him, probably in self-defence. Maybe to save her life. Dylan suspected that Curtis had been getting more violent towards Lucie, but she was very loyal to her husband and Dylan never saw any proof. He'd tried to talk about it one time, but Curtis had gone crazy. In that one brief episode, Dylan had seen a glimpse of what life must be like for Lucie. To his shame, he'd backed off. And he'd been too big a coward to challenge Curtis since.

Now Lucie was gone. And Dylan didn't know if she was dead or alive.

* * *

Curtis was alone in his hospital room when Dylan pushed open the door. 'Hey! How you feeling?' he asked in a bright, cheery voice.

'Hell you think I'm feelin'?'

'Glad to be alive?'

'When I could've been dead, thanks to that sweet girl I married. Is that what you mean?'

'What are you talking about, Curtis?'

'Don't act cute, Dylan. Lucie did this to me, didn't she?'

'How would I know that, Curtis? I wasn't there.'

'It's coming back to me now. We started fighting about money. I was hungry and she was, like, whining I don't give her enough money to buy food. What a crock! Then she told me, as if she'd found a cure for cancer or something, that she had the solution to all our problems. She was getting a job. Cleaning offices. She had arranged an interview in Manhattan. Without saying a word.'

'Maybe she's just trying to help.'

'Yeah, right! Like I'd let her go waltzing off into Manhattan every day! To clean offices?' He patted the bedcovers. 'This is the result. She's crippled me.'

'Curtis, that can't be right. Lucie wouldn't hurt a fly.'

'Well, she did a damn good job hurting me. And now she's run away. Proof she's guilty, wouldn't you say?'

'We don't know for sure she's run away. You said she was going to Manhattan. It's crazy in there.' Dylan didn't want to say what he was thinking.

'You think she's dead.'

Dylan searched for a response. Came up blank. He lowered his head to hide his emotions.

'Yeah, I thought so. Well, I don't think she is. But it might only be a matter of time.'

'What do you mean, a matter of time? You still got concussion?'

'I'm perfectly compos mentis. What I mean is, if she ever shows her face again, I'll kill the bitch.'

Dylan left at that point and considered staying away, but the next night Curtis called.

'Dylan?'

'Hey, Curtis. How you doin', buddy?'

'Don't ever ask me again how I'm doin'. I can't walk, take a piss, screw my wife, or any other woman. How would you be doin'? Buddy.'

It crossed Dylan's mind that his friend would never beat another woman either. Small mercies. 'Sorry, Curtis.'

'Yeah, you ain't as sorry as me,' said Curtis, the aggression gone from his voice.

Dylan shook his head, glad his friend couldn't see the pity on his face. Curtis wouldn't take kindly to people feeling sorry for him.

He'd been the same when he'd ruptured his Achilles. God help anyone who'd offered him sympathy, especially another athlete.

Dylan made his voice upbeat. 'It's good to hear from you.'

'Listen, I need you to track down my wife.'

'But I've no idea where she is.'

'She been home yet?'

'Last time I checked there was no sign.'

'Well, you've got to find her.'

'Did you ever think that maybe if you hadn't been beating up on her, none of this would have happened?'

'You're taking her side? I don't believe this. She's left me crippled and you're feeling sorry for *her*?'

Curtis's voice was rising. Maybe this wasn't the time for home truths, not while the guy was so vulnerable. 'Look at me! I can't even wipe my own ass.'

Dylan didn't like the picture that came into his mind. 'Woah! Too much information there.'

'You know what I'm saying. I need to find Lucie. She needs to come back and look after me. Unless you'd like to volunteer for the job?'

Dylan refused to react. 'Why would she want to do that, Curtis?'

'Doesn't matter what she wants. She's my wife. It's her duty. She took a vow to love me, in sickness and in health. You heard her. You were there when she said it.'

'Yep, I was there. I heard you vow to love and cherish her too. Look how that turned out.'

'Dylan, don't be a smart-ass. Help me or don't help me. I'll find her. And when I do, well, I've got a pretty good idea that'll convince her to stay. And a backup plan if she refuses.'

Dylan could think of one, but not the other. 'Yeah, what's that?' he said.

'If she won't stick around to help me, I'll threaten to turn her in to the cops.'

'And the backup plan?'

'Trust me, you don't want to know.'

CHAPTER 18

Cleaners. Lucie had been dreading something like this. It was bound to happen sooner or later. Women like Charlotte Gillespie didn't usually soil their hands performing their own domestic duties.

'Rob? Tell them thanks, but I don't need any cleaning done today.'

'Sorry, Ms Gillespie. They're already on their way up. I checked their ID, don't you worry. It's all good.'

'Can't you stop them, Rob? I don't feel well.'

The doorbell rang. Lucie stopped breathing. She hung up the intercom handset and listened to the voices outside the door. It sounded like a football team. So many voices, all male. One of them was bound to know Charlotte. If Lucie let them in, it was game over.

She wouldn't answer the door. They'd get fed up waiting and go away, eventually, thinking no one was home.

The bell rang again.

This was stupid. She dragged her hair out of its ponytail and pulled it forward onto her cheeks and forehead. Raising one hand to her face she opened the door with the other.

A bunch of young guys stood in the hall, the United Nations in white overalls, armed with brushes, mops and crates of cleaning products. Each wore a broad smile and a cap with the logo 'K n K'.

'Kleer n Kleen at your service, ma'am,' said a short, wiry guy who looked a bit older than the others. He gave a small salute and marched in past her, his colleagues trooping at his heels.

Lucie held her arms out to try and keep them at the door. 'Hold on,' she said, 'I don't really need any cleaning done, thanks. Can you come back next week?'

'Sorry, ma'am,' said the leader. 'The only paperwork we got is for today.' He produced a sheet of pink paper from his hip pocket and waved it at Lucie. 'Don't say nuthin' about next week. We'll be outta here in two hours, max.'

Lucie decided the easiest thing would be to let them go ahead. What harm could it do? If they wanted to clean an already clean apartment, well, fine.

'Hey, Boss? Lady watching TV. What we do?'

'Ma'am? We can leave this room till last, if you prefer. Or were you planning on leaving now we're here?'

Lucie shrugged and shook her head. Before she could ask him to explain, another cleaner emerged from the bedroom.

'Should I get the cartons, Chief?'

'Yeah, and take Zak with you.' He looked around the room and said, 'There's a lot of stuff here.'

This was making no sense at all. But at least nobody was paying her any undue attention. All she had to do was bide her time. They'd soon be gone. Lucie sat down, grabbed a handful of popcorn and tried to pick up the storyline of episode two.

When the guys came back with the paper boxes, Zak paused by Lucie's side and pointed at the TV. 'Yay, the one where Stanford introduces Carrie to Derek. Love it.'

Lucie offered him the popcorn but he shook his head. 'Sorry, boxes to pack.'

The credits were running when Lucie thought about what he'd said. 'Boxes to pack'? She ran to the bedroom. The bed had been stripped bare, its pillows and throws stuffed into a box which Zak was about to close and tape. Two 'cleaners' had made a good start on clearing Charlotte's beautiful clothes from the shelves in her closet. One was piling sweaters into a carton while another had begun to remove shoeboxes from their stacks on the back wall.

By the tall cabinet where Charlotte kept her lingerie a huge guy with a beard was holding a lacy bra and tiny scarlet panties against his overalls.

'Hey, look, Marco,' he joked, 'just your style.'

'What are you doing?' asked Lucie.

Like a guilty schoolkid, the lingerie guy hid his hands behind his back and blushed.

'Leave that stuff alone!'

'Sorry, lady,' said the shoe remover, looking up from his boxes. 'Boss say everything go.'

Lucie realised there was more to this than a weekly clean and polish. Trying to keep the panic out of her voice, she said, 'Where is your boss?'

'He in bathroom. Boss! You needed out here.'

Lucie pushed open the bathroom door. The smell of bleach caught in her throat. Every cupboard and drawer lay open, empty and pristine and the boss, his face covered by a mask, was on his knees in the shower.

Lucie pointed to the box in the middle of the floor, stuffed full of make-up, toiletries and towels. 'What's going on here?'

Looking as if he wasn't delighted to be disturbed, the boss stood up, removed the mask from his mouth and with a ping of elastic let it drop under his chin.

Lucie repeated her question, a little less assertively this time, aware of how vulnerable she could be, alone in a house full of strange men.

The boss gave a long-suffering sigh and pointed to the logo on his cap. 'Like it says, ma'am. We're clearing and cleaning.'

'But you can't.'

'Look, lady. Why don't you go watch your movie and give the guys a chance to work? We'll be outta your hair before you know it.' He smiled. 'You going abroad or what?'

Lucie struggled to find an answer that might make any sense at all. 'What makes you ask that?'

'Cos that's what most of our clients do.' He paused. 'Well, not the dead ones, obviously. You going somewhere nice?'

Lucie thought fast. 'Meant to go to Europe, but with ... you know?' She left the rest of the story for him to make up.

The man nodded, his mouth a slant of sad resignation. 'Ah, 9/11. I get it. And now you ain't going, huh?'

Lucie said nothing.

'And that's why you don't want us in here today, taking all your stuff away to storage?' He looked at the box on the floor. 'Oh man, we messed up. Why didn't you say something?'

'I thought you were just going to clean the place.'

He suddenly rushed from the bathroom, pushing past her, shouting, 'Guys! Stop what you're doing. Drop everything. We made a mistake. Put all the stuff back where you found it.'

Lucie could hear the groans, the complaints, one or two cuss words.

'It's okay,' she said, keen to see the last of Kleer n Kleen. 'If you guys empty the boxes and take them away, I'll put my things back.'

'You sure, ma'am?'

Lucie nodded, trying to look as if she didn't mind having an entire apartment to put to rights, when all she wanted to do was watch some TV and pig out on popcorn.

One good thing came out of it, though. She found Charlotte's laptop.

Lucie had been a real technophile when she was at college but when the laptop she'd had as a student died on her, she and Curtis had been unable to replace it. Before money became too tight for such treats, she'd occasionally go into an internet café, buy herself a cup of coffee and log on to check emails. Eventually Lucie's flow of mail dried up. She gradually lost contact with all of her friends and had no reason to log on.

It was ages since she'd touched a computer. She unzipped the bag and removed a glossy new laptop, hoping she'd remember how to use it.

The machine booted up a treat but then, of course, it wanted Charlotte's password and Lucie couldn't oblige. For what seemed like hours she tried, worried she'd guess once too often and get locked out for good. No joy. She shoved the laptop in its bag and chucked it, in frustration, to the back of the closet.

The sky beyond the glass wall was darkening towards twilight. Smoke drifted and mingled with the corals of sunset as though the whole city were ablaze. It was far too beautiful a backdrop for tragedy.

Without TV to remind her, it would be easy to forget that only a few blocks away rescue workers were risking their lives to search burning rubble for survivors.

CHAPTER 19

Lucie's days started to take on a pattern. She rose when she woke and jogged for half an hour on Charlotte's treadmill while she listened to Charlotte's music on Charlotte's Walkman.

She showered and dried her hair, set a place at the breakfast bar, brewed some coffee from freshly ground beans and sat up to enjoy her first meal of the day. The food deliveries looked like working out well and she'd decided that soon she'd start adding one or two items she fancied and leave out things she didn't enjoy. She was aware that changes would have to be made gradually if she were to avoid arousing suspicion, but the grocery boy seemed to take her at face value. She'd been brave enough to dispense with the disguise on his second visit and the young man hadn't batted an eyelid. As far as he was concerned, she was Charlotte Gillespie.

When she'd washed up her breakfast things she did some housework. Kleer n Kleen hadn't got to the cleaning part before she'd flung them out and the apartment was in need of a little dusting.

She was no closer to working out why Charlotte would want her place emptied and cleaned to a surgical standard. Putting everything back in its place had given Lucie the chance to explore nooks and crannies, keen to find out as much about Charlotte as she could. She'd come across well-organised paperwork relating to many of the financial aspects of Charlotte's life and discovered that she owned her apartment. Lucie was relieved there would be no landlord snooping around, making inspections or looking for rent arrears. She'd also unearthed a little sketchbook, which seemed full of abstract doodles. Lucie was admiring Charlotte's artistic skills when she noticed some pages had numbers and symbols incorporated into the drawings. With the fingers of her left hand crossed, she typed the first set into the laptop and bingo, she was in.

A second series proved to be the passwords for Charlotte's online banking. Statements showed a business account from which a staggering amount had been withdrawn just over a week ago. Lucie wondered what on earth Charlotte had bought with that much money. A house in the Hamptons? A more upmarket apartment, say, in Paris, France, or Monte Carlo? A checking account showed an outrageous balance and a monthly deposit that made her eyes water. It was more than she and Curtis lived on for a year.

Every time Curtis came into her mind, she made a real effort to push him back out again. She was also pushing to the back of her mind any thoughts of what the future might hold for her. A hundred times a day she told herself to live in the moment and enjoy the predictability and pattern of this new life.

What she *had* learned about Charlotte was that her wealth seemed to come at the cost of a love life. She was certainly unmarried. And if she had a boyfriend, he never stayed over. Nor were there any special birthday cards or gift tags with romantic messages. After Kleer n Kleen's visit, Lucie had found a neatly organised photo album, but not one picture of a guy, not even Matthew. Plenty of girlfriends. Charlotte celebrating birthdays and baby showers. She'd been a very pretty bridesmaid several times but, as Granny would have put it, never the bride. An official race photo showed Charlotte finishing the New York Marathon. As she crossed the finishing line, arms raised in triumph, the clock on the gantry displayed an impressive three hours twenty. No wonder she looked so proud of her medal in the series of personal photos that filled the next few pages. At least one skiing trip was recorded and several sunny vacations featured a smiling Charlotte but there was no sign of a companion. Lucie wondered who had taken the photos.

There was no album showing the happiest times in Lucie's adult life. Even her wedding day had gone unrecorded, because she'd been afraid the baby was already showing. And there had been no skiing trips or sunshine holidays for her.

She should have married Josh. He'd been really keen before Hurricane Curtis hit her life and laid waste to her plans. Josh was all that Curtis was not. Straight, floppy hair streaked blond from summer weekends at Martha's Vineyard, skin a golden tan from crewing on his father's yacht. Josh would be an expert in child medicine by now. She could see him with a perfect wife and two matching children, spending Sunday afternoons looking at dinosaur bones in the Museum of Natural History. They'd buy the kids books as souvenirs then go to the coffee shop and eat toasted teacakes before heading home for bath and bedtime stories.

She'd hardly given Josh a thought in the almost-decade since she'd seen him. She'd only agreed to go out with him in the first place because she thought it might impress her father. To be honest, she'd found him a little bit boring, probably the reason why Curtis had seemed so enticingly dangerous by comparison. In reality, Josh was probably screwing his medical secretary nowadays. Or he was already divorced because his wife had an affair with the bohemian house-painter who'd come recommended by one of the friends she met every week for lunch. Those kids, if they ever existed, would be well past the cute toddler stage by now. They'd be pre-pubescent brats with braces on their teeth and 'issues'.

Lucie did a quick calculation. Because she did it so often, the answer always came easily. Her own sweet baby would be seven, had he or she lived. Lucie had never found out whether she'd been carrying a boy or a girl. The night she'd miscarried, the midwife had offered to tell her the sex of her tiny dead baby, but Lucie hadn't wanted to know and Curtis hadn't been there to ask. For some reason she'd always imagined a little girl, called Evangeline.

Lucie plonked down on the white leather sofa and started to weep. She didn't know for what or whom she was crying – a lost baby, a lost mother, a lost life. Maybe she was crying for all the lives that had been lost? While she was lucky enough to survive? Surely she shouldn't be crying, she should be laughing and singing, dancing in her underwear, rejoicing in her new-found freedom.

She dried her eyes on the duster. She was going crazy, stuck in this apartment with nothing but a TV and her own thoughts for company. She needed to see real human faces, not just the ones on television. It was time to get in touch with life again, before she lost her mind.

CHAPTER 20

Dylan's heart sank when he saw the open door up ahead. Yesterday, by the time he'd finished work and ridden the subway, the place had been closed for the day. He could have made it in time, but he chose to stop and check the posters of Lucie he'd stuck up anywhere he could get a space. Finding them again was like looking for a needle in a haystack and Dylan suspected some of Lucie's photos had been removed to make space for other faces. It was hard to feel annoyed about it. Everyone was desperate for news of their loved one.

As he'd scanned the rows of faces, looking for Lucie, he hoped against hope that one of his posters might have a message from her. A scribble that told the world she was safe.

He'd spent so long looking he'd ended up in a mad rush. And when he'd found the address given to relatives searching for information he'd been too late. In truth, he'd been more delighted than disappointed to find the door locked. The longer he could put off knowing the truth the better.

Every day Dylan prayed that Lucie might still turn up, alive and well. Even if she didn't come back to Curtis, even if Dylan never saw her again. That was all he cared about.

Curtis didn't feel the same way. He was adamant they had to find out, one way or another. He'd shouted at Dylan for messing up the day before, and had accused him of deliberately wasting time so Curtis wouldn't get the information he wanted. He'd even accused Dylan of knowing the truth and keeping it from him.

The only truth Dylan was keeping from his friend was how much he'd like to walk away and leave him to get on with it. This wasn't the first time he'd asked himself why he put up with

Curtis's abuse. It had been a long time since Curtis was fun to be around. The easy-going, laugh-a-minute companion that Dylan had hero-worshipped since childhood had somehow morphed into a bad-tempered oaf who beat up on his wife. Not the type of person Dylan liked to spend time with.

Dylan had other friends and had it not been for Lucie, he would have long since given up on Curtis. But Lucie had kept him close. At first it was so he could be near her and latterly it was to watch over her. Now he had to stick around in case Lucie came back and needed his support, if not his protection. Also, Dylan didn't have it in him to turn his back on Curtis now. Even if he had brought his misfortune upon himself.

The office was dingy and smelt of pine disinfectant and dust. A line of dejected-looking people straggled its way through the hall towards a counter and left by a side door. A child was crying and a woman hushed and soothed it in an embarrassed voice. A man on his way out sobbed openly, shaking his head as he walked towards the exit.

Dylan stood in line and tried not to think the worst. Not everyone was being given bad news. A family passed him, hugging each other, their relief and joy clear for all to see. Dylan envied them their good news more than he'd envy a million-dollar win on the sweepstake.

'Next.'

Dylan stepped up to the desk.

A woman with grey hair and a kind face greeted him with a weary smile. 'How can I help you?' she said.

'I'm trying to find my wife, Lucie Jardine. I was told to come here.'

'How are you spelling that, sir?'

Dylan spelled out Lucie's name and the woman noted it on a slip of paper.

'Does she have any middle names?'

Dylan panicked. He didn't know.

'That's all right, sir,' said the woman. 'Can you tell me your wife's maiden name, please?'

'It's McBride. She was, I mean, she *is* Scottish originally.'

'That's nice. Do you have some ID?' she asked him.

He pushed the dog-eared, soiled remains of Curtis's driver's licence across the counter. The woman, who looked reluctant to touch the card, barely glanced at it. 'That's fine, Mr Jardine,' she said, leaving it for him to pick up. 'I'll just be a moment.'

When she came back she gave a little cough, and said sadly, 'I've found your wife, sir. I'm very sorry.' She handed Dylan a computer printout.

There it was.

In black and white.

Confirmation of Lucie's death. September eleventh, two thousand and one.

Dylan bit down hard on his lip till he felt his teeth piercing the skin. The pain shooting through his chest was like a bolt of electricity, blocking out every other sensation. He clasped his chest, as if he could hold together his breaking heart.

'Sir, are you okay?'

He shook his head.

'I'm so sorry. This is such a terrible way to find out.'

He'd tried to prepare himself for this news, but Lucie's loss hit him harder than he'd imagined possible. If this was grief, it was a deeper, more devastating pain than any emotion he'd felt before, even when his dad died.

Dylan thought of Curtis and wondered how he'd react to this news. Time would tell, but so far Curtis seemed to be grieving not for Lucie, but for himself and the life he'd squandered. There was no sign of any regret for the way he'd treated Lucie.

Maybe her death would move Curtis to show genuine grief for his wife. Dylan had no way of knowing what was going on in his friend's head. Whenever he communicated it was in a rant, a raging tirade about the injustice of what had been done to him and how Lucie would have to pay.

Someone muttered about the time it was taking for the line to move along, and Dylan realised he was holding up the queue.

'Can you tell me how she died, please?' he asked.

The woman shook her head. In a low, official-sounding voice she said, 'I'm sorry, sir, because of the scale of the 9/11 tragedy, there weren't too many details logged.' She consulted a single sheet of paper. 'All I can tell you is your wife was found on Murray Street. She was already dead, I'm afraid. There was no suspicion of foul play. Your wife appears to have suffocated in the dust cloud. She wasn't the only one to succumb. Unfortunately, a number of our fellow citizens appear to have died in the same way.'

As if to prove how damaging the dust cloud had been, someone in line behind Dylan started to cough uncontrollably.

'Can I see her?' he asked.

The woman shook her head. 'I'm so sorry. That won't be possible.'

'Why not? I'd like to see her, please.'

The coughing stopped and the child's crying too. The silence seemed to amplify her whispered words. 'It's too late, I'm afraid. When no one came forward to register she was missing …'

She seemed unwilling to finish the sentence. Dylan waited.

'I'm afraid the records show your wife's body has already been cremated, sir.'

Dylan's breath stopped for a second then caught on a sob. He slapped his hand over his mouth.

'I'm really sorry, sir. The city morgue was overwhelmed, as you can imagine. Bodies could only be kept for so long and if no one came to claim them, those whose identity had been established were cremated. I am so, so sorry for your loss.'

Dylan blinked hard and chewed on the inside of his lips. Taking his hand away from his mouth, he attempted a smile for the woman. He felt sorry for her. What a job.

Lips welded tight, he nodded to accept one last apology and left the office, passing people who looked as distraught as he felt.

So Lucie was gone. How could he accept he'd never see her again? It didn't seem real. Only a few days ago he'd made her laugh at some silly joke his mum had heard at the grocery store. Lucie's laughter was rare as gold these days. When he managed to coax a smile from her, Dylan felt like a prospector panning a stream. Making Lucie laugh was like finding a glistening nugget amongst the silt.

He stood on the street and looked up at the sky where smoke still drifted. At the heart of Ground Zero a fire was burning that seemed impossible to extinguish. Exactly how Dylan felt.

CHAPTER 21

Lucie had only one connection to the outside world apart from television – the newspapers that were delivered each day to Charlotte's apartment. Even so, she would probably have stopped reading them by now, were she not worried sick she might have killed Curtis. Every morning she dutifully skimmed each paper searching for a report, but she was growing tired of seeing nothing but photo after photo of destruction and suffering. It seemed there was only one item worth covering, as far as the New York dailies were concerned, and she wondered if other crimes had stopped since the eleventh or if they were going unreported. As the days passed and nothing appeared in the papers about a man found murdered on his kitchen floor or a nationwide search for a fugitive wife, Lucie began to hope she might have got away with it. Either Curtis was still alive, or the death of a drunk in a suburban slum wasn't newsworthy.

Lucie had flicked through the pages of *The New York Times* and was working her way through the *Post*, scanning for her name or Curtis's, when the words Glasgow and Scotland leapt off the page at her. The newspaper flopped to the floor like a broken kite. She steadied herself against the counter then bent to retrieve the jumble of pages.

Lucie spread the paper on the kitchen counter and smoothed the page with the flat of her hands. She reread the full article. It made no sense.

Accident investigators have revealed that the incident which closed the Lincoln Tunnel for several hours on September 10th was due to driver error, the most likely cause of which was fatigue. The driver is thought to have just landed at Newark after an overnight flight from Glasgow, Scotland. She has been identified as Margaret McBride. Mrs McBride was taken to Hackensack UMC where she remains in a very serious condition.

Lucie stared at her hands, their palms blackened with newsprint. She wiped them on her jeans and inspected them again. They were no cleaner. She grabbed the *Times* and searched each page thoroughly, but there was no coverage of the accident or mention of her father. What had happened to him? And why was Mum driving? Dad was always the driver. Lucie carefully tore out the article from the *Post* and laid it to one side. Then, on hands and knees, she gathered the piles of scattered pages and rolled them into a fat, untidy bundle.

She got to her feet, feeling as stiff as an old woman, and leaned on the wall with one hand while she raised the internal phone to her ear.

Rob answered right away. 'Ms Gillespie, good morning. What can I do for you?'

'Could you come up and collect a pile of old newspapers, please, Rob? Put them in the recycle bin for me?'

'Of course I can. I'll be right there.'

When Lucie hung up she noticed the black handprint on the wall beside the phone but felt too weary to do anything about it. Was Mum driving because Dad refused to come after all?

Lucie had a few happy memories that featured her father, but not many. He was always working, or so it seemed. She remembered how Mum would dress her up in frilly frocks with white shoes and socks. She could recall her granny and other women fussing over her, saying things like, 'Isn't she the brawest wee lassie you ever saw?'

Occasionally Mum had a reason to take her to the yard and Dad would hoist her into his arms and show her off to the drivers. 'What do you think of my wee princess, boys?' he'd say. 'This one'll break some hearts, eh?' Then, as if to please her father, the men would pinch her cheek or tousle her curls.

She once heard one of the men muttering, 'She's a bonny wee thing, right enough, but a daughter's no good to McBride.'

Later, when Mum was tucking her into bed, she'd asked, 'Why am I not good, Mummy?'

When Lucie stopped being sweet and biddable, her father had stopped calling her his princess. His disapproval had grown as fast as she did. When Lucie reached high school age, he seemed to find it impossible to praise her. His resentment at having no sons was plain for Lucie to see. She was 'just a lassie'. A boy would have made him proud. He never said that in so many words, but the subliminal message was loud and clear.

No matter what her achievement, he never seemed impressed. When, aged fourteen, she showed him she could drive a lorry, he wasn't proud. He was outraged and almost sacked Old Sandy for teaching her. When she started to excel at distance running he'd taken an interest in her wins, but he never went to see her run. The trouble really started when she began to talk about getting a place in the American scholarship system. Dad refused point blank to give his permission. She'd cried herself to sleep night after night, but he wouldn't be swayed.

Then there was the way he'd reacted to Curtis and the news of the baby. She'd shed a few floods that time too.

She hadn't seen Dad for years, and although it was distressing to be rejected by her parents, he'd been no real loss. The lack of a mother in her life had been much harder to bear, especially when the going got rough.

She remembered the day she'd finally plucked up enough courage to call home. She had to tell them she was pregnant. She needed to ask them to send her money, so she had no choice but to tell them Curtis had lost his job. Because of the baby. She couldn't see her father's face but he'd sounded fit to explode. After a lot of unintelligible shouting she heard him growl, 'Tell her to get rid of it.'

Mum said, 'I'm sorry if you heard that, Lucie. Your dad doesn't mean it.'

'I mean every bloody word!' he bawled. 'It was bad enough she got mixed up with the likes of him in the first place. Now we're to be humiliated by our unmarried daughter giving birth to a wee bastard? Thank God she's at the other side of the world, that's all I can say.'

'Jim! How can you talk like that?' Lucie's mother had covered the phone, but Dad's voice was too loud to be muffled.

'I'm only saying what should have been said months ago, when she first got involved with him. A man that takes advantage of his students? Gets them pregnant? No wonder he's lost his job. He deserves to be struck off, or whatever it is they do to unethical teachers. And as for sending them money? Well ...' Whatever he'd been planning to say was lost in some sort of scuffle.

'Give me the phone, woman. Let me talk some sense into her.'

There was a pause, then he came on the line. 'Listen here, Lucie. That's not the right man for you. Can't you see that? If you have his child, you'll be tied to him forever. Here's what we'll do. First thing in the morning, I'll send a ticket for a first-class flight home. You come on back here and we'll forget this ever happened.'

'What about the baby?'

'Your mum can see Dr Wilson and make arrangements.'

When Lucie had refused to have an abortion, her father tried everything in his power to make her change her mind, including guilt-tripping about her mum's mental health. He even stooped to bribery at one point, and when that too failed, he lost his temper and told her he hoped he'd never set eyes on her again.

Lucie could still hear her mum's anguish as she begged her husband to reconsider, but Big Jimmy McBride was a not a man to be dissuaded once he'd made a pronouncement.

Lucie had phoned back the next day to tell her parents that she and Curtis planned to get married. The baby would be born legitimate. Curtis was standing by their daughter and would do the right thing.

Lucie had never been in any doubt that he would. Although he was angry about losing his job and devastated that Lucie would not be able to run in the American championships, he had seemed pleased about the baby.

Lucie explained that the wedding ceremony would be small and the celebrations modest. She asked if they'd please come. She'd like her dad to give her away.

But instead of softening, her father became more entrenched in his position and neither Lucie's tears nor her mother's could move him.

His voice rose as he issued his ultimatum. 'If you insist on staying with that reprobate and having his child, we're finished with you. Whether he marries you or not. You've let me down, Lucie, and your mum. I'm just glad your granny never lived to see this day. She'd have been black-affronted. Now, make up your mind. Come home and get rid of it and we'll forget any of this ever happened. You can finish college here, get on with your life and we'll never speak of it again.' He paused, waiting for her to agree, she supposed, then said, 'Or—'

'There's no need to tell me what the "or" is, Dad. I've heard enough.'

'I haven't finished!'

'Please, Jim!' wailed Mum. Lucie could picture her, dragging at his arm, distraught.

'Or ...' His voice was low and much more frightening than all his screaming and shouting. 'If you stay with him, don't *ever* come back. You will not be welcome. And your mother,' he said, as if he was threatening his wife, 'will not be making arrangements to come and see you. You'll be dead to us.'

Dead to us. Curtis might be dead too. Her granny always said deaths come in threes.

CHAPTER 22

After a shower and a strong cup of coffee, Lucie felt brave enough to phone the hospital.

The switchboard operator's tone was curt and Lucie was forced to listen to a xylophone version of 'Greensleeves' three times before the woman came back on the line.

'Sorry you had to wait so long, but it's been crazy here since Tuesday.'

When Lucie said she was calling for an update on Mrs Margaret McBride's condition, the receptionist's tone dropped a few degrees from cool to chilly. 'I'm sorry, who did you say you are?'

Lucie didn't answer.

'See, unless you're a relative and a pretty close one at that, we can't divulge patient information.'

Lucie thought about it. 'I'm her niece.'

'Your name, please?'

Lucie's confidence deserted her. She put her finger on the button, very gently, terminating the call and hoping the woman would think they'd been cut off.

Lucie made a fist and knocked on her forehead. She should have decided what she was going to say before she called the hospital. She thought about trying again but fear of the dragon on the switchboard put her off.

She'd been looking for a reason to leave the apartment. Now she had one.

Even with the most compelling reason in the world, the thought of venturing beyond these four walls made Lucie cringe.

What if someone saw her and knew she was an impostor? They would call the police.

Lucie considered ringing a lawyer; maybe she ought to confess everything and ask for help. Good idea, up to a point. Until Lucie saw herself being put in the back of a police car, with some cop's hand on the top of her head. She thought about spending months in jail waiting to come to trial and knew she couldn't go through with it. Life with Curtis had been hard, but not hard enough to prepare her for jail. She didn't know much about prison, other than what she'd seen on TV dramas and documentaries, but she knew enough to convince her she wouldn't survive a day.

She wondered if she could simply ring a lawyer's office and ask to speak to someone, make an anonymous enquiry, but when she rehearsed the conversation in her head it sounded ludicrous. She could ask her mum's advice. Except Mum was fighting for her life, by the sound of things.

Another cup of coffee would help her think. She couldn't contact anyone in the outside world without identifying herself as Lucie Jardine, but she had to remain incognito for as long as she could. At least till she had proof that Curtis was alive.

Stimulated by caffeine her thoughts raced off in all directions. Why not call the police in her old neighbourhood, give them the address and ask if they had found a dead body? She tutted with impatience as that thought screeched to a dead-end halt. Soon she had run through every scenario she could think of and discarded all of them. Lucie sighed heavily. For all her plotting, she'd achieved nothing but a headache from too much strong coffee.

But it had served a purpose. She had identified her priority, beyond which nothing else mattered.

Her mind was far from clear, but at least it was made up.

An hour later, with make-up disguising the fading remains of her bruises, Lucie was ready to go, but too scared to open the door. She took another last look in the mirror. And peered through the peephole for the tenth time. All clear, but what if a neighbour's door opened at the same time as hers?

'Come on, Lucie,' she whispered. 'You can do this. For Mum.' With a deep breath she opened the door and stepped out. The hallway was silent as she tiptoed towards the elevator, praying it would be empty when it stopped at her floor. A green light flashed on the wall above her head and she could hear the mechanism working in the shaft. A hydraulic hiss announced the elevator's arrival but the doors seemed to take forever to open; when they did, they revealed a man in a business suit who seemed intent on the *Financial Times*. He didn't raise his head until the doors started to close again. He looked puzzled as she let the elevator go without her, but it was clear he didn't recognise her.

She tried to see herself from the man's point of view. She had chosen dark clothes that would blend into the Manhattan crowd, but nothing too new or too stylish. She did not want to stand out and was aiming to look like any other young businesswoman on her way to work. Now she had drawn attention to herself by acting suspiciously. What normal person waits for an elevator and then doesn't get in? Maybe the man was talking to Rob right now, alerting him to the fact that there was a stranger hanging about on floor forty.

She darted back to the apartment and slammed the door behind her, gasping for breath as if she had outrun an attacker. As she waited for her heart to slow she wondered if she were having some sort of a panic attack. Maybe she was turning into one of those sad people you saw on the programmes Curtis used to watch. People who lost their nerve for facing the outside world, so they didn't ever leave the house. Just stayed in and ate their way to an early death, by which point they were so enormous they couldn't be removed from their home without a crane and a crowd of neighbours watching. One Ton Wonders, Curtis called them.

Was she turning into a recluse? How ironic would that be? To escape from her life with Curtis only to end up trapped by her own fears, terrified to leave the building in case anyone recognised her. Had she run from one prison straight into another?

That wasn't going to happen. She'd be better off owning up to murder and being sent to jail. At least there she wouldn't be in solitary confinement.

Lucie stood up tall and concentrated hard on getting her breathing under control. 'In for six, out for six,' she whispered, trying to focus like she used to do before a big race. Gradually her heart slowed and her breathing returned to normal. She went to the kitchen, poured a glass of cold water and took it to the huge window.

She had to get out and face the world, before the prospect became too big for her. Fear had trapped her once before, kept her with Curtis when she knew he was no good for her. Even when the love between them had gone, buried with their poor wee baby, she'd been unable to leave. It was clear to Lucie now that she'd suffered some sort of postpartum depression. When she'd mentioned it to Curtis as a reason for her lethargy, tears and mood swings, he had scoffed. 'How can you have the baby blues if you haven't got a baby?'

With hindsight it was easy to see how Curtis had chipped away at her self-esteem, but things were different now. She was different. And if she was strong enough to fight Curtis and win, she was brave enough to walk out of this building.

It couldn't be that difficult. All she needed to do was not think about it. Focus on the breathing and the little things. Normal, everyday things. Like shoes.

The shoes she'd chosen, a pair of Charlotte's plain black pumps, were a little on the narrow side, already squeezing her toes, but they'd be fine for an hour or two.

Determined to keep her mind off her fears, Lucie watched her feet walking along the hallway. She had a flashback to the red-soled Louboutins she'd seen discarded on the street just before the dust came down.

The elevator began to slow and Lucie's heart began to race. She had survived the dust cloud, she could survive this. Focusing on the elegant shoes on her feet, she stepped into the lobby. It wasn't enough to wear Charlotte's shoes. Until she made it through the lobby and out into the street, she had to *be* Charlotte.

Rob greeted her from the desk with a cheery good morning. 'Sorry I had to bother you about the grocery guy and the cleaners.

Security is high and I'm on strict orders to let no one into the building without checking.'

'Fine,' said Lucie, smiling back.

'You have a great day now, Ms Gillespie.'

Nice to be living in a place where everyone was protected from harm. Well, unless some crazy terrorist flew a plane into the building. Lucie looked up at the sky, empty now where once the towers had stood. Manhattan looked wrong without them. Sure, there were enormous buildings all around but nothing that tall, or that special.

The air smelled like a burnt saucepan and, though there was no dust that she could see, Lucie could still smell it. That odour would stay with her forever, the way some aroma-memories did. Like the baby soap Mum always used when Lucie was tiny. The merest whiff of it used to make her feel happy, loved and secure. She had bought a bar when she first knew she was pregnant, but eventually threw it in the bin. Baby soap without a baby had no magic.

There was a guy lounging against the apartment block opposite, one trainered foot flat on the wall behind him. His casual style looked out of place amongst the business types. A tourist, on his way to Ground Zero? The wreckage was attracting as many visitors as Times Square, according to one snippet of a TV report.

When he saw her, he pushed off the wall and start walking in her direction. She hurried towards the subway, glancing back once she got to the end of the block. He was gone. She exhaled loudly then smiled, feeling silly. Why on earth would anyone be following her?

On the subway, where no one ever made eye contact with anyone, Lucie continued to concentrate on shoes – old ones, new ones, polished ones, dull ones, ten-dollar shoes like she used to wear and two-hundred-dollar shoes like the ones on her feet, which were starting to hurt already, threatening blisters.

It was good to be out in the world again, an anonymous traveller like everyone else on the subway train. When Lucie reached the hospital, she felt more alive than she had for months. As she walked through the front doors, she threw back her shoulders and attempted to smile, knowing she would have to appear confident if she was to get the information she needed. Two women sat at a reception desk, their attention on the monitors in front of them. Lucie eyed them up, trying to decide which one to approach.

The younger of the two was well made-up with long, glossy hair that she kept running her fingers through. The other was much older, a small, mousey-looking woman who could have been anyone's favourite aunt. Both looked up as Lucie approached the desk. She had the feeling the younger one was sizing her up, appraising the clothes she was wearing, making a judgement. The older woman smiled warmly and Lucie moved towards that side of the desk. She noticed the young woman tossing back her hair and returning her gaze to the screen, her interest in Lucie apparently over.

Mousie removed her spectacles and said, in a voice as warm as her smile, 'Help you, dear?'

Lucie's face felt like it had frozen. 'Hi,' she said, then cleared her throat. 'I'm looking for Margaret McBride. I believe she's a patient here?'

'Let me just check for you. Do you know which station Ms McBride's in?'

'No, not exactly. I think she might be in Intensive Care. I was hoping you could tell me.'

Mousie gave her such a long look, Lucie began to wonder if she'd picked the wrong receptionist.

'We're not really supposed to divulge that information.'

Lucie took a snap decision. 'She's my mum. She's badly hurt. I only just found out.'

'So many of the patients we have with us right now were injured like your mom. What a dreadful thing to happen to our city.'

Lucie had been planning to play for sympathy by telling the woman how her mother flew all the way from Scotland to see her but had a crash on the way in from the airport. Now it seemed she wouldn't have to.

Lucie swore a tear came into the woman's eye before she put on her glasses and looked back at her monitor. She scrolled down, clicked twice and said, 'Can you give me your mother's full name and date of birth, please?'

Lucie tried to remember what year her mum had been born and crossed one finger over another as she said the month and the day of her mum's birthday and took a chance with the year.

Mousie nodded and Lucie felt like a schoolkid who'd got the right answer to a hard question.

'Try ICU station three. Go to the end of the corridor, turn right and you'll find the elevators and the stairs. Take either one to the third floor and Intensive Care is through the double doors on your left. And I hope your mom will be okay, dear.'

Lucie wanted to hug the woman. She followed her directions and stopped when she came to the double doors, scared to go any further.

Lucie leaned forward to take a peek through the glass panel. Suddenly both doors swung open, like curtains on a stage. She expected all eyes to be upon her but no one gave her a second look. Nurses rushed about, intent on their work, doctors consulted notes at a central desk and, on a bank of seating, a man appeared to be comforting his weeping wife.

Lucie sneaked her way along a row of windows, peeping into patients' rooms. There was no sign of her mother.

CHAPTER 23

One of his cell phones rang just as the entrée was being served. 'Oh, really, darling. Must we have those things at the dinner table?'

His friend Ray came to the rescue. 'Business is business, Diane. You know that.'

Diane, in perfect hostess mode, raised her glass to her guest with a coquettish smile. 'Well, of course ah do, Raymond,' she said, her best southern drawl exaggerated for his benefit. 'But don't y'all agree it's just a teensy bit tiresome during dinner?' She pronounced it 'dinnah'. Her accent was the first thing about Diane he'd fallen in love with. The second was the size of the estate she would inherit on her daddy's death.

'My daddy, may God rest his soul, would never take a phone call once his guests were called to table. It's just downright bad manners.'

Their dinner guests laughed. Everyone loved Diane, especially when she turned up the heat on that Southern Belle charm.

He checked the phone and walked backwards out of the dining room saying, 'Sorry, everyone. I really need to take this.'

'Speak!' he barked into the phone, once he was out of earshot. 'Boss?'

'Didn't I tell you not to ring me unless it was urgent?'

'It is urgent, Boss.'

'It better be.' He tapped the fingers of his free hand on the mantelpiece. The smell of perfectly roasted beef drifted from the dining room and straight up his nose. His famished stomach rumbled in anticipation of the feast to come.

'Well, for God's sake, spit it out, man. I've got dinner guests waiting. You couldn't have picked a worse time to call.'

'Sorry, Boss.'

'What is it? You got something?'

'Yessir.' The guy sounded like a kid at Christmas. One who'd got all the presents on his Santa list. And then some. 'She's there.'

His stomach gave a lurch, all desire for food gone in an instant. This was the last thing he expected. 'You sure about that?'

'Yessir, I'm sure. I saw the woman with my own eyes, walking out the building, just like you said she might.'

'You sure it was her?' He'd never thought, for one minute, that Charlotte would appear. He'd simply been crossing t's and dotting i's. That's why he'd got Ray to find him a low-grade nobody of a private eye. Somebody who'd disappear back under a stone after a couple of days' reconnaissance of Charlotte's building. All Ray and his private dick knew, a mistress was cheating, and some proof was needed.

'Definitely, Boss. I have a picture of her right here in my head. I haven't seen her close up, but it's her all right. What did you say her name is?'

'I didn't. You don't need to know her name.'

'It's just, she was chatting to the doorman like she's known him all her life. I was gonna check with him I've got the right person.'

He shook his head and tried to keep his temper. Where the hell did Ray get these guys? Stupid or what?

'And let her know I'm having her followed? That's about the dumbest idea I ever heard. Don't you go near that doorman. Or her, you hear me?'

The youth became sycophantic. 'Sure thing, Boss. Sorry, Boss.'

Time to tone it down. He didn't want this guy getting suspicious about Charlotte and why she was so important. As far as this second-rate sleuth was concerned, Charlotte was just another two-timing gal with an angry lover checking up on her whereabouts.

'Sorry, Boss. I'll keep a low profile from now on.'

He hated crawlers. 'You even know what that means?'

The guy ignored the jibe, proof he didn't understand. 'She didn't come out with another guy, Boss. I know that for sure.'

'Well, that's all I need to know. You sure she didn't see you?'

'She didn't see me, I swear.'

'I hope not.'

'Boss, pardon me for saying this, but you don't sound too happy. Will I still get paid?'

'Sure you will. Your contact will be in touch and you'll get paid. I'm a man of my word. Good job.'

'Anythin' else you need, Boss, I'll be glad to help out.'

He killed the call without answering. As far as he was concerned, this bozo just did his last job.

All the guy had been asked to do was watch the apartment block for a few days and let him know if a woman answering Charlotte's description appeared with a man.

It had been a setback, not to mention a shock, to hear the professional cleaning crew had been turned away. They were supposed to erase all trace of Charlotte Gillespie. Pack up her belongings, drop them at a storage facility and clean that apartment till it shone like no one had ever lived there. The only difficulty he had anticipated was their gaining access to the building, but the doorman had examined their ID and it checked out. Security had never been tighter in New York. Everyone was terrified of everyone else. The man living next door. The passenger sitting opposite you on the subway. The solitary kid hanging out on the street corner. Any one of them could be a terrorist.

He hadn't anticipated the cleaners being sent away. By the woman who lived in apartment 40/1. The woman who was supposed to be dead.

He didn't understand how the guy he'd hired to get rid of Charlotte had managed to get his hands on the ribbon and key if he didn't kill her. Whatever else he'd done, it was clear he didn't finish her off.

Charlotte had run back to the sanctuary of her home. She would assume *he* had died in the North Tower, and if she loved him as much as she claimed, she'd be devastated by his loss. Not to mention the loss of her business premises and most of her employees. The woman would be an emotional wreck. A very rich one, but a wreck nonetheless. He almost felt a little sorry for her.

Charlotte's business colleagues were gone, vaporised. She had no close friends these days. All her girlfriends, she said, had got married and had babies, moved out to the suburbs or closer to family – while she'd been busy working or working out, training for marathons. And then, of course, she'd had to find space in her life for him, so there wasn't much room left for girly get-togethers. He'd been so flattered by her affections that he'd broken his no relationships rule. To begin with, an illicit affair had suited Charlotte perfectly. She wasn't looking for a husband. She was already married, she said, to the business she'd built up from nothing. Now Gillespie Solutions was gone, but Charlotte Gillespie was still around to make trouble for him. What a balls-up.

He flopped into a Louis XIV armchair by the fireplace and chewed on his fingernail. He'd expected to be very relaxed, and very rich, by this stage. With not a care in the world more serious than which bathing suit to pack for his hard-earned vacation.

Now he'd have to deal with the cheating scumbag who caused this mess. That man had taken a lot of money for a job he didn't complete. Charlotte should be dead by now.

It was his own fault he'd been made a fool of. He should know better than trust low-life trash. Problem was, only low-life trash would be prepared to kill a woman at short notice and in broad daylight. To make a few thousand lousy bucks. The money didn't matter to him. It was more important to find out what went wrong. And why Charlotte was still alive.

He'd hoped to keep his hands clean, but he hated loose ends. And this loose end was big enough to unravel the whole garment. He preferred everything nice and tidy. You didn't get to be rich by ignoring the details.

There would be a lot of deals to be brokered in the forthcoming months. When the stock exchange opened again he could expect to net more income than the GDP of many a small country. Then there were the reinvestments, not to mention the big bucks to be made from keeping America's citizens safe in their beds at night. He had too much riding on this to leave anything to chance. Or to anyone else. He had to sort this out himself.

He'd catch up with Charlotte later.

Right now, what he needed was an explanation as to why she was still alive. And once he'd got that explanation? Well, he hoped the ass-wipe enjoyed his money while he had the chance. A reckoning was on the cards.

He selected another phone and made the call.

'Remember me?'

'Sure. You got another job for me?'

'The biggest of your life. Meet me tonight, nine o clock.'

'No deal, man. I ain't goin' into no Central Park after dark. You crazy?'

'I never mentioned Central Park. Listen up. I'll give you the address in a minute. And make sure you come on foot.'

* * *

Diane was not going to be happy. He opened the ornate doors that led into the dining room. Dinner was in full swing. He was glad they hadn't waited for him. Except Ray, who looked a little anxious, all their guests seemed to be having a good time, laughing and chatting.

He coughed to get attention and everyone looked at him, including Diane, whose face was cloudy as a winter sky. She shook her head slowly from side to side, her expression saying, 'Don't you dare.'

Smiling broadly, he announced, 'Friends, I cannot tell you how sorry I am, but I'm going to have to ask you to excuse me.' Without further explanation, he gave a bow that would have done credit to a courtier and backed out of the room.

He could hear their disappointment as he pulled the double doors towards him. Diane's dinner parties were always fun, she made sure of that. Everyone knew how prestigious it was to receive a dinner invitation from himself and Diane and he was proud of their social standing. And he enjoyed the role of host. It suited his personality.

He could hear Diane's voice on the other side of the doors. 'Well, I do declare, that man will be the death of me with his business dealings at all hours of the day. Still, who says we can't have a party without him?'

Their guests, as expected, responded with much laughter and a tiny round of applause. If he were a less confident man he might think he wasn't wanted, but he knew this was all part of Diane's act and her very special way of supporting him. He often had 'business' to attend to late at night, and Diane, bless her, never asked any questions.

CHAPTER 24

He'd left his car miles away and taken a taxi for a few blocks, completing the last half mile on foot. This was a part of town that tourists were advised to avoid, but he wasn't a tourist. He was a New Yorker, born and bred, and not from the privileged part he had people believe. He was the American Dream, a poor white boy made good, and he was proud of it. But in a quiet, personal way. Unlike some self-made men of his acquaintance, he never boasted about his journey from the gutter to the glitz. Not even his wife knew about the poverty he'd grown up in.

He found the rendezvous, a warehouse that was owned by one of his companies. Empty now, no longer needed, but not yet ready for reselling. He could afford to wait till the value increased.

What he couldn't wait for was to get to the bottom of this Charlotte thing.

He freed the heavy iron door of its padlocks and hauled on the handle. The rusted hinges shrieked their reluctance to cooperate and the screeching echoed across the deserted lot. He waited in the shadows. When no one appeared, he stepped from the murk of the street into a darkness several shades deeper. The place smelt of damp and decay. He wondered if the roof needed a repair. He hoped it hadn't been broken into by junkies looking for a place to squat. He listened hard for a few minutes. All he could hear was the scurrying of some creature he'd rather not identify. His eyes were adjusting to the dark but there was little to see, apart from the skeleton of an ancient shelving system that had been too much bother to move.

He crouched down, back against the wall, and waited.

He liked to be early. For everything. A board meeting, a billion-dollar deal, an assignation with a mistress. Being early gave him the chance to be prepared. And it gave him power.

He said nothing when the door creaked opened and his contact crept in, silhouetted for a moment against the meagre streetlight. He watched the man look around, at a clear disadvantage. Just the way he liked it. When the door banged closed, the warehouse was plunged back into blackness. He waited, long enough to make the other man nervous, then flicked a switch on the huge flashlight he was carrying. A megawatt beam lasered through the darkness, illuminating and startling the guy he'd come to meet.

The man stepped back as if shot, covering his eyes with both hands.

'Fuck! Get that light outta my face.'

He held the flashlight steady and said nothing. He had the power.

He let a few long seconds pass before he slowly lowered the beam. It dropped like a dying spotlight, concentrating its light in a blue-white pool at the man's feet.

He waited for him to approach, noticing the exaggeration of the arrogant swagger. Sure sign of nerves.

'You got another job for me, chief?'

'Could be. Once we tie up a few loose ends from the last job.'

Half-lit from below, the guy's face was hard to read. The expression on it might have been surprise, but whether feigned or genuine, it was impossible to tell.

'I hired you to take out Charlotte Gillespie.'

'Yeah, and I did.'

'You sure about that?'

'Of course I'm sure. What the hell is this?'

'Intelligence tells me she may still be alive.'

'Dude. I don't know what you're talking about. You got the key, didn't you?'

This guy was hiding something. He knew it. He'd seen enough bluffing in his time at the board table.

'Yes. But that proves nothing,' he said. 'You could have ripped that ribbon off her neck and made a run for it. You get paid without getting your hands dirty. Result.'

The guy protested, stammering and stuttering, cheating vibes coming off him like gorgonzola in a heatwave. He was holding something back.

'You came highly recommended. I heard you were one of the best.' Flattery was a useful tool.

The bravado was back. 'I *am* one of the best. And your woman's dead. She died on 9/11, like all those other poor bastards. Perfect cover up for both of us.'

'Perfect cover up for you, you mean. You got paid for a murder and all you did was steal a key. You can see why I might feel I've been ripped off, can't you?'

'Listen, man. I killed the woman. Suffocated her. It was real easy. With all that dust in the air. She hardly even struggled.'

'Maybe you killed *a* woman. The problem is, you didn't kill the right woman. And now there she is, walking around Manhattan. She could cause me a whole lot of trouble I can't afford.'

The hitman said nothing, seemed to be thinking of his next move.

'And the way I see it, I'm due my money back.' He raised the torch and shone the beam right in the guy's face, saw the panic there. The man closed his eyes and turned away from the blinding light.

'I can't pay it back. I owed that money and it's gone. But I swear to you, I took out the woman you wanted dead.'

He said nothing.

'Trust me, man. She's dead.'

'Unfortunately, you can't prove it, can you?'

'I got some proof,' said the dude, reaching for his back pocket.

His own hand went automatically to his waistband, but stalled there when the hitman produced not a gun, but a photo ID card on a lanyard. He jerked his wrist and the plastic card bungeed to the end of its nylon cord and dangled there. The beam of light picked out Charlotte's face and the name of her company.

'This is the target, right?'

He nodded. 'I asked you to take the key. Nothing else.'

'And you got the key. But it always pays to have a little backup plan. Call it insurance for the future.'

'So you were planning to keep it so you could blackmail me?'

'Hey, that's not such a bad idea.'

'Don't even think about it,' he growled.

'No, nothing that fancy. There's always a market for fake ID. A free pass into the North Tower at WTC? That would've been gold to somebody planning to steal a few laptops or dip a few purses. Now there is no North Tower. But plenty of saddos out there will be wettin' themselves for something like this. Memorabilia. Worth good money.' He jerked on the string and flipped the card into his hand. He waved it around, like someone teasing a small child. 'Now do you believe I got the right woman?'

It was often wiser to say nothing in tense negotiations. Wait to see what the other guy's next move would be.

The lowlife turned his face to the light and paused, like a soloist ready to perform. His tone defiant, he said, 'I been thinking, I bet the cops would be interested in why a nice gentleman like you would want a nice lady like that murdered.'

He'd heard enough. He slowly raised his right arm into the shaft of light, illuminating simultaneously the gun and the shock on the poor guy's face. A soft echo of muffled gunshot floated to the roof and back and it was done. He bent to disentangle the nylon cord from the dead fingers that held the ID like a pass to the underworld.

He fetched some old burlap from the shelving and threw it over the body. It might be found when the building was demolished, but the warehouse would guard his secret for a few years. It would be a long time till this area was scheduled for redevelopment. He'd make sure of that.

With all his senses on high alert he locked and padlocked the door, urging his trembling fingers to hurry up. Then, fighting the desire to throw up on the sidewalk, he walked the few streets back to the district where he'd been dropped by the cab.

Once he'd hailed another and was safely inside, he expelled a long, shaky breath and began to consider his next move. There was no doubt left in his mind that the hitman believed he'd murdered Charlotte. He had certainly incapacitated her enough to remove the key and the ID from around her neck. That much was self-evident. But then the dust cloud came down and hid everything. He'd watched it himself on TV, several times. It had blacked out all vision for a few minutes, according to witnesses who'd been in the vicinity and got caught up in it. The white dust had been so thick it was impossible to identify people or places, even after it cleared.

It had made for good television footage, seeing all those New York citizens transformed into walking snowmen. Very visual. He'd even seen one of his employees interviewed on CNN – and hadn't recognised the guy until he'd heard the voice. A man he'd known for twenty years, white from head to toe and indistinguishable from every other businessman on the street.

It wasn't impossible that Charlotte had recovered and crawled off under the cover of the dust cloud, back to her apartment. She had asthma, after all, so maybe the hitman thought he'd suffocated her, when she was just suffering a severe asthma attack. She'd become breathless one night after a particularly athletic bout of sex. He'd found it strangely stimulating at first and taken some credit, thinking his prowess had given her a particularly satisfying orgasm, but it had quickly become scary to see her gasp for air as if she were dying. The minute she'd got her inhaler and taken a few puffs, she bounced back and soon felt well enough for a rematch.

His sources told him she was still living in her apartment, so it didn't look like she was planning on taking off. Or going to the cops. First thing he had to do was get close enough to find out what was going on. Then he could take action.

CHAPTER 25

Lucie rose from a night spent worrying about her mum and dragged herself to the shower.

After all that angst about leaving the apartment and getting herself to the hospital, she'd managed to make a complete mess of things.

She'd been just about to slip out of Intensive Care when someone called, 'Excuse me! May I help you?'

'No, I mean, yes. Em, sorry. I seem to have got a bit lost.'

A young doctor, about her own age, stood smiling at her. 'It's a confusing place. Took me six weeks to find my way around. Where is it you want to go?'

Lucie picked the first place she could think of. 'The cafeteria,' she said, feeling a blush crawl up her neck.

'You *are* lost.'

As he gave her directions, Lucie backed off saying, 'Thanks, sorry to trouble you,' and hurried away.

When she found herself alone in the elevator, she gave her head three bangs on the metal wall. How could she be so stupid? Why hadn't she said she'd come to see Mrs McBride? She didn't have to give details. The doctor had been friendly and kind. He didn't look the type to interrogate somebody about their reasons for visiting.

She'd thought about going back to the mousey lady on reception and trying again. But then she'd get caught out in her lies. If her mother was no longer in ICU wasn't that a sign she was getting better? Maybe she'd even been discharged? There was another alternative but Lucie preferred not to dwell on it.

All night long she'd tossed and turned, angry with herself for being such a wimp.

She'd made a terrifying trip into the outside world and a nerve-wracking visit to the hospital, and still she knew no more than she did this time yesterday. Worse, she was no closer to a plan for seeing her mother, despite a night spent agonising over the problem.

In the bathroom mirror her reflection was tired, but with the bruises fading every day, she looked better than when she'd first got here. Her hair, responding to Charlotte's colour-enhancing shampoo, was sleek and glossy, and she'd put on a little weight too. Not surprising with the amount of good food sitting there in the refrigerator, asking to be scoffed. Lucie patted her tummy and gave her mirrored self a little warning to watch her weight. She had no idea how Charlotte ate that sort of food on a regular basis and fitted into the clothes in her wardrobe. One thing was certain, they wouldn't fit Lucie for much longer unless she did something about her diet, or increased her exercise.

The novelty of using Charlotte's treadmill had quickly worn off and the prospect of getting on it again was unappealing. Lucie had always preferred to run in the open air. She wondered if the Manhattan air would be safe to breath. What she'd give right now to be running through a bright Scottish morning, gulping down the fresh autumn air.

She wouldn't be able to run far today, not till she built up some real fitness. How long was it since she'd had a proper run? Even if she had been able to afford running shoes, the neighbourhoods she'd lived in with Curtis weren't the kind of places where housewives went jogging.

Kitted out in the finest of running gear, Lucie told herself to be brave and stepped out into the hallway. She'd found some brand-new trainers that Charlotte hadn't even taken out of their box. Without socks, they were a good fit and her feet made no sound as she padded towards the elevator.

This time she made it inside without too much of a panic and hit the button for street level.

'Good morning, Ms Gillespie,' said Rob. He grinned at her as she crossed the lobby. 'Off out for a run?'

Head down, she waggled her fingers in goodbye, keen to get out of the door before she lost her nerve, or met any neighbours who might know Charlotte.

She stopped, almost colliding with the plate–glass doors. Without making it obvious, Lucie looked for a handle or some button she needed to press. She waved her hand around in the air, hoping to trigger some invisible sensor. Nothing happened.

'Rob? Something wrong with the doors?'

'Not so far as I know, Ms Gillespie. How about you step back and try again?'

Lucie obliged, stepping back and forth like a cha-cha dancer, but the doors remained closed.

'I'll just go check the control panel, Ms Gillespie.' Rob ambled off as if he had all the time in the world.

Lucie felt her courage draining away with every second she had to wait. She started to breathe to the count of six again in the hope of calming herself down.

When Rob reappeared at the end of the hall, unhurried, Lucie stepped up to the doors, keen to get through them and go. The sensor, wherever it was, failed to react and the doors stayed closed.

At the back of the lobby a discreet ting signalled the arrival of the elevator. Two men and a woman got out, in silence. None of them looked at Lucie. Rob wished them a jovial good morning and apologised for the problem with the doors.

'I can't stand around here all morning,' said the woman, without returning Rob's greeting.

Apparently, this was not the kind of apartment block where people got friendly. Maybe Charlotte knew none of her neighbours. Perhaps everyone who lived in a place like this was engrossed in his or her own life, all too busy working themselves to death to chat to the person next door.

'It's Ms Landsbury, isn't it?' asked the young doorman reverentially.

The woman nodded abruptly, her expression severe and judgemental.

'I'm very sorry, Ms Landsbury. I've no idea what's going on. I've never really worked with this type of door before.'

'This is unacceptable. You're a doorman, for God's sake. If you can't open doors, what are we paying you for? You need to do something. Fast.' The woman opened her Louis Vuitton and removed a Blackberry. She turned her back on the doorman and her neighbours and began an intense conversation.

'This can't be the only exit, Rob,' said one of the men, his tone friendly and reasonable. 'The trash doesn't go out this way, surely?'

'No sir, it doesn't, but I just checked the service door and someone seems to have parked so close up against it I can't get it to open more than an inch.'

'What kind of an idiot would do that?' asked the man, looking to Lucie for agreement.

The other guy said, 'Rob, I can work from home for an hour or so. Would you call me, please, when the doors release?'

'Sure thing, Mr Baumler. And I'm sorry for the inconvenience.'

'That's okay, fella. Not your fault.'

'Well, whose fault is it?' demanded the woman, looking as if her phone call had brought the direst of news.

Lucie was losing her nerve. It was bad enough standing in Lycra leggings and T-shirt next to this perfectly made-up, divinely dressed woman, but Lucie was panicking in case somebody spoke to her. She was fighting the temptation to run back upstairs to the safety of the apartment but that might be unwise, given they were all effectively trapped in the building.

'What if there's a fire?' asked the woman, as if she'd read Lucie's thoughts. 'Have we learned nothing from 9/11?' She looked at Lucie, as if for backup, but Lucie glanced away, uncomfortable with the crass reference to such a raw wound in the city's side.

To avoid any contact with her new neighbour, Lucie turned to Rob. 'Maybe there's a code you need to put in or something?'

'I already tried everything I could think of, but I'll try again, Ms Gillespie. And the super should be here any minute. He'll know how to fix it.'

Oh God, now he'd said the name out loud. Lucie waited for the well-dressed woman to denounce her with a strident, 'She's not Charlotte Gillespie.'

'Hang on,' she said, peering at Lucie's face. 'Did he just say Gillespie?'

Lucie nodded, unsure what else she could do.

'Are you, by any chance, related to the Westchester Gillespie's? From Sterling Hill?'

Great. Now the rudest woman in New York wanted to chat. Lucie tried to look interested, vacant, pensive. Anything but terrified.

'What are you, twenty-nine, thirty? You'd be about the same age as Miriam? Tall girl. Great tennis player.'

Lucie started to slowly shake her head, as if she were doing a mental inventory of all the high-society folk she knew. 'I don't think so.'

At that moment Rob walked in front of the doors and, as if by the magic of sesame, they opened.

Her new best friend dismissed Lucie with a regal flap of her hand as she charged out the door. Or maybe her arm was already raised for a cab. In any case, it was clear her interest in Lucie was over.

* * *

Lucie was shaking as she stepped outside. She waited in the doorway for a moment, wanting to be sure her neighbour had gone. The air was still tainted with the odour of smoke, but it was good to be outdoors and Lucie turned her face to the warm sun, glad to be alive, and still free.

She'd promised herself, since the day of the catastrophe, that she would stay away from the World Trade Center, but today something seemed draw her towards the smouldering skeleton at Ground Zero. Everyone on the street seemed to be heading in the same direction and it was easier to walk with them and go with the flow than try to battle against it. What attracted people to the scene of a tragedy? She'd never understood drivers who slowed down as they passed a road accident, so keen to witness a horror they endangered themselves and other drivers.

This – 9/11 – was like the world's worst car wreck, dreadful beyond imagination. And there were plenty of rubberneckers in New York keen to have a look, it seemed. Some folks were obviously trying to get to work but the sidewalks were thronged with people watching rescue workers, medical staff, police officers, as they went about their grisly task of looking for survivors.

Lucie had seen enough and was ready to jog away in the opposite direction when she overheard a conversation start up between two women beside her.

'He was on the ninety-sixth floor, South. We were so proud of him when he got that job. The youngest broker in company history. He was only twenty-six. And now he's gone. I can't comprehend it. I stand here every day praying he'll walk out, covered in dirt and dust, unrecognisable to anyone but me. I'll call his name, "Jamie!" He'll look around, then, when he sees me, his eyes will light up and he'll shout, "Mom!" and come running out of that wreckage, right into my arms.'

The woman broke down and, touched by her sadness, Lucie turned slightly and watched. The two strangers, joined by tragedy, hugged and appeared to take comfort from each other. That kind of thing didn't normally happen in the streets of this city. She heard the second woman say quietly, 'I know what you're going through. I dreamt last night they'd found everyone alive, safe in some secure underground bunker, and my Amelia walked out, just like your son, and said, "Momma, sorry I'm late." Just like it was any old normal day and we were going for lunch.'

Lucie looked around with more compassionate eyes and saw that these people were not rubberneckers here for a cheap thrill at the expense of someone else's loss. They were desperate grieving mothers, sisters, fathers, wives, husbands, even a few children. Many people carried pictures, family snaps of loved ones, their likeness so enlarged, every pixel stood out. Pictures of happy times, a woman with a new baby in her arms, a smiling man, his face illuminated by a candle-covered cake, a couple in Santa hats. Each one a snapshot of a life brought to a sudden, ugly, premature end. Lucie was aware of how many young faces were pictured, faces like hers, and knew again the rush of relief and gratitude that she'd never made it to that interview. At the time, running from Curtis, she'd felt her whole future depended on getting that job. Lucie said a silent prayer of thanks to a God she'd stopped believing in some years before. She turned and made her way courteously through the bystanders, murmuring her apologies and avoiding eye contact, scared of seeing more pain and despair.

When she had enough clear space to break into a jog at last, Lucie felt so lucky to be alive she was worried it might show on her face. Would anyone in Manhattan ever feel it was okay to smile again? Especially if, like her, you were one of the fortunate few.

Curtis must have been found by now. Dylan would have been round to the house, called the cops. She felt guilty that poor Dylan had to be the one to find his friend, but Lucie felt neither guilt nor sorrow for Curtis and when she remembered the grief of those sobbing mothers, she knew her heart had become hard as the sidewalk beneath her feet.

CHAPTER 26

Diane was in a mood. And it was all his fault.

She'd been in bed when he got home. It had been his intention to come straight back and pick up his role of dinner party host right where he left off. But once he'd dealt with the smug little schmuck, he'd felt too sick to socialise. Killing someone, even a douchebag like that guy, hadn't ever been his intention. He'd only taken the gun along in case he needed to defend himself. But the minute blackmail was mentioned, he'd been left no choice.

Instead of going home, he'd gone to a bar to drink the adrenaline out of his system and formulate a plan. His dark mood had lifted by the time he got back, and, to his relief, the dinner guests had departed. He'd climbed into bed and cuddled up close to Diane. Sex was another great way to neutralise excess adrenaline. He'd slid his hand under her nightgown, the stroke of warm silk arousing him as he swept his palm over her stomach and downwards. When she groaned quietly he took it as a sign she wanted him and his fingers had explored further till she moved away, saying sleepily, 'No, please don't.'

He knew better than to try to force himself on her.

By morning, despite his sleep being disturbed by dreams of warehouses and gunshots, he was dying to make love to her, but Diane was taking her time to thaw. They'd played this game before and it was usually worth the wait. When she gave in, and she always did, she made sure he had a good time. But for now, she was making him pay.

'Those dinner guests were *your* business contacts, not *my* friends,' she complained. 'You had no right going off like that and leaving me to hold the fort.'

'Diane, you were born to play hostess. I've never seen another woman welcome guests as graciously as you. It's effortless.'

'It may look effortless to you, but it was hard work after you left. That awful Miriam flirting with anything in pants and Raymond with his terrible halitosis, breathing all over me.'

She was sitting up in bed now, delectable in a gossamer-thin negligee, a ruffle of marabou around her neck. The pale pink colour showed up her skin to perfection. Diane never let the sun touch her face and her complexion was still smooth as silk. He suspected she spent a fortune on face creams too, but hell, they could afford the best and she deserved it. Besides, he needed his wife to look good. She was like the First Lady of the New York business world.

'And just what are you smiling at, may I ask?' she said, sounding cross.

'I'm smiling at that lovely pout of yours, but don't go spoiling your pretty face with frowning. You'll get wrinkles.'

'Well, no wonder I'm frowning. What kind of a husband leaves his poor wife with such a bunch of boring people?'

'The kind of husband who makes his wife very rich.'

When she smiled, he moved closer and pulled her down under the covers. As she slid towards him, the silky nightgown rose up and exposed her naked thighs. This time she didn't say no.

Diane's cheeks were blushed when they drew apart and he knew he was forgiven.

'Still love me?' he asked.

'Of course, always.' She kissed him and he believed her.

'Good. Because I've got to go away for a day or two. Got some out of town business to attend to.'

The pout was back. Her lips were irresistible. He kissed them, over and over, saying between each touch, 'Sorry, sorry, sorry,' till she gave in to him again and all was good.

* * *

He rode into Manhattan on the subway. Not his usual choice of transport, but he'd given his driver a few days off and didn't want to be seen in any of his own cars. He wanted to slide into the crowd for a while, to take stock. He couldn't risk involving any more bozos, not after the blackmail episode. The last thing he'd expected was to be tying up loose ends by himself.

How to do it, though, that was the problem. Without arousing suspicion. As he'd nursed a Scotch or three in the dark corner of that dive of a bar last night, he'd run through various scenarios in his head. He had to make some sort of contact with Charlotte, that was paramount, but he couldn't just turn up at her apartment. For one thing, he wasn't supposed to know where she lived. She'd been adamant about meeting him in hotels, said she was protective of her private space and never took anyone there.

He, however, always made it a priority to find out all he could about potential partners before he considered sharing any type of venture with them, business or otherwise. That way he didn't get any nasty shocks further on down the road. It had been months since he'd followed Charlotte home to Fitzgerald Square. Just to make sure she was who she said she was.

He rubbed his gut. His ulcer had been bothering him since he'd found out Charlotte was alive. Drinking didn't help, of course, he knew that, but this pain was different from his usual gastritis. If he didn't know himself better, he'd say it was nerves, but that was nonsense. He was unshakable, had nerves of steel. That was what everyone always said about him.

This was more than a business deal gone sour. This was a woman who knew far too much about him and his family. And she could tell the world any time she chose.

He had to stop her, one way or another, before she went public with her knowledge.

CHAPTER 27

He looked over his shoulder, suddenly sure he was being watched, but no one seemed to be paying him any attention. He told himself to calm down and strode off in the direction of Charlotte's apartment.

Apart from television footage, this was the first time he'd seen Manhattan close up since the towers fell. The skyline was like a jigsaw puzzle with pieces missing and he deeply regretted the fact that such splendid buildings had gone. He could still remember how proud he'd been the day he'd moved his business into WTC. The most iconic buildings in the world, now erased from the cityscape. But they'd be rebuilt, bigger and better, and he had many fingers in the pies of the construction industry.

The sidewalk was busy with people staring at walls of pictures. Excusing himself he picked his way through the crowd. Grieving relatives, he supposed, but not this many. The others were sightseers. This public outpouring of grief had all started over in England with Lady Di's death. Outside her palace in London, people had left a sea of flowers, candles and little cuddly toys. He couldn't see the point.

He looked at the wall of faces. All shapes, sizes, and colours, united by the fact that they all happened to be in the same place when they died. Some of the fliers were like the Wanted posters that fluttered in the breeze of Western movies. Some were like the kind of signs folk stuck to lampposts when their cat went missing. 'Please come home. We miss you.' Others were bald statements of fact, like the cops might issue. John Doe. Height: Six foot three. Hair: brown with blond streaks. Going a little grey at the sides. Eyes: Brownish green. Age: Forty-seven. Weight: Two hundred and five pounds. Weight, for Godsake. What was the relevance of the man's weight?

He shouldn't judge. People did the strangest things at a time like this and if making these posters helped, well, who was he to criticise?

This might be the ideal time for him to be seen donating some money. After all, along with his premises in the North Tower, he'd lost most of his workforce. Not that he gave a damn. He didn't know most of them and those he did know by name meant little to him. But it would be an appropriate gesture for someone in his position to make. Might even start a groundswell of donations from other benefactors. He'd get Diane to make the arrangements. She was brilliant at that sort of thing. Maybe they could get a photo shoot organised with Diane at his side looking sad and beautiful as they handed over a huge cheque to relatives of the lost ones. The nervous pain nagged at his belly. Plastering his face all over the newspapers might not be the cleverest thing he could do at the moment.

If Charlotte were lying low, biding her time before going to the authorities, he'd be wise to keep a low profile too. She must be sure he was dead, lost with his faithful employees, like a captain going down with his ship. The longer he could keep her thinking that way, the better. At least until he could get a hold of her and work out what she was up to.

Fitzgerald Square. This was the place. Now he was here, he wasn't quite sure what to do. He couldn't hang about outside her apartment block, like a stalker, waiting for her to appear. Someone might call the cops. And yet, how else was he ever going to find out what the hell she was planning to do next?

He needed to get himself a vantage point. Somewhere he could sit and keep an eye on the building without looking suspicious. He found a coffee shop and chose a little table on the sidewalk from which he'd look like Joe Ordinary enjoying a latte in the pleasant September sunshine.

At first it was quite relaxing, sitting there sipping coffee, people watching and listening to the chatter of other New Yorkers. There seemed to be only one topic of conversation, as far as he could hear, and that was the audacity of terrorists striking right at the heart of their country.

After a while, the novelty of sitting still wore off, the appeal of eavesdropping paled and he became bored. He requested another latte from the pretty young waitress and, on her suggestion, added a chocolate muffin to his order. Anything to occupy him while he waited for Charlotte.

'Can I freshen up your water glass for you, sir?' asked the waitress as she pocketed her order pad and tucked her pencil into the loose chignon of hair on the top of her head. She was cute.

'No, I'm good, thanks,' he responded with a smile, wondering if she'd be up for some fun, but there was nothing in her demeanour to suggest she might be interested in anything he had to offer, other than a decent tip. He turned his attention back to the block on the other side of Fitzgerald Square.

He was peeling the paper case from his muffin and licking chocolate off his fingers when the futility of what he was doing occurred to him. How long could he sit here, or anywhere else, waiting for Charlotte to walk out the door of her apartment block? He had no idea what the woman's daily routine was, even when he was seeing her regularly and she had a job to go to. He knew she liked to jog. She'd told him so, one time when he'd been clutching her buttocks and admiring their pertness. But he didn't know if she ran in the morning or in the evening. Could be she preferred to work out indoors, on a treadmill, like many who disliked the polluted city air and refused to exercise in it. He could sit here all day and never see her.

Just then, as if he'd willed her to appear, the Lycra-clad figure of his erstwhile mistress stepped into the street and jogged off in the opposite direction.

He leapt to his feet, spilling coffee and knocking his muffin to the ground. He steadied the table then took off down the street in pursuit.

The cute waitress shouted, 'Hey, you haven't paid,' but he couldn't afford to stop.

'I'll be back,' he called as he ran, not caring whether she heard.

Sprinting had never been his strong point and he was carrying the after-effects of too many business lunches, but he had to keep Charlotte in his sights.

There she was, up ahead, making for Central Park probably, but he was losing her and it was hurting to breathe. His chest felt like he was zipped into a jacket ten sizes too small and he couldn't expand his lungs. He was running out of air and she was getting away.

He stopped, breathed in till it hurt and shouted, 'Charlotte!'

She didn't react in any way. He tried again, louder this time, but that tight little butt disappeared round a corner as if he'd never opened his mouth.

He doubled over and leaned his forearms on his legs, gasping for breath. There was nothing he could do. He wasn't going to catch up on her now, not in this state.

When his ragged breathing had stilled a little he straightened up and began to walk back to the café to get the check. The waitress was clearing his table and looked relieved when he appeared at her side, apologising for taking off.

'Could I trouble you for a glass of water, please?'

'Sure. Like, right after you pay,' she said, all trace of her earlier smiles gone.

He grabbed some bills from his wallet to show her his good intentions. When she held out her hand he gave her a bundle of notes, uncounted, and collapsed on the nearest chair. 'Keep the change,' he said, 'But can I get that water quick, please?'

He'd regained both his breath and his composure before he'd drained the glass. How long could someone spend jogging round a park? Five minutes would be too long for him, judging by the state of his heart and lungs. Obviously sex was not sufficient exercise for a man of his age. He'd have to do something about his health soon, if he didn't want to die of a coronary. He made a mental note to see his physician and try to get fit after all this Charlotte nonsense was settled. The next bozo he hired would be a personal trainer. Someone who'd knock him into shape again.

'Sir? Can I get you something else?'

He shook his head.

'It's just that, we'll, like, need this table pretty soon. Like, for lunch and all?'

'That's okay, I need to be going anyway. Thanks for the water and sorry about earlier.'

Her smile was back.

He was walking away, still thinking about the pretty waitress when Charlotte appeared, running straight towards him. He stopped and waited for her to spot him, wondering how she would react. Closer and closer she came and still she didn't seem to notice him. She was almost upon him. Her name was on his lips but he hesitated too long. She slowed to a walk and turned towards the doorway of number thirty-two.

CHAPTER 28

Running in the park had given Lucie a chance to think things through. She'd come up with a solution.

All she needed to do was phone the hospital and pretend to be a relative calling from Scotland.

While the phone was ringing, Lucie pictured Mousie, the kindly woman on the front desk who had been so helpful yesterday. At the sound of a man's voice, Mousie's face vanished like condensation from a mirror.

'How may I direct your call?'

'I'm not sure. I thought my mother, Margaret McBride was in ICU, but ...'

Before she could finish the line filled with static and she thought she'd been cut off.

'Mrs McBride is in station three. Connecting you now.'

Lucie cleared her throat and tried to remember the lines she had rehearsed to the rhythm of her running feet. 'Good morning,' she said, rolling the r for effect. 'Could you tell me how my mother's doing, please? She's Margaret McBride.'

'Oh, are you Lucie?'

That was not on the script. 'No, sorry, that's my sister. I'm Mhairi. I'm calling long-distance from Scotland.'

'Your mom's well as can be expected.'

Lucie felt a surge of relief.

'We have your mom sedated so she had a peaceful night. Did you say your name was Marion?'

'Mhairi.'

'Well, Marie,' said the nurse, 'I don't know if you're able to come see your mom?'

Lucie had an answer prepared. 'I'd like to, but getting a transatlantic flight right now ...' She left it hanging there, so it wasn't a lie.

'I can imagine. Still, if I were you, I'd come sooner rather than later.'

'Oh my God, what's wrong? You just said she had a peaceful night.'

'Your mom's been seriously injured.'

'Is she in pain? Please tell me she's not suffering?'

'No, no. Don't worry about that. But there is one thing?'

'Yes?'

'I don't really know how to say this ...'

The nurse faltered and Lucie dreaded her next words.

'Your mom keeps asking for Lucie. I don't know if it's possible for Lucie to come?'

'I don't see Lucie much these days, but I'll pass that on.'

'That's great. I've a feeling it will mean a lot to your mom.'

Lucie rang off, so overcome she couldn't even say bye.

She had to get changed and head to the hospital. But the thought of it made her ill. She stood before the bathroom mirror and chastised herself. Was she so scared of Curtis, or the consequences of what she'd done to Curtis that she wouldn't go and see her injured mother?

She was turning into Charlotte. Poor, self-contained, unattached Charlotte, who had no one. If her mum didn't pull through, Lucie would be alone in the world too.

It might be a risk to go to the hospital and declare herself as Lucie, but what was the alternative? Stay here, a prisoner of her own making, till the papers announced that her mother had died? Was that the way she wanted to find out she was an orphan?

And what if seeing her would help Mum recover? What was it the nurse had said? 'Seeing Lucie will mean a lot to your mom.' Something like that. Perhaps being reunited would give her enough strength to claw her way back to fitness. When she got better, the two of them could go home. Maybe they could do some travelling together first. A cruise, perhaps, to help Mum convalesce. Mum had always fancied a cruise but Dad insisted he couldn't leave the business. Mum said the truth was he got seasick in a rowing boat but wouldn't admit it.

Buoyed by optimism, Lucie jumped in the shower and scrubbed vigorously at her skin, as if she could slough off the veneer that was Charlotte. She'd been crazy to think this arrangement could work long term. Far better to help Mum recover and then face up to the Curtis situation. With Mum's support, she'd come through it.

As she made her way to the hospital, she tried to banish all memories of the last time she'd spoken to Mum and Dad. She didn't want to think of her father's cruel words, or her mother's weakness. Having lived with a domineering, manipulative man herself, Lucie now understood a little better why her mother had so often deferred to her husband. To 'keep the peace'. Life was easier that way.

Mousie was on duty at the desk, ruffling through papers. If the woman noticed her, she showed no sign of recognition.

Lucie hurried towards the little crowd of people waiting by the elevators. As a set of doors slid open a man stood back and allowed her to go in ahead of him.

'Which floor?' he asked her.

'Third, please.'

The man pressed 3 and a couple of other buttons, acknowledging her murmur of thanks with a smile that looked kind.

At the third floor he said, 'Your stop.'

The elevator had already moved off before she had enough courage to push open the double doors marked ICU and step up to the nurse's station.

Behind a counter a young nurse was tapping away at a keyboard, her eyes locked on a computer screen. She hit the return key like a maestro reaching the final note of a piano concerto. Her cheeks puffed as she blew out a huge breath.

When she noticed Lucie watching she flushed a deep red and said, 'Sorry, that's the bit of the job I like least – I hate computers.' Her mouth turned down at the corners and Lucie smiled.

'I'd like to see my mother, please. Mrs Margaret McBride. I came as soon as I could. Mum's been asking for me.'

'Ah, you must be Lucie? Would you like to take a seat? I'll fetch one of the doctors.'

CHAPTER 29

The nurse came back a moment later with a young woman who looked far too young to be responsible for all those very sick people. Her hair was tied in a ponytail high on her head, her face clean of make-up. Her eyes were weary but they brightened as she introduced herself.

'Hi, I'm Doctor Meyer. I've been taking care of your mom.'

'Is she going to be okay?'

'She sustained a severe fracture to her pelvis in the collision which required immediate surgery. The procedure was fairly lengthy but straightforward and your mom appears to have come through it well. That's really all we can say at the moment. She's going to need time and rehab but we're hopeful that in a few months she'll be good as new.'

'She'll be able to walk and everything?'

'Of course. She may want to give up the ballet ...' Dr Meyer smiled and Lucie felt her trust grow.

'Try not to worry. I promise we'll take very good care of your mom. Before you know it she'll be ready to fly back to Scotland and you can take her home.'

The doctor led Lucie to the side of a bed where a woman lay asleep. Lucie didn't recognise anything about her. Her hair was blonde with greyish roots while Mum was dark, like Lucie. This woman's face, albeit swollen and bruised in places, was thin, almost haggard. Lucie's mother, like Granny, had a round, rosy face. Lucie was about to tell Doctor Meyer she'd made a mistake, when the doctor gently touched her patient's arm.

'Mrs McBride,' she said, 'your daughter's here to see you.'

The woman in the bed opened her eyes and the corners of her mouth rose. Lucie would have known those hazel eyes and that smile anywhere.

'I'll leave you two to talk,' said Doctor Meyer. 'Please press the buzzer if you need anything.'

Lucie pulled a chair close to the bed and touched her mum's cheek. Her skin, always so soft, felt dry and flaky. 'Oh, Mum,' she murmured.

'I had a crash. Too tired.'

'How come you were driving, Mum? Why wasn't Dad with you?'

'We've separated.'

'What? When was this?'

'About two years ago.'

'Why didn't you tell me?'

'I was too ashamed. And worried you'd blame me.'

'Why would I blame you, Mum?'

'I left him, Lucie. When he cut you off, it nearly broke my heart. At first I played along, thinking he would soften once the baby was born. But then we heard nothing from you.'

'I'm so sorry, Mum. I should have kept in touch. But Dad made it clear he wanted nothing to do with me, or Curtis. I thought you felt the same.'

'I kept on at him. Every day, nagging at him, but you know your dad. He wouldn't budge from his position. We fought about it constantly. I became chronically depressed. Couldn't get out of bed. Didn't wash. Wouldn't look at him. The pills helped a bit, I suppose. But the damage had been done by then and eventually your dad found solace elsewhere.'

'You're joking! What a bastard.'

Her mum cringed and Lucie remembered she didn't like bad language.

'He's not, Lucie. I drove him to it. When you left for America, he was just as heartbroken as I was.'

'He had a funny way of showing it. He wouldn't even come to see me off at the airport, remember?'

'That wasn't because he didn't care, sweetheart. It was the opposite. Your dad's a typical Scottish man of his generation. He doesn't like to show emotion. He can't help it. It was the way he was brought up.'

'Mum, it's the twenty-first century.'

'I know, I know, but your Granda was just the same. Laying down the law and expecting everyone to obey without question.'

'At least Granda loved you.'

'Oh Lucie, your dad worships you. He always has, from the day you were born. Do you not remember him calling you his wee princess?'

'So why did he cut me off when I got pregnant? How is that love?'

'Two reasons, I think. The main one was anger. He was angry with you for going away in the first place. He was raging that you got pregnant and wasted the opportunity you'd fought so hard for. And he was apoplectic that Curtis abused his position of trust.'

'What was his other reason for telling me I was "dead to him"?'

'He was mortified. Believe it or not, Lucie, when you left, your dad did a fair bit of crowing about how you were away to America for specialist coaching that you couldn't get in Scotland. He told anyone who'd listen that you'd be coming home with an Olympic medal round your neck. Probably gold.'

'And then I phoned to tell him I was pregnant and ask him for money because my boyfriend had lost his job for diddling his student.' Lucie sighed, understanding for the first time how big the shock and disappointment must have been to her parents. 'Yeah, I can see why he'd be gutted.'

'He felt all the men were laughing at him. High and Mighty McBride with his wee lassie up the spout, no better than any other.'

'They were right.'

'The only way your dad knew how to cope was to pretend you didn't exist. But I heard him, crying in bed at night, when he thought I was asleep.'

'I wish I'd known. I'd have got in touch long before this.'

'Well, we're in touch now. That's all that matters, isn't it?'

The huge lump in Lucie's throat meant she could only nod.

'Don't think for one minute your dad doesn't love you, Lucie, please. He's basically a good man. He'd welcome you with open arms. You're his only child.'

'But you said he had another woman.'

'Yes, he has now. But I'm not sure I can blame him. I was a bitch, pecking at his head all the time. And then the depression came, and I wouldn't even speak to him. No wonder he fell for somebody soft and loving.'

'What did you do?'

'I left him to it. Moved out.'

'You went through all that on your own? Oh, Mum. I am so sorry.'

'It's not your fault. I tried my best to trace you, but you seemed to have disappeared. I'd given up hope of ever seeing you again.'

'And then you got my letter?'

'Eventually. When it was forwarded to my new address. About three months after you'd sent it. You must have thought I didn't care?'

That was exactly what Lucie had thought, but none of it mattered now. 'Of course you care. You came all this way, on your own. That's really brave. But, Mum, whatever possessed you to drive from the airport? Couldn't you take a cab?'

'All part of the new, independent me. I planned this whole trip, you know, all by myself. Booked it on the internet.' She paused as if for approval.

'Wow,' said Lucie, 'that's impressive.'

'You know your dad used to make all the arrangements whenever we went anywhere. He always said I'd mess it up. I was determined to prove to myself that I can do anything I want to do. And what I really wanted to do was to whisk you and the wee one off for a road trip, so I rented a car. Turns out your dad was right after all.'

'Mum, I hate to ask, but, did you remember to take out travel insurance?'

The blank expression on her mother's face gave Lucie the answer she'd been dreading.

'Oh, for the car, you mean? Yes, it was covered. I even paid extra. And I didn't bring any valuables.'

When Lucie didn't comment, her mum's face clouded over. 'Oh, no. Don't tell me I've messed that up too?'

Lucie ran her fingers lightly over her mum's brow, smoothing away her frown. 'Don't worry about it, Mum. It's no big deal,' said Lucie, thinking the opposite. There was little point in worrying her. 'Listen, I like the sound of that trip you'd planned. I'd love to travel up the coast. See Martha's Vineyard and Nantucket. But first you need to get back on your feet. Did the docs give you any idea how long it might take?'

Mum grimaced. 'They say it could take up to three or four months before I'm back to normal.'

Lucie whistled. 'Looks like we're going to have plenty of time to think about our road trip.'

'And to get to know each other again.'

'Mum, when you're better, can I come home with you, please?'

'Aye, of course, pet. For as long as you like. But what about your own family?'

Lucie shrugged her shoulders and hoped Mum would sense she didn't want to talk about it.

'Och, we can have a good long chat about all that tomorrow. Bring me some photos, eh?'

Lucie felt a surge of gratitude and love. She leaned forward and gathered her mother into her arms. When Lucie squeezed her in a hug, she heard the sharp gasp of pain and let go.

'Mum, I'm hurting you! Will I get the doctor to give you something for the pain?'

'No, no, no. It makes me sleepy. I've waited too long for this. I don't want to miss a moment.'

'I love you, Mum. And I'm so sorry for all the hurt I've caused you. If I could turn the clocks back, I'd listen to you and Dad.' Lucie couldn't hold the tears any longer.

Slowly, as if every inch was agony, her mum raised her hand and stroked Lucie's hair, just like she used to when Lucie was little.

'Hush, little baby, don't you cry,' she sang, her voice as sweet as Lucie remembered.

CHAPTER 30

Dylan had been unable to go to work the day after he'd found out about Lucie's death. He'd gone straight from the information office to his mother's home, seeking comfort. Mom had been great, although he hadn't been able to tell her the real reason he was so upset. As far as his mother was concerned, he was mourning a favourite colleague who'd gone to a business meeting in the North Tower and never made it out again.

Mom had seemed glad of the chance to mother him again. She'd cooked him mac'n'cheese, the same comfort food she'd cooked when he was a little kid falling off swings all the time. While they ate, she regaled him with one story after another about the search and rescue operation that was going on only a few miles from where they sat. She seemed to be fascinated by facts and figures and quoted random information like someone talking about a favourite hobby, not a biblical-scale disaster.

'Can you believe there are more than three hundred and fifty dogs searching for people who are trapped? I mean, where do they keep all those dogs? And how do you train a dog to go into a dark, scary place below a collapsed building?'

'I've no idea, Mom,' he'd replied, not wishing to offend her. He was beginning to regret his decision to come here rather than go back to his own apartment.

'And did you know people also died on the street that day? Folks just going about their business, nothing to do with the World Trade Center. Hit by debris that fell from the burning building. Else they got smothered in that awful dust that came down like a snowstorm. Can you believe that, Dylan? I mean, how unlucky can one person get?'

It was too much. 'Mom,' he said, 'I don't mean to be rude, but would you mind if I just went to my room now? I'm kind of tired.'

'Sure, son. You go ahead. I need to call Lanie about something before she goes to bed.'

He'd started to help clear the table but his mom had shooed him out of the kitchen with the promise of a cup of cocoa, with mini-marshmallows and cream, as if he'd earned a treat.

He'd lain there staring at the ceiling, brooding over his mother's words. 'How unlucky can one person be?'

Lucie had her whole life ahead of her. She could have made up for the time lost with Curtis. Time wasted on a man who didn't appreciate her. It was ironic that she put up with abuse for so long, and when she finally plucked up enough courage to retaliate, she'd picked that day, of all days, to make her bid for freedom. Dylan couldn't help wishing she'd taken a few more punches that night and stayed put. She might have been injured, but at least she'd be alive now. And he'd have got the chance to quit being such a coward. He could have stood up to Curtis, challenged him properly this time, physically if necessary. He could have offered Lucie an escape route, a safe haven. If not with him, then with his mom. Dylan knew his kind-hearted mother would have taken Lucie in.

Instead, it looked like she'd hit back and run for it. And she'd run out of one hell straight into a disaster zone, as if tragedy was stalking her.

What he'd give for a chance to put things right.

As he'd lain grieving in his childhood bedroom, the tears had run over his temples and into his ears. The pillow had still been damp when he woke in the morning.

A mixture of sadness and anger had made visiting Curtis impossible that day, but Dylan could put it off no longer.

So many of his fellow citizens were affected, but Curtis was too wrapped up in his own misery to show any emotion for anyone else. And all this talk about taking his revenge on Lucie by having her killed? Dylan found it difficult to listen to that stuff, even though he believed it was nothing but idle talk. Curtis might be tough, a big shot when it came to hitting his wife, but he was no killer.

In any case, Dylan was sure Curtis believed Lucie was alive. Probably thought she was keeping a low profile, staying out of his way for as long as she could.

He should tell Curtis that Lucie was dead. Today. Not put it off any longer.

That would put an end to Curtis's stupid talk about having Lucie 'taken out'. Maybe he'd stop talking about Lucie altogether. Now, that would be a result.

But what if Curtis really did believe Lucie was alive and would come back to him eventually? Would the news of her death come as a shock? A shock that was too big for him to deal with in his current state? Curtis had been making progress but he was still fragile and Dylan didn't want to be the one to cause a setback in his recovery.

He was no closer to making a decision when he quietly opened the door to the room Curtis was sharing with three other men. At first Dylan thought the room was empty. Then he saw Curtis sitting alone in the corner. Staring at the wall.

Dylan had met Curtis on their first day at kindergarten. At break time Dylan had been crying, sad to be separated for the first time from the mommy he adored. Another little boy had called him a crybaby. Curtis pushed the bully over on his butt and said to Dylan, 'I know a joke. Want to hear it?'

Dylan had wiped away his tears with the cuff of his favourite Mickey Mouse sweatshirt and nodded. Curtis had told him the kind of joke only kindergartners find amusing.

'What do you call cheese that's not yours?' asked Curtis, giggling in anticipation.

Dylan didn't know the answer.

'It's Nacho cheese!'

The two of them had laughed till Dylan's tummy hurt. They'd been best friends ever since.

To see his hero, loyal, charming, funny, outrageous Curtis sitting there helpless was too much for Dylan. He wished for a sleeve to wipe his eyes but had to make do with the back of his hand.

Sensing someone in the room, Curtis looked round, his eyes wide and fearful. The strong, always ready for a fight Curtis looked vulnerable. Probably for the first time in his life.

'Thought you weren't coming back,' said Curtis.

'Came to see you're okay, buddy.'

'Well, you've seen.' Curtis spread his arms wide. 'Do I look okay to you?'

'I didn't mean that, Curtis,' said Dylan, his voice so full of pity he could hear it himself.

'Hell *did* you mean then?'

'I just meant, well, I thought you might like some company. Maybe cheer you up a bit. I haven't been around for a couple days. Sorry about that.'

'Yeah, I bet you're *real* sorry.'

Dylan thought he'd never heard so much bitterness in one sentence. He tried again. 'Well, I'm here now.'

'To cheer me up? So what do you suggest? Go for a run? Shoot some hoops? Or maybe we could head on out to a bar? Grab a few beers then pick up some hot girls and screw their brains out?'

Curtis was shouting louder than Dylan had ever heard him, even on the side of a running track.

'Never gonna happen! You got that, Dylan? Never gonna happen!'

The door opened and a nurse stuck his head into the room. 'Everything okay in here, guys?' he asked.

'Just peachy, thanks,' said Curtis, lowering the volume. 'Catching up with my ole buddy Dylan here.'

When the nurse left and closed the door behind him, it was as if the air had gone out of the room and Curtis too. He sat slumped in his chair, head down.

Dylan wondered if Curtis had been waiting all day for someone to scream at, to vent his frustration. Maybe he'd feel the better for it, in which case, Dylan was prepared to take the flak.

'Know what, Dylan?' Curtis said, his voice quiet and resigned. 'Never thought I'd hear myself say this, but I wish you'd just let me die.' He gestured at his legs. 'Instead of this shit.'

'Don't say that, Curtis.'

'Why shouldn't I say it? It's true.'

'You don't mean it.'

'Oh yes, I do. This is it for me. I'll die a pathetic, hopeless cripple. And not a day too soon.'

Curtis sounded like his life was already over.

Dylan stood helpless, trying not to watch as the tears rolled down his best friend's face. He didn't know which was kindest, to step forward and comfort his weeping friend, or to leave and let him regain his composure in privacy. In the end he chose to say nothing, respecting what little dignity Curtis still had, but he laid his hand gently on Curtis's shoulder and left it there.

'Sorry, Dylan. None of this is your fault.'

'I hate to see you this way, Curtis. I wish there was something I could do.'

'There is. I told you. Help me find Lucie. I didn't mean all that stuff I said about getting her killed. I miss her. I love her. Please, Dylan, help me.'

'I've been trying, Curtis.'

Curtis looked up at him, eyes red-rimmed. 'Did you find her?'

Dylan looked at his friend, opened his mouth to tell him what he'd found out about Lucie and shook his head. How could he kick a guy so far down he wished he was dead?

'Come on, man. Tell me!'

'Curtis, I think Lucie's gone for good.'

'I knew it,' he spat. 'She's run home to her mommy, hasn't she?'

'No, she hasn't run anywhere.'

Curtis let out a bitter snort of laughter, devoid of any humour, and said, 'Well, I'm sure as hell not running anywhere either.'

CHAPTER 31

Lucie was so helium-hearted she had to resist the urge to skip along the hospital corridor. She'd stopped at a flower stall on the street and bought ten yellow chrysanthemums. Their heads were like big smiley faces. They were Mum's favourite flowers, but Lucie had always hated them. Ever since she was small and found one full of earwigs in Granny's garden. Lucie had thrown the flower away and screamed hysterically because Bernie Yates at school told her earwigs crawled in through your ears and ate your brains. Granny said, 'Well, they'll no get much to eat in wee Bernie's head.'

When Lucie had calmed down, Granny gave her a stick of rhubarb as consolation, and a little bowl of sugar to dip it in. It was a very special treat of Granny's that Lucie had to keep secret from Mum, who disapproved.

'Hi,' she said to the nurse on desk duty. 'I've come to see my mum.'

'Cool. Who's your mom?'

'Margaret McBride.'

The smile didn't leave the nurse's face, but it changed, like one of those lights you can dim, eliminating all the brightness. Lucie felt something drop deep in her stomach.

The nurse came round to Lucie's side of the counter. She put her hand gently on Lucie's back and said, 'Would you like to come and take a seat?'

Lucie held out the bouquet of golden flowers. 'I've brought Mum these. They're her favourite.'

'They're beautiful. If you wait here a moment I'll fetch Doctor Meyer.'

When the doctor came and sat beside Lucie, she knew something was seriously wrong. Yesterday's twinkle had gone from the doctor's eyes. In a low, gentle voice she said, 'I'm very, very sorry.'

Lucie grabbed the doctor's arm. 'Please. No. Don't tell me she's dead.'

The doctor nodded, the slightest movement of her head. Her tired eyes looked full of sadness.

Lucie tried to take it in. 'How long ago?'

'About an hour.'

'An hour?' said Lucie. 'I missed her by an hour?'

The doctor nodded.

'Was anyone with her?'

'We were with her.'

'Was she in pain?'

'No. No pain. You have my word on that.'

Lucie felt like a child, longing for a hug. From her mother, from this stranger, anyone would do. She'd never felt so lost and alone in her life.

'I saw her yesterday. She seemed fine. We talked about going back to Scotland together. And now she's gone? I don't understand how that can happen.'

'As you know, your mother sustained a pelvic fracture in the crash. As a result, a blood clot formed, probably in one of the deep veins of her leg, and caused a blockage in a blood vessel in her lungs. It's known as a pulmonary embolism or PE. Sometimes a PE causes chest pain or breathlessness but your mom had no symptoms. About an hour ago, your mother suffered cardiac arrest. My colleagues did everything they could, but I'm afraid they were unable to save her. And we had no contact details to get in touch with you. I am very sorry.'

'I screwed up. If you'd had my phone number, I could have been here with her when she died. I would have made it here on time, wouldn't I?'

The doctor shook her head, sadly and silently.

'If she'd stayed in Scotland, she wouldn't have had the car smash. If I hadn't got in touch and begged her to come and see me, she'd still be alive. This is all my fault, isn't it?'

'Lucie, you mustn't think like that. Your mom was ecstatic to see you yesterday. She told me she could die happy now she'd found you again. She could never have guessed what was going to happen this morning, but those were her words, I promise you.'

Lucie looked into the doctor's eyes, appealing for affirmation. 'Did she really?'

'She did. Your mom was glad she came to the States and found you, so don't beat yourself up, please. There's no point. Now, is there someone we can call for you?'

Lucie shook her head, suddenly conscious of tears dripping from her chin. She hadn't even known she was crying. 'Nobody.'

The nurse reached for a box of tissues, ripped out a handful and gave them to Lucie.

'Would you like to see your mom?' asked the doctor.

Lucie sniffed loudly, wiped her eyes and stood up, saying, 'No, thank you.'

'There's nothing to be afraid of. She looks very peaceful, as if she's asleep. Are you sure you don't want to see her?'

Lucie shook her head. 'I can't. Please don't make me.'

'That's okay. People often feel the same way. Why don't you sit here for as long as you need? If you change your mind, just tell the nurse. We have some paperwork we need to go over with you, but we can leave it till tomorrow if you like.'

A pager attached to the doctor's waistband started to squeal impatiently. She checked it and rose to her feet, saying, 'I'm sorry. I have to get this.'

'What's the paperwork?' Lucie asked the nurse.

'Insurance stuff, usually. You're Mrs McBride's next of kin, right?'

'I don't know. I suppose I am. There's my dad, I guess.'

'Well, don't you worry, we'll get it sorted out. We have your mom's things ready for you to take away. Her bag, clothes and so on. I'll just go get them for you.'

The last thing Lucie wanted right now was another woman's possessions. Even her mother's.

She was at the swing doors when she remembered the chrysanthemums. Glad to be rid of their acrid smell she laid them on a chair. Maybe the nurse would put them with Mum.

Lucie waited for the elevator, trying to dry her eyes with damp scraps of disintegrating tissue. For the seconds it took to descend to ground level, she covered her face with her hands and gave into an urge to howl like an abandoned child.

She felt the elevator come to a standstill. When the doors opened, she blundered out, bumping into people. Someone fended her off and Lucie stumbled. Strong arms caught and held her upright till she was steady on her feet.

'Hey! Are you okay?'

Lucie leaned against him, this stranger, and wept. She felt firm hands gripping her shoulders. Not pushing her away. Keeping her from collapsing.

When she straightened up, embarrassed and apologising, the man took a pristine cotton handkerchief from his pocket and handed it to her.

'Go ahead,' he said. 'Please.'

Lucie wiped her eyes and dabbed at her nose, still sobbing. 'My mum just died,' she cried, 'and I wasn't there.' The last vowel tailed off into a sorrowful whimper.

The man opened his arms and, as if she'd known him all her life, Lucie stepped into them and continued to weep against his chest. She felt him patting her back, the way her mother used to comfort her when she was small. The memory was too much.

CHAPTER 32

It could not have worked out better for him had he planned it all in advance.

On the way to the hospital, he'd been unable to decide if the girl he was following was Charlotte. She looked very like Charlotte, was wearing similar clothes and shoes, but something about the way she held herself was different. On the few occasions he'd seen Charlotte walk anywhere, into meetings or across the North Tower lobby, she had an aura of something he found hard to identify from memory. It was a confidence, an awareness of herself as someone powerful – he recognised it in himself and others. That aura was probably what had drawn him to her. But this girl had looked different, as if she was out of her comfort zone somehow.

Now, holding her in his arms, at a discreet and respectable distance, of course, he knew this wasn't Charlotte. He didn't know this girl but she showed no sign of wanting him to let her go. In fact, she seemed to be finding solace crying onto the chest of a complete stranger in the middle of a very public place. However, people were starting to look and he was beginning to feel a little uncomfortable.

He eased her away and said in his gentlest voice, 'Hey, come on now. Let's see if we can get you a glass of water or something.' With his hand just touching her elbow, she allowed him to lead her across the entrance hall of the hospital to a little coffee shop in the corner. He settled her at a table for two and said, 'What can I get you? Coffee?'

She shook her head and dabbed at her nose with his handkerchief.

'You go ahead and have a good blow, if that would help. Sure I can't get you something to drink? You should sit for a moment.'

In a tiny voice, completely unlike Charlotte's, the girl said, 'Water, please.' She spoke with a slight accent, Irish or Scottish.

Stepping away from the table he heard an enormous honking sound. Well, that was one handkerchief he wouldn't be using again in a hurry.

When he'd navigated the counter and the queue to pay, the young woman gave him a wan smile. He nodded to her, hoping she would find it encouraging and supportive.

'I took the liberty of getting myself some coffee. Do you mind if I join?'

'No, of course, please,' said the girl, pointing to the seat beside her. She took a sip of water and said, 'Thanks for being so kind.' She held out the sodden hankie with a smile of apology.

'Keep it,' he said. 'I insist.'

The girl wiped her nose again and put the cotton square in her jacket pocket. 'I'm so sorry. You must think I'm completely mad.'

He shook his head. 'Not mad, just very, very sad. I'm terribly sorry for your loss. Has your mother been ill for some time?' Before she could answer he added, 'Forgive me. I have no right to ask such an intrusive question. We haven't even been introduced. Sorry.' He held out his hand and said, 'Richard Armstrong.'

She took his hand and shook it but did not give her own name in return. Interesting. Most people he met replied automatically with their name when he introduced himself.

He tried again. 'My friends call me Rick.' He smiled encouragingly, but still she didn't tell him her name. Better not to force the issue.

With the saddest look he'd ever seen, the girl began to talk. 'My mum was involved in a road accident.'

'That's awful. I'm so sorry.'

'She was driving. But she'd just got off the plane. She was tired.'

'Had she been on vacation some place?'

The girl shook her head and dabbed away fresh tears. 'She flew all the way from Scotland. To see me. It's my fault.'

Scotland! He knew it. He hadn't the time to listen to the dramas of this girl's life. But he was curious about her.

'You're not to blame for a road traffic accident. They happen all the time.'

'Yes, but she wouldn't have been driving if it weren't for me. I haven't seen my parents since I was eighteen. I sent my mum a letter, because I didn't know what else I could do. I had to get away.'

'Away from what?'

'Away from my life. I was going to beg them to forgive me and take me home with them. I didn't get the chance.'

'They came for you. So it's clear they already forgave you.'

The girl shook her head sadly. 'No, they split up because of me. Mum left him. She came alone. When the accident happened, she was driving to see *me*. All to prove she was an independent woman.'

Oh Jesus, this was getting more like a country and western song by the minute. The sooner he got out of here, the better.

'And now the hospital wants to talk to me about insurance and stuff.'

'Did your mom have insurance?'

The girl looked at him as if he was mad. 'No one comes to the States without travel insurance. Everybody knows that, right?'

'Right.'

'Everybody except my mum, it turns out.'

CHAPTER 33

Dylan dumped the paper cup on the table. Scalding coffee sloshed over the edge and burnt his hand, but his brain barely registered the pain. This must be what people meant when they talked about seeing a ghost. You saw a loved one walking towards you through a crowd on the street. Only to be hit with the reality of bereavement when the 'ghost' got close enough for you to make out the features. You wondered how you could possibly have made such a mistake.

There she was. Lucie's ghost. Sitting at a table in the corner. Deep in conversation with a man. Husband, older brother, perhaps. She seemed very upset, and the man, looking kind and concerned, appeared to be consoling her.

Lucie didn't have a brother. She was an only child. Maybe that's why she'd been such an independent spirit when he'd first met her. Not every eighteen-year-old was brave enough to leave her family and cross the ocean by herself. Especially when her family were so dead against it. But Lucie had been full of spirit. Determined to chase her dream of running against the best runners in the world, and beating them.

She was well dressed, this young woman, in clothes that looked more expensive than anything Lucie had owned. Her hair was shorter and looked shiny and soft, cared for in a way Lucie's hadn't been for a long time. She'd got into the habit of tying her hair up in a permanent ponytail, not caring how it looked. Also, this girl had a dark mark on her neck, like a birthmark she tried to hide with make-up.

Dylan had to look away. Not because his mother had always said it was rude to stare. Because it hurt, deep in his chest, to watch this Lucie lookalike. The strength of his feelings came as a shock. He knew he was grieving. He knew she'd left an unfillable hole in his life but he hadn't realised, when she was alive, just how strongly he felt about her. She'd always been Curtis's. End of story. So he'd switched off his emotions around Lucie and tried to treat her as a friend.

But the way his heart leapt in his chest when he saw this girl, the blush that was flooding his face, the deep, devastating sense of loss proved she'd meant much more to him than friendship.

He tried to focus on his coffee cup and raised it to his lips, but the coffee that had seemed so necessary five minutes ago had lost its appeal. Besides, he was feeling nauseous. The moment he put his cup down his gaze returned to the girl. She was leaning on the table, her face in her hands. The man said something to her and she raised her head to looked him.

Dylan felt like he'd touched a live cable. He'd know that profile anywhere. He'd studied it often enough when Curtis and Lucie had been so engrossed in each other they hadn't even noticed he was in the room. The curve of her cheek that he'd always longed to stroke. Her cute little nose that wrinkled when she smiled at something he'd said. Her hair so dark, and skin so pale it looked like porcelain. Her bone structure so fine it made him wonder how she didn't shatter when Curtis hit her.

He had to go to her. She was obviously upset and in need of comforting.

As Dylan approached their table, the man spotted him. His expression changed. The message was easy to read. This is private.

CHAPTER 34

He became aware of people at neighbouring tables watching the little drama unfolding at his own. A tall guy, his face flushed, rose from his seat and walked towards them, coffee cup in hand. He seemed very intent on the young woman, as if he recognised her. God Almighty, could this be the bozo he'd hired? Still stalking her? Coming over to check him out?

He leaned over to pat the young woman on the back and flashed the guy a look. He hoped it said, 'Back off.'

'At least you got the chance to see your mom,' he said to her, his eyes still on the bozo, making sure he got the message.

'No, I didn't.' She started to cry again and reached into her pocket.

'But didn't you just come from seeing your mother right now?'

She gave a huge sob, and wailed, 'I was too late. I didn't see her. Didn't get the chance to speak to her. To tell her I love her. No matter what happened in the past.'

This was becoming more intriguing by the minute. But interesting though her story might be, there was only one piece of information he needed. And he'd already got it. There was no vestige of doubt left in his mind. Whoever she was, this girl, she wasn't Charlotte Gillespie. He'd got it wrong and so had the idiot who'd been watching her. It was clear now that he'd spotted this girl and mistaken her for Charlotte. An easy enough mistake, perhaps, for someone with only a description and a brief glimpse at a photo to go on. But this wasn't Charlotte. Charlotte had no family. She was alone and a loner. At least that's what she'd always told him.

He couldn't hang about here all day waiting for this kid to stop crying. So he drank his coffee as quickly as its temperature allowed then said, 'I'd better be going. Will you be okay by yourself? Is there someone who can come and fetch you? Your husband or boyfriend, maybe?'

The young woman looked up at him, her eyes overflowing. She was really quite appealing, in a childish way. 'No one,' she whispered. 'I'm all alone now. An orphan, I suppose.' She gave him a sad little smile.

'I'm afraid I really must be going.' He got to his feet and held out his hand to her. As she took it, he said, 'Again, I'm very sorry for your loss. But I'm pleased to have met you, Miss?'

She hesitated, as if wondering whether she ought to reveal her name to a stranger. She appeared to make up her mind, smiled a teary smile and said, 'Sorry. Rude of me when you've been so kind. My name's Gillespie.'

CHAPTER 35

Straightening his jacket, he stepped up to Intensive Care reception, where a man stood, watching him. Suspiciously, he thought.

Time for a smile and a helpless look. 'Sorry to trouble you, but I think I just saw someone I know leave ICU.'

'Oh yeah?' said the man, with a straight, serious face. He did not sound encouraging.

'Yes, but I can't find her anywhere in the hospital. Could you tell me if she came back in here?'

The guy shook his head. 'No idea, sir.'

'Her name's Gillespie?'

No response.

Scratching his chin in fake puzzlement, he sought a different approach. 'I wonder, could you tell me the name of the lady who passed away in here about an hour ago?'

'Yes sir, I could.'

'Oh, that's super,' he said, trying to sound grateful.

'But I'm not going to.'

'What do you mean?'

'I mean I'm not going to disclose information about any patient unless you're a close relative. Got it?'

'Hey, come on,' he said, reaching for his wallet.

The man tensed, as if he expected a gun to appear.

'Steady, fella. I'm just reaching for my billfold. Thought maybe you could use a few dollars. Call it a tip, if you like.' He removed a fifty, folded it in half and held it out.

The guy glanced down, quickly, but his eyes lingered long enough to register the value of the note. He would take the bribe. They always did.

'Sir, I'd sure like to help you.'

Gotcha. He'd never seen anyone refuse a fifty-dollar bill in his life.

'But, if you don't get outta here in five, I'll call security and have you removed.'

Not the reaction he'd expected. 'Come on, bud.' He held up the note. 'I'll double this. All you have to do is tell me the answer to one question.' Sliding another fifty dollars from his wallet, he said, 'You don't even need to speak. Just nod and you're a hundred dollars richer.'

He could see the guy hesitate. Almost hear him doing the math in his head. Working out how much fun he could have with a hundred dollars. Or how many pairs of shoes it could buy his kids. Or how it would help pay for his momma's medication.

He went in for the kill, 'The woman who just died? Mrs Gillespie?'

The guy looked him in the face, reached for the money and without dropping his gaze, took it. Then started to count, 'Five.' A heartbeat later, 'Four.'

On three he dropped the money.

On two the green bills fluttered silently to the floor.

So there was still one incorruptible man in New York City.

He was surprised. And more than a little impressed. But no wiser.

CHAPTER 36

Lucie sat on for a while after the kind stranger left. She drank her water and wiped her tears. Each sip she swallowed seemed to recycle itself as a teardrop and roll down her face.

Notes of conversations from surrounding tables floated to her like barely heard fragments of music. Upbeat voices, happy laughter, delighted chuckles from a toddler hiding behind his mother's chair.

Lucie looked around, in search of another tearful face, another sad, bereaved soul. She'd never felt so desolate and unattached in her life and longed to see someone else suffering as she was, just so she'd know it was normal to sit in a café and weep into a stranger's handkerchief. She unfurled the damp cotton, looking for a dry corner to wipe her eyes. One section felt less soggy than the rest and she spread it out between her fingers, preparing for another mighty nose blow. Feeling an embroidered monogram, she flattened the fine material and examined the letters. Three cursive initials intertwined, just like the ones Granny used to stitch every year for her son-in-law. It was a Scottish tradition, when Lucie was small, maybe it still was, to give hankies for Christmas. Lucie had owned a collection of little monogrammed squares of her own, but they'd been lost long ago, used as bandages for broken dolls or parachutes for teddies, anything but their intended purpose.

The kind stranger's initials were so delicately worked, she had difficulty making them out. As if she were reading braille she traced each letter through the maze of scrolls and curls, deciphering a double s and a very elaborate m. Feeling a little guilty for defiling such beautiful craftsmanship, Lucie blew her nose as hard as she could, rolled the handkerchief into a ball and stuck it into the pocket of Charlotte's jacket.

On the journey back to the apartment, Lucie stared at the reflection of her sad face in the window of the subway carriage. How had it come to this? On September eighth she had a mother, a father and a husband. Now she had no one. For the first time since the bust-up with her parents, Lucie realised that she'd been expecting a reconciliation at some point in the future. Maybe not so much with her father, those bridges had gone up in flames long ago, but with her mum, surely. She'd never stopped to consider the details of that reunion but she'd been confident it would come about one day. Ironically, she'd always imagined a touching scenario at her sick father's bedside, as he lay there asking her forgiveness, but some vague premonition had stopped her imagination in its tracks. A dark, superstitious 'be careful what you wish for' warning had drawn curtains over the scene before she could take it to its conclusion.

There would be no reunion now. If only she had made some attempt to contact them sooner, instead of staying silent, like a sulking child.

At first, she'd been fired up by a mixture of anger and righteous indignation. It was bad enough that her father had tried to stop her coming to the States. If it had been up to him, she'd have given up running and got stuck into accountancy textbooks. How dare he tell her how to live her life? What right did her father have to dictate her choice of partner? Given a chance he'd have treated her like a Third-World bride, promised to the son of a local business associate. Curtis had made a costly mistake, but Dad wasn't prepared to give him a chance. Who knew, maybe if her parents had made an effort to welcome Curtis, things would have turned out differently. They could have been one big happy family by now, looking forward to the holidays. She could see them all tucking in at a big dining table, in a joint celebration of Thanksgiving and St Andrew's Day. Curtis and Lucie, smiling at their beautiful seven-year-old daughter and adorable twin boys.

She could see those kids, in cute tartan outfits, and her parents, doting on them, hardly able to believe their good fortune.

The train pulled into an above ground station and Lucie's reflection vanished, and with it the dream of what might have been. When she was pregnant, Lucie had been sure her mum would try to stay in touch. But apart from sending a big money order, she'd obeyed her husband's command that she sever all contact with their daughter. At the time Lucie thought the cash was a salve for her mother's conscience, but she'd taken it anyway. She'd spent it, thank God, on a health insurance plan that covered her and Curtis and their family for any eventuality. Curtis couldn't have paid for her care when she lost the baby. At that tragic time, when Lucie needed all the support she could get, she had missed her mother terribly. It felt like a double loss.

Lucie was glad she hadn't mentioned the miscarriage yesterday. Better Mum died thinking she had a living grandchild.

The terrible months that followed the baby's death seemed like a grey blur now, best forgotten. Lucie began to feel better, physically and emotionally, but things had started to go downhill with Curtis by then, and shame had kept her from contacting her parents. The thought of her father crowing that he'd been right all along was too much. Each time she dialled their number, she killed the call before it could connect. Finally, she'd let it ring through only to find their number was unobtainable. It was a clear message: 'We're out of your life.' She and Curtis had been forced to change apartment soon after and the link was broken.

And now Mum was gone. If only she'd stayed at home. What Lucie wouldn't give to have her parents, estranged from her or not, alive and happy in Scotland.

And what about Curtis? Did she wish *him* alive? Was it better to have one person who cared about her, even if he had a strange way of showing it, than this desolation?

CHAPTER 37

'Is everything as you wished, sir?'

He looked around the ballroom. On a dais at the far end, where, on happier occasions, a band might play, a modern lectern had been set up with microphone and lighting. An overhead screen bore the brightly projected name and logo of his company. Large, round tables, surrounded by golden chairs, had been set up. Each was prepared, not for a wedding feast or a corporate banquet, but with a plain white cloth and an unlit candelabra which held aloft a numbered sign. The numbers corresponded to the floors occupied by his company at its World Trade Center headquarters in the North Tower. More than two hundred people were thought to have reported for work on those floors on the morning of 9/11. None of them had been seen since.

'It looks great,' he said. 'Can you just make sure there are plenty of refreshments on offer and keep the food coming, please. As long as they're eating, I'm paying.'

'Certainly, sir. I'll see to it personally.' With a Prussian snap of his heels, the manager gave the tiniest of bows and excused himself.

Waiters, immaculate in white shirts and waistcoats, carried trays of sandwiches and laid them on tables at the side. Bottles of Coke and Evian reclined in huge buckets of ice. Had there been bubbly chilling too, it might have looked like the firm's annual Christmas party.

Just inside the main door, a table had been set up with information packets, including lists of hospitals and investigative tips. He'd managed to get a hold of several grief counsellors who were standing by, should anyone wish to speak to them, and some small seminar rooms had been set aside for that purpose. Another table was piled with missing person reports and a place had been provided, with pens, to fill them out. Already a few people were gathering around it and many more were streaming into the ballroom. Some went straight to a numbered table and sat there, as if waiting to be served. Others worked their way around the room, speaking to one and then another as they went. Yet more were pinning up home-made posters of their loved ones with a 'Have you seen?' heading in bold pen or print. One young woman, a stars and stripes bandana covering her hair, was directing two children to a space where they might pin up their hand-crafted poster.

He coughed to clear a lump that had inexplicably formed in his throat. Although he believed his actions were absolutely the right ones, it was hard to be this close to the bereaved. He turned away and left the ballroom. He'd find a quiet place to look over his speech and return when people had settled and got some of that raw emotion out of their system. This wasn't going to be easy for anyone.

As he made his way through the main doorway, a woman caught his arm. 'You're Michael's big boss, aren't you?'

His face must have made it clear he had no idea who Michael was.

'Michael Mulholland? My son? Worked on the ninety-seventh?' She pointed at the table marked ninety-seven as if that might jog his memory. 'You probably knew him as Micky?'

When he smiled and nodded, although he'd never heard of the guy, she grabbed his hand. 'Have you seen him? Have they found my boy?'

Cradling this stranger's hand in his, he said quietly, 'I'm so sorry, Mrs Mulholland. I haven't seen Micky. But I do know him. Great guy! Real asset to Langdon.'

With a final shake of her hand he extricated himself and walked away. He could do without any more encounters of that sort.

In the lobby he met Diane, who was hugging a sobbing woman as if she were a close relative. Diane was so good at this stuff. It was a gift, an innate ability to empathise with people and give them comfort. She smiled at him over the woman's shoulder, just the briefest raising of her lips to let him know she'd seen him. Nothing overt that might be noticed by others and cause offence. He waited until she was free then went to her side.

'God, Diane, this is awful.'

She gave him a sympathetic look. 'Well, of course it is, honey. But just imagine how much worse it is for these poor, unfortunate folks here.' In an elegant gesture she pointed out the people who were still making their way into the ballroom.

'How am I going to get up there on that stage and speak to them?'

'I'll be right there with you, for moral support.' To prove her point she took his arm and squeezed it tightly as she walked with him through the wide doorway. She was as calm and collected as if they were sweeping into a ball, guests of honour arriving after the others. 'Remember, honey,' she whispered, 'you're here to help these folks. They all know none of this was your fault.'

The room was noisy, everyone talking at once. A child crying, another giggling hysterically. But there was an atmosphere in the room that he found hard to identify. A group of women near the door moved aside to let him and Diane through and as they passed one of them grabbed his arm and said, 'Have you seen my husband, Graham Carter? He was real strong, a bodybuilder. I believe he may have made it down to the basement.'

He shook his head and tried for a sorrowful look. 'I'm so sorry, ma'am. I haven't seen Graham.'

The woman looked as if he'd just taken away her last shred of hope and he realised then what was creating the buzz in the room. It was hope. These people had come here in the hope that he could tell them something or do something that would help them.

As he climbed the two steps onto the dais and turned to help Diane step up, he thought he'd never had to do anything so difficult in his life. Was this some sort of karma at work? Was this how he'd be made to pay for his actions? God, he wished it was over and he could get out of here.

Gradually the room stilled as people took a seat or turned to face the stage to give him their full attention. Apart from the crying baby, the huge room fell silent, waiting for him to speak.

Checking the mike was on he tried to say hello and found his voice letting him down for the first time in a long career of public speaking. He cleared his throat and tried again.

'Hello, everyone, and welcome. Thank you so very much for coming along this afternoon. I hope you've been able to help yourself to some refreshments and that you've found our information packs helpful.'

There was a muted rustle of agreement from his audience but his overwhelming impression was that they were impatient. Keen for him to get on and say whatever it was he had to tell them.

He gave another nervous cough, then began. 'As many of you already know, the headquarters of my company, Langdon Associates, was located in office suites on floors ninety-five through ninety-eight of the North Tower. You may also know that since 9/11 we have been trying to ascertain exactly how many of our employees were in the building that morning. We know that many colleagues went to vote in the mayoral primary on the way to work and thus were delayed. Many others took the kids to their first day of school that morning and were also delayed. Added to that, at eight forty-six, when the first plane struck, we would not have expected our full workforce to be at their desks.'

'Please get to the point,' someone shouted from the back of the room, drowning out a woman who had shrieked when he'd mentioned the plane. She wailed pitifully in the background, while he filled his lungs with air, having learned somewhere that oxygen helped with nerves.

'The point I'm trying to make,' he said, 'is that we are fortunate so many of our colleagues were not at work when this tragedy occurred. However, that fact has been making it extremely difficult for us to give the authorities accurate figures of how many of the Langdon staff are still missing.'

He dragged his hand across his mouth, felt sweat on his upper lip. He'd spent so long planning what he should say and still he was getting it wrong. He stole a look at Diane, who managed, without altering her expression one bit, to give him the strength to carry on.

'That's why it is so vital that everyone fill in a missing person's form before they leave today.' He indicated the tables at the back of the room and there was a scraping of chairs as people turned to look. 'Please help yourself to the pens provided and complete your form in as much detail as you can. If, that is, you haven't already done so.' Some members of the audience rose and went to fetch the forms, as if they were worried the supply might run out if they didn't grab one right away.

Once the room had settled again, he took a handkerchief from his pocket and mopped his face. This was the part he had been dreading most of all.

'I'm going to be completely honest with you now. And I promise to tell you all I know.'

An expectant hush fell on the room. He felt as if he were about to announce the winner of a sweepstake instead of preparing to deliver the worst news imaginable.

'It's just been confirmed that the bodies of two of our employees have been found and identified by their dental records. Two people who were on our floors. I have to tell you that the search and rescue services, NYPD and the Fire Department are no longer looking for survivors. I've been advised to make this as clear to you as I can. They are now in the process of finding your families. That's all they can do for us now. I am so sorry.'

Several people slumped over their table, or clung to their neighbours, the picture of despair.

A young woman stood up and screamed at him. 'Don't you dare take away our hope. Don't you dare!'

Another distraught voice shouted, 'You can't tell us there are no survivors. Nobody knows that.'

Other voices joined in. 'Yeah, who says so?' 'They don't know shit!' 'I don't believe that.' 'Not true!'

He felt the atmosphere in the room change and wished he'd taken the advice of the hotel manager to have some security standing by. He tapped the microphone, trying to get some order.

'We're all on the same side here, people,' he said, somewhat plaintively. Was that a touch of desperation he could hear in his voice? Jeez, this was godawful.

'How can we be on the same side? Who have you lost?' This from the sweet mom in the bandana.

Before he could decide what, if anything, he ought to say, a big burly guy close to the front stood up and demanded, 'Why weren't you in the office that morning? You're supposed to be the boss.'

This was starting to get ugly. He looked towards the doors, measuring how far he had to run and at the same time hoping the manager might have sent some guys from security after all.

When he felt a gentle push he looked down and saw Diane, elbowing him to the side, just a little, managing to make it look like a planned move rather than a rescue. She looked expectantly at the crowd and, to his astonishment, people stopped shouting and stared at her, as if wondering what was coming next.

Her voice smooth as melting honey, she spoke quietly into the microphone. Like calming oil on troubled waters, her soft southern accent seemed to soothe and within moments everyone in the room was listening.

'My husband was on his way to work early on that awful morning, despite the fact he was suffering from a terrible migraine headache. When the pain made it dangerous for him to drive, he turned around and went back home. Please don't be mad at him. He's already mad enough for everyone. Mad at the terrorists who did this to us.' She gestured around the room, implying that they were all one big family. 'Mad at those towers for tumbling like they did.' She shook her head as if she couldn't believe what they'd all seen with their own eyes. Then, after a perfectly timed pause that would be the envy of any politician alive, she said in a low, confidential tone, 'Can I tell you something?' As if she were sharing the most private secret, she said, 'Most of all, he's mad at himself for turning back that morning. He wishes, each and every day, that he'd been in there with his folks, in that tower.' On the last word, her voice broke and it seemed to him that somehow this amazing woman had made everyone in the room feel sorry for him. She wiped her eyes with a scrap of lace and looked at him, smiling sadly.

It was time for him to step up to the plate. He had to be the one to do this. 'Ladies and gentlemen. Please be assured that we, Langdon Associates, will do everything in our power to help you in any way we can. We have counsellors here today that you can speak to if you wish. We have set up a relief fund with financial assistance, available right now, for those of you who may already be in need of support at this time. And I promise you one more thing. This firm will work tirelessly to rebuild and establish a new global headquarters in Manhattan. No terrorist is going to destroy what your families worked so hard to create. You have my word on that.'

To his surprise, he felt tears on his cheeks, real tears. Perhaps it was those that made the people nearest the stage start to applaud. He would never know, but the mood had swung again and, this time, he felt like the good guy.

At table number ninety-eight a man stood and shouted, 'What the hell are we doing here, eating sandwiches and drinking fancy French water? We should be out there, looking for our loved ones. Come on!'

The man stormed from the room and like revolutionaries rushing to the barricades, a small army of people followed.

He turned to Diane and exhaled the longest breath of his life, his shoulders drooping as his lungs emptied. She hugged him and whispered, 'Well done, honey. You're a saint.'

If only she knew.

CHAPTER 38

The sun was up when Lucie woke from the first full night's sleep she'd had in months, maybe years. Since she'd moved into Charlotte's apartment, her sleep, if she slept at all, had been snatches between random sounds in the building. Perhaps it was sheer exhaustion that had made her sleep through till morning. More likely it was the fact that she could see a guaranteed escape route. Not just a light at the end of the tunnel, but a whole new future. In a familiar landscape.

She'd thought of it just before she fell asleep and her dreams had been of Scotland, as if her subconscious mind wanted to convince her it would work. She knew she was dreaming because the sky was azure and the sun was shining as her private jet flew over the Firth of Clyde. Everyone she'd ever known was gathered at the foot of the aircraft steps, waiting to welcome her home. She appeared at the door of the aircraft, dressed like a visiting princess, and the hordes went mad with excitement. She swept elegantly to the foot of the steps where she took off her red-soled shoes so she could kneel to kiss the ground. The crowds cheered and paparazzi shouted her name as they jostled and fought for the best shot. The Provost stepped forward, in velvet, mink and chain, to shake her hand and introduce her to the guests of honour.

Granny came first, with a bouquet of rhubarb and a two-pound bag of sugar. 'I couldn't think whit else tae bring ye,' she whispered, as Lucie kissed her rouged cheek. Then Dad, smiling through the tears as he silently gathered her into his arms. Over his shoulder Lucie scanned the line. Looking for someone. Not sure who. Curtis was there, handsome as ever, joking with school friends, running friends, people from her past. Some faces were familiar, others less so. She started to push through the crowd, becoming frantic in her search. She saw Dylan. Standing taller than the others, and a little apart. He smiled and said, 'Stop. Let me help you.' But Lucie ignored him and pushed past. She had to keep looking. And looking. Till she woke.

Lucie had never been kicked in the stomach, but she imagined it felt like this. An unexpected, low blow that knocks all the breath out of you.

Mum. Gone. This time, for ever.

It was like being told all over again. She replayed in her mind the sad way Doctor Meyer had looked at her. The barely perceptible nod that confirmed Lucie's fear. She remembered wanting to scream 'That's not fair.' She'd been given a wonderful gift and had it been snatched away hours later. No wonder she felt wronged.

The hospital staff would be expecting her today. Expecting a daughter to want her mother's possessions. Anticipating a close relative would be keen to sort out the paperwork, pay the bills, do the decent thing. Imagining Lucie had dumped the flowers and run off because she was too distraught to stay. Believing she'd be back to talk about insurance.

Granny had a saying, 'Ye make yer bed, ye lie in it.' If Lucie had been prepared to put up with her lot and accept the consequences of the choices she'd made, things might have been better. She'd still be miserable, but at least her mum would be alive. Living the new, independent life she'd finally made for herself. Pity she'd left it too late. And yet, didn't she tell the doctor she'd die happy because she'd been reunited with Lucie?

Last night Lucie had been sure she'd found the solution. Nothing had changed since then. In her dream, Dad had been smiling. He'd welcomed her with open arms, just like Mum said he would. Lucie knew it was just a dream, but in the afterglow she could feel her dad's arms around her. She'd believed herself forgiven, loved, safe and secure. All feelings that had disappeared from her relationship with Curtis.

Maybe accepting the bed you'd made was enough for the stoics of Granny's generation, but it hadn't been good enough for Mum, and it certainly wouldn't do for Lucie. This was a new millennium, after all. Women didn't accept their lot anymore. They didn't lie in the bed they'd made and feel sorry for themselves. They leapt out and took on the world.

Lucie was thinking like a self-help book. And about time too. She threw back the covers and opened the curtains to a new dawn.

Her mind was made up. She was heading home to Scotland. Putting all this chaos behind her. Miss Gillespie would pay for the flights. And Dad's arms would be open wide to welcome her back.

CHAPTER 39

'How's the patient today?' Dylan asked.

All four women at the nurses' station smiled at him. The senior nurse, a straight-talking black woman old enough to be his mother, said, 'He's grumpy as a bear with its ass on fire.' Dylan loved Nurse Abigail. She'd had the measure of Curtis from day one and knew exactly how to handle him.

Everyone hooted, apart from the youngest nurse, a pretty little thing about Dylan's own age. 'He is not grumpy!' she said indignantly.

'Is too,' chorused the others.

'Don't you be taken in by those dark, brooding good looks of his, missy,' said Abigail with a complicit smile at Dylan.

The young nurse blushed to the roots of her baby blonde hair. Dylan hoped Curtis wasn't making a move on the nurses now. It would be a sign that he was feeling better and that was good, but the last thing Curtis needed was another woman to abuse.

Dylan thought it best to make light of the situation. He slapped his thigh, cowboy style. 'Hell, ladies,' he said with a salacious grin and a phoney accent, 'good looks ain't everythin!'

They were still laughing when Curtis appeared at the door of his room. 'You havin' a good time there, Dylan?' he shouted.

'Did warn you,' said Abigail under her breath.

'I heard that,' Curtis shouted again, less aggressively.

Dylan raised an eyebrow at the nurses and took a deep breath. 'Wish me luck,' he muttered.

'Gonna need it,' said Abigail.

'Heard that too,' Curtis called. He turned his chair and wheeled off down the corridor towards the day room where patients were encouraged to sit and engage with others or in therapeutic activities. Curtis had refused to participate.

If the nursing staff were to be believed, Curtis preferred to sit alone all day and brood. It meant he was usually ready with the vitriol the moment Dylan arrived.

'You're a lucky bastard, strutting about on those legs of yours while I'm going crazy in here.'

Looked like today would be no different.

'Can you imagine how long an hour takes to pass when you're sitting here watching the clock?'

There was an impossibly fine line between sympathy and pity. Curtis sought one but could not tolerate the other. Dylan decided to steer clear of both and try humour.

'Now I don't know how you feel about this, Curtis,' he said, 'and I certainly wouldn't want to point an accusatory finger and call someone a cheat. But nobody should be slam dunking in wheelchair basketball.'

Curtis didn't even attempt a smile. 'Have you lost your mind, Dylan?'

Dylan shrugged. 'I thought maybe you'd like to hear a joke.'

'A joke about guys in wheelchairs?' Curtis patted his hands together, like a genteel lady watching an opera performance. Dylan hadn't known applause could look and sound sarcastic.

His face felt warm, a sure sign he was blushing. 'Sorry, buddy. Bad taste.'

'You think?'

At least the usual rant had been diverted, or so it seemed. Dylan tried some talk about the Giants but Curtis didn't engage, beyond a few non-committal grunts. Finally, there seemed nothing left to talk about but Lucie and how she had ruined his life.

'Would you swing by the house one more time, Dylan?'

'Curtis, what's the point?'

'I could use some of my stuff, but hey, if it's too much trouble for you, just say the word.'

'I didn't say that. I asked you what's the point, as in what do you hope to achieve?'

'Some sort of evidence as to where the bitch has gone and if she ever intends to come back is what I "hope to achieve".' Curtis curled his fingers in the air, visual aids in case his tone wasn't sarky enough.

Dylan wondered how long he could put up with the constant sarcasm. 'Any idea what I should look out for?'

'See if there's food in the fridge. Check if the toilet's been cleaned.'

'How do you expect me to tell if Lucie's been cleaning the toilet?'

Curtis banged the flat of his hand against his brow. 'See if you can smell disinfectant! For chrissakes, Dylan, don't go giving up the day job any time soon. You have no future in the private eye business. Why don't you rummage through her underwear drawer and see if all her panties have gone?'

Dylan gave him a look. 'Seriously, dude?'

'Okay, maybe not the panties. Hell, Dylan. Use your initiative. See if her passport's still there.'

'Still where?'

'It's hidden behind the bathtub. Low down on the left-hand side, where the taps are.'

'Why does she keep it there?'

Curtis laughed, more like a villain than a clown. '*She* doesn't keep it there. I do.'

It took a moment for Dylan to work out the implications of what Curtis had just said. Even for him this seemed extreme. 'You confiscated her passport?'

At least Curtis had the good grace to look a little uncomfortable, but not much. 'Not sure I'd use the word confiscated. Seems a bit over-dramatic.'

'What other word would you use? Man, I don't know you anymore. You took your wife's passport? Why?'

'Hell do you think? In case she left me.'

'You're a sad bastard now, Curtis, but you were sad long before this happened. I just didn't know it.'

CHAPTER 40

The screen door hung dejected as ever. As Lucie tried to ease it open the last rusted hinge gave up and the door clattered to the ground. She jumped back, out of its way, and waited for Curtis to shout abuse from inside.

She knocked on the front door, gingerly at first. Then more loudly. She tried the handle and was surprised when the door opened. She'd been hoping Curtis would be home so she could see he was fine, but hoping he wouldn't be there so she could take what she needed and leave.

She stepped inside and called, 'Curtis?' She didn't like the way her voice wavered on his name. It made her sound scared and she was trying so hard not to be.

No answer. He must be sleeping. Good. If she was lucky she could grab her stuff and go. She'd been planning to pick up some clothes, so she could leave Charlotte's in the apartment, but if that meant going into the bedroom, forget it. She *had* been hoping to retrieve Mum's letter from under the mattress, but that wasn't her priority.

A quick look round the living room reminded her how little she and Curtis had to show for their years together. She was glad Mum hadn't seen the way she was living.

The place smelled the same as ever. Musty and faintly damp. But it was tidier than she remembered. That was reassuring.

And there was no sign of the skillet.

Lucie checked the floor. If she'd killed him, wouldn't there be a chalk outline of his body, or did that just happen in movies? The place didn't look like CSI had been here combing for clues to a murder. Lucie sagged with relief. 'Thank you, God,' she whispered, earnestly.

She opened the kitchen cabinet where the skillet was kept. There it was, clean and innocent. She had nothing to worry about. The police don't put murder weapons back in their place, that much she did know.

She tiptoed to the drawer where they kept their paperwork. The squeaky drawer they called it. Lucie held her breath. The old drawer allowed itself to be coaxed open, obligingly quiet for once. At the last moment wood screeched on wood, reluctant to part. Lucie held herself rigid, like a kid in a game of statues. The house remained silent. Outside a car whooshed past and a dog barked till it was gone. Lucie's hand was shaking as she started to leaf through the papers in the drawer. Most of it was junk mail that should have gone straight in the trash. There were takeout menus, vouchers that were years out of date, a birthday card Curtis had given her two years ago and recycled last year. She wouldn't be around to see it make a third appearance.

Lucie fumbled through paper, till her fingers touched the bottom of the drawer. Where was it? She always kept it in here, didn't she? What about that spate of burglaries in the neighbourhood? Had she moved it then? Curtis always joked that no self-respecting burglar would climb in their window, but Lucie had been spooked. She carefully lifted out the contents of the drawer and sat them on the countertop so she could go through them one by one. The drawer was soon filled to the brim again, but Lucie hadn't found what she was looking for.

The only other place she kept anything of value was in the bedroom. Should she come back another day, when Curtis was out? But what if he locked the front door and she couldn't get in? Anyway, she didn't want to wait. She wanted to find her passport, book a flight and get going.

She sneaked to the bedroom door and listened, her ear as close to the wood as she dared. Nothing. Good sign or bad? If he was deeply asleep, he'd be snoring. She stood for a whole minute, counting off the seconds in her head, listening for bedsprings creaking or bare feet slapping the floor. Still nothing.

She could dash in like a SWAT team, grab stuff from the drawer beside the bed and run for it. He might not even wake up. And if he did, she could be gone before he realised what was happening.

She touched the door handle but didn't turn it. He might have another woman in there. A woman who would wake up and scream. They'd call the police and keep her here till the cops arrived.

There it was again. That fear of Curtis. The same fear that had kept her a prisoner in this squalid little house. Lucie had vowed she'd never be scared of him again. She was going in.

Taking a huge gulp of air, she turned the handle, pushed the door and ran towards the bed. The empty bed.

She was about to let out a whoop when she heard the front door open.

CHAPTER 41

Dylan had promised himself he'd do this one last favour for Curtis and then he was done. With Lucie gone there was nothing to tie him to Curtis anymore. The guy was becoming increasingly hard to like and, looking back, it seemed to Dylan that their friendship had always been a one-sided affair. It was a bit like unrequited love. Something Dylan was becoming quite the expert in. And he'd had enough.

The subway ride had given him time to mope and the walk through Curtis and Lucie's neighbourhood did nothing to lift his mood. He skirted broken pavements and avoided uncollected trash, sad to see cars so rusted they'd never drive a highway again and houses with cardboard for windows. He felt sorry for Lucie. She deserved far better than this.

The screen door had given up and lay sprawled like a drunk across the doorway. Dylan stepped over it and into the house. He planned to spend as little time here as possible. This room gave him the creeps. He'd had no choice but come back to hide the evidence that might have condemned Lucie. Otherwise he'd not have set foot in the place again. He preferred to put the whole traumatic episode to the back of his mind and had decided that this would be his last visit. Even if Curtis came back here to live.

Best get it over with. Find the T-shirts Curtis wanted, pick up some socks and underwear and of course, Lucie's passport. He'd start with that.

The bath panel came off with a crack as the plastic split in two. Not that it mattered. Neither Curtis nor Lucie would ever soak in this old tub anymore. Dylan cast the pieces aside and stretched into the dark recess, hoping there was nothing more harmful than spores lurking. He walked his fingers along the floorboards towards the corner. His thumb touched a polythene bag and he dragged it into the daylight. There it was. Lucie's passport. Not the familiar navy blue of the United States but the deep burgundy of the European Union with the golden insignia of Great Britain. Dylan leafed through till he came to the photo page. His heart sank in his chest when he saw Lucie's face. The regulation pose, staring straight into the camera, made it feel like she was looking into his eyes. 'Oh, Lucie,' he murmured. He wasn't going to part with this. It was all he had left of her. He discarded the plastic bag and stuck the passport in the back pocket of his jeans.

Next stop the bedroom. And then he was out of here.

The first thing he noticed was the open door. He'd made a point of closing them all last time he was here. A silly habit he'd got into as a child believing it prevented a fire from spreading. He stopped short of the doorway, feeling a shiver on the back of his neck, as if his hair was rising. If there was someone in there, he did not want to get involved in any sort of confrontation. The guy could be a thief, a squatter, an addict. Anyone could have wandered in here, just as he did. Carrying a knife, a gun or a needle. None of which Dylan wanted to see.

He should leave. Now. Curtis could live without socks.

Dylan listened, unable to shake the feeling that he was not alone in the house. Curiosity made him edge forward.

Suddenly he was knocked against the wall as someone barged out from behind the door and made a run for it.

Instinctively, he grabbed. Clutched at a jacket. Heard the material rip.

'Lucie!'

She stopped and turned towards him, a fraction at a time.

'Jesus! I thought you were …' He couldn't say it.

'I thought you were Curtis!' She started to laugh, but in a frantic, overexcited way. He'd never seen her like this before.

She looked at his hand clinging to her jacket and he let the fabric drop. She looked straight into his eyes then made to run. He was too fast and caught her arm.

She writhed and squirmed like a toddler in a tantrum, but he held firm.

'Lucie! I have to talk to you.'

She turned away from him and he saw the mark on her neck. The same as the girl he'd seen in the hospital.

His fingers went to the mark, barely touching. 'Was this Curtis?'

'Please let me go, Dylan. Before he comes in.' For maybe a second, maybe a minute, they stood staring at each other, he wary, she beseeching. 'Promise me you won't run?' He let go, expecting her to bolt like a wild animal freed.

She said simply, 'Thank you,' and rubbed at her arm.

Terrified he might have hurt her, he said, 'Sorry, Lucie,' and held his hands up, palms towards her. He took a step back, as if to prove he meant her no harm. 'I guess you've had enough rough handling to last you a lifetime.'

Her hand went to the mark on her neck.

'Want to tell me about it?'

When she didn't answer, he said, 'Not here. Come on, let's go find ourselves a coffee.' He put his hand on the small of her back, not pushing, just for reassurance.

They found a place a couple of blocks away. Lucie chose the most secluded table. She sat with her back to the wall and her eyes on the door, as if she were afraid someone might burst in.

'You look terrified, Lucie. What are you so afraid of?'

She whispered, 'Curtis.'

'Curtis doesn't know you're here.'

She leaned across and grabbed his hand. 'So he's alive?'

She looked so happy, Dylan felt like he'd been stabbed through the heart. How could she still care about that asshole after the way he'd treated her?

'Of course he's alive. Why wouldn't he be?'

Lucie's face crumpled. 'Thank you, God,' she whispered, closed eyes raised to the ceiling. Her gratitude sounded heartfelt. It was clear she still loved the guy.

Dylan said nothing. There was nothing left to say, really.

'Oh, Dylan,' she sighed, her eyes full of tears. 'What a mess I've made of my life.'

He wanted to reach out and wipe her tears away. He clasped his hands tightly in his lap to make sure they'd behave.

'Well, I've got time to listen,' Dylan said, 'if you want to talk.' He settled back in his chair and crossed his legs. 'Why don't you go ahead and start at the beginning.'

She recounted the drama that had unfolded in the kitchen of the little house. He noticed she missed out a few details, like the skillet and how it came to be on the floor. It was easy enough to fill in the blanks from what he'd seen for himself or been told by Curtis.

As she spoke, Dylan tried to work out how much he ought to tell her when it came his turn to talk.

'Then, well, you know what happened to the Twin Towers.'

He nodded sadly.

'So, I never did make it to my interview in the South Tower. For which I will be eternally thankful.'

'Amen to that.'

Lucie give him the tiniest smile he'd ever seen.

'Why didn't you go home?' he asked.

'I'm never going back to that life. Not ever.' Lucie shook her head as she spoke, 'I *can't* go back. He might kill me next time.'

'I'm sure he won't.' Total lie. Curtis threatened daily that he'd kill Lucie if he ever set eyes on her. How he planned to achieve that was something they'd never discussed. Maybe this would be the right time to tell her Curtis was paralysed, that he could never hurt her again. Dylan decided to say nothing. He'd examine his motives later. Right now it was important to keep her here, keep her talking.

'Where have you been living? I don't imagine you can afford the Waldorf?'

That teensy little smile again. 'I'm staying with a friend. We went to school together.'

'Do I know her?'

'No, she wasn't one of the runners. Anyway, she's happy for me to stay until I get a job and find a place of my own.' He could tell she was doing her best to sound upbeat and full of purpose.

Reaching for his wallet, he said, 'Do you need some money? I can help you out.'

'It's okay. I don't need your money.'

'Cool,' he said, trying to sound non-committal.

As if sensing she'd hurt him, she added, 'Thanks, Dylan, but I'm fine. Charlotte has plenty of money.'

'Charlotte?'

'The friend I'm staying with is from a very wealthy family.'

She lowered her gaze, stared into the coffee she was cradling in her hands, stealing its warmth.

'Family,' she said, wistfully. 'Yeah. Back to the story. I don't know if you knew I'd arranged to meet my mother that day?'

Dylan shook his head, wondering if he was supposed to know that. 'Your parents were here? That's amazing.'

'Yeah, except my dad didn't come and my mum ended up driving. Straight off the plane. She was so tired she caused an accident that shut the Lincoln Tunnel for half a day.'

'I heard about that. Is she okay?'

Lucie shook her head, biting her lower lip so hard he feared she'd draw blood.

'Is that why you were at the hospital a few days ago?'

Lucie looked up, the sudden movement causing her coffee to swill around in its cup. She put it back on the table and stared at it. Avoiding his eyes, he thought. As if she was hiding something.

'I saw you in the coffee shop.'

'Why didn't you speak to me?'

He considered telling her he'd heard her say her name was Gillespie, but thought better of it. He didn't know why. 'You were already talking to someone.'

Lucie nodded, still staring at the coffee cup.

'And you were very upset,' Dylan prompted.

'Yes. I was. I am,' she said, at last, her voice breaking.

Dylan said, 'Is your mom going to be okay?'

Lucie chewed her lower lip and shook her head, wordless. Tears streamed down her face. Without waiting for permission his hand stole across and touched her cheek, his thumb gently wiping at her tears.

'I'm so sorry, Lucie.'

'I didn't even get to say goodbye, Dylan. I was too late.' She gave him a teary smile. 'My granny always said I'd be late for my own funeral.'

Wise woman, that granny. Lucie had missed her own funeral by several days. Dylan decided this was not the time to tell her.

CHAPTER 42

Lucie poured a glass of Californian Zinfandel and sat staring out at the evening sky, wondering if Mum and Granny were up there somewhere. It was hard to believe they were in heaven, even harder to believe that wherever they were, they were gone. For good.

'What will you do now, Lucie?' Dylan had asked her.

'Oh, I guess I'll stay with Charlotte for a while. See how things pan out, job-wise. To be honest, it's just such a relief to get away from Curtis and feel safe for the first time in years.'

'It was that bad, huh?'

She'd felt it was important to justify her actions to Dylan. Maybe because he was Curtis's friend. Maybe because it mattered what he thought of her.

'It's got pretty bad recently but that's the first time I've been afraid for my life. Curtis had his hands round my neck, Dylan, strangling me, like he really wanted me dead.'

'Why didn't you ever fight back?'

'Oh, I used to. When it first started. Then I worked out it just makes him madder. Realised it was easier to take the beating. But this time I had no choice. If I hadn't defended myself, I believe he might have killed me.'

She had omitted the fact that *she* might have killed *him*. Or that she didn't care at the time. Instead she'd enquired after his health. 'So, he's okay?'

Dylan had seemed to hesitate, as if he wasn't sure what to tell her.

'He was out cold when I found him on the floor that morning. They took him to the hospital and all.' Another pause and hesitation. Then Dylan said, 'He'll live.'

They'd exchanged a look that told Lucie there was more to this.

'Is that why you were at the hospital the day mum died, the day you saw me? Were you visiting Curtis?'

'Yeah.'

'Is he still there?'

'Do you really care, Lucie?'

She had shaken her head. No, she didn't care. And for that reason, she had asked no more questions. Whatever had happened to Curtis, he'd had it coming. She couldn't find it in her heart to feel any sympathy for him. The man had almost taken her life.

'Will you tell him you've seen me today?' she'd asked.

'Do you want me to?'

'No. definitely not.'

'In that case, I won't tell him. He doesn't need to know.'

She'd felt such relief, and such gratitude to Dylan, she'd leaned over the little table and kissed his cheek. His face lit up, like a frog kissed by a princess. She felt guilty about lying to him. Still, she reminded herself, his loyalties would be likely to lie with his injured friend. Not with the wife who'd laid him out and run for the hills. Best to keep her own counsel.

When they'd parted outside the coffee shop, Dylan had pressed a scrap of paper into her hand.

'Lucie,' he said, 'this is my cell phone number and the number of my mum's place. She'll take a message. You may have to listen to her chat for a while. Boy, does she like to talk!' He'd rolled his eyes and made her laugh. Then he'd got all serious again and said, 'Please, Lucie, promise me you'll call? Even if it's just to let me know you're okay, give me a call, yeah? Don't just disappear again.'

She'd hugged him and whispered, 'As long as you promise you won't ever mention me to Curtis.'

He'd promised. And she trusted him.

Curtis was alive. She was off the hook. No longer facing the threat of a murder trial.

That meant she had no need to hide anymore. No need to go on pretending to be Charlotte. No need to spend every waking minute worrying in case someone found out and exposed her for the fraud she was.

Fraud. She hadn't really thought of it like that. Fraud was a punishable offence. How punishable?

Half an hour on the internet taught her as much about fraud as she needed to know. And a lot more than she wanted. Fraud was an offence punishable by law in New York. Fraud came in many forms, as it turned out. Criminal impersonation, identity theft – she was guilty of both.

Then there was larceny. Okay, maybe she hadn't deliberately stolen Charlotte's bag. But in the eyes of the law, she might as well have mugged the woman. After all, she'd made no attempt to hand the bag over to the police, either on 9/11, or since.

And there could be no denying that she'd stolen Charlotte's identity. Her internet attorney was black-and-white clear on that one: *A person is guilty of identity theft in the third degree when he or she knowingly and with intent to defraud assumes the identity of another person by presenting himself or herself as that other person, or by acting as that other person or by using personal identifying information of that other person, and thereby obtains goods, money, property or services.*

The description applied perfectly. Charlotte continued to pay for the food and flowers that were delivered to the apartment. Food Lucie ate. Whether or not stealing a few yogurts and drinking a glass or two of wine made her guilty of identity theft in the third degree was a moot point. But she had been spending Charlotte's cash. Money she knew wasn't hers. Guilty as charged.

When she reached the part that said: *Identity theft is punishable as a Class A misdemeanour in its most basic form and a court will impose sentences of up to one year,* Lucie felt sick. She could almost hear a court judge intoning the terms of her punishment.

Her hands trembled on the keypad. She was in deep trouble.

When there was a possibility she'd done something awful to Curtis, she'd been scared. But that was more like a dark dread, an anxiety. Even in her darkest days she'd been able to hang on to the hope that she'd get off with it, plead self-defence or whatever. This was different. She had no defence against these charges. She was scared and this time her fear was so gut-clenching it made her bowels want to empty.

She imagined how it would sound to anyone who didn't know the circumstances.

The accused, Lucie Jardine, practically a derelict, finds a woman lying in the street. The suspect believes the woman may be dead, but instead of getting medical help, she leaves the woman lying there, unaided, and takes her bag. She goes through the bag and finds the woman's address. She goes to the woman's home and deceives the doorman into granting her access. She wears the woman's clothes, eats her food, drinks her wine, sleeps in her bed, spends her cash. She answers to the woman's name and gives that name to a stranger who asks what she's called. Basically, she *becomes* that woman. The charge: Identity theft. The verdict: Guilty. Guilty. Guilty.

Lucie leaned her elbows on Charlotte's laptop and put her head in her hands. She ran her fingers through her hair and tugged on two handfuls till the roots hurt.

She'd been so naïve.

This morning her biggest concern was whether or not she could risk sneaking into her own house to look for her passport. She'd been scared of being arrested and charged with attacking her husband.

This afternoon she'd learned that Curtis was alive. She'd thought she had nothing to worry about. She was in the clear.

Now she *knew* she was a criminal, a felon, a fraud. A woman who could be charged with, and found guilty of, several serious offences.

And without her passport, she'd no way out.

CHAPTER 43

Dylan had stopped by the nurses' station with a box of doughnuts, since this would be his last visit. Nurse Abigail, whose size implied she was partial to a doughnut or three, was laughing at something Dylan had said. It was nothing to do with Curtis, but he must have heard Dylan's voice, for he appeared in the corridor, and he did not look happy.

'Hey, Dylan! You here to see me or the nurses?'

'Oh boy,' muttered Abigail. 'Rather you than me, mood he's in today.'

Dylan shrugged, resigned to one last tirade from Curtis. After today, it wouldn't be an issue any more. 'Better go, ladies,' he said, with a rueful smile.

As he followed Curtis towards the day room, the wheelchair suddenly performed a neat three-sixty-degree turn and stopped to face Dylan. Curtis's skill in handling the chair was improving daily.

'You'll be doing wheelies in that soon,' Dylan had remarked one day. The compliment hadn't gone down well with Curtis. Judging by the look on his face right now, he wasn't in the mood to be told his U-turns were looking good.

'Listen to me,' he said. 'I don't appreciate you making fun of me with the nurses.'

'Loosen up, Curtis.'

'Don't you come waltzing in here and tell me to loosen up.'

'First of all, we weren't talking about you, as it happens. And second of all, if I want to goof around with the nurses, I will. Where's the harm?'

Curtis pointed to his legs. Muscle wastage made them look smaller and weaker every time Dylan visited. They were starting to look like a kid's legs tacked on to a man's body.

'This is the harm,' said Curtis, jabbing at his thighs. 'Did you forget that, when you were having your little joke on the way in?'

'We didn't mean any offence, Curtis. Come on, man. Lighten up.'

Curtis didn't come back at him this time for having the audacity to suggest he lighten up. Dylan was surprised. Maybe he should have been more assertive years ago. 'What's on your mind?' he asked, keen to move on.

'I wanna know how you got on. Was she there?'

'Was who there?' Dylan was playing for time. He knew that, but all the lines he'd rehearsed on the subway seemed to have deserted him. An angry Curtis had always had that effect on him.

Curtis snorted. 'The queen of England! Who the fuck do you think? Lucie, you shmuck!'

'No. She wasn't.'

'Dammit! I was sure she'd be back by now.'

Dylan said nothing. Discretion was always the better part of valour when dealing with Curtis. He'd learned that a long time ago.

'Did you speak to anyone?'

Dylan shook his head. It wasn't a real lie, if he didn't say anything.

'Hell you mean, no? That's the reason you went. To find out if anyone had seen her sneaking around. Or noticed lights on. You seriously telling me – wait a minute, you didn't go, did you?'

'I went, Curtis. Lucie wasn't there. And I didn't see any of your neighbours. Let's face it, they're not really the type to pop round with a freshly baked pie and an enquiry about your health.'

'Okay, okay. No need to be a smart-ass all the time. Did you check the place like I told you? Looking for signs she'd been there?'

'What kind of signs?'

'Come on, man. Work it out for yourself. Clues. Did you look for clues?'

'Like what?'

'I dunno. Was there fresh milk in the fridge? Was there trash in the bin? The toilet tissue. Is the roll smaller since the last time you were there?'

'Are you serious? You really expect me to check the toilet paper?'

Curtis laughed, breaking the tension. 'Well, maybe not. But the coffee maker. Has it been used recently? The stove? The skillet.' He stopped. Went quiet, as if something had just occurred to him.

'You okay, Curtis?'

Curtis scratched his head. 'Yeah, I think so. Just got a weird, what ya call it? Day-ja something or other.'

'Déjà-vu. Yeah, I get that sometimes. Everyone does. They say it means nothing.'

'Sure feels funny though, doesn't it?'

Dylan nodded, wondering how he could change the subject. 'Say, some of those nurses are cute. Have you noticed?'

'Hard to miss them when they get up close and personal.'

Dylan's surprise must have shown on his face for Curtis laughed a second time.

'Yeah, close enough to wash your face and wipe your ass.' He laughed again, but this time the bitterness was back. Dylan's change of subject had misfired badly. Had served only to remind Curtis that he'd be depending on nurses for the rest of his life. And that it was all Lucie's fault. And that Dylan still hadn't found her.

'Anyway, sorry. I looked pretty much everywhere. I don't think Lucie's been back. I brought you those shirts and socks you wanted.' Dylan tossed a plastic bag into Curtis's lap.

'Did you find her passport?'

Dylan's hand went to the pocket of his jeans. Touched the material, feeling for the reassuring shape of the passport. 'No, I didn't,' he said. 'Sorry.'

'Did you look where I told you? Under the bathtub?'

'I practically tore the bathroom apart. It wasn't there.'

'And you say nothing else in the house has been touched?'

'Not that I could see.'

Curtis slammed a fist into his thigh, a new habit. It looked painful but Curtis continued to punch, feeling nothing. 'How can you stand there and tell me she hasn't been back when her passport's gone? Of course she's been back. And now she's got her passport, she's free. I'll bet she's gone already.'

'Where would she go?'

'Hell would I know? Mexico? Canada? Bonnie Scotland?'

'Did she have any money?'

'Bitch has been stealing from me for years, it turns out. Keeping me on short rations for months now. Whining at me, 'There's no food, Curtis.'

'Come on, Curtis. That's not fair. Lucie didn't whine like that.'

Curtis ignored him. 'All the time she's siphoning off money from the housekeeping to buy fancy duds so she can go for an interview. In Manhattan? She's made an ass of me.'

He went quiet for a moment, thinking. 'You bastard!' he shouted. 'Were you in on this? Did you help her to get away from me? Are the two of you planning to jet off together?'

'Don't be ridiculous, man.'

'What's ridiculous? You've wanted Lucie all along. Don't think I didn't notice. But you couldn't compete with me. Till now.' Curtis clapped his hands, starting quiet and slow. 'Congratulations. She's all yours,' he said, increasing the speed and the volume.

Curtis was still raving when Dylan left and closed the door behind him.

CHAPTER 44

He'd searched the obits and death notices in all the city papers for days. Looking for an explanation. That young woman he'd met at the hospital. He could only assume she was the same one he'd mistaken for Charlotte in the street that day. Not Charlotte, of course, but certainly a close relative. A cousin, perhaps, possibly even a sister.

It didn't make sense. Charlotte had no siblings. No living relatives, she'd said. At least none that she knew of. Why would she keep a mother and a sister secret? And if that was their mother who just died in the hospital, why wasn't Charlotte there too? And what about that Scottish accent?

An obit would give information about relatives of the deceased. And if the funeral were to be held locally, the girl and Charlotte would turn up. He was planning to be there too, in the background. But no death had been intimated for anyone called Gillespie. He couldn't understand it.

There was more to Charlotte than met the eye.

He'd begun to wonder what else she'd kept from him.

Could she have been playing him? Using him to her own ends while allowing him to believe it was he who was calling all the shots?

When the insurance companies paid out for the losses incurred on 9/11, Charlotte would become extremely rich. Add that payout to the profits from the put options alone and Charlotte would be phenomenally wealthy. 'Beyond the dreams of avarice' was the phrase she always used.

What if she'd been working to her own plan all along? Was she biding her time, waiting to go to the authorities with her story?

And yet why would she do that? It was in both their interests to keep quiet about the information he'd fed her before 9/11. And how he'd come by it. She'd nothing to gain and a whole lot to lose by going anywhere with her knowledge.

Maybe it was time to do what Charlotte wanted and leave Diane? He wouldn't be the first in their circle to trade his wife for a younger model and, once the initial shock wore off, everybody would get over it. Except maybe Diane.

God, he was going round in circles, driving himself mad and getting nowhere in the process. He needed to give up trying to second-guess this young woman, whoever she was, and concentrate on finding her. Her mother's funeral would be the ideal place. If only he could find the damn funeral.

Maybe he'd already missed it? It might have taken place the day he and Diane met with the families of his employees at the Pierre. Admittedly, he'd taken his eye off the Charlotte ball while that meeting was being organised.

He rechecked the papers. Beginning with the day he'd been too busy meeting the families. When he drew another blank, it dawned on him. The Gillespie girl had said her mother had just flown in from Scotland. The body must have been repatriated for burial. He'd never met a Scot who wasn't sentimental about Bonnie Scotland. Of course Mrs Gillespie would have been flown back home.

He was about to close the *Times* when a short article way towards the back caught his eye. It identified the driver of the crash that had closed the Lincoln Tunnel and caused traffic mayhem. She was Margaret McBride, thought to be a tourist on vacation from Scotland. It went on to say that Mrs McBride had died as a result of injuries sustained in the accident.

McBride? This had to be the same woman. Yet the girl had said her name was Gillespie and her mother had just died. Following a road accident. And a flight from Scotland. It could be a second marriage, of course. He had to work out the connection between the girl crying in the hospital and Charlotte.

He was going to have to track down Charlotte and this sister of hers. Or whoever she was. The only way he could do that was to engineer another meeting and hope the coincidence didn't cause too much suspicion.

With the towers gone and his business headquarters with them, he was finding it difficult to get the time to do anything. He had entire mountains of paperwork to deal with. Even if 'dealing with' only meant adding a signature to myriad documents, it still meant he had to turn up at one office or another, or work from home.

His intention had been to take a vacation with Diane towards the end of September and he'd been looking forward to escaping from the city for a while. He loved the city, but it could be an exhausting place. He'd had his eye on the Seychelles, or the Maldives, where he and Diane had found it easy to relax in the past. At the moment relaxation was an impossibility. From the minute he opened his eyes, he was wired. If he wasn't worrying about WTC, he was fretting about whether his insurances would pay out, if he might get some of the rebuild contracts and whether his investments would come good when the stock markets opened again. This delay had not been part of the plan. The shares should have been bought or sold by now and the profit made and banked overseas. Every day that passed made him more vulnerable.

But the problem weighing heaviest on his mind was Charlotte, and with good reason. She was the loose end that should have been tied up, trimmed off and forgotten. Instead she was still out there, not just a loose end, but a loose cannon. On a hair trigger.

His best bet, he reckoned, was to catch the girl when she went out for a jog. He imagined runners to be creatures of habit, inclined to run at roughly the same time on roughly the same routes. All he had to do was be patient. There was no other option. He wouldn't rest until he worked out what was going on and solved the problem. His need to tie up loose ends was compulsive and this one was so dangerously loose, his whole life was in danger of unravelling like a poorly knitted sweater.

Thinking it wise to avoid the same coffee shop as before, he found another, not quite as close to Charlotte's apartment building. He struck up a conversation with the barista and led him to believe he was a lonely widower who was desperate to get out of his apartment and into the world. He was welcome, according to Alfonso the barista, to sit and chill over a couple of coffees and the newspapers for as long as he liked.

It looked as if his vigil would prove fruitless. He'd sat here most of the morning. He was about to give up and head back to the office when saw the girl jogging along the opposite side of the street. He slapped a few dollars of a tip on the table, much more than was justified. 'See you, Alfonso.'

Although she wasn't running fast, trying to chase her would be pointless, for all sorts of reasons. A better strategy would be to find a place where he could ambush her on her way back to the apartment.

He followed her for as long as he could keep her in his sight. Suddenly she made a left and disappeared. He could only hope she'd come back the same way. With his fingers tightly crossed he turned the corner too, on the lookout for a doorway or lobby he could step into without looking suspicious.

Then he saw it, a church, its beautiful broad steps spread out like a welcome. The answer to his prayers. The thought made him smile and an elderly priest on the top step smiled back, encouragingly.

A church – what better place to wait, hiding in plain sight, the best subterfuge of all. He nodded to the priest on his way by and looked inside. The church was busy but unlike many others in the neighbourhood that had become centres for rescue activities, this building seemed to have remained a place of worship and a sanctuary from the mad world outside. Most of the pews had at least one occupant, many sitting with heads bowed. Quiet organ music played soothingly in the background, a requiem, Mozart if he wasn't mistaken. The smell of incense took him back to his childhood.

He felt a light touch on his elbow.

'Why don't you go on inside, my son?' asked the priest.

'Um, I don't really have time right now, Father.'

'That's all right. Now you know we're here, perhaps you'll look in on us again? When you've a bit more time?'

'I will,' he said, putting his hand in his pocket. He produced a twenty-dollar bill. 'Take this in the meantime, will you, Father?'

He slipped the cash into the priest's hand and left through the huge wooden door. There were several people sitting on the steps. He wouldn't look out of place if he joined them. He found a spot with a good view of the street and sat down to wait.

Soon she came into view and stopped at the cross street. He called, 'Charlotte!' When she didn't respond, he waited until she had crossed, out of the traffic, then shouted again. He tried 'Miss Gillespie,' but that didn't get her attention either. Maybe she was listening to a Walkman. He waited for her to pass, close enough for him to see there were no wires, no earphones. He shouted again. She faltered, stopped for a second, just enough to tell him he was right to be suspicious. When he called out a third time, 'Miss Gillespie!' she turned and faced him.

She looked more afraid than inquisitive as he went down the steps towards her.

'It is Miss Gillespie, isn't it?' he smiled tentatively, as if he wasn't sure he'd got the right person. 'We met at the hospital recently?'

When she didn't react, he said, 'Richard? Richard Armstrong? I gave you my handkerchief?'

She laughed nervously and bent over, hands on knees, to get her breath back. 'Sorry,' she said between gasps of air, 'I was daydreaming. Makes the run go by faster. Sorry, I remember you now. You were very kind to me.'

He laughed like a jovial uncle. 'Oh, my goodness. It was nothing. How are you?'

'I'm coping. Running helps.'

'I thought the events of the eleventh might have made it extra difficult for people in your position?'

Her eyes widened. She looked ready to bolt. 'I don't know what you mean.'

'Sorry, I didn't mean to be intrusive, but I was thinking it might be hard to arrange your poor mother's funeral, under the circumstances.'

The girl looked at a complete loss.

'Oh, I'm sorry. That was indelicate of me,' he said. He remembered there were insurance issues. 'How did you get on with that other matter?'

Again, she looked as if she had no idea what he was talking about. Had he got the wrong girl? Was someone cloning Charlottes in a lab somewhere?

'Forgive me. It's none of my business. The thing I really mean to say is, I'm very sorry for your loss.'

'Thanks. That's kind of you.'

'I expect you've got lots of friends and family to see you through this difficult patch?'

The young woman smiled and shook her head. 'Afraid not,' she said.

'Losing a loved one can be a lonely time. I speak from sad experience.'

'I'm sorry to hear that.'

He lowered his head, as if overcome with emotion, and put a little catch in his voice. 'I lost my wife a few months ago. I've never felt so lonesome in my whole life.'

He was delighted to feel her touch his arm.

'Oh, poor you,' she said, in a sad voice that sounded sincere. 'Had you been married for long?'

'Ten years this month. But I feel as if I'd known her forever. She was my better half, that's for sure.'

'You must miss her.'

'Every minute of every day.' He pointed to the church. 'I'm not the most religious, but I find coming here a real comfort.'

The woman started to jog on the spot. He took the hint. 'Oh, don't listen to me,' he said. 'I'm just feeling sorry for myself. Sorry, I shouldn't have interrupted your run.'

'Don't worry about it. It's good to see you again. I'm glad of the chance to be able to say thanks. You were really kind to me the day my mum died. I'm just sorry I can't return your lovely handkerchief.'

'Not a problem. Listen, I didn't catch your first name?'

'It's Charlotte.'

'Charlotte?' Shock made him repeat her, like a parrot. 'Charlotte? That's unbelievable.' Recovering quickly, he said the first thing that came into his head. 'That was my wife's name.'

The girl seemed taken aback. It was time to move. Before this got any more awkward. He needed time and space to think.

'Okay. Bye then. Charlotte.'

With a little wave of her hand she jogged off in one direction and he walked away in the other, satisfied with the encounter. He passed a young man tying a laminated photo to a lamppost. At his feet lay a bag filled with similar posters. Someone else on a quest.

'Good luck, fella,' he said. The man handed him a photo and said he was sure his wife was alive but she'd lost her memory.

He crossed the street and headed for the nearest subway, stuffing the photo in a trash can as he went. The first part of the job was done. He'd made contact with the mystery woman. Now he had to work out why this girl was masquerading as Charlotte Gillespie and how much she knew about the woman she was impersonating.

CHAPTER 45

Dylan had made up his mind. He would wish Curtis good luck. Shake his hand, for old times' sake, and walk away. Nurse Abigail wasn't on duty. Pity. He'd have liked to say goodbye. He'd grown fond of the woman. How anyone could work with guys like Curtis day in, day out, he'd never know.

The cute blonde nurse assured him Curtis was on excellent form today. Been telling her jokes, making her laugh. 'He's a funny guy,' she said. Dylan could hear an admiration in her voice that made him worry for her.

'If you say so.' He headed off towards the day room.

'Hey there, buddy,' Curtis greeted him with a grin. 'Good to see you.'

He must have thought the better of his accusations the previous day. Or realised that he couldn't afford to lose his only friend.

'Hey, Dylan. Listen. That stuff I was saying? About you and Lucie? Forget it. I didn't mean any of that shit.'

'Sure. Anything you say.'

'You're way better than that. I should've known.'

'It doesn't matter, Curtis. Really.'

Curtis's face lit up. It was clear he thought he'd been forgiven. Like every other time he'd offended Dylan. It was that easy.

As if they were two best buddies catching up, Curtis said, 'Grab a chair. Come sit by me so I can tell you my plans for when I get out of here.'

Dylan had not intended to stay, but he thought there was no harm in listening to Curtis's plan. Knowing what Curtis had in mind for the future would only make it easier to walk away for good.

'That health insurance Lucie set up with money from her folks? Their "kiss-off" cash, she called it.'

Dylan didn't really know what Curtis was talking about but he was beyond caring so he nodded anyway.

'Just before she lost the baby?'

Dylan remembered asking Lucie at the time if they could afford the hospital bills and offering to help out. 'Yeah. Is it going to come good for this?'

'It is. And not only that.' Curtis sounded as if he'd done something really clever. 'The plan will help me get set up once I leave here. Nothing fancy, just "appropriate to my needs".'

'Well done, Lucie, for having the foresight to set that up. You'd probably have squandered the cash if you'd got your hands on it.'

Curtis didn't rise to the bait. 'Yeah,' he said, quietly. 'Speaking of Lucie. You wanna hear what I've done about her?'

'Not sure there's much you can do about Lucie, is there?'

'I can call the cops.'

'You wouldn't!'

'Bet your sweet ass I would. And I did. Told them what she did to me and that she's been back to the house to grab her passport. I expect they're watching for her at La Guardia and JFK right now. Not to mention Newark, which would be my bet.'

'What did they say?'

'They said they'd find her. And when they do, they'll throw the book at her. Those were the cop's exact words. He was a former track athlete, the guy who booked in the details. Said he remembered my name from back in the day. Reckon he felt sorry me.'

'Yeah, well,' said Dylan, keeping his voice neutral.

'But you haven't heard the best bit.' He paused like a stage comic waiting to deliver his punchline. 'You ever hear of CVC?'

Dylan shook his head.

'Crime Victim Compensation. Reckon I could be eligible for a minimum ten grand. Could be as much as ten times that, for life-changing injuries like mine.' Curtis gave a little whoop, as if a slot machine had paid out.

Dylan knew he ought to feel pleased for his friend, but his heart had hardened to the point where he didn't care anymore.

He'd never considered himself malicious, but something about Curtis's smug grin made him want to wound in whatever way he could. He inhaled deeply and blew the air out through his lips. It made a whistling sound as it went.

'Curtis, buddy, there's no easy way to say this. So I'm just gonna get it out, okay?'

Dylan crossed his fingers. A childhood habit he thought he'd long since grown out of. 'Thing is, there's no point in the cops looking for Lucie.'

'Hell you talking about?'

'They won't find her. She's dead.'

'Fuck.' The word came out on a long, soft whisper. Curtis sagged in his chair, as if the muscles of his upper body had also withered, but taken only seconds to waste away. He folded his arms and raised one hand to clasp his face, making it hard for Dylan to read his expression.

'She died on 9/11.'

'In the towers?' Curtis pumped a fist in the air and started to whistle 'I'm in the Money'. Incredible. The man had just been told his beautiful young wife was dead.

'Christ, you look like you're pleased! I can't believe it. Were things really that bad between you two?'

A familiar expression stole across Curtis's face. It was the same sly look Dylan had known since they were kids. Whether he was swindling Dylan out of a favourite toy or wangling the lion's share of their Trick or Treat candy, Curtis had always been expert in pulling fast ones.

'Hell you implying, man? Things were great. I loved my wife.' Curtis paused for dramatic effect and wiped an invisible tear from the corner of his eye. 'I can't believe she's gone for good.' He covered his face with both his hands and sniffed loudly.

Dylan waited, intrigued by the performance and keen to see what would come next.

'So how come they know for sure she was in the World Trade Center?'

'I didn't say she was in WTC. She was found in Lower Manhattan, on Murray Street, to be precise.'

Curtis's hands, and then his smile, dropped off his face. He shook his head, as if he couldn't believe what he was hearing.

'They're paying out to the families of people who died in the towers. And she has to get run over by a car. Typical.'

'I didn't say she got run over, man. I said she died in the street.'

'So she *was* a victim of 9/11?'

'Her body was found by the cops. That's all I know. Sorry.'

Curtis looked like he might burst into tears. He sniffed loudly.

Dylan berated himself for being cynical. 'Curtis, this must be a terrible shock. I'm sorry to be the one to tell you. But, I need to ask, why did you look pleased when you heard she'd been killed?'

Curtis sighed, as if he'd been asked to explain quantum physics to a particularly stupid child.

'Because I thought I was in the money. Twice over.' His voice was so cold that Dylan knew his cynicism had been justified.

'I thought there might even be enough money to make up for this.' He banged his hands on the metal sides of the wheelchair. The sound reverberated angrily around the little room, one bang for each word. 'This total fuckin' mess!'

CHAPTER 46

Lucie smoothed the iron over a white blouse of Charlotte's. The smell of hot, fragranced linen rose to her nostrils, a homely scent that reminded her of her childhood.

Even with state-of-the-art equipment, doing laundry was tiresome. At least she didn't have to wash Curtis's foul-smelling socks and underpants ever again. Their ancient washer had packed in six months ago. Lucie had been forced to wash everything by hand, even their bed sheets. There was a Clean Rite Washeteria within walking distance but Curtis didn't believe in wasting good beer money. Not on something his wife could do for nothing. As a result, the place had a permanent smell of damp washing.

She'd been trying to avoid thinking about things. She was working her way through Charlotte's collection of bestsellers. She also spent hours on Charlotte's laptop, surfing the net. Some days her only contact with the real world was Friends Reunited. She'd managed to trace a few folk she'd gone to school with back in Scotland. Most of them had kids by now. Some were even on their second husband. Gluttons for punishment. One would be more than enough for Lucie.

She eased the shirt on to a hanger, glad to be done. Surely someone as well off as Charlotte had sent her clothes out for laundering? Lucie could do the same but she was keen to use as little of Charlotte's money as possible. The thought of having to go to an ATM was horrifying. But when the cash ran out, she'd have no choice. Using Charlotte's card would feel like serious fraud.

Much of her time on the internet had been spent on researching her chances of avoiding a jail sentence. They did not look good.

She could claim to have lost her memory. That was feasible. She did bash her head when she fell in the street. It was not uncommon, apparently, to sustain memory loss from a head injury.

Or, she could plead temporary insanity brought on by the events of 9/11.

She could say she remembered the dust chasing her until she fell and hit her head. She'd talk about how she opened Charlotte's bag believing it was hers. Believing she was Charlotte. Official records would show where Charlotte's body was found. It would be clear that Lucie was a victim of the dust cloud, just like Charlotte. The only difference was that Lucie's lungs were better able to cope with the polluted air.

It would not be difficult to convince people that she'd gone a little mad as a result of her traumatic experience. Waking up with your legs wound round a dead woman would be enough to freak anyone. All she had to do was convince the experts that she'd lost her mind, or her memory, maybe both.

But wouldn't they have tests they could run? Lucie wouldn't be the first criminal to use madness as a get-out-of-jail-free card.

She needed to do more research. Look into the kind of tests used to check for insanity. Then she could work out a way to get around them. How hard could it be to pretend she'd gone a little bit mad?

Lucie lifted the basket to put it away and spotted the handkerchief lying on the bottom. She placed the square of linen on the ironing board and smoothed it out. Her fingers traced three letters. S, S and M.

She drew the hot iron over the handkerchief, folding it as she went. She ended with a small smooth square with the initials in the corner. Strange letters to have on your hankie if your name is Richard Armstrong. Maybe she'd ask him about it, if she ever bumped into him again.

It had been a long time since she'd been in the company of anyone so charming and solicitous. An image of Dylan's kind face came into her mind and she felt instantly guilty. Dylan was caring, but he could hardly be described as suave and sophisticated, like Rick.

She tried to recall the handsome stranger who had come to her aid that awful day in the hospital. From their first meeting she'd had only the vaguest of impressions of the man. He'd felt solid, anchored, something she could cling to until she recovered enough to carry on. Lucie smiled at the clichés that were piling one on top of the other, but often a cliché was the most apt way to describe something. And Rick had felt like a rock.

When she first met Curtis, he'd still been strong and muscled, even though his sprinting days were behind him.

Dylan was slimmer, his chest not so deep, his arms not so bulky. But on the few occasions he'd given her a hug, she'd felt safe and protected. Dylan was one of the good guys, no doubt about it. He was a true friend. Loyal to Curtis and Lucie over the years. But he was hardly a looker. With sandy hair and cheeks that looked permanently embarrassed, Dylan was a regular boy next door. She'd rarely seen him out of baggy denims, sweatshirts and sneakers.

Rick oozed sophistication with his expensively groomed dark hair and designer stubble. In the hospital that day, even in her grief, she'd been aware that he smelled gorgeous. Of something citrusy, piney, leathery.

Curtis didn't believe in cologne.

Curtis was in the past.

She needed to leave him there.

However this whole mess turned out, one thing was sure. Her marriage was over.

Lucie laid the folded handkerchief on the console table in the hall. Maybe she'd take it with her the next time she went for a run, just in case she bumped into Rick again.

CHAPTER 47

'Come on, Dylan. Pick up,' Lucie muttered, tapping her nails on the worktop.

She didn't even give him time to speak. She'd rehearsed her lines and was keen to say them before she lost her nerve.

'Hey, Dylan. You said to call if I needed anything?'

'Sure. Whatever you need.'

'I need my passport. But I don't want to go back to the house in case Curtis catches me. Could you take a look for me, please? Or can you find some excuse to ask Curtis if he's seen it?'

'Why do you need your passport, Lucie?'

'I'm going home.'

'To Scotland?'

'Yes.'

'You taking your mum back?'

'Well, you see. I'm not sure. That's the other thing I wanted to ask you. Could you call the hospital for me?'

'I guess. If you need me to.'

'Can you call and find out what's happened to my mum, please?'

'What do you mean?'

'She had no insurance.'

'I see,' said Dylan, in a way that confirmed what Lucie feared. She had a problem on her hands.

'See, I need to know what's happening. I can't bear the thought of her lying in some hospital morgue, unclaimed. Or even worse, being disposed of.' Lucie tried to keep her voice strong. She wanted Dylan to believe she was in control.

'What is it you want me to do?'

'Call up and ask what the position is.'

'They won't talk to me, Lucie.'

'I've thought of that. You can pretend to be my brother. Phoning from Scotland. Everyone knows international calls are expensive so you can cut to the chase.'

'What is it you want me to say?'

'Find out how much her medical bills are. And what happens if she can't pay. And how much it would cost to send her home. Repatriation, it's called. And ask what happens if she stays in the States, does she get buried or cremated or what? Can you do that for me, Dylan?'

'I can try.'

'Thank you so much. You're such a good guy.'

'Why the sudden decision to go home?'

'Well, I've been thinking. You told me Curtis is okay, so there's no need for me to hole up here any longer. My friend Charlotte's really nice and all, don't get me wrong, but I'm going stir crazy. There are only so many DVDs you can watch in a day.'

She'd expected Dylan to laugh but he said nothing. The line was so silent, Lucie wondered if their call had been disconnected.

'Dylan?'

'I'm here, Lucie.'

'You won't tell Curtis you've seen me, will you?'

Another silence on the line.

'I'm not sure how to tell you this.'

'For God's sake, Dylan!' She couldn't help being impatient. 'Tell me what?'

'Curtis thinks you're dead.'

CHAPTER 48

Dylan was angry with himself.

He had told Lucie about Curtis sending him to find out why she hadn't come home on September eleventh. He'd told her Lucie Jardine had been found dead on Murray Street. A victim of the dust cloud.

'Why didn't you tell me this before?' Lucie had asked.

'Think about it,' he'd said. 'You were sitting right there in front of me, large as life.'

'Are you sure it was me they found? I mean, are you sure I'm the Lucie Jardine who's been declared dead?'

'Looks like it.'

'Well, I guess I'm just going to have to rise from the dead. I'm sure it can all be sorted out. One way or another. I can't be the only Lazarus walking around this city at the moment. There must be few people showing up who were assumed dead.'

'You were more than assumed dead, Lucie. A body was found with your ID. How did that happen?' Why did he have to sound so accusing? He'd only been trying to understand the mix-up.

'I have no idea! Dylan, you had to be there. It was chaos. One minute I was walking along, in a hurry to get to my interview on time. Curtis had made me late and I was frantic in case I'd blown it. The next minute I heard this noise, and it was ... like this avalanche of white stuff racing towards us. No one knew what it was. Everyone just ran for their lives.'

Lucie had wittered on, as if she couldn't stop. 'I dropped my bag. Tripped and fell over. Bumped my head. Lost consciousness for, I don't know how long. When I came to,

I couldn't see a thing for dust. Next thing, a policeman was shepherding everyone out of the area. I tried to tell him I needed to get my bag, but he wouldn't let me go back for it. He just kept saying, over and over, like a robot, "Go north. Go north."'

'And your bag got picked up later? And matched up with the wrong woman?'

'There's no other explanation. Is there?'

Lucie had been very matter of fact. Something about her tone had made Dylan uneasy. He wouldn't have said she was lying. But.

'Did you tell Curtis you'd seen me?'

'No.'

'So he still thinks I'm dead.'

'Yes.'

'Is he distraught?'

Dylan hadn't been sure how to answer that one. So he'd said nothing.

'Fine!' The word was spat out like something poisonous. 'That's made my decision a whole lot easier. You get me my passport, Dylan. I'm going to sort this shit out. Then I'm going home.'

He could have told her he had her passport in his pocket. But he didn't because she mustn't know he'd been underhand.

He could have told her Curtis was paralysed. But he didn't because he was scared she'd go back to him.

He could have told her his loyalty was so strong that he'd covered up a crime scene for her. But he didn't because she'd have to work that one out for herself.

Worst of all, he didn't tell her he loved her. Because he was a pathetic fool.

And now she was leaving.

Well, maybe that was the best thing. Keeping secrets to protect her was getting too difficult.

None of it was his responsibility, far less his fault, and yet he was constantly embroiled in the drama of their lives.

He should come clean to the two of them. Then wash his hands of them. Friends were supposed to make you happy, not fill your life with stress.

Lucie could do what she wanted. If she chose to go back to Curtis, there was nothing Dylan could do about it. Maybe it was time to cut them both loose and let them drag each other to hell.

CHAPTER 49

His resolution didn't last the night. He texted his boss to say he'd be a little late. Then he rang the hospital. Finally he tried the number Lucie had called him from.

He was about to give up when she answered, her voice hoarse and sleepy.

He wasted no time on small talk. 'Morning, Lucie. I made that call you wanted.'

'Great. Thanks, Dylan. You're a pal.'

'Good old Dylan. That's me.'

Lucie didn't respond.

'Okay, so here's the deal. Turns out you don't need to worry about your mom. Her passport stated her next of kin is your dad. They contacted him and he's stepped up to the plate. Everything's been taken care of. Your mom has been repatriated for burial in Scotland.'

'Good. That's what she would have wanted.'

Dylan heard the catch in her voice and his heart softened. 'You okay? Lucie?'

Between sniffs she said, 'My mum told me my dad isn't a bad man. She also said he'd welcome me back with open arms. I didn't believe her but now I think that might be true. Did you find my passport?'

'I've got it.' No need to elaborate.

'Oh, thank God.'

She sounded so relieved Dylan wished he'd told her sooner.

'Is it still valid? Please tell me it's still valid.'

She must be desperate to get away.

'I know it's in my maiden name, but if I book the ticket in the name of Lucie McBride, no one will be any the wiser, will they, Dylan?' She was childlike in her eagerness.

Oh God. Why did he have to be the one to dash her hopes?

'Lucie, there's something I haven't told you. Something you need to hear.'

'You make it sound ominous.'

'It's about Curtis.'

'Dylan, you need to understand this: my marriage is over. I have absolutely no further interest in Curtis.'

'What I have to say might affect that, Lucie.'

'I can't imagine how, but go ahead and say whatever it is you've got to tell me.'

'Remember I told you I saw you at the hospital the day your mom died?'

'Yes.'

'Well, Curtis is still in hospital.'

'What's wrong with him? Alcoholic poisoning?'

'No. He's paralysed.'

'Paralysed?' she said, as if Dylan was joking.

'Yes. From the waist down.'

'What does that mean?'

'It means he'll never walk again. And he'll struggle to live independently.'

There was a long pause. Dylan waited to see what Lucie would say next. 'That's awful. I feel sorry for him,' she said. Her voice was quiet and flat, devoid of emotion.

'You should.'

'What do you mean by that?'

'I think we both know what I mean.'

'What are you accusing me of, Dylan? It's not my fault Curtis had an accident.'

There was an aggression in her voice that Dylan had never heard before. 'I'm not accusing you, Lucie, I'm suggesting it might not have been an accident that caused his paralysis.'

'Meaning what?'

He had to hand it to her. She was cool.

'I found him lying in a pool of blood. At first I thought he'd just fallen down drunk and bashed his head. Wouldn't be the first time. Then, when he tried to get up, he couldn't move his legs. It was a nightmare, Lucie. I'm no neurological expert, but it was pretty obvious, even to me, that his spine had been injured.'

'And you think that was me? Are you crazy?'

In a flat tone he said, 'I found the skillet.'

'Ah.' A tiny sound, acknowledging her guilt.

'You must have known you'd hurt him, Lucie. That skillet weighs a ton.'

'That's why I didn't hit him over the head with it. I know real life's not like the cartoons. Real people don't get bopped with a frying pan, see a few stars then charge about as normal. Even as I feared for my life, I knew that.'

'But you did hit him with it.'

'As hard as I could, but on his back, not on his head. I didn't want to kill him. I just wanted to stop *him* killing *me*.'

'So it was self-defence?'

'Dylan. You don't really believe I set out to paralyse him?'

'No, Lucie. I don't believe that for a minute. Never did.'

'What do the police believe? I know they haven't taken the skillet. I checked.'

'I washed it and put it away. Before the cops got there.'

'You covered up for me?'

'What else would I do?'

'Thank you, you've saved my life.' She started crying, very quietly, as if she didn't want him to hear. Dylan thought the sound might break his heart. He listened, saying nothing, giving her time to compose herself.

'Can you meet me somewhere with my passport, please? I've got to book a flight and get out of here.'

How to tell her? 'Lucie, listen. There's something else you need to know. The police had no reason to continue with an investigation. There were no witnesses and there was no evidence. I thought we'd got away with it. But then Curtis started to remember what happened. He called the police. Lucie, he's pressing charges.'

'Shit! All the more reason for me to hurry. Can you come right now?'

'Lucie, he claims they're watching the airports.'

'Wait a minute. Did you tell him I'm still alive?'

'No, I didn't.'

'The cops won't go after a dead person. Will they?'

'I don't know. Are you prepared to take that chance?'

She didn't answer.

'Can I ask you a question? That day in the hospital? You were talking to a man in the coffee shop?'

'Yeah?'

'The reason I didn't speak to you that day? I heard you tell the guy your name is Gillespie.'

She didn't deny it.

'I can't work out why you would you do that.'

Several long moments passed before Dylan realised she'd hung up on him.

CHAPTER 50

L ucie couldn't face breakfast. Her conversations with Dylan had made her sick to the stomach.

It wasn't fair to hang up on him like that. He was such a lovely guy, doing his best to help her. Lucie had been reeling from shock and desperate to hit out, like a beaten boxer throwing a final punch. If she hadn't hung up, she'd have said stuff she'd be regretting by now. And Dylan didn't deserve that.

And then there was the guilt. Her loss of control had cost Curtis the use of his legs. A runner who'd never walk, far less run. If someone were to tell her she'd never walk again, she'd want to die. No question.

She remembered her throat closing down as his hands tightened on her windpipe, cutting off her air supply. How much longer before she stopped breathing? Would he have realised what was happening in time to save her life? She'd had no choice but to save herself. Most people might think paralysing her husband was taking self-defence a bit too far.

Lucie wondered what would happen if she were to come forward and confess. Would her dad be willing to pay for lawyers to defend her? It was a big ask, under the circumstances. Even if he did, it was still likely she would go to prison. Curtis would blame her for attacking him and causing his paralysis. He would lie and cheat. Beguile the ladies in the jury.

She was screwed. Caught in a trap, again. And Curtis was the one keeping her there. Again.

Lucie looked around her luxury apartment with its magnificent view, its soft leather sofas, the glass table, the glossy kitchen and its state-of-the-art appliances. As traps went, this was a beautiful one, she had to admit. And if her life had worked out differently, if she'd never met Curtis, maybe this was the kind of life she'd be living.

She'd longed for a better life when she was caught up in her abusive marriage. When she was confined to that grotty little house, practically starving. Suffering the degradation of having to depend on Curtis for every morsel she ate. She'd dreamt of designer clothes and gourmet food, smooth Egyptian sheets and a luxury bathroom. And here she was. Not by the route she'd imagined, but she was still here, and still alive.

In the rotten game of poker that her life had been so far, this was the hand of cards she'd been dealt. It was up to Lucie how she played them.

Why should she own up to injuring Curtis when he had wounded her so often and got away with it? If she stepped out of the shadows now, who knew what she'd be getting herself into? At worst a prison sentence and at best a melee of legal wrangles that could swallow up all her dad's money.

Maybe the best thing was to wait. It was only a matter of time till the police traced Lucie Jardine to the morgue. The thought made Lucie shiver. She wondered about writing her own obituary and putting it in the papers. Would that throw the cops off the scent or bring them baying to her heels?

Maybe she could send Curtis some money, anonymously. Compensation for the life-changing injuries she'd caused him. Payment for her freedom. She need have no further contact with him.

She wasn't trapped. She had choices. That alone put her ahead of where she was before 9/11. She had reconciled with her mum. She knew her dad wasn't bearing a lifelong grudge. And she was no longer shackled to Curtis.

Poor Curtis. He was the one who was trapped. While she was free to do as she wished.

He might have set the police on Lucie Jardine, but no one was looking for Charlotte Gillespie.

CHAPTER 51

He reckoned he needed to let a couple of days pass. Then she'd come looking for him. Probably with the handkerchief as an excuse. It wasn't arrogance on his part, just a lifetime's experience of working with people and studying women. He'd learned, as a small child, how to be likeable. He'd been one of the popular kids all through school and always had a girlfriend. He'd never chased after a woman in his life, not even Diane, and she was the one whose affections he'd been most determined to win. Charlotte too had taken little work before she was eating out of his hand, prepared to do anything for him.

Playing it cool had always been his strategy for success and he was sure this girl would be no exception. She would come to him, if not today, then tomorrow or the next day. As long as he could find the time to lie in wait, she'd show up. He was certain of it.

He looked around for the little priest who'd been so welcoming the first day. Yesterday he'd greeted him like a long-lost friend, but there was no sign of him today. Did priests get days off?

It was best if no one noticed him making contact with Miss Mystery Girl, assuming she showed up.

He checked his watch and then drew his sleeve down over its expensive face. He had plenty of time. Adopting an attitude of prayer, he dropped his head while he ran through his plan. He'd try to get her to meet him for a coffee or a drink. It would be vital to get her complete trust, then he could set about finding out who she was and what she knew.

He was wondering whether God, if he was watching, could be fooled by fake prayer when a quiet voice whispered, 'Rick.' It took him a moment to remember his assumed name. He opened his eyes and, like the answer to a prayer, there she was, sitting in the pew beside him, dressed for a run. This close up, he could see she wasn't Charlotte, but the resemblance was strong.

'Hello,' he murmured. 'What are you doing here?'

She indicated her leggings and sweat top and said, somewhat unnecessarily, 'I was out for a run.'

He smiled his most disarming smile. 'I can see that.'

She blushed in a very endearing way. 'Sorry, bit obvious, isn't it?'

He nodded, still smiling. 'Shall we step outside?' he asked, indicating the many people praying around them. 9/11 had probably done wonders for the churches in New York. He'd be willing to bet they hadn't been this busy in years.

Like a newly married couple they walked along the carpeted aisle and out through the big doors into daylight.

'How nice to see you again,' he said. 'Do you always pop into church during a run?'

She laughed, as he'd intended, and said, 'No, actually I was looking for you.'

Such refreshing honesty. This just got better and better. 'Really? I'm intrigued.'

'I'd planned to bring your hankie in case I saw you today. But I forgot to pick it up on the way out. When I passed the church I thought I'd see if you were around so I could tell you …' She stopped, all of a sudden, without finishing her sentence and blushed again. Mystery Girl was getting more attractive by the minute.

'I'm babbling, aren't I?' she said.

He nodded, very solemnly and they both burst out laughing. He couldn't believe how well this was going.

'Sorry. Talking too much has always been a fault of mine.'

Couldn't be better.

As if to prove her point, the girl kept chattering. 'Do you think you'll be here again tomorrow? Because if you are, I could bring the handkerchief with me. I won't forget it next time and I could give it to you then. My granny always said, "neither a borrower nor a lender be", so I'm honour bound to return it.'

He shook his head and was delighted to see her look a little disappointed. Of course he could be here tomorrow, but he was a great believer in striking hot iron and he had every intention of using this situation to his advantage.

'Not tomorrow, I'm afraid. But hey, listen, it's just an old hankie. There's no need for you to bother returning it. I have others. Forget about it.'

She looked crestfallen. He said nothing, waiting to see how she'd react.

'No really, I'd like to. Maybe I'll just stick it in my pocket, in case I ever bump into you again.' She lifted her top, revealing a few inches of pale, skinny abdomen as she pointed out a miniscule pocket in the leggings. She laughed and said, 'It might be a bit crushed once it's been squashed in there, but at least you'll get it back.'

He laid his hand gently on her shoulder, noticing how birdlike she was. Had Charlotte ever been this skinny? 'Listen, do you have to be somewhere? You want to go grab a coffee?'

As if realising he'd overstepped some mark, he removed his hand and said, 'Sorry, that was dumb. Of course you need to be somewhere.'

'The only place I need to be right now is in the shower, but once I've freshened up I could meet you for a coffee.' She paused, unsure of herself. 'If you have time, that is?'

He looked at his watch, making it seem like he was a busy man trying to come to a decision about something. 'You know what,' he said suddenly, 'I can make time. I mean how long does it take to drink a latte?'

They laughed again and parted on the church steps with a plan to meet up later in a coffee shop he knew. He was surprised to hear she didn't know the place because he'd deliberately chosen one near Charlotte's apartment. It all added to the intrigue and the challenge, but he knew that, given the opportunity, he'd soon work out what was going on.

He watched her cute little ass run off down the street and called his driver to tell him he wouldn't be needing the car for the next hour or so.

The coffee smelled real good, but he settled himself with a glass of water. While he waited for her to show up, he considered what might be his best approach. Having heard how chatty she could be, he was pretty confident he could just let her talk. Eventually she'd tell him all he needed to know. Depending on what she revealed, he'd either disappear from her life or stick around and cause her a whole lot of trouble.

He was beginning to think she wasn't coming when she rushed in, breathless, pink and quite adorable. This was no Charlotte. She was as soft and warm as ice-maiden Charlotte had been diamond hard. He gave himself a little mental warning not to get too fond of this girl. Whoever she was, she had no place in his life.

They got a couple of lattes, hers a predictable skinny. She began to rummage in her bag. 'Damn,' she said, then looked up at him in apology. 'Sorry, I could have sworn I'd put it in here.'

'What?'

'Your handkerchief. Isn't that why we're meeting? So I can return it?'

'Don't worry about it. I have plenty more.' He produced one from his pocket, so clean and white it almost sparkled, like an ad for washing powder.

She took it from him and examined the corner. 'They're beautiful. This looks hand-embroidered but I can't work out the monogram.'

He looked at her, knowing his face was showing his incomprehension. 'Sorry?' he said, genuinely confused.

'Your initials? R and A? Yet the monogram on the hankies show a double s and an m.'

He guffawed like a fool, relief making his laugh far louder than usual. A woman at the next table gave him a disparaging look, but he ignored her rude stare and concentrated on telling a credible lie. 'Yes. Well, there's an explanation for that. These handkerchiefs belonged to my grandfather, Steven Mulholland. My grandmother did the embroidery, apparently. We found stockpiles of them in a closet when she died. My mother believes Gramma kept making them for years after Gramps died. I didn't have the heart to see them thrown away.'

She seemed to buy it. 'Oh, that's so sweet. I thought it was vintage linen. What was his middle name?'

He blurted a name, regretting it immediately.

'Nice names,' she said, then added, 'but I also like Rick.'

'What's yours?' he countered, hoping to catch her off guard.

'Lucie. Charlotte!'

'Lucie-Charlotte? That's pretty.'

'No, I thought you meant my middle name. It's Lucie. Please, just call me Charlotte. Everyone does.'

That pretty blush was back again, this time going down her neck and inside her blouse. It reminded him of the one Charlotte had worn the night he'd ripped the button off in his haste to get his mouth on her breast.

'Okay, Charlotte. What do you do?'

'I guess you'd say I'm between jobs.'

He leaned back in his chair and crossed his legs, aiming for a relaxed, non-threatening look. 'Right, and what line of business are you in?'

'Oh, this and that.'

He nodded, as if this and that was a recognised profession, and gave himself some time to think. He could offer her a job, get his PA to create some menial position for her, but that might become problematic if he had to get rid of her later on. Plus, if he let her into the workplace, she'd be bound to find out more about him than was wise. Like his name, for example. Better to wait and see if she took the bait he planned to dangle in front of her pretty little nose.

Time to try a different tack. 'How long have you lived in the city?'

'Pretty much most of my life, one way or another.'

Was he imagining things or was this girl prevaricating as much as himself? This could take longer than he'd expected if she kept it up.

'Isn't that a hint of a Scottish accent I hear?'

'Yes, I meant most of my adult life. I came to the States when I was eighteen.'

'That's right. You said.'

'I did?'

'That day in the hospital.'

'Oh yes. The day my mum died.'

'Did you manage to get her insurance issues sorted out?'

'Yes, it's all good.'

When he was sure she wasn't going to elaborate, he said, in his gentlest voice, 'Would I be right in guessing you're alone in the world now?'

'If I stay here, I am.' She compressed her lips as if she were struggling to keep her composure. He leaned over and patted her hand. 'We're in the same boat.' She didn't move her hand away.

'No children?' she asked.

'No. My wife's illness made that impossible, I'm sad to say. You?'

She shook her head. 'Me neither. No children. No spouse. No siblings.'

He squeezed her hand and said, 'Oh, poor you. But I bet you've got loads of friends.'

Again she shook her head. 'I lost touch with everyone a while back. Oh, listen to me! How pathetic do I sound?'

Knowing he was taking a risk he took her hand in his and said, 'Well, Charlotte. You could always make new friends.'

'I could use one right now.'

'So could I, as it happens. I've become a bit of a recluse since my wife died, to tell you the truth.'

He looked down at the table, hoping to give the impression of a guy too shy to ask. He took a sip of his coffee and glanced at her face. 'Tell me, Charlotte,' he said, 'how would you feel about having some dinner with me? Not a date or anything, just two new friends meeting up to share a meal. I find dinner just about the hardest time of day. We could grab some pizza, whatever you like.'

She hesitated for the longest time. 'Thanks, but I'm not sure.'

'Oh, sorry, have I offended you?' Before she could answer, he babbled on, as if he'd expected her to turn him down and was letting her off the hook. 'Is it inconvenient? It's too short notice, isn't it? Sorry, I shouldn't have asked. It's just, I've so enjoyed …' He let his voice peter out, as if he'd lost his nerve.

She laughed, a charming sound, more a girlish giggle than adult laughter. 'I'd love to. Why not?'

When they parted for the second time that day, he could hardly believe his luck. He'd anticipated a real problem in getting close to this girl, but she was making it easy. All he had to do now was find out who she was. And why, in heaven's name, she was complicating his life by pretending to be Charlotte Gillespie.

CHAPTER 52

Lucie felt as excited as a teenager with a first boyfriend. This would be their third date, not counting the coffee they'd had together. They didn't call them dates. They called them 'friendship nights'. He said dating felt disloyal to his wife, whom he referred to as 'the love of my life'. It was a bit too soon, he said. She knew he appreciated her understanding. And she had nothing to complain about. Their arrangement suited her.

She'd been determined not to get involved with Rick. One coffee, she'd told herself that first day. Return his hankie and bye. But he'd made her laugh. And she had cheered him up, he said. He'd made her feel witty and clever, as if they were helping each other get through the horror of bereavement.

When he talked about the heartbreak of losing his wife, Lucie found herself comparing him to Curtis. According to Dylan, Curtis had received the news of her death with barely a tear. He'd been so caught up in his own misery. But Rick was bereft. It was clear to see.

She'd wondered once or twice if he'd think her cold-hearted. She'd been bereaved more recently than Rick. Sometimes Lucie doubted her ability to love. Then she'd remind herself that she hadn't seen her mum for years. There was no bond between them anymore. Why would she be distraught at her loss?

It suited her very well that Rick was a long way short of getting over his wife. She was not even close to getting over Curtis. For entirely different reasons, of course. She was in no hurry to find herself another man. Never would be too soon if all they were all like Curtis.

But she knew that wasn't the case. Rick was the living proof. And so was Dylan. The day she'd called back to apologise for hanging up on him, he'd been lovely. And when she'd thanked him for hiding the skillet, he said, 'I'd do anything to keep you from harm, Lucie. Please don't ever forget that.'

She'd told him of her decision to stay away from Curtis for good. She didn't mention the fact that she was looking into ways of getting some money to Curtis to help him have some quality of life. It would have sounded too much like a pay-off, a salve for her guilty conscience.

The truth was, Lucie would send the cash but Charlotte would be the philanthropist. She wouldn't ever know how generous she'd been.

Lucie's longer-term plan was still to try to find a job. Anything that would allow her to save up enough money for a fare home. For some reason she couldn't quite understand, it was important she pay for the ticket herself. Finding work had proved to be more of a challenge than she'd expected. For every job in New York there seemed to be a queue of applicants and, of course, without proof of identity, never mind qualifications, Lucie was no better than an illegal immigrant. Even the lowliest underpaid jobs were out of her reach without proper paperwork.

Rick had suggested he might have something for her, if she could wait a week or two till he sorted out some little details. Lucie still wasn't too sure what Rick did for a living, but it was definitely finance and business-related and seemed fairly high powered. It certainly paid well, judging by his generosity on their 'friendship nights'.

'Let me spoil you a little,' he'd said the first time. 'It's been a long time since I bought a lady a drink.'

She didn't tell Rick it had been a long time since anyone had bought this lady a drink, unless you would call a can of cheap beer a drink.

Dylan had called yesterday with some very good news. Curtis had moved into custom-made accommodation and surprise, surprise, he had not moved in alone. Apparently he'd taken along a cute, blonde nurse who had looked after him in hospital. He was likely to need twenty-four-hour care and it was easier to have his nurse stay on the premises. Lucie wondered where he was getting the money but decided not to ask. The prospect that she herself might have ended up as his full-time caregiver was too awful to contemplate. Good luck to them, she'd said to Dylan.

He was doing well. He'd got a promotion at work and was seeing someone. He would not give her any details, claiming it was far too soon to get excited, although his mum was apparently checking out wedding outfits in her Sears catalogue.

Were it not for the constant worry of being exposed as a fraud, Lucie thought she might almost dare to feel happy at times. If she weren't so lonely. Some days she felt as trapped in her new life as in her old one. It was crazy to compare the two. She might be lonely living Charlotte's life but at least she was safe from harm. No violent man was ever going to hurt her in this beautiful apartment. When she went to bed she could rest easy. No drunken husband would be pawing at her in her sleep. Living up here on the fortieth floor, where the only sound to be heard was the air con or the refrigerator, Lucie often felt like she wasn't living in the real world at all.

All afternoon she'd been trying on different outfits from Charlotte's wardrobe. She wanted to look especially good tonight. She had finally decided on a little black dress she'd first tried on hours ago. Since then she had luxuriated in the tub and spent ages fixing her hair and nails. She was pretty much ready to go, apart from putting on her make-up and slipping into the dress. She had picked out some black patent sandals earlier. They were pretty enough but she felt the dress, and Rick, deserved better. What she needed was a pair of sexy killer heels.

Charlotte's shoes were kept, tissue wrapped, in their original boxes. The end wall of the closet looked like an upmarket shoe shop. Lucie pulled down a Jimmy Choo box she had avoided earlier, thinking the shoes too expensive to borrow. But tonight felt, somehow, like a special occasion. She opened the lid and took out the matching dust bag with its iconic lettering. Lucie reached inside and removed a shoe. She raised it to her face and inhaled the smell of luxury. She placed the shoe reverently on the floor and slipped her foot inside. Her toe jammed on a wedge of tissue paper. Lucie prised it out and tried the shoe again. Still something was blocking her toes. Being careful not to spoil her freshly manicured nails, she inserted two fingers and caught hold of a little piece of plastic. It was an SD card from a camera. Was this where Charlotte kept all her photos and private stuff?

Charlotte had clearly taken trouble to conceal the memory card, and Lucie was keen to know why. She checked the time on the bedside clock. She really should be putting on her make-up. Getting ready to leave in fifteen minutes. Not booting up a laptop to have a nosey at someone's personal data.

'Curiosity killed the cat,' Granny would say if she could see her now.

While she waited for the laptop to start, she mused on the idea of cats having nine lives. Granny had never been able to explain that one.

Rick was constantly asking her questions and Lucie was struggling to come up with anything remotely interesting to say about herself. Being married to Curtis for the last seven years had not given her much that she could talk about. She had no vacations to recall, no family weddings to describe, no Thanksgiving dinners or special Christmas stories that she could share. Her life had been arid as a desert in July. She was beginning to feel uncomfortable each time Rick asked her anything about it. She could make stuff up, but the problem with fake memories was, they were hard to remember later. She was sure to be caught out.

Maybe the contents of the memory card would round Charlotte out a bit, make her seem more like a real person. Anything would be better than nothing.

To Lucie's disappointment, the screen remained almost blank. No albums of Costa Rica vacations, photos from Adele and David's wedding or memories of Christmas. All that appeared was a tiny folder icon named 'Please Open Me'.

Lucie checked the little clock in the corner of the screen. She couldn't afford to spend too much time on this. She should leave it till morning.

The trouble was, she was intrigued now. Desperate to find out why would Charlotte go to such lengths to hide something that said Please Open. Lucie was sorely tempted to take a quick look before she went out. Whatever was in the folder might prove fascinating enough to share with Rick. Might even make him laugh.

She could dress and put on make-up in less than ten minutes if need be. Even if she were to turn up a little late, it would do no harm to keep Rick waiting.

She double clicked on the little folder. And felt like Aladdin in a cave with no treasure. There was nothing inside but one single Word document. No photos, no videos, no scans. This was promising to be a complete waste of time. Expecting little, Lucie opened the document. What appeared on the screen looked like a letter.

Dear Stranger,
If you're reading this, it's because I'm dead.

Lucie stopped and blew out hard. What the hell was this?

She told herself it had to be some kind of a joke. She hoped it was, for the last thing she needed right now was any more drama.

Lucie moved the cursor to the corner of the screen and closed the document. She took her fingers off the trackpad and rubbed them over her temples, as if she had a headache.

Her old life suddenly seemed very simple and uncomplicated and for a second Lucie wished she could go back to it. She could deal with the occasional beating, and the poverty she'd got used to a while ago. But this? Just when she'd been beginning to enjoy life. It was too much.

She couldn't leave something like this unread. She opened the letter again and started to read.

Dear Stranger,

If you're reading this, it's because I'm dead.

I've been wondering who might find the memory card. (Ain't that one sexy pair of heels? Great hiding place, don't you think? Was pretty sure no woman could resist a peek.)

You're unlikely to be a man, unless you have very small feet and a proclivity for cross-dressing, so that leaves only a few options.

You may be a female detective, or a cleaner or even a volunteer in a goodwill store. Whoever you are, please keep the Jimmy Choos, if they fit you, with my blessing. (That includes you, the cross-dresser!)

In return, I want you to do something for me. Check the calendar. If it says September 2001, the likelihood is my life ended on or around the eleventh. Probably in the North Tower of the World Trade Center.

Lucie clapped her hand over her mouth, stifling her own gasp. She reached for the arrow key that allowed her to scroll to the foot of the document. It was signed Yours, Charlotte.

Charlotte had predicted her own death. And not only that, she'd predicted the timing of her death. And got it right. Lucie's stomach contracted with a lurch that made her feel sick.

Charlotte, this woman whose life had ensnared Lucie, had also predicted the tragedy that struck the North Tower. Perhaps not the detail, but certainly the possibility of lives lost. Lucie shivered. How could anyone have foreseen such an unlikely event as a plane crashing into the iconic landscape of her home city? It wasn't possible.

The woman was crazy. And yet, she'd been right about her own death. Maybe not the place, but, when Lucie thought about it, Charlotte had probably been on her way to the towers, same as herself. Had the planes struck a bit later, Lucie would have been in the South Tower and Charlotte could have been in the North Tower, where she'd have died, just like this spooky letter predicted. Lucie scrolled to the top again, searching for a date. There it was: 9/10/2001. Charlotte had written this the day before 9/11.

Lucie pushed the laptop away, as if it was contaminated. She was too nauseous to read any further.

She had to tell someone about this, get some advice, some help. That would mean revealing her deceit and dishonesty, but she couldn't keep something like this to herself. Lucie had never felt so alone in her life.

It was time for her to go and meet Rick but he'd have to wait. A letter from a dead woman was far too compelling to resist.

I don't know why it's important to me, since I'll be dead if you're reading this, but I'd like someone to know, even if you're the only one in the whole wide world, that I'm not a bad person.

Oops, beginning to sound a bit maudlin, Charlotte. (I'm trying for a cool, ironic tone with a touch of black humour. Just so you know.)

This letter is like an insurance policy. Insurance – the only thing you ever purchase that you never, ever want to use. I mean, can you think of one other item that falls into the same category? 'Okay,' you'd say to yourself, 'I must have that Mulberry bag, but I really hope I don't ever get the opportunity to use it.'

That's why I'm allowing myself to be flippant. I have to hope no one ever reads this, because the alternative is too horrific to contemplate. And not just for me. So it doesn't matter how I write it. The important thing is that it gets written and that you read it, please.

I'm not a bad person, not really. I'm vain and I'm greedy. And probably selfish, but since I'm alone in the world, that's possibly not surprising. Vain, greedy and selfish. That's me.

I was also perfectly happy, working hard, focused on building my business empire, enjoying my success and the sweet, exotic fruits my labour brought me. Then I met the man who changed my life and caused my death.

* * *

Lucie thought of the one and only time she'd seen Charlotte, dead in the street, shrouded in white powder. How could her death have been caused by anyone? Surely she breathed in the dust? There was no time to use her inhaler. She suffocated. Or she collapsed and hit her head. She died. But she wasn't murdered.

Hadn't she said something about the likelihood of her death occurring in the North Tower? Lucie scrolled back up the page to confirm.

This was starting to read like the ramblings of a madwoman. The whole upbeat, detached tone was at odds with such a sombre message. It didn't ring true.

Lucie knew she should leave it. And yet she couldn't resist reading on.

* * *

At first he was just another charming colleague, a potential co-investor, a handsome man to be seen with at corporate events. I knew he was married. He never hid that fact from me. He frequently spoke of his wife and always with affection. He and I started to meet occasionally, in hotel rooms. It was fun. He was a caring, considerate lover.

I was satisfied. By him and our relationship. He knew Matthew was the only man I'd ever wanted to marry. Would have married. If President Bush had declared his ceasefire one day earlier.

He knew I wasn't looking for a husband. He used to joke that I was already married to my business, and he was right. But then I began to yearn for more. I wanted what his wife had. And worse, I began to feel broody.

He didn't lie to me. He said he'd been clear from the start. He loved his wife and would never leave her. Besides, she was the one with the money, so he couldn't leave her or she'd make him penniless. I tried to persuade him that we could live on the proceeds of my business, but he wouldn't hear of it. Swore he wouldn't touch my money.

Then, suddenly, he changed his mind. He told me about a 'once in a lifetime' business opportunity that he'd heard about. He'd been given some insider information that would allow him to predict the market and buy options on shares. It sounded too good to be true so I demanded to know his source. He kept smiling and saying 'classified'. He refused to tell me at first, just wanted me to sign a huge cheque and become his fellow investor. He promised me the millions we'd make would secure our future together. He predicted untold wealth, more than enough to guarantee his freedom and to ensure we'd live happily and luxuriously ever after. The only problem was, I'd have to wait a few weeks for him to leave his wife and to see a return on my investment.

Well, do I seem to you like the kinda gal who walks blindfold into anything, far less a million-dollar deal? (That should read millions, not million, by the way.) I didn't build Gillespie, Manders and Moffat into a World Trade Center business by doing what others suggested. (FYI – there is no Manders or Moffat, I just liked the triple-barrelled sound of the name.)

Now, don't get me wrong. I'm not averse to a bit of insider trading. My God, you have to take the breaks where you find them in the world of business and finance. I learned that lesson long ago.

No. I needed to know more. Where did he get the information on which he wished to bet megabucks, his and mine?

He wouldn't tell.

And I wouldn't invest until he did. I can be stubborn, but I can also be very persuasive, in ways that it wouldn't be proper to go into here. Just let's say, I knew what he liked and what his wife didn't. (!)

So he told me. And I was shocked.

At first I said no. Under no circumstances. But he won me round. Like I said, I'm vain, very selfish and very, very greedy.

I withdrew the cash. He purchased the options and our bets were placed. The die was cast and we planned our future together, symbolised by two keys to the safe deposit box we co-rented to keep all the paperwork secure, not to mention secret. I wore mine on a silk ribbon, 'close to my heart.' And we waited for fate to play its part.

And right there, that was the problem. The waiting.

Remember I told you I'm not a bad woman? Well, I guess I just forgot that for a while. Got caught up in someone else's dream and lost track of what's right and wrong.

I told him I couldn't go along with it. I couldn't stand by and do nothing while people died. People I knew. People I employed. People *who trusted me for their livelihood. Suddenly I had not just their livelihoods, but their very lives in my hands. And I couldn't do it.*

I expected nuclear-sized fallout when I said the words, 'I can't sacrifice my workforce.'

He said nothing in response. Said nothing at all for a while. As if he were thinking carefully about what I'd said, considering my point of view, he closed his eyes. Then he whispered, 'Thank God for that.'

I hugged him, kissed him, blessed him. This wonderful man that I loved.

'So what are you thinking?' he asked.

'I'm going to go in tomorrow morning and send everyone home. On paid vacation.' The vacation bit hadn't been part of my plan, I'd just thought it up. Originally I was going to hire decorators but that wasn't the solution. One, it was too short notice and two, it meant bringing other innocents into the building. Paid vacation was a brainwave. Expensive, but inspired.

'Can you afford that?' he asked.

'Maybe not now, but when our investment pays out, yes, of course I can.'

'Then I'll do the same,' he declared, as if he were making a menu choice not a decision that would save many lives.

'You will?' I asked, wondering how I ever got lucky enough to find him.

'Yes, I will. It's been bothering me too. We've stayed away from work for the last couple days, but others have been in there, at risk. I keep seeing faces of guys I've known for years, dependable, loyal workers who'd die for me. Shoot, I've met their wives and kids. I even employ some of their kids. It's been ripping my heart out, thinking of what might happen to those good people. And now you've come up with the solution, you sweet angel.'

He kissed my brow, as if he were bestowing a blessing on me, and we hatched our plan and made our arrangements. We would safeguard ourselves as much as possible by staying out of the North Tower until most workers would be at their desks. We'd go into the building about ten-thirty to let our respective workforces know that they should go home, on full pay. We were calling it preventative sick leave, a precautionary action to pre-empt an outbreak of Legionnaire's Disease that had hit one of their colleagues and might be coming from the air conditioning on our floors. In other words, we were protecting our workers from potential harm, being good guys. We'd tell our folks about symptoms and advise them to see a doctor if they developed any.

Then we'd hightail it out of there and hope they did the same. He seemed to be very worried that our workers might tell others and there would be a stampede, but I thought that unlikely. Most people tend to look after Number One and apart from those with relatives working in the Tower, I was sure everyone would be out of there fast as kids from a schoolroom. 'If I know New Yorkers,' I said, 'most of them will be straight out the door and off to see a doctor, symptoms or no symptoms.'

We laughed and agreed to meet for coffee afterwards near the bank. He said to be sure to wear my key, in case he forgot his, so we could retrieve the documentation we'd need. I dangled the key on its silken string and told him not to worry, I never took it off.

And I never did. Apart from that once, to open the box.

And now, dear Stranger, I have one more favour to ask of you. Will you please go to the safe at the back of my closet. The combination is in my sketchbook, worked into the drawing on the last page. Inside the safe you will find a little envelope. The contents are self-explanatory and the rest will soon become crystal clear.

Good luck and thank you.

Yours,

Charlotte.

PS I can't tell you (obviously) how much I hope you never get to read this, my dear Stranger.

* * *

Lucie felt like she'd been hit by a runaway train. What the hell was this? And what should she do about it? Who was this guy? And if he and Charlotte were lovers, why hadn't he come looking for her? Lucie remembered the arrangement Charlotte had made to meet her lover/business partner at the bank. Of course, he must have died in the North Tower, along with all the colleagues they'd planned to save.

Lucie scurried to Charlotte's closet. If it had a safe, Charlotte had it well hidden. The only way to find it would be to move or remove every item of clothing, every bag and every shoebox. That would take hours.

What Lucie needed to do right now was get ready to go meet Rick, enjoy the company of another human being. Living alone could drive you mad. If she wasn't careful she might end up as deranged as Charlotte.

She'd tell Rick about this over dinner. He was a man of the world. He would know what to do.

Lucie closed the file, removed the memory card and shut down the laptop. Then, not sure why she was hiding it, other than the fact that Charlotte had gone to great lengths to do the same, she put the little gadget back where she'd found it, in the shoebox.

CHAPTER 53

The longer it took for her to arrive, the more irritated he felt. He was unused to being kept waiting, plus it had been difficult to get away tonight. Diane had seemed suspicious, probably because the pattern of his days had changed so drastically since the eleventh. Instead of heading off early each morning to beat the traffic and get into WTC by seven o'clock, he was sleeping later than usual then having a leisurely breakfast before dealing with important calls and doing some paperwork in his study. He imagined this would be what it felt like to be retired, not that he ever intended to retire. He agreed with whoever first observed that golf was a good walk spoiled and as for tennis, well, he couldn't see the point. Any activity that involved hitting or kicking a ball seemed like the very definition of time wasted. He wouldn't be seen dead with a putter or a tennis racket but he would die with the *Financial Times* in his hand. That was what his associates said of him. And they weren't wrong.

A life without business deals would be no life at all. He loved the cut and thrust of business. That was his sport, and, played well, it could be as bloodthirsty as bullfighting.

Diane rarely asked where he was going or questioned his reasons for leaving her alone, but tonight she had been unusually demanding. The events of 9/11 had unsettled his wife. Like many of their friends, she felt that the security they'd always taken for granted had been undermined. The wealthy probably felt more threatened than the poor. He knew from childhood experience that poor folks didn't have time to worry about threats to national security. Too busy worrying where their next meal was coming from. Or in the case of his momma, her next drink.

He had managed to erase most of the memories from the early part of his life and he had no idea why he was revisiting that terrible time tonight. For most kids the memory of being taken into an orphanage would be a traumatic event that left them damaged for life, but for him it had been a turning point. He'd been properly cared for, clothed, well-fed, and, for the first time in his young life, he'd been happy and contented. But even so, when the Millburns adopted him he'd felt like the luckiest kid alive. As well as a mom and dad he had acquired a big brother, one who doted on him and promised to always protect him. Having a family had given him the chance to make something of himself and he had risen to the challenge.

As a successful young entrepreneur he'd met Diane's father through a business deal. Diane had been lined up to marry a young man who'd been her 'beau' almost since childhood, until she had fallen victim to the charm offensive of her father's youngest business partner.

He looked at his watch for about the twentieth time, it seemed, and had decided to give up and go home to his wife when the maître d' appeared at his table with his date in tow. The head waiter seated her and bowed obsequiously before snapping his fingers to summon the sommelier.

'I am so sorry,' said Mystery Girl, and puffed out her very pink cheeks. 'I was running late and then I couldn't get a cab.'

She was sweet and apologetic, making it difficult to feel angry with her, and those rose petal cheeks were so appealing he wanted to lean over the table and kiss her face.

'Don't worry. You're here now.' He turned to the waiter. 'Champagne, please. My usual.'

'They know you in here?'

'I often have clients here for business lunches.'

She leaned forward and rested her chin on her upturned palm. 'You never did tell me exactly what it is you do.'

He fought back the desire to boast and impress her. The less she knew about him the better. 'I'm in finance.'

'Have you thought any more about that job you said you might have for me?'

He winked at her and said, 'Leave it with me.'

The champagne arrived and made it easy to change the subject. They clinked glasses and toasted 'the future'. That was vague enough to be appropriate while subliminally suggesting a continuation of their relationship. 'Charlotte' repeated the toast with enthusiasm and drank most of the glass in one go. She replaced the slim-stemmed flute on the table and giggled apologetically.

'Oops, bit thirsty after my rush to get here. Sorry.'

He raised his hand mere inches and a waiter appeared to refill her glass.

'Don't give it a second thought. I'm delighted to see you like champagne. It's not to everyone's taste.'

'I love it. I'd forgotten how much. But I'd better warn you, the bubbles make me a bit silly sometimes.'

'That sounds like fun.'

It also sounded like a godsend. He'd been racking his brains trying to work out how he could find a solution to the Charlotte problem before too much more time passed. He had to find out what this young woman was doing in Charlotte's apartment before the situation got any trickier. Diane was in danger of suspecting him of having an affair and he was in danger of proving her right. Maybe it was the girl's resemblance to Charlotte that turned him on or maybe it was the fact that she was like a new, improved version of Charlotte – younger, softer, fresher, and a good deal more naïve. Had it not been for the fact that he was playing the part of grieving widower, he'd have made a move on her long before now. The only woman he'd ever wasted this much champagne on in the past was Charlotte and that had turned out to be a good investment. Or at least it would, if the NYSE ever opened again.

It was worth the cost of the bubbly to sit across a table from her. She was so enchanting that he sometimes forgot the whole reason for his involvement with her. In his heart of hearts he was still hoping to discover that this was all a mistake. Maybe there were two Charlotte Gillespies living in that apartment block who happened to look very similar. Perhaps he was getting soft in his old age, but it would be nice to find out that this young woman had no connection to Charlotte whatsoever. Then he could keep her on to fill the vacancy of mistress.

Her glass was soon ready for another refill. 'The flutes in here are very small,' he reassured her, while putting his hand over the top of his own glass to show the waiter he had enough.

'But you're not drinking,' she said with a moue of disapproval that made him want to kiss her there and then.

'Keeping a clear head. Busy day tomorrow.'

The champagne worked its magic and she became not silly, but witty and beguiling, if a little on edge. It was a pity the bubbles hadn't loosened her tongue, but the night was still young. He continued to ply her with questions over dinner, but her answers seemed guarded. He was sure she was hiding something.

When they were offered dessert she said, 'Oops, I'm far too tiddly for pudding,' and giggled into her hand. When he asked for the bill and suggested he take her home, she seemed more grateful than wary.

During the short cab ride, she rested her head on his shoulder. She smelt divine, her perfume the same bewitching fragrance as Charlotte used to wear. He inhaled deeply and felt more aroused than he had since his last night with Charlotte. This girl's vulnerability made her even more difficult to resist. He turned his face to her hair and breathed deeply, enjoying the silky softness against his cheek.

When the cab stopped at her apartment building, he woke her gently. 'Time for bed, I think,' he whispered. When she snuggled even closer, he took it as a sign and helped her out on to the sidewalk. The glass doors to the building slid open and a young doorman stepped from behind a huge marble desk.

'Good evening, Ms Gillespie,' he said, and managed to imbue the simple greeting with a whole lot more. He appeared to be asking if she was okay about this man he'd never seen before going up with her. 'Have you had a pleasant evening?'

She seemed to sober up instantly and said in a very dignified voice, 'Hello, Rob. I'm having a lovely evening, thank you. Off duty soon?'

'Another hour.'

'Well, goodnight then.' She gave the doorman a little wave as they made their way to one of the elevators.

He was in.

Although he'd never seen Charlotte's apartment, it was somehow just as he'd imagined. Or perhaps she'd once described the view from the wonderful floor to ceiling windows. By night the view was a myriad of lights, some bright like beacons, others twinkling like stars in a distant galaxy. He stood respectfully, waiting to see if he was expected to stay.

'Shit down, Rick.' Realising what she'd said, she collapsed onto the sofa in a giggling fit and covered her face with her hands. 'Oh sorry,' she said, making an obvious effort to enunciate. 'Please, take off your jacket. Can I get you something to drink?'

She seemed to be concentrating very hard on each word. He hoped she hadn't sobered up too soon. He needed her compliant. 'I'll join you in a glass of wine if you like, thank you.'

'Shertainly, shir,' she replied, followed by another fit of hysterics. When her laughter petered out, she lay there, eyes closed. He wasn't sure whether or not she was asleep – it was hard to tell. He decided to try an experiment.

'Lucie,' he said in a gentle, sing-song voice.

She opened her eyes immediately and smiled at him. 'Yes?' she said, innocent as a toddler.

'Time for bed, Lucie.'

She didn't argue, either with the name or with the suggestion. 'Lucie's sleepy,' he said, like a parent to a tired child.

'Lucie's sleepy,' she agreed.

Perfect. Guessing which door was the bedroom, he led her through. She leaned on his arm, trusting, willing and very vulnerable.

He sat her on the bed and knelt to slip off her shoes. How women walked in these things he'd never know. He stood to unzip her dress and help her out of it. She reached for him and he pulled her into an embrace, holding her upright with one arm, while he hauled back the comforter. Gently, he lowered her onto the bed and, with the greatest effort he'd ever made to resist temptation, covered her up.

She stirred a little. 'Thank you for looking after me,' she said, melting his heart.

He kissed her forehead. 'You're welcome, Lucie.'

Her eyes opened wide and he saw fear in them.

'No, I'm Charlotte,' she said. 'Charlotte's my name.'

'I know, you told me. Lucie Charlotte.' Her startled reaction told him he was on to something. Her real name was Lucie.

'Night, night, Charlotte. Sweet dreams. I'll stay right here by your side.'

When her breathing had settled into a rhythm he walked into the closet and started flicking through the clothes. He recognised several outfits. This was definitely Charlotte's apartment. There was no doubt about it. As if further proof were needed, the next item he touched was a white shirt. Out of curiosity, he counted the buttons. One missing. Charlotte hadn't been lying when she said she didn't sew on buttons.

Who the hell was the girl in the bed, and, more importantly, how much did she know about Charlotte? And him?

As quietly as he could, he searched the apartment, cringing when doors creaked open or drawers banged shut. He found the laptop on a bookshelf in the lounge. He knew Charlotte never left her laptop out of its bag, she had a thing about it, so the girl in the bed must have been snooping. With his heart lodged somewhere in his throat, he opened the lid and hit the on switch. As expected, it was password protected. He'd hoped to have a quick look to see what kind of websites had been browsed since 9/11. You could tell a lot about a person from a quick check of their browsing history. He'd had a purge in one of his offices where he felt the workers were spending too much time online and not enough time working. It was astonishing what people will access, especially from their workplace. The exercise had not only increased productivity, it had earned two men a termination of their contract.

This, however, was a waste of time without a password. A thought occurred to him. It was worth a try.

He crept into the bedroom. 'Lucie Charlotte,' he whispered, until she came close enough to the surface to be responsive. 'Can you remember the password?'

'What?' she said groggily.

'The password?'

'No passwords.'

He was leaving the room when she started to mutter.

'I know a password.'

He listened carefully as she reeled off a string of random characters, but her voice was quiet and far too blurred by alcohol for him to catch them.

He hurried back to the bed and knelt at its side. Trying to keep his voice light and encouraging he said, 'What did you say, my darling? What's the password?'

He sat on the edge of the bed and waited but the girl appeared to have gone to sleep. He gave her shoulder a gentle shake, but she seemed to be out of it. So drunk she was almost unconscious. He'd get nothing more from her tonight. He might as well head home and surprise Diane by getting back early.

He leaned over to give Lucie Charlotte's cheek an affectionate kiss. She looked so innocent lying there. 'Goodnight, Princess,' he whispered.

As if a deeply buried memory had been stirred, she murmured in a little girl voice, 'Daddy calls me Princess.'

'Princess Charlotte?'

'No, silly, Princess Lucie.' She sounded like a child, impatient with a stupid grown-up. 'I've got a secret.'

Now this could be interesting. 'Have you, Princess? What sort of a secret?'

'A secret letter.'

'Really?' he asked indulgently. 'And who's your secret letter from? A fairy? Or another princess?'

'It's from Charlotte.'

He felt like he'd been sprayed with dry ice. The hairs on the back of his neck were standing up like hackles.

'Where is this secret letter, Princess?'

'Not telling,' she sang, ''cos it's a secret.'

Her voice faded away to nothing. He shook her, desperate to know if she was asleep or awake. She was impossible to rouse, deeply asleep. He gave his head a shake, trying to clear it and make sense of what he'd heard. Surely it had no meaning. Surely he was reading something into nothing.

He couldn't take the risk.

Grabbing the comforter in two hands he raised it towards her face. 'Sorry, Princess,' he whispered, 'I think your fairy tale might be over.'

CHAPTER 54

Lucie woke uncomfortable. She was wrapped, almost smothered in a blanket or comforter. Too tightly. Her arms were trapped by her sides, like a swaddled baby. Or a shrouded corpse.

She opened her eyes but her head hurt far too much and she closed them again. She became aware of sound and listened. She could hear breathing. That was wrong. She should be sleeping alone.

Had her taste of freedom been nothing more than a drunken dream? Had there been no fight after all, no escape, no suffocating cloud of dust? No Charlotte, no dying Mum, no deaths? Would she turn over and see Curtis, able-bodied, beside her?

'Charlotte?'

It was real.

'Charlotte, are you awake, honey?'

Oh God. Oh God. As if her life wasn't complicated enough.

'Honey?'

She rolled over.

'Open your eyes.'

'I'm afraid.'

'What are you afraid of?'

'Everything. What I said last night, what I did last night. What *we* did last night.'

She felt a gentle touch on her cheek. 'There's nothing to be afraid of.'

He was lying on the bed. Not in the bed, on top of it. And he was fully clothed. Well, not fully clothed. He'd lost his jacket and tie. Did he take them off in the bedroom or before? She had no idea. Was he even wearing a tie last night? She couldn't remember.

She was clothed too, minus the LBD. Again, no recollection of having removed her dress. This was bad.

'Rick?'

'Yes, my darling?'

'How much did I have to drink last night?'

'I'm far too much of a gentleman to answer that.'

She remembered a second bottle of champagne coming to the table, only because of the mental arithmetic she did about the cost. And how long she and Curtis could have lived off the same amount.

'Did we empty the second bottle of Dom Pérignon?'

He laughed, as if she'd said just the cutest thing he'd ever heard. 'You don't remember?'

She groaned. 'No, I don't remember. It's been a while since I had anything stronger than a beer. I guess it went straight to my head. I'm so sorry.'

The gentle fingers were back. This time stroking her forehead. She closed her eyes.

'Headache, huh?'

'Mother of them all.'

'It happens.'

'Please tell me I didn't embarrass you.'

'How could you ever embarrass me?'

'God, I don't know. By doing something crazy or saying something awful.'

'You really don't remember *anything*?'

'Nothing after dessert, which I don't think I ate. See, there you go! There's one embarrassment right away.'

'So you've forgotten our first real date?'

His voice sounded so sad. 'Including the tender, beautiful way we made love?'

Her eyes shot wide open. 'Oh God. We didn't, did we?'

'Would that really be so terrible, if we did?'

She looked at his kind face, felt his soothing fingertips on her brow and realised she felt safe. She could see a future. Maybe the hell of the last few years was meant to be. So she could come out the other side ready to appreciate a good man.

'Would it, Charlotte?'

The room swirled like a slow-moving carousel. Last night was coming back to her. That bizarre letter from Charlotte was hiding right there in the closet.

Lucie put her hands over her face, and pressed on her eyelids. Sequins of light sparkled in her head and her stomach roiled.

'Darling? I didn't mean to upset you.'

'You didn't upset me. I just remembered something.'

'Something you want to talk about?'

Should she tell him about Charlotte's crazy missive? She'd intended to talk to him last night over dinner and ask his advice, but the evening was going so well and she didn't want to spoil it. More importantly, she didn't want to explain that *she* wasn't Charlotte. Before she knew it, she'd got too drunk to talk about anything.

It was all too complicated to think about right now with her head hurting and her stomach threatening to rebel. 'Maybe later,' she said.

'Sure. Listen, I owe you an apology. I was teasing you about last night. Nothing happened.'

'If you say so.'

'You really don't remember?'

'Not a thing.'

He smiled at her, but the look on his face was wrong somehow. He looked relieved.

Why relief? Had something happened after all? Something he was glad she'd forgotten?

'I didn't lay a finger on you, I promise,' he murmured. 'I wouldn't, ever. Unless you wanted me to.'

Lucie's mouth filled with saliva and she swallowed quickly. Breathing hard, in and out, in and out, she tried to control a panic that she didn't understand.

She threw back the covers and sprinted for the bathroom. Like a baseball player skidding onto last base, she slid on her knees to the toilet bowl. She spewed up last night's dinner, gagging on bile and self-loathing.

Fate had thrown her a lifeline. With a gorgeous, caring man anchoring the other end, willing to haul her to a better life. And she had to go and ruin everything by getting drunk. She was as big a loser as her husband. They were well matched.

When there was nothing left in her stomach, she got to her feet and washed her face. As she opened the bathroom cabinet, trying to avoid her reflection, Rick's voice startled her.

'Are these what you're looking for?'

He was standing in the doorway holding out some pills and a glass of water. She noticed he had put on his jacket and tie. He looked suave as Bond and just as out of place in the foul-smelling bathroom. 'Can we get out of here, please?' she said, mortified.

In the kitchen she swallowed both pills with a sip of water.

'You need to drink more than that,' he said, slipping a robe around her shoulders. Was there no end to his thoughtfulness?

'Why don't I refill that glass then maybe I could make you a cup of coffee?'

She clasped her hand over her mouth. 'No coffee,' she muttered through her fingers.

He laughed. 'I guess not. Maybe later. What you need right now is to get back to bed and sleep this off.'

She nodded. No suggestion had ever made better sense. She drank a second glass of water, enjoying its cool, clean taste and the way it soothed her raw throat.

He opened his arms, offering a hug she couldn't resist. As she leaned into him, she looked up and whispered, 'Sorry.'

He leaned down and kissed her forehead. She was glad he hadn't gone for her rank mouth. She wished she'd had time to brush her teeth or at least swill some mouthwash around. The thought of Listerine made her gag and she stepped away from him.

'Everything okay?' he said.

'It will be when I've sobered up and regained some composure. If that's possible. I am *so* sorry.'

His smile was like a benediction and she relaxed. She'd been given another chance.

She took his hands in hers, as if they were about to exchange vows at an altar. 'You know you said you wouldn't, unless I wanted you to?'

He nodded, solemn.

'Are you sure you're ready?' she asked.

He looked puzzled.

'What do you mean, ready?'

'I mean, sorry to be tactless, won't it feel a bit like cheating on your wife?'

He heaved a sigh, as if he'd just realised what she meant.

'I didn't think I'd ever be ready to replace my wife,' he said sadly, 'but then I didn't think I'd ever meet someone as fabulous as Charlotte Gillespie.'

'Yeah,' she said, drawing the word out to give her time to think. 'Let's talk about that before we take this relationship to the next level.'

'Talk about what?'

'Em, there are a few things you don't know about me.'

'Well, of course, that's what makes you fascinating. Want to tell me?' He poured her another glass of water and sat down on the sofa.

She tightened the belt of the robe and sat beside him, curling her bare feet underneath her so she could turn and face him. It was time to be honest.

His phone jangled, breaking the confessional atmosphere. Lucie's aching head throbbed at the sound and she covered her ears.

'Sorry, I've got to take this,' he said, rising. He moved away from her to stand staring out at the city while he listened to the voice at the other end. A woman's, judging by the pitch. Lucie listened but couldn't make out individual words. She thought the woman sounded angry. Was this the 'dead' wife? Surely not. Rick was too nice, too caring, too genuine. Too bereaved.

'You're right,' he said quietly, his tone appeasing. 'I apologise. Start without me, please. I'll be right there.'

He flipped his phone shut and put it in his pocket. 'I'm sorry, I have to go.'

'Who was that?' Lucie asked, wishing she didn't feel, or sound, so suspicious.

'My PA. I've missed an important breakfast meeting.'

'That's my fault. No wonder she sounds annoyed.'

'You could hear her?'

'Not her words, but I could tell she was angry, yes.'

He grimaced. 'She can be a bit domineering at times. But she and I go back a long way. We're like an old married couple. She puts up with me and I let her off with a lot because she's the best PA in the city.'

He sat down beside her. 'What was it you wanted to tell me?'

Lucie shook her aching head then flapped her hand instead. 'Oh, it's not important. Anyway, you'd better scoot. Or she'll have your blood, by the sound of things.'

'Correct. But listen, you and I have unfinished business. How about dinner?'

'Tonight?' She shook her head once then groaned and placed her hands on her temples.

'You have plans?' He looked frustrated, or maybe just terribly disappointed.

'I plan to sleep off this hangover. Then try to undo the damage I've done to my system. No fine dining for me this evening, but thank you.' She hoped he wouldn't think she was giving him the bum's rush. 'Could you maybe give me a couple of days?' she asked.

To her relief he said, 'Sure. Same place?'

'Where I made a complete fool of myself last night? Mmm, maybe not such a good idea.'

He laughed. 'You didn't make a fool of yourself, but we can go somewhere else if you prefer.'

They made arrangements to meet at the weekend and he kissed her, on the lips this time.

'See you soon,' he said. 'I look forward to hearing all your secrets.'

Lucie closed the door behind him. She made it to the bathroom just in time.

CHAPTER 55

The bedroom was filled with the russet glow of sunset before Lucie felt brave enough to face the day, or what was left of it. She rose and watched from the window as light after light came on against the darkening sky. The city was like a grand lady dressing for the evening in sparkling jewels.

A deep rumble from Lucie's stomach reminded her that she'd lost most of last night's dinner. She cringed at the memory. How could she let herself down so badly? Getting blind drunk on a date. Even at high school she knew better than that.

She stayed under the shower till she felt cleansed of the previous night's mistakes and then dressed in the baggiest, slouchiest garments she could find. Nothing in the refrigerator was tempting, other than the makings of a sandwich. She grabbed the near-full bottle of wine from the fridge door and with a vow of 'Never again,' sloshed it into the sink. She poured a glass of fresh orange juice and downed it in one.

Sandwich in hand, Lucie headed for the closet and retrieved the memory card she'd hidden last night. She was intrigued. Why would a grown woman write such a thing? She had to have another look.

Password. She shivered, as if a cold finger had touched the back of her neck.

Lucie's alcohol-fuelled dreams had been a crazy collage. Of being trapped in high towers. Of her legs tangling in silky ribbons as she tried to run. Of secret messages she couldn't decipher and passwords she couldn't recall.

She inserted the SD card into Charlotte's laptop.

The letter was there.

A quick skim was enough to satisfy her that she hadn't dreamt the whole thing.

The proof would be if there was anything in the safe that matched Charlotte's description of 'a little envelope'.

First she had to find the safe, and the combination of numbers that would allow her to open it. Lucie looked for the second time at the number of possessions in Charlotte's closet and her heart sank. Her hangover was wearing off but the last thing she felt like doing was moving a whole bunch of hangers and boxes in the search for Charlotte's safe.

She flopped on to the bed and lay staring at the ceiling. She imagined Charlotte lying there, thinking about the deal she'd made with her lover that he'd promised would seal their future together. Charlotte tossing and turning. Battling with her conscience. Then the Damascene moment that made her decide to put the safety of her employees before her own happiness.

What did Charlotte and her lover know in advance of 9/11? What could they know?

Lucie had to find out.

She found the safe hidden behind stacks of shoeboxes at the back of the closet.

The code was easy now she knew where to find the four numbers. She keyed them in. The door released and swung open as if on a spring. Lucie could see nothing. She put her hand in and felt around. The safe was empty. Someone must have got here before her. The Kleer n Kleen guys, maybe? Was that why they were here? Did Charlotte's accomplice send them in? Lucie shivered at the thought of those strangers in here going though Charlotte's belongings. What had she got herself into?

She lay on her stomach and reached inside, running her fingers over every surface. Just to make sure. Her fingernail caught on some Scotch tape and she peeled it off. A small envelope dropped onto the floor of the safe.

Lucie grabbed it, rolled onto her back, and tore open the envelope. When she sat up a little silver key fell into her lap. It was unlike any key Lucie had seen before. The shaft was cut on each side in a complicated pattern. The top was engraved with a number and had a hole for a chain to go through, or a ribbon. This must be the key Charlotte had worn round her neck. The key she said she never took off. So what was it doing here?

Lucie turned it over and over in her hand. She had no idea what she was supposed to do with it. She checked the envelope and found a small card, embossed with the name Danisticus Financial and a downtown address. It was printed, in upmarket gold ink, with Charlotte's name and a number that matched the key.

Charlotte had said the contents of the envelope were self-explanatory and that the rest would make sense.

It looked like Lucie was meant to take this key to the bank named on the card. She didn't know whether to be excited or terrified. She wished she had someone to turn to. Someone who'd go with her to open this box. Someone who'd know what to do with whatever she found inside.

The stress was too much for Lucie's stomach. The sandwich decided to reverse its journey through her digestive tract. This time she made it to the bathroom with a split second to spare.

When she had recovered enough to speak, she reached for the phone.

CHAPTER 56

Curtis was sitting in a flash-looking wheelchair.

'How do you like my new wheels?' he asked, when Dylan was barely through the door. 'Specially adapted for agility and ease of movement in a restricted environment.'

'You quoting the sales blurb?'

'Indeed I am. And it's all thanks to that *mystery benefactor* I told you about.'

'You find out any more?'

'Not a thing. Thought at first it had to be a hoax. Some kind of sick prank. But Carol-Anne banked the cheque for me and it cleared. One hundred thousand dollars. Kerr-ching!'

'Was there no name on the letter?'

'Duh! Wouldn't be a mystery benefactor if I knew the name, would it?'

'Was there no clue to who sent it?'

'Three initials at the bottom of the note. SSM. That was it.'

'Nothing else? No name on the cheque? A signature?'

'Dunno. Who cares? I can ask Carol-Anne if you're that interested.'

'Nah, doesn't matter. I'm pleased for you. You're looking good, by the way.'

Curtis did look good – fit and toned, his arms strong and muscled, putting Dylan in mind of one of those amazing wheelchair warriors you saw charging through the streets on Marathon day.

Something else had changed, harder to identify than the improvements to his physique. Dylan listened to him talk about his plans to go back to school. He seemed determined to make something of himself, despite his situation. He sounded serious about grabbing this second chance he'd been given.

'So, buddy, there you have it. Curtis Jardine's life plan. Version two. I may only be half the man physically, but believe me, I plan on being twice the man I was before the accident.'

Dylan noticed how Curtis now referred to the reason for his paralysis as an accident. He seemed to accept it as the hand he'd been dealt, however unfairly.

As if he'd been reading Dylan's thoughts, Curtis began to recite.

'Life handed him a lemon,
As Life sometimes will do.
His friends looked on in pity,
Assuming he was through.
They came upon him later,
Reclining in the shade
In calm contentment, drinking
A glass of lemonade.'

Dylan noted the quiet enthusiasm in his friend's voice. 'Did you write that?' he asked.

'Hell, no. It was on a poster in one of the rooms at the rehab centre. I had plenty of chance to look at it and think about what it meant. One day I realised I'd learned it off by heart, without even trying. Good, eh?'

Dylan wasn't sure if his friend meant the poem or his recitation of it. Didn't matter really. The answer was the same. 'Great.'

'Well, I plan not only to drink lemonade, or even open a lemonade stand. I plan to run a chain of lemonade stands.'

As they laughed like old times, Dylan was glad he'd not given up on Curtis.

'Curtis, it's good to see you positive about the future.'

'Thanks, buddy. You know, crazy as this sounds, I feel like I've got something to look forward to.' He patted his thighs. 'Even with these useless mothers.' His wide, optimistic smile faded. 'You know what, Dylan? One of the things I've learned?

We can't turn back the clock and if you think like that, you'll end up crazy.'

He touched the tip of his finger to the corner of his eye, as if he'd got some dust in it. 'Man,' he said, 'I can't tell you how much I wish Lucie didn't have to die that day. She'd have left me, anyway. I know that. Who could blame her, after the way I treated her? But what I'd give to see her walk through that door right now.'

If Dylan came clean about Lucie, he could lighten Curtis's burden, but his loyalty to Lucie was too strong.

'Wanna know the best thing to come out of all this?' asked Curtis.

Dylan shrugged.

'Meeting Carol-Anne when I was in hospital.'

'She good?'

'She's amazing. Looks after me better than I ever looked after myself. And you know what's really great about her?'

'Apart from the fact she's young, cute and blonde?'

'None of that matters, man. What matters is that she's always there for me, good days and bad. And don't get me wrong, I still have plenty bad days too, but it seems like she cares. Lucie didn't care.'

'How can you say that? Lucie worshipped the ground you walked on.'

'Yeah, maybe at first, but not at the end.'

'And whose fault was that?'

Curtis hung his head. Dylan didn't enjoy seeing him look guilty and embarrassed, but he couldn't let his friend rewrite history and learn nothing from the past. 'You gonna control that temper of yours with Carol-Anne?'

'Sure. Been working on the temper thing.'

'Man, it's about time.'

'Listen, Dylan, nobody knows better than me what an asshole I've been all my life. I'm sorry for the way I treated Lucie. And you.'

'She deserved better.'

'You both did. Seriously, I'm very sorry. I wish Lucie were alive today, so I could tell her. But that's never gonna happen. Like I said, you can't turn back time.'

How would Curtis react if Dylan told him it *could* happen?

'Maybe it was Lucie's destiny all along, to die that day. I'll tell you, she did me a big favour dying where she did.'

'How come?'

'I could have as much as half a million dollars coming to me from the 9/11 victim compensation fund that's been set up. I'll never need to worry about money.'

'But I thought you already got enough money to set you up? From the mystery man? You've got a nice place here, you can afford to go to school and pay Carol-Anne to help you.'

'Sure. That rich bastard, whoever he is, helped me out some. And I'm grateful.'

'Then why would you take money from a 9/11 victim compensation fund?'

Curtis looked at him as if he'd gone crazy. 'You're kidding me, right?'

'You're not a victim.'

Curtis flushed, his cheeks turning bright. The warning sign was all too familiar to Dylan. 'I don't look like a victim to you? Of course I'm a fuckin' victim.'

'And what about Lucie?'

'What about Lucie? Lucie's dead, man. You told me so yourself. She died on 9/11. That makes me eligible for compensation.'

Dylan heard a door open behind him. A gentle voice said, 'Everything okay in here?'

Curtis growled, 'Yeah.'

'Need me to do anything?'

Curtis breathed in deeply and exhaled slowly, his mouth puffing out like a blowfish. When he'd completed three of the long breaths, he said calmly, 'Thanks, Carol-Anne, but I'm fine. We're fine.' He looked at Dylan, a challenge in his eyes, and said, 'We fine, buddy?'

'Sure,' said Dylan, and turned to look at Carol-Anne. For such a young, slight person, she seemed to exude a confidence that was reassuring. She beamed a broad smile, whether for Dylan or for Curtis, it was hard to tell.

The door closed quietly again and the two of them were left alone. Dylan didn't know what to say next.

'You trying to say I shouldn't take that money?' demanded Curtis, his voice quieter but still full of aggression.

Dylan considered his next words carefully. Curtis may have learned to manage his anger, but it was hard for Dylan to break a lifetime's habit of diplomacy.

'I guess I'm wondering if there might be folks out there who need the money more than you do. Maybe I'm wrong, but I thought that cheque you got was enough.'

'How much is enough?'

'I don't know, Curtis.'

'No, that's right, man. You don't know. You have no idea what it's like to know you'll never walk again. So don't you dare walk in here with your perfect legs and tell me I'm not a fuckin' victim!'

Against his better judgement, Dylan persisted, although he wasn't sure why. 'That's not how it works, Curtis. The fund's not there to compensate you for your injuries. That's not what it's for. The 9/11 fund is supposed to compensate the bereaved, to make up for the loss of their loved ones.'

'I lost a loved one!'

'You lost a wife that you beat senseless. You're the reason she was in Manhattan that morning.'

Curtis stared at him. He was nothing, if not smart. 'Hell you know all this?'

Had he said too much? Blown Lucie's secret after all these weeks?

He'd learned from his friend how effective it can be to go on the attack when your instinct is to be defensive. He took a step towards Curtis and loomed over him.

'You really think no one knew what was going on? Sure, Lucie did her best to cover up the bruises or hide them under her clothes. But who wears long sleeves when it's eighty degrees outside? You've been beating up on her for years. I should have done something about it long ago.'

Despite the wheelchair, Curtis did not look cowed. He stuck his face defiantly upwards and said, 'Yeah, but you didn't, did you, Dylan? Too much of a pussy. Same old, same old.'

Dylan stepped back, defeated and deflated. He wasn't here to fight with this man he'd known for twenty-five years. 'Lucie went to Manhattan to look for a job. She was trying to find a way out.'

'Out of what?'

'Her life.'

'Hell was wrong with her life?'

'Oh, come on, Curtis! Not five minutes ago, you said, "She'd have left me. Who could blame her," you said, "after the way I treated her." You treated her no better than a slave.'

'Yeah?'

'Yeah.'

'Well, she's free now. Free at last, and I'm gonna take the money. Money I'm entitled to because, on September eleventh, thanks to those terrorists, my wife died.'

'You can't do that.'

'Watch me, buddy.'

'But Lucie's ...' Dylan's brain caught the traitorous words before they could tumble disloyally out of his mouth.

Curtis was on it like a snake. 'Lucie's what, Dylan?'

Dylan's phone rang, startling both of them.

Curtis recovered first. 'Gonna get that?' he demanded.

Dylan patted himself down like a self-frisking cop. He fished his phone out of his back pocket just as the ringtone stopped jangling. In the silence he checked the little screen then switched the phone off. He'd call her later. This was more important.

'Don't take the money, Curtis, It's wrong.'

'No, *you're* wrong, man. That money's mine, by rights, and I'm gonna make sure I get every penny that's due me. Might even screw a bit more than I'm due, if I play the poor crippled widower.' Curtis laughed like a cartoon villain. He sounded so convincing Dylan wasn't sure how much of it was an act.

'You haven't changed at all, have you, Curtis?'

'Oh, I've changed all right. Got shit for legs, but that's not the only change. I'm never gonna be poor again and if there's money in any fund I can get my hands on, then I'm sure as hell taking it. You got a problem with that?'

Dylan looked his friend in the eye and nodded. 'I've got a problem with you, Curtis. Full stop.'

CHAPTER 57

Lucie woke a hundred times in the night. Each time she hoped it was morning and when the alarm dashed her hopes, she flopped back down onto her pillow and squeezed her eyes shut. She felt like a child on Christmas Eve, willing the hours to pass until she could rise and find out what surprises the day had in store.

She was meant to fly home tonight. She had a ticket booked in the name of Charlotte Gillespie. She'd booked a return so it looked like a short business trip. No need for lots of luggage. She'd also booked business class. Might as well live it up, while she had the chance. And she had planned on using Charlotte Gillespie's passport. No one would challenge her. Passport photos were often notoriously bad likenesses.

Now she didn't know what to do.

Foreboding squirmed like a snake in her gut. She recognised the dark apprehension from her life with Curtis and those awful days that followed their last fight. She remembered the same tense, nauseous feeling as she crept about this apartment, convinced someone would appear and blow her cover. The horror she'd felt each time a door banged or the elevator stopped on her floor.

Finally she rose, made herself a coffee and sat to watch the city come to life. It crossed her mind that whatever she found today might mean she couldn't fly out tonight. Part of her was hoping that might be the case. In a way she'd be sorry to end to this make-believe life she'd been living.

It was silly to think she could she keep up the pretence of being Charlotte Gillespie. Equally silly to allow herself to dream of a future with Rick. A future where he knew everything there was to know about her and still loved and wanted her. She had fantasised about taking the place of his wife, imagined sliding seamlessly from this life into a new one. Forgetting her vow to never become dependent on another man as long as she lived.

Lucie showered in Jo Malone lather and let the zesty scent of lime and mandarin push her worries to the back of her mind. She dressed in one of Charlotte's business suits and tried the Jimmy Choos, for luck. She tucked the little card and key in the inside pocket of her purse and with a wistful look at the apartment, she closed the door behind her.

'Morning, Ms Gillespie,' said Rob, as she approached his desk. 'Something I can do for you?'

'Yes, please Rob. Could you call me a cab?'

Now the time had come, Lucie's nerves were getting the better of her. In the cab she held her hands out and watched them tremble. She dropped them into her lap and tried to still one with the other. She had no idea what was waiting for her at the bank, but feared it wouldn't be good. The actual process of accessing Charlotte's safe deposit box was freaking her out too. What if someone at the bank knew Charlotte and recognised Lucie as an impostor?

She needn't have worried. She handed over her little card, showed her key and was escorted in an elevator that seemed to plummet to the centre of the earth. She fought her instinct to flee from the vault and run back up to daylight. Serge, the young man who was accompanying her, unlocked and led her through two doors, which he then re-locked behind them. Lucie tried not to think about fire escapes. Serge ushered her into a chamber that looked nothing like any room she'd ever seen before. Every wall was covered, floor to ceiling, with numbered metal doors. Some were shallow as a letter box and others were the size of gym lockers.

Serge seemed to know exactly where to find Charlotte's box. He checked the number on the door, made sure it matched the little card and handed it back to Lucie.

'Your key please?' he said, his voice echoing slightly.

Lucie handed over the key and Serge inserted it, and one of his own, into twin locks. He turned both simultaneously. The door opened and he handed Lucie her key before removing a grey oblong box with a black lid.

'Would you like to use a private room, ma'am?'

Lucie nodded. 'Please.'

'This way.'

At the end of the corridor he unlocked yet another door and stepped into a small, windowless room. He carefully laid the grey box on a table in the middle of the floor, saying, 'I'll be right outside. Just ring the bell when you're done.' He closed the door behind him.

The room was completely bare apart from the table and one chair. Lucie sat and tried to gather enough courage to open the box and unleash whatever evil lurked within. She was convinced nothing good would come of this. Perhaps she should just ring the bell now and leave. Granny would say this was none of her business. 'Remember what curiosity did,' she'd remind Lucie.

With a great, deep breath she released the lid and folded it back. On top of a pile of documents rested a cream vellum envelope. Someone, Charlotte presumably, had written in calligraphic handwriting, 'To be opened once you have perused the contents of the box, dear Stranger.'

Lucie dutifully laid the envelope on one side and removed from the box a sheaf of printed papers. They looked like receipts for options purchased on shares by Scott Millburn and Charlotte Gillespie. Lucie flicked through the sheets. Page upon page was dated seventh September 2001.

They'd been short selling. Millions of dollars invested in buying push options. On shares in major world airlines. A similar amount spent on call options. On shares in Munich Re and Swiss Re. The names meant little to Lucie but she knew that these 'options' were essentially bets that a company's stock was about to rise, or fall, dramatically.

She delved deeper into the paperwork and found a densely worded legal document that looked like the deeds to a house, fortunately not Charlotte's apartment. Below these lay sheet after sheet of evidence that this Scott Millburn had borrowed huge amounts of money from various sources at the end of August. Whoever the guy was, he appeared to have a lot riding on this gamble on the stock exchange. He must be pretty sure it was going to pay off.

A sobering thought occurred to her. If this Scott was the man Charlotte was due to meet in the North Tower, it was more than likely he was now dead.

Where did that leave Lucie? She'd just impersonated a dead woman and, under false pretences, had accessed the contents of a safe deposit box which appeared to contain evidence of criminal activity. Lucie had swum so far out of her depth she was drowning in deceit.

She glanced around as if there might be someone who could help her. She wished she'd brought Rick along. He would know what to do.

All that remained in the box was a manila folder. Lucie lifted it out and opened it. Charlotte smiled at her from a large glossy photo in *Avenue* magazine. Against a background showing the logo of NYSPCC, Charlotte posed for the camera with a young man. Two things struck Lucie. The first was how young, vibrant and glamorous Charlotte looked. The second was how much Lucie resembled her. No wonder people had been easily taken in.

Underneath the photograph ran a line which identified Charlotte as a guest at the Annual Fall Benefit of the children's charity. Lucie studied the photo and felt a deep sadness for the loss of Charlotte's life. She wondered if the man pictured was Charlotte's mystery lover and business partner, Scott. He was handsome. Lucie could see the attraction.

She flipped through *Avenue* looking for more photos of Charlotte. She stopped at a photo that showed a group of four people, elegant in evening dress. Charlotte and her partner stood, champagne glasses in hand, beside another couple. A beautiful woman on the arm of a tall, handsome man. Lucie recognised him immediately. It was Rick. This must be his wife. They made a strikingly good-looking couple. How sad that he'd lost her.

Charlotte Gillespie of Gillespie, Manders and Moffatt and Simon Hood of Simmonds Hamling with Mr and Mrs Scott Millburn of Langdon Associates.

That couldn't be right. It should say *Mr and Mrs Richard Armstrong.* Another photo showed a group raising slim flutes in a toast. This time Charlotte and Rick were standing together, smiling at each other instead of to camera.

A column down the side of the photo identified guests from left to right: *Jonathon Grieves with Meredith Brown, Andrew Capaldi, Genevieve Duval, Charlotte Gillespie, Scott Millburn and Jeremy Warren.*

Lucie put a finger on each face and moved it from the left, one person at a time, as she checked off the names. She read them again, this time in reverse, moving her finger from the right. She had no need to read beyond Charlotte's name. The man she knew as Rick had to be this Scott Millburn.

She felt sick and looked around desperately for a bin or some other container that could save her dignity. Nothing. She ripped a tissue from the pack in her bag and rammed it against her mouth, swallowing furiously until the wave of nausea ebbed away.

Heavy-hearted, Lucie packed all the papers into the box, keeping the magazine till last. She tore out one photograph, which she stuffed into her purse. Then she took Charlotte's envelope but, instead of opening it, she tucked it in her bag too. There would be time enough later to study both. Trying to remain composed, she closed the box and rang the bell by the door.

CHAPTER 58

Dylan had expected to arrive first, but Lucie was waiting for him at a table right at the back. She didn't wave to attract his attention. Just nodded when he noticed her.

He made to sit opposite, but she touched a chair beside her own and said, 'Can you sit here, please?'

As he sat down he caught a whiff of citrusy fragrance. It smelled expensive. She moved her chair so close to his, their thighs touched. Lucie didn't seem to notice. Or if she did, she wasn't embarrassed.

'Can I get you a coffee? Tea?' he asked, and tried to catch the waiter's attention. This place was always busy, but the tables were well enough spaced for a private conversation, or a business deal.

'Water,' said Lucie. 'Anything, thanks.'

He placed their order then leaned on the table, a little uncomfortable with the way they were sitting. 'So, Lucie,' he said, 'what can I do for you?'

She clutched at his forearm. 'Dylan, I'm scared.'

He believed her. Lucie was no drama queen.

He patted her hand, hoping to reassure, though he'd no idea what was going on. 'Curtis can't hurt you anymore.'

Her eyes were wide. She shook her head, frantic. 'It's not Curtis.'

He'd never seen her look this frightened, even that day at the house, when he'd startled her out of hiding. 'Lucie,' he said gently. 'Tell me what's going on.'

She looked around the coffee shop, like a spy in a movie. 'I'm in big trouble, Dylan,' she said, 'I don't know what to do. I need help.'

The waiter appeared and placed a steaming espresso on the table. 'One coffee. And a San Pellegrino.' He unscrewed the cap and poured. The water sparkled and fizzed in the glass. 'Enjoy.'

When he'd gone, Dylan swivelled on his seat so he was almost facing Lucie. 'Okay, deep breath and tell me all about it.' He lifted his cup and kept his eyes on her face while he sipped the boiling coffee.

She spoke so quietly he had to strain to hear her. 'I need you to go to the police about something really bad. But you can't go till I've left the country.'

'Lucie, what have you done?' He regretted the words the moment they left his lips, but she didn't seem offended.

'It's not me. Well, it is me. I mean, I've done some stuff that's illegal, but that's not the really bad thing I'm talking about.'

'Sorry, you're not making any sense. Can you slow down and go back to the beginning?'

'I don't know where to start. It's such a mess.'

'Okay. Let's take it one step at a time. Do you want to start with the really bad thing or do you want to tell me what it is you've done that's illegal?'

She hesitated.

'Before you say a single word, know this. Whatever it is you've done, I will stand by you.'

'Really?'

'You have my word on that.' He put his arm around her and gave her a quick, friendly hug then let go. 'Come on now. Let's hear it.'

'I've been lying to you. I'm not living with a friend. I'm living in a stranger's flat.'

'Nothing illegal about that, unless maybe the stranger hasn't given permission.' The look on her face told him he'd guessed right. 'Ah, the stranger doesn't know.'

Lucie shook her head. 'She's dead.'

Dylan prayed he wasn't about to hear a confession of murder. He wasn't sure he could stand by a murderer, even Lucie.

'God, Dylan. I didn't murder her, if that's what you're thinking.'

'Phew, that's a relief.' He wiped imaginary sweat from his brow and gave her a fake smile.

'I found her dead in the street. Remember I told you about losing my bag?'

'In the dust, yeah.'

'Well, I picked up Charlotte's, that's her name, by mistake. I realised I'd the wrong bag but the policeman wouldn't let me go back.'

'I remember. What did you do with it?'

'I was going to take some money. Just enough so I could get home, but it felt like stealing. I couldn't do it. So I got her address and I went to her apartment to give the bag to her family. I thought maybe they could lend me some money. I'd have paid it back. You know I would.'

Dylan nodded. 'Of course I do. What happened?'

'Remember all those people who got caught in the dust? How they looked?'

'Like snowmen.'

'You couldn't tell one person from another, right? Well, I get to the address and this doorman comes out and says, "Miss Charlotte, I'm so glad you're safe." I try to tell him I'm not Miss Charlotte, but my throat's all closed up with the dust and I can't. So he takes me inside and before I know it, I'm in this apartment and the door's shut.'

Lucie stopped and gulped at her mineral water. She choked and Dylan patted her on the back till she stopped spluttering.

'And you stayed?'

She nodded, as if afraid to try her voice.

'Go on. I'm listening.'

'No one came or phoned or anything and I waited till it was almost dark. I had nowhere to go and I was scared to leave in case I'd get stranded on the street.'

'That's fair enough.'

'I meant to leave the next morning, but by then I was too scared. You know why?'

Dylan had no idea.

'Because I was afraid I might have killed Curtis. I know this sounds awful, Dylan, but I didn't stop to check on him. I just walked out and left him unconscious. I was scared to rouse him in case he'd punish me, stop me getting to Manhattan.'

'For your interview?'

'Not just that. I was supposed to meet my mum afterwards.'

'Oh, Lucie. I'm so sorry.'

'Anyway, I've been lying to you. I knew I'd hurt Curtis. And since I'm being honest, you might as well know that I didn't care. Are you shocked?'

'Not really. I know how badly he'd been treating you. I'm only sorry I didn't do something to stop him before it ever got to that stage.'

Lucie shrugged, as if to exonerate him. 'I decided to stay in Charlotte's apartment, just till the dust settled.' She looked at him apologetically. 'Sorry, no pun ...'

'... intended. I know. How did you survive?'

'Charlotte gets all this luxury food delivered. And flowers. I was worried the delivery boys would know I wasn't Charlotte, but they didn't.'

'How come?'

'I look like her.'

'Wow! What are the chances?'

'I know. So it was easy for me to stay. It was like heaven, Dylan, after living with Curtis, scrimping and saving on food. I've been trying, for months, to get enough money to escape, and the only way I could do it, without making him suspicious, was to cut down on my food.'

'You were starving yourself?' Dylan groaned. 'Oh, Lucie, why didn't you say? I'd have given you all the money you needed. My mom would have taken you in. We'd have kept you safe.'

'But you're Curtis's friend.'

'And you think that meant you couldn't trust me?'

She didn't answer, but her eyes said everything.

'Lucie, what would you say if I told you I'd have walked away from Curtis long ago if it hadn't been for you?'

Lucie gave him a sad little smile. It was impossible to tell if she believed him.

'I had to do it myself. I've been a victim long enough. Far too long.'

'I get that. I just wish you'd have let me help.' He drained his coffee cup and concentrated a moment on the grains in the bottom, so she wouldn't see his face. 'So what happened next?'

'I was trying not to use Charlotte's money. Then, after Mum told me my dad would be glad to see me, I decided to go back to Scotland.'

'Which is why you were looking for your passport?'

'Yes.'

Dylan decided not to complicate things by telling her how long her passport had been in the pocket of his jeans.

'But then you told me Curtis had the cops watching the airports, so I lost my nerve. By then I'd started spending Charlotte's money.'

A connection sparked in his brain. 'How much of Charlotte's money?' he said.

'Em, quite a lot.'

'Like a hundred thousand dollars?'

'I felt bad about him, Dylan. I wanted to do something to help. I knew the health plan would cover hospital costs, but I couldn't send him back to that hovel. He wouldn't have coped. It wasn't fair. I loved him once.'

Dylan's heart soared at the finality of that past tense, but he couldn't condone what she'd done. 'So you paid him off with a hundred grand of someone else's money? You can't do that.'

'Why not? What difference does it make? She's dead. She's hardly going to notice. And I'll be gone before anyone finds out. Are you worried they'll take the money back off Curtis?'

'Yeah, maybe. But I'm more worried about you.'

'No one will be able to trace the money Curtis got. Don't worry, I made sure of that.'

Dylan shook his head in despair at her naivety. 'Is that the illegal stuff?'

'That's the larceny part of it. No, sorry, grand larceny. Then there's identity theft, fraud, criminal impersonation. They'll throw the book at me. Oh, and faking my own death. Let's not forget that one.'

'Okay, I get the picture. Is this the really bad stuff you were talking about?'

The terrified look was back on her face. It had relaxed while she was concentrating on her story. 'I found papers of Charlotte's. She's been involved in a scam to make money by insider trading. With a boyfriend.'

Dylan felt so relieved he actually laughed out loud. 'Lucie, that kind of stuff goes on all the time. How do you think this Charlotte person had a hundred grand lying around for you to donate?' He touched her cheek. 'You're so sweet. And I love that you're naïve. Is this the reason you want to leave the country? Because you've uncovered insider dealing?'

She started whispering, her voice an icy-cold hiss. 'Charlotte's boyfriend. He's the guy you saw me talking to in the hospital that day.'

'You know him?'

'No. That's the scary thing. And he gave me a false name.'

'You think it wasn't a coincidence, bumping into this guy.'

She shook her head.

'So, let me get this straight. You're pretending to be Charlotte? Her boyfriend spots you and follows you to the hospital? He strikes up a conversation?'

'Correct.'

'And you told him your name was Gillespie?'

Lucie nodded, looking shamefaced.

'What did he talk to you about?'

'When? That first time?'

'You saw him again?'

'I met him in the street. When I was out jogging.'

'Didn't that strike you as strange, Lucie?'

'I didn't really think about it at the time. We went for a coffee. He seemed nice, he was kind to me.'

She sounded as if she liked this guy.

'I told him my name was Charlotte.'

'And he didn't react?'

'Not so I noticed.'

'Was that the last time you saw him?'

'I've seen him a couple of times. We went out for dinner.'

Dylan felt ridiculously jealous.

'I had a bit too much to drink. He took me home.'

Dylan dreaded what was coming. He wanted to kill this nice, kind stranger.

'I didn't do anything, if that's what you're wondering.'

'And now you've found out this guy was Charlotte's boyfriend?'

'Lover. She wanted him to leave his wife.'

'Boyfriend, lover, whatever. He knows you're pretending to be his girlfriend, who hasn't been seen since 9/11, yet he doesn't mention the fact?'

Lucie didn't say a word. Just sat and stared at him as if she was thinking about this stuff for the first time. 'And now you've found out the two of them have been making shitloads of money on insider dealing? Which is highly illegal, in case you don't know.'

'I do know.'

'Not looking good, is it?'

'You haven't heard the worst part.'

'It gets worse?'

Lucie nodded.

'Come on then. Spill!'

'They knew about 9/11. Before it happened.'

Dylan scratched his head. Called the waiter and ordered more coffee. One for Lucie, without asking. He was trying to process what she'd just said, wondering if she'd been affected by her fall. He didn't want to dismiss what she was saying, but it was so fantastic, he was worried about her state of mind.

'Lucie, do you realise the implications of what you're saying?'

'Yes, I do. Which is why you need to go to the police.'

'Hold on a minute. *I* need to go to the police?' He could imagine the reaction if he turned up at the local cop shop with this story.

'Yes, I've thought about this. I'll tell you where to find the proof then you can take it from there.'

'Why me?'

She looked at him as if he was the one who'd lost his mind. She rose from the table and reached for the suitcase she'd stowed behind her chair. 'Because I've got a plane to catch. Or at least Charlotte has.'

CHAPTER 59

He'd been surprised to get her call. It had taken an effort of will to disguise his delight at being invited to the apartment. He was thrilled to have created so much trust that she seemed keen for him to come visit.

Now he'd found out what he needed to know, he'd been wondering how and where he would deal with her. There were still a couple of pieces missing from the puzzle. Fairly big, key pieces, like where all his paperwork had gone.

He'd told Diane he'd be out of town. Out of state in fact, possibly for a few days. He had business associates all over the country and sometimes he felt the need to see the whites of their eyes, so she was long used to his business travel. She had even come with him on a few trips in the early days, if the destination was somewhere she found appealing. That novelty had soon worn off and nowadays she was more inclined to do her own thing.

Fortunately, he'd managed to reassure her, with much spoiling and fuss-making, that there was no other woman in his life. She had almost caught him out with her morning phone call after his all-nighter in Charlotte's apartment.

Although he'd planned to have a follow-up date with 'Charlotte' that night, it was just as well she'd said no. The change to his plan, while irritating at the time, had worked in his favour. He'd had more time to find out all he could about the mystery girl who was posing as Charlotte Gillespie.

It had also given him time to go to the bank to retrieve the receipts he would need when the damned markets opened again. The cab had dropped him this afternoon, not at the Federal Reserve where Diane's family had banked forever, but at a nearby branch of Chase, where no one knew him. As he'd paid off the cabbie, he felt grateful to have chosen that branch. The one in Five World Trade Center he used to use now lay buried in a mountain of rubble. He felt sorry for anyone with valuables stored there. They'd be lucky to ever see their stuff again.

Having shown the card that proved he had his co-renter's permission to access the safe deposit box without her, he'd been taken to a private room and left alone with their box. The box he'd last seen when Charlotte was alive. The box that was now empty. All receipts, the deeds of the house that had been in Diane's family for generations, everything had gone.

His plan to take the money and run had already been scuppered by the NYSE being closed for so long, the longest closure since the Depression. Not that it mattered now. He couldn't trade anything without paperwork. If those papers didn't turn up soon, he, his business, his family and his marriage would be mouth deep in manure. It was bad.

The only person who could have stolen them was the lowlife he'd hired to kill Charlotte. And now he was dead. That was a mistake. He ought to have been more vigilant, knowing someone else had Charlotte's key in his possession. All the stuff in the box should have been checked before he killed the guy. This could prove to be a costly and dangerous mistake.

He would have to try very hard to keep his temper with his mystery girl, whoever she was. Somehow or other, and this was the part he didn't understand, this girl had managed to weasel her way into Charlotte's life and assume a new identity.

He needed to get this Lucie, if that was her real name, to fill in the blanks for him. Then he could deal with her. He would not rest easy, could not, until he made certain she hadn't uncovered and revealed any information that could compromise him and Bill. He mentally crossed out the word 'compromise' and replaced it with 'destroy'.

His best theory tied in with what he already suspected. The moron he'd employed to take out Charlotte had botched the job and left her alive. Lucie must have come across Charlotte in the street, maybe tried to help her. Charlotte must have told Lucie where she lived, probably asked to be taken home. What he needed to find out from Lucie was, what else did Charlotte tell her? Did she, for example, tell Lucie his name and reveal her reasons for knowing him?

Where was Charlotte now? Maybe Lucie could tell him if Charlotte was hiding some place. Recuperating, biding her time before she revealed all she knew and brought about his downfall. Maybe Lucie would be able to tell him who had emptied the safe deposit box?

He needed to know if Lucie had discovered anything in Charlotte's apartment that could implicate him. As far as he was aware, Charlotte had been as circumspect as himself about their affair. To his knowledge, she did not even have a photo of him and certainly no 'billets doux' or little personal gifts like the ones he gave Diane. He'd had time to check the apartment the other night, while Lucie slept, and had found nothing that connected him to Charlotte. It would have been better had he been able to access her laptop, but knowing Charlotte as he did, he couldn't imagine her being so careless as to have anything incriminating on a computer that she left lying around the house. It wasn't her style at all. Still, he should have taken the laptop when he had the chance.

Now the contents of the safe deposit box had gone missing, he was really worried. As if he hadn't been worried enough hearing Lucie, half-asleep, talking about a secret letter from Charlotte.

Soon he'd be in a position to find out what Lucie knew. High up in that apartment he'd be able to grill her, torture her if need be, and there would be no witnesses. Once he was satisfied she hadn't blabbed about him to anyone, it would be bye-bye Lucie.

He asked the cab driver to stop at a flower vendor's cart so he could buy her some flowers. He picked the biggest bunch on offer and jumped back in the cab. He had already picked up a chilled bottle of Moët. He could only hope she hadn't sworn off alcohol for life.

With his eyes covered by dark glasses and his face hidden behind the huge bouquet of lilies, he asked the doorman to ring Lucie's number.

'You can go on up, sir. Ms Gillespie is expecting you, fortieth floor.'

Lucie answered his knock as if she'd been standing behind the door waiting. He presented the bouquet with a 'Da-da!' that echoed down the hallway.

'Thank you,' said Lucie, her reaction somewhat muted. Perhaps she was embarrassed by his trumpeting. 'These are lovely.'

He held out the champagne. 'Do you want me to put this in the refrigerator or would you like a glass right now?'

'I'll have a small glass,' she said, 'to welcome you to my apartment. Properly, this time.' She made a funny face, mouth turned down like a clown.

'Hey, forget about it. Do you think I've never had too much to drink?' As he popped the cork and poured the wine he told her a made-up story about running stark naked down a hotel corridor one night.

She laughed, more nervously than he'd heard her before.

They clinked glasses and he raised his to his lips, watching to see how much she would drink. She took the tiniest of sips, like a kitten lapping a drop of milk, and he had the distinct impression she was being careful. Either she had not yet forgotten her hangover or she was taking very great care to stay sober tonight.

CHAPTER 60

'Oh, excuse me,' said Lucie, rising from the sofa. 'I'm a terrible hostess. Let me just fetch some snacks.'

While she opened a pack of peanuts and tipped them into a bowl, she ran through her plan. She would start by seeing how honest he was prepared to be with her. Then, depending on his reaction, she would confess about Charlotte and take it from there.

'Won't be a minute,' she sang out, disguising the sound of a drawer opening. She retrieved what she needed and pushed it up her sleeve, like a cheat preparing for a poker game. She adjusted her cuff and patted herself down, making sure there was nothing about her to make him suspicious. She checked her watch, lifted the little bowl of nuts and trilled, 'Coming,' as she bumped the drawer closed with her hip.

She settled deep into the comfort of the soft leather and faced him.

He smiled disarmingly, and said, 'This is nice, just the two of us.' He patted her knee once then withdrew his hand, the perfect gentleman. Panic snatched at her stomach. What if she'd got this all wrong?

She smiled back, studying his face. Remembering the photos. Comparing the two. She hadn't got it wrong. 'I agree. It's lovely to meet informally like this. We can get to know each other better.'

'Mmm,' he murmured, leaning forward to put his glass on the black marble table. He put his arms round her, gathered her towards him and moved in for a kiss.

Despite herself she softened, her mouth welcoming him while her brain warned against giving in. She felt like she was back in college, determined not to let the boy go too far, but having to fight her own body, not his.

She eased away from him. 'I'd like to talk for a while before we, you know.' She dropped her gaze, coyly.

He heaved a great sigh and said, 'Okay,' but he looked like a kid who'd just heard there was no Santa Claus. She laughed, releasing some of the tension that was making her shoulders ache. Without thinking, she massaged the back of her neck and he immediately touched the tight spot and soothed it with a gentle, caressing stroke. It would be so easy to succumb to his charms, but she caught his hand, gave it a quick kiss and replaced it on the back of the sofa.

'You remember, the other morning, I said there were a few things you don't know about me?'

'Yes. I remember,' he said, an adult indulging a child.

'Well, I've been wondering. Is there anything I don't know about you?'

His eyes narrowed and the smile he gave her took a long time to reach them. 'Sure, honey,' he said, his voice artificially bright. 'Loads of stuff. Let me think. I hate pastrami. I've never been to a baseball game in my life. I can't swim. Um, cats bring me out in hives. I love the holiday season. What else would you like to know?'

'I'd like to know what your wife's doing tonight.'

Shock, disbelief, suspicion all flitted across his face before his features settled into a picture of sadness. 'My wife's dead. You know that.'

She shook her head. 'Don't think so. Mrs Diane Millburn? Last seen in the society pages of the *Times*? Dressed in Versace, hosting a benefit lunch at the Pierre? All proceeds to the families of 9/11 victims?'

He said nothing.

'Also in last November's edition of *Avenue*? Photographed with you at the Fall Benefit for NYSPCC. Ring any bells?'

He shook his head, stony faced. Doubt drenched her like an icy shower.

She had to keep going. It was time to produce her 'proof'. First she showed him the photo. Then with a magician's flourish she snatched the white handkerchief from her sleeve and waved it playfully in front of his nose. Best to look as if she could see the funny side.

'Mr Millburn, I believe,' she said in a theatrical voice, showing him the initials on the handkerchief. 'Mr Stephen Scott Millburn, known to his friends as SS?'

She was relieved to hear him laugh. 'That goes way back to my childhood. My friends were all reading war comics and thought it was very funny. The name stuck.'

'I spotted you in those photos and thought, wait a minute, that's not SS Millburn, that's my friend, Rick Armstrong.'

'Then you remembered the hankie and did the two plus two sum?'

She nodded. 'How could you say all that stuff about a dead wife? Weren't you superstitious that something might happen to your real wife? What about karma?'

'Who's karma?'

She gave him a look that told him she was being serious.

'I have no time for superstition and I don't believe in karma.'

She shrugged to hide the shiver that raced up her spine. 'Okay, if you say so.'

'Are you angry with me?'

'That depends on how honest you plan on being, *Richard*.'

He had the good grace to look sheepish. 'Oh, we're back to that?' He spread his arms in an appeal. 'Gimme a break. What guy tells his real name to every random person he meets in a coffee shop? Shoot, most people in New York don't ever speak to strangers, far less reveal their name.'

'Fair enough, but when did you mean to tell me?'

He stroked his fingertips down the side of her face. 'Tonight. Before we made love. So you'd call out my real name.'

She moved her face away. 'A bit presumptuous, don't you think, *Rick*?'

'Enough already. Call me Scott, please.' He gave her a puppy dog look that was far too practised to be spontaneous. 'Am I forgiven?'

'That depends. Are you asking me to have an affair?'

'Will you?'

'I might. But only if I'm certain you're being completely honest with me.'

'That works both ways, Charlotte-Lucie.'

Did he put a special emphasis on the Lucie? Her plan was to tell him about Charlotte but this confessional stuff was proving harder than she'd imagined. She tucked her feet underneath her, and turned to watch his reaction to her words.

'Okay, here goes. I'm not Charlotte.'

He tipped his head, curious.

'And this isn't my flat.'

He nodded, as if he understood. 'You just rent it. Cool.'

'No, I don't rent it. I live here for nothing, as if I own it.'

'Okay, getting confused.'

'This is Charlotte's flat.'

'Got that.'

'I'm pretending to be Charlotte.'

'Now you've lost me. Could you maybe start again?'

Lucie started with the dust cloud. She told him about taking Charlotte's bag by mistake and about the doorman mistaking her for Charlotte and letting her into the apartment. She ended her tale with the day her mum died, the day she'd met Richard Armstrong. 'The man with the strong arms.' She waited for him to speak.

'Your mom, *did* she really die that day?'

Lucie nodded, too sad, suddenly, to answer him.

'I'm terribly sorry for your loss.'

Lucie wiped her tears on the white handkerchief.

'Wow, that's some story,' he said. 'What do you plan on doing now, if you don't mind me asking?'

'Well, I *was* planning on flying back home to Scotland. To see my dad and try to fix things between us. Actually, I was meant to leave three days ago.'

'What made you change your mind?'

She pointed at him. 'You. But I have to tell you, I almost went, when I found out you were married.'

'I'm glad you stayed. Might I ask what your plans are now?'

She tried to sound flirtatious. 'Well, I guess that depends on you and how good you are at keeping secrets.'

'I'll keep *your* secrets if you promise to keep mine.'

'You have more?' She feigned shock. 'How many secrets can one man have?'

'Oh, you'd be surprised.'

There was an edge to his tone she hadn't heard before.

'Go on then, Scott, surprise me,' she said, fluttering her eyelashes.

'Now why would I want to do that?'

'Because if I'm about to embark on an affair with a married man, I'm going to have to believe that *I'm* the only secret he's keeping.' She leaned forward and kissed the tip of his nose. She was playing for time, scared he'd try to take it to the next level before she was ready.

'So,' he said, spreading his arms wide, 'why don't you go ahead, ask me anything.' He eased the front of his trousers, 'but you better be quick about it. These pants are starting to feel a little tight.'

'Okay, is this your first extra-marital affair?'

He sat upright, tense and alert. 'What is this, a divorce hearing?'

In a deep, grave voice, like a judge's, she said, 'Just answer the attorney's question please, Mr Millburn.'

He sniggered, indulging her. 'Yes, your honour. This is my first affair.'

'So you didn't have an affair with Miss Charlotte Gillespie?'

All sign of tolerance vanished from his face. 'What the hell are you talking about? I'd never even heard of Charlotte Gillespie until I met you.'

'That's not true, is it?' She shook her head sadly, as if *she* were the wronged wife. 'You and Charlotte go a long way back, at least five or six years.'

She could almost see his brain working, trying to select the best response to her accusation.

'As business partners, yes.'

'Nothing more?'

'Nothing more, I swear.' He was trying to look trustworthy and honest, she could tell. 'Why on earth would you ask that?'

'Oh, it was just something she said.'

Now he looked alarmed. 'Said? Said when? Where? In the street? I thought you said she was dead?'

'Did I?' She was beginning to enjoy this, the sparring, the mental challenge of keeping one step ahead, the danger.

'How much do you know, Lucie?'

'About what? Your business? Enough to get you in trouble, I guess. If I ever told anyone. But why would I? It's not for me to judge. My father's a businessman. I imagine he's been involved in some shady deals in his time. I admire a good business brain and I suspect yours is one of the best.'

She'd thought he'd be far too clever for flattery. But like the conceited crow sweet-talked into dropping the cheese, Scott Millburn dropped a bombshell.

'Did Charlotte tell you about our joint venture?'

'Some,' she said, 'but I'd rather hear it from the mouth of the master.' She reached for her glass and made herself comfortable, as if she were looking forward to a good piece of gossip. 'Go on, talk dirty to me.'

She tried to sound coquettish and enticing. She licked her lips and said, 'Talk dirty, filthy lucre to me. Call it financial foreplay.'

Evidently it was working. He reached for her breast, but she drew back. 'Uh-uh,' she said, pouting, 'not till I hear how brilliant you are.'

She touched and teased, posed and promised while he confirmed pretty much everything she'd found in Charlotte's letter and her safe deposit box. He seemed, after a point, to lose himself in the telling, as if he were describing a holy mission or a crusade. Not one of the biggest, most ambitious stock market frauds in history.

When he paused for breath, she asked him, for there were still some gaps she needed him to fill, 'How did you know the hijackers were planning to fly the planes into WTC?'

'Well, sorry, little lady. That would be classified,' he said in a corny, movie-style voice, with a smile to match. As if he couldn't help showing off, he added, 'But it helps to have friends in high places. No pun intended.' He laughed at his unintentional joke.

'How did you know what stocks to buy and which to sell?'

'Remember, Charlotte and I didn't actually buy or sell the shares, we bought *options* to buy or sell them. When their value fell or rose significantly.'

She wanted him to name the companies involved. 'I get that, but how could you tell which shares to buy options on? It seems like a bit of a crapshoot to me.'

'No, no, no,' he said, patiently, as if she were his student. 'It's simple contrarian investing. Take the airlines, for example.'

'Which airlines? There are so many.'

'You're right, and almost any airline in the world had shares worth buying a put option on. How many people do you know who were prepared to fly after 9/11? I mean, you don't expect to get on a plane and have it fly you straight into the side of a building. But it happened. So people have developed a fear of flying which means losses for airlines, especially American Airlines and UAL, the ones whose planes were actually used in the attack on WTC.'

'Okay, I understand. It's not very ethical, is it?'

He spluttered into his champagne and choked out the words, 'Ethics are a luxury I can't afford.'

Lucie gasped. Then as if the idea had just occurred to her she said innocently, 'Oh no, please don't tell me you deal in arms too?'

'Are you serious?' He wagged his finger at her, teacher-like. 'First rule of business?'

'I don't know. Supply and demand?'

'Correct.' He seemed genuinely pleased with her. 'Supply and demand. America at peace is no good for business, is it?' He waited for her answer.

'You want America at war?'

'Right again. Since we got all touchy feely with the Russians, our political masters have become complacent. Americans need a new bogeyman.'

'Al-Qaeda,' she said in a whisper.

'Got it in one.'

'A terrorist attack on American soil. Citizens terrified to sleep at night. The politicians need to keep them safe.' She stopped, realising the implications of what she was saying, 'Oh my God. You think America will go to war over this?'

'I sure as hell hope so. Otherwise I've wasted an awful lot of money trading options in armaments.'

'Profits of doom.'

He laughed. 'Very smart.'

'Let me take another wild guess, you own shares in insurance companies too?'

'Reinsurance, to be precise.' He nodded, smug and self-satisfied. 'Millions of dollars on put options for shares in companies like Munich Re and Swiss Re. They're bound to take a big hit when they have to pay out billions of dollars. Like the airlines.'

She shook her head in genuine astonishment. It was hard not to be impressed. 'Wow, my father was never in your league.'

'No, he wasn't. But then, few are.'

'Scott,' she said quietly, 'what about all the people who died when the towers came down?'

His head dropped. She felt a pointless pang of relief when he looked up at her and said, 'Well, I feel terrible. Of course I do. I'm not heartless.'

She must have shown some doubt for he seemed compelled to explain. 'Listen,' he said, 'I tried to keep casualties to an absolute minimum.'

'But you lost your own employees. Wasn't that why your wife was organising a benefit lunch?'

He nodded. 'Regrettably some of my workforce had to be present in the North Tower, to avoid attracting suspicious attention. But don't worry, Diane and I will make very sure their families are well looked after.'

'You're a regular Andrew Carnegie.'

'What did you say?' he asked sharply.

She mustn't antagonise him. 'Sorry, I'm just having a bit of trouble getting my head round all the dead people. I could have been one of them, you know. I was on my way to the South Tower.'

'You were? Why?'

'Does it matter?'

'Yes, I'd like to know.'

'I had an interview for a cleaning job. If I'd been half an hour earlier, I'd have been dead. It's like you were playing God. You knew this was going to happen and yet you did nothing.'

'What was I supposed to do?'

'You could have sent your employees home.'

He looked at her suspiciously. Had she said too much too soon?

'Don't you think that might have looked a bit odd? It could have started a panic. A mass exodus.'

'Would that have been so bad? Saving all those lives. You could have been a hero.'

He shook his head as if she didn't understand. 'I couldn't do that, Lucie.'

'Why not?'

'It would have compromised my source.'

'So you preferred to let folk die?'

'Collateral damage. Regrettable but unavoidable. Like the civilians unfortunate enough to die on the surrounding streets. Ever heard of Baron de Rothschild?'

She shook her head. 'Why? Who's he?'

'He was the man who said: "Buy when there's blood in the streets, even when it's your own blood."'

'Or Charlotte's.'

He didn't answer, seemed to be reflecting. Although he made frequent use of words like unfortunate, she could see no regret in his demeanour. Wasn't that the sign of a psychopath or a sociopath or some other kind of maniac you wouldn't want to be sipping champagne with?

'Listen, I might seem like a monster, but would you believe me if I told you there's an altruistic motive behind all of this?'

'That might be a big ask.'

'I know, but it's true.'

'I *knew* all along you were really one of the good guys.' She smiled quickly, hoping he hadn't noticed her sarcasm. 'Go on. I'm listening.'

'Well,' he said, his voice deep and serious, 'I don't think terrorism is the biggest threat to America. I believe it's something much more insidious that will destroy this great country of ours.'

'Drugs?'

'They're in the mix, but I think they're a symptom of the ailment, not the cause.'

'What is it then?'

'It's unemployment. If people have no work, they have no self-respect. If they have no self-respect, they don't respect other people, or their property or their rights. Keep heading down that highway and you're heading for hell. Have you ever seen pictures of the Great Depression?'

'When Wall Street crashed?'

'October 1929. Industrial production dropped by almost fifty per cent, building practically stopped. By 1932 there were thirteen million unemployed. You know how many unemployed we have right now, in 2001?'

Lucie had no idea. Even though her husband had been one of them. 'Two, three million?'

'Almost six million and that's without a recession. What happens the next time the banks fail? And they will, you mark my words. We live in a boom or bust economy. There's another collapse on its way. Can you imagine what that will be like?'

Lucie shook her head. He was really fired up now. Evangelising like a preacher. 'Let me tell you. There will be anarchy. America has changed since the thirties and people won't meekly accept their fate next time a depression comes along. They won't be prepared to live in shanty towns like Third World folks. They've come to expect better and they'll take what they believe is their right. Poverty won't be a working-class problem next time around.'

He stopped for a minute, as if deep in reflection. 'You ever been poor, honey?'

'No, I haven't.' It was a lie, of course, but she wasn't going to tell him that. She didn't entirely disagree with his theory about unemployment. She'd seen the changes in Curtis when he got laid off.

'Well, I have. And I'm never going back there.'

'I appreciate that, but I don't understand how something as awful as this can help the economy.'

'America didn't recover from the Great Depression until December 1941. Any idea what happened then?'

'If I were to hazard a guess, I'd say something to do with the Second World War?'

'And you'd be right. It took a war to help this great nation make a recovery. The United States entered the war in Europe at the end of 1941 and the economy recovered soon after.'

'So you and your people in high places are starting a war?'

There was a messianic fervour in his voice and his eyes. 'Not so much a war as a period of economic growth. America will become strong enough to withstand any attack from terrorists, should they be foolish enough to try. But they won't. Terrorists are like bullies. They pick on the weak. They attack countries that don't have the wherewithal to defend their citizens.'

'And what about New York and its citizens?'

'New York will recover. A new, better WTC will rise from the ashes, creating jobs and manufacturing opportunities for years. Can you imagine how many workers and how much material and investment a building project this size will involve? How much wealth it will create?'

'For you and your cronies?'

'Please, I prefer the word associate or fellow investor.'

'Okay,' she said brightly, 'which brings us neatly back to Charlotte.'

'Yes, lovely Charlotte. Pity she lost her nerve, or got religion or some damn thing, I don't know what the hell happened. Anyway, she begged me to evacuate our own people.'

'What did you say?'

'I agreed we should.'

'So why didn't it happen?'

'I told you, we couldn't do anything suspicious. It would have compromised my source.'

'That source must be pretty well connected. Who is he? Or she?'

'I can't tell you that. Anyway, no one knew for sure the attack was going to happen.'

'And yet you invested millions of dollars in the possibility.'

'It was a bet, a gamble, like all investments. Some pay out, some don't.'

'And this person, your contact, really meant more to you than Charlotte?'

'Charlotte brought it upon herself. She made me choose.'

'Between her and your contact?'

'Between her and Diane.'

Lucie sipped at her champagne. She was getting close, but not close enough. 'This is delicious,' she said, for want of anything safer to say.

'Moët. Glad you like it.' He took a mouthful and swallowed. She watched his Adam's apple move up and down. 'Now,' he said, replacing his glass on the table, 'it's time for us to talk about Lucie. I assume that is your real name?'

'I've just told you Lucie's story, *my* story,' she said with a little smile, hoping she looked trustworthy.

'It seems to me you've missed out some of the best bits. Like why you'd want to steal someone's identity. You do know that's breaking the law, don't you?'

'So is insider trading, isn't that what they call it? But unlike you, I haven't done any harm, have I?'

He laughed, dismissing her plea. 'I don't think the law will see it that way, Lucie.'

'Maybe not.'

'Why didn't you want to go home?'

'I don't know what you mean.'

'I mean, home to your husband.'

Lucie felt the bottom drop out of her stomach. This was getting scary. How could he know that stuff? 'Who have you been talking to?'

'Oh, it's amazing what you can find out if you have the right contacts in the right places.'

'Such as?'

'Such as the rehab centre your poor husband was living in after you crippled him. And the nine one one team who found him almost dead on his kitchen floor.' He looked around. 'I can see why you'd prefer it here, Lucie. Much nicer than your old place.'

'It was self-defence. I thought he was going to kill me.'

'What *did* actually kill you, Lucie?'

'I have no idea what you're talking about.'

'Lucie Jardine, née McBride, is officially dead. Did you know that? I'm just curious about what happened. I thought you'd be the ideal person to tell me.'

This was not on Lucie's plan. She decided the best thing would be to remain silent.

'Taking the Fifth, are we?'

Lucie said nothing.

'Probably wise. Fraud, identity theft, assault, faking your own death. I hope you know a good lawyer, Lucie. You'll need one. I would say you're looking at ten to fifteen for that lot. Quite the little felon, aren't we?'

He started to edge closer to her. 'Any more secrets you'd like to share before we get down to business? I think that's probably enough foreplay, don't you? Enough for me, anyway.' He took her hand and pressed it on his erection. She tried not to snatch her fingers away or let her revulsion show. The last few years with Curtis had prepared her well. She moved her hand firmly back and forth till he groaned, eyes closed.

Lucie slid backwards an inch or two and removed her hand. 'You won't get away with it, you know. Charlotte left evidence.'

His eyes flew open. 'Spilling her guts to some stranger in the street before she died? That isn't evidence.'

'You didn't expect her to die in the street though, did you? Your plan was to send her to her death with all those other sad, unsuspecting souls in the North Tower.'

He laughed. The most sinister sound she'd ever heard, like something from a horror movie, only far more credible. 'Oh, Lucie. You're so naïve. Not only did I *expect* Charlotte to die in the street, I made it happen.'

'No. You're lying.'

'Charlotte died in the street because I planned it that way. I paid someone to kill her. Then, when I found out he didn't do the job the way I asked, I killed him.'

Lucie tried to slide away from him but he grabbed her by her forearms and trapped her.

'You're the only person left who can betray me now. You're a loose end, Lucie, and I don't like loose ends. I prefer everything nice and tidy. Which is why, once you've told me all you know and I've had my fun with you, I'm going to kill you too.'

'You can't do that.'

'Oh really?' he sneered, 'and why not?'

'Because I know where to find all the documents. I can prove you acted on classified information to make exorbitant amounts of money through insider trading.'

He dropped her arms and pulled back from her. 'It was you that emptied the box.'

'You're wrong. It was Charlotte.'

'Why would Charlotte do that? I thought she loved me.'

'I think she did. But you didn't love her back.'

'I love Diane. Always will. Charlotte knew that, but she refused to accept it. She got too greedy.'

'So why didn't you walk away?'

'I needed her investment. A chance like this comes along, you beg, borrow or steal to put everything you can on it.'

'I get that, but why did you promise her you'd leave your wife once the investments made good?'

'I was playing for time. She threatened to tell Diane about the affair.'

'And it was Diane's money?'

Scott nodded. He let go of her arms.

'I still don't understand why you had to have Charlotte killed. She went along with you on the insider dealing, gave you her money to invest. You were partners in crime. Surely that was enough leverage to have on her?'

'Have you any idea how much I have riding on this? Everything. Every penny that Langdon Associates owns, and millions that we don't. Shoot, I've even put the house on it. Diane's family home. Can you imagine what that means?'

Lucie tried to imagine Scott and the lovely Diane surviving in the kind of places she'd lived in with Curtis. 'Still,' she said, 'how can that justify killing Charlotte? And then killing her killer?'

'You just don't get it, do you?'

His face was turning red, his eyes filling as if he might burst into tears.

She shook her head, tried to look sympathetic and encouraging.

'Charlotte was going to ruin everything.'

'By sending the workers home, you mean?'

'No, that would have been dangerous enough. But what she threatened was much worse. I had to get rid of her. She left me no choice.'

Lucie chose her words carefully, knowing how vital it was to get this right. 'How did she threaten you, Scott?' she asked gently.

'She said if I didn't agree to evacuate our floors, she would go public.'

'And say what?'

'She threatened to go to the media and tell the world that a terrorist attack was anticipated.'

Lucie sensed there was more to come. 'And?'

'She threatened to reveal my source.'

'And your source is someone very important?'

Scott looked her in the eye. 'He's very important to me.'

'More important than Charlotte and thousands of poor innocent people?'

He said nothing. Lucie *had* to find out more.

'They all had *family*, Scott. For every casualty, every statistic, there's a distraught mother, father, or wife. Some are out there in the street right now, waiting for news. Hoping against hope that someone will find their precious sister. Their lost brother.'

Still not a word, although he did look as if she'd touched a nerve.

'Can you imagine that, Scott? Losing your brother in a catastrophe, with the world watching?'

'You don't get it,' he said again, his voice quiet and weak.

Lucie had never heard him sound vulnerable. It was time to push. 'Get what? That you could have saved hundreds of people from losing their beloved sons and daughters, sisters and brothers?'

'That's just it. I couldn't.'

'Of course you could. But you were too greedy, weren't you? You went ahead and sacrificed the lot of them. To make a fast buck.'

Scott shook his head. 'You don't understand. It wasn't that simple.'

Lucie's voice rose in appeal, 'How could it *not* be simple, Scott? Make the call, warn people, save lives.'

'And sacrifice my own brother?' he said quietly. Far too quietly.

'What did you say?'

'I said, would you have me sacrifice my brother? The brother I've idolised since I was four years old? Because that's what you're asking.'

'Your brother? What's he got to do with it?'

Scott nodded, sniffing loudly and wiping his eyes and nose with the back of his hand.

'He was my source.'

'He told you about 9/11? Who is he? A terrorist?' She laughed. Scott didn't.

'How could he know about it?' she asked. 'Scott? How could he know about it?'

'He's in the CIA.'

Lucie gasped, her shock genuine. 'The CIA knew about 9/11?'

Scott nodded, looking grim.

'And your brother told you?'

Another nod.

'So you could make money? I don't believe this.'

'No, not so I could make money. Bill was looking out for me. I'm his kid brother. When we were young, he promised he'd always protect me. He always has. It's as simple as that. He wanted to make sure I'd stay away from WTC till it was all over.'

'*You'd* stay away? What about everyone else?'

'He was protecting me, his family. It's all he could do.'

'And you were protecting him? By killing Charlotte?'

'Of course I was protecting him. I still am. That's why you're going to tell me what Charlotte did with all those important documents of mine. I need those. You can see that, can't you, Lucie? I bet they're right here in this apartment, aren't they?' His voice had taken on a persuasive, seductive tone. He stroked her face then caressed her neck. His hand moved towards her breast and she caught his wrist.

Lucie had been prepared for all kinds of reaction, but she hadn't anticipated his becoming amorous at this stage. 'Are you for real?'

The sleazy smile vanished from his lips. 'What?'

'One minute you're threatening to kill me and the next you're making a move on me?'

'And?'

'And it's not going to happen. How can you expect me to find you attractive after all you've just told me?'

'Some women like dangerous men. Charlotte did.'

'And look where it got her.'

He laughed. 'I like it when you're feisty, Lucie. It's very sexy.' He reached for her again and she tried her best not to squirm out of reach and run for it. 'There's one thing I can't work out. One loose end. You know how I feel about loose ends. Tell me, sweet Lucie, what made Charlotte betray me?'

'By moving the contents of the box, you mean?'

'Yes. And that night you were drunk you said something about a secret letter. Was that true? Did she leave a letter?'

Lucie nodded.

'Why would she do that?'

'She left it as insurance, in case she didn't survive.'

'She didn't trust me?'

Lucie shrugged. 'For what it's worth, she did say she hoped the letter would never be found. So she wanted to believe in you.'

'And yet she still emptied our box? Did she tell you why?'

Lucie wasn't sure she had enough courage to say what she'd planned.

'Come on, you know, don't you?'

'She didn't trust your sudden changes of heart. One minute you weren't leaving Diane and you wouldn't take Charlotte's money. The next you wanted her to invest millions and you were promising a future together.'

'I thought she believed me.'

'I think maybe she did.'

'What did I do wrong?'

'You agreed to evacuate your workforce, but only after she forced you into it. Even then, she didn't trust you to go through with it.'

'How the hell could I?'

'Charlotte was going to. She was on her way.'

'Which is why I had to stop her.'

'Which is why she was right not to trust you. And why she wanted to make sure you wouldn't get away with it.'

'Okay, Lucie, enough talking. Time for some action.'

Before she could react, he tore open her shirt and stuck his hand into her bra, pulling it away, leaving her nipple exposed in his palm. He lowered his face, his mouth open to kiss her breast, when he stopped. 'You little bitch! You're wired!'

Everything seemed to happen at once. She screamed, the door of the apartment burst out of its frame and slapped onto the floor. Heavy-booted feet charged over it towards her. A deep voice roared, 'FBI.' Lucie was dragged off the sofa. Three huge, Kevlar-clad agents surrounded Scott and pointed their guns at his head.

'Great job, Lucie. We got every word. This guy's gonna get crucified. And his brother.' As he spoke, Agent McKenna moved behind the sofa and leaned over to fasten handcuffs on Scott. 'On your feet, sir,' he demanded. Scott stood, his eyes never leaving Lucie's face while he was read the Miranda. She wanted to look away but he seemed to mesmerise her.

When McKenna stopped speaking, Scott said, in the most reasonable of tones, 'This isn't over, Lucie. We have unfinished business. Where will you hide this time? Who will you become now? Not that it matters. I found you once, I'll find you again.'

'You chose the right to remain silent, asshole. Remember?' McKenna gave him a shove in the back and Scott stumbled forwards. 'Get him out of here.'

Agent McKenna put his arm round Lucie's shoulders. She was shaking.

'You did good, young lady,' he said. 'Real good. Cool, calm and in control. Just like we asked of you. You'd make a great agent.'

Mc Kenna laughed and Lucie knew she should smile but when she tried, her face crumpled. She burst into tears.

McKenna gave her a hug. 'Now, listen to me,' he said, squeezing her shoulders. 'Don't you go losing any sleep over what Millburn just said. You did exactly the right thing. Your friend Dylan advised you well. Now leave everything to us. I promise you we'll take the very best care of you. You can forget about Millburn. Trust me, he's going away for so long, they'll not only throw away the key, they'll knock down the prison and build a new one before he's due for parole.'

EPILOGUE

9/11 Memorial
Manhattan 2011

It had become a habit of hers, visiting the memorial, waiting for this day, knowing it would come soon. She had got to know most of the staff who checked the visitor passes, still, she was relieved to see one of her favourites on duty today.

'Hi, Lesley,' she said, removing her sunglasses. She opened her bag for inspection.

Lesley barely glanced inside. 'Mrs Millburn! How are you today?'

'I'm good, thanks.'

The woman stood aside to allow her to pass and turned to greet the next person in line.

Diane was surprised to see so many people on the plaza. More than usual, probably brought out by the unseasonably warm sunshine. She replaced her oversized sunglasses and scanned the crowds, hoping she'd be able to spot them. She was a little concerned she may have got the wrong day, or the wrong time. Her source was never inaccurate; they'd be here. She headed for the South Pool.

A group of school kids streamed past her, all dressed in matching yellow sweatshirts. A harassed-looking teacher followed on, trying to hush his charges, but succeeding only in adding to the noise.

Diane was glad when they were herded off towards the opposite side of the pool and serenity was restored. With the sounds of the city playing in the background like a muted soundtrack, all she could hear was the rushing of water into the vast reflection pool below. No matter how often she visited, Diane never failed to be moved by the expanse of this space that would never be filled again.

When she heard a child's voice she moved away a few yards and rummaged in her bag, her head lowered. She took out a mirror and checked her reflection. The last decade had etched its story onto her face and the less said about her poor hair the better. She patted and smoothed today's coiffure, a nondescript, unremarkable grey bob.

'Up, Daddy! Up!' the child insisted.

Diane couldn't resist a peek as the man hoisted his toddler son onto his shoulders. The little boy yelped with delight and raised his arms to the sky, as if he were trying to be as tall as a tower.

The children seemed excited. From all accounts, this was their first visit to New York City. Their first visit to any city, for they were country kids, from Humble, Texas, where Mommy taught preschool and Daddy sold real estate. Angelina's new love was horseback riding and little Ethan had so many play dates it was hard to keep track. The original All American Family.

'Me too, Daddy. I want to be a tower,' said the little girl, hopping up and down impatiently. Her tumble of blonde curls bounced in time with each jump.

'Sorry, Angelina,' said the man, 'I can't put both of you on my shoulders. Why don't you go help Mommy look for her friend?' He pointed to his wife, dark head bent as she studied name after name on the vast bronze plates that commemorated the lost. Or at least, some of them.

His daughter's scowl changed to a smile. With her father in tow, she ran off calling, 'Mommy, can I help you?'

As Diane watched, Mommy turned and opened her arms. The child jumped into her embrace. Astonishingly, the mother managed to stay upright; her daughter was tall for her age and sturdy like her father, while her mum looked like a strong wind could blow her over. She had looked more robust in the few photos Diane had seen and her hair had been lighter, surely.

Taking a small rosebud from her bag, Diane made a show of searching for a name as she edged closer to the woman who'd haunted her day and night for the last ten years.

'What's making you smile, Daddy-o?'

'Oh, just the kids, you, all of this.'

Mommy glanced around and up towards the skyline. 'Yeah, pretty amazing, isn't it? When you think back.'

'Hey,' Daddy said gently, and touched her arm. 'No dark thoughts, remember? We agreed.'

Mommy nodded but her smile looked sad. 'I know I promised and I'll do my best, but it's hard not to feel sorrow here.'

Holding his son secure with one hand, Daddy put his arm round his wife's shoulders and hugged her to him. 'I know, my love.'

'Mommy!' screamed the little girl.

'Shhh,' the parents hissed in unison, unwilling, apparently, to have their children show a lack of respect in this place of sanctity. Diane approved.

The child frowned, as if she were unused to being scolded. 'But I've found your friend, Mommy.'

The parents hurried over, the toddler jiggling on his father's shoulders, laughing. The girl smiled at her brother and rose on tiptoe to reach the name on the plaque. 'Look, Ethan. This is Mommy's friend. I found her.' Her little finger carefully traced, one by one, letters cut into the metal parapet. She spelled aloud as her finger moved, 'L, U, C...'

Mommy knelt to clasp her child in a tight embrace and kissed the top of her blonde head. 'Yes, sweetheart,' she said, 'you found her. Thank you.' Standing, she placed her hand flat on the dark metal surface, on top of the name they'd been looking for, and lowered her head, as if in prayer, although she was not a churchgoer.

'Can we put a flower in her name?' The little girl pointed towards a row of names, each one marked with a rosebud stem.

'No, my darling. No flowers,' said her father. 'We'll just stay quiet for a little while and let Mommy remember her friend.'

Daddy gathered his daughter to him. They stood in silence, listening, it seemed, to the gush of water dropping into the heart of the memorial and the hushed voices of the people who had come to pay their respects to the lost.

'Family hug!' demanded the little girl. Mommy hoisted the child into her arms and they hugged like footballers in a huddle till the boy started to bounce on his father's shoulders and shout, 'Airplane, Daddy, Airplane.'

Diane watched as all four looked up at the airliner soaring across the sky, like a giant silver seabird flying to the ocean. It seemed to be heading straight for the newly completed One World Trade Center, a sparkling glass spike that reached defiantly for the clouds. The plane passed safely behind the tower and made its elegant way west.

Daddy looked at his wife.

She was laughing at him. 'Did you just hold your breath?'

Daddy nodded, looking embarrassed.

'Me too. Ridiculous, isn't it? That plane's miles away.'

'Mommy, mommy,' squealed the little girl. 'Is that our airplane? The one that's taking us to Europe?'

'I sure hope not, honey, or we've missed it.'

'Our plane's tomorrow, Angelina. You and Ethan, me and Mommy, we'll be flying high in the sky this time tomorrow.'

'Are you scared, Mommy?'

The woman embraced her daughter, showering her golden curls with kisses until the child squirmed away from her.

'Scared? Now, why would I be scared? There's nothing for us to be scared of. Not a single thing in this whole wide world. I'm excited. We've got a whole new adventure waiting for us in Europe.'

'Come on, kids,' said Daddy. 'Who wants ice cream?'

He lifted his child over his head and placed the boy gently on his sturdy little legs. 'Hold Ethan's hand, please, Angelina. Make sure he doesn't run off. I want to give Mommy a special hug.'

Mommy clung to him, burying her face in his chest. Daddy held her tight, just like he always did when she looked worried. As if he realised new identities weren't always enough to protect good folks from life's evils.

Mommy raised her face at last and her husband kissed her, ignoring the kids' screams of 'Yuck, Daddy!'

Mommy took her man's face in her hands and whispered something into his ear.

Diane moved a little closer to the pair, openly watching now.

'What did you say?' Daddy asked, grinning. 'I can't hear you for all that water.'

'I love you,' she said. 'I always will.' She silently mouthed the name. 'Dylan.' And kissed him on the lips.

Mommy obviously didn't understand how easy it was to lip-read a word that began with D. A foolish and careless mistake for her to make after all this time. She was letting down her guard, relaxed perhaps by the thought of escaping to another continent.

'Want me to give you a moment?' asked Daddy.

Diane held her breath until the woman nodded.

Diane exhaled, controlling her breathing, as she'd been shown. She checked her pocket. It was there, at her fingertips, ready to use.

Mommy touched the memorial, like a benediction. Diane moved in close and, her hand hidden from view, took aim. At such close range, two shots would be all she needed to end this here and now. One through the heart for the woman and one through the roof of her own mouth. Revenge, fast and sweet.

'Mommy, come on!'

As his little body pushed past he jostled Diane and his mother said, 'Ethan, say sorry to the nice lady.'

The child looked up and smiled at her. His eyes were as blue as her own.

'Sorry, nice lady,' he said, in the voice of an angel, and took his mom by the hand.

The little family walked away, without looking back, focused on ice creams and dreams.

Diane stuck the rosebud into the L of Lucie Jardine's name, patted the cold bronze and whispered. 'See you on down the road, Lucie.'

They paid Diane no attention as she flipped open her phone and said, 'It's Plan B after all. Meet you in Europe.'

THE END

A NOTE FROM BLOODHOUND BOOKS

Thanks for reading Till The Dust Settles. We hope you enjoyed it as much as we did. Please consider leaving a review on Amazon or Goodreads to help others find and enjoy this book too.

We make every effort to ensure that books are carefully edited and proofread, however occasionally mistakes do slip through. If you spot something, please do send details to info@ bloodhoundbooks.com and we can amend it.

Bloodhound Books specialise in crime and thriller fiction. We regularly have special offers including free and discounted eBooks. To be the first to hear about these special offers, why not join our mailing list here? We won't send you more than two emails per month and we'll never pass your details on to anybody else.

Readers who enjoyed Till The Dust Settles will also enjoy

Undercurrent by JA Baker

Care To Die by Tana Collins

ACKNOWLEDGEMENTS

I never planned on becoming a writer but a story got into my head. Rita Costick told me I should write it. Rita, my friend, I am forever in your debt.

Writing is a solitary business. Getting published isn't. I am grateful to so many people for helping me along the way. My critical friends, too many to name here, read my stories and tell me, honestly, what they think. I hope you all know how much I appreciate you. Joining Ayr Writers was a big step, but I'd not have made it this far without your support and I'll always be grateful for it. Special gratitude is due to Caro Ramsay and Michael J Malone who have always said this day would come and whose faith and advice are invaluable to me. I must thank my pet surgeon, Stef Young, without whose knowledge Curtis would not have suffered such convincing injuries.

Finally, boundless thanks to all at Bloodhound Books. What a team!